FLINCH

R O B E R T

PANTHEON BOOKS / NEW YORK

FLINCH

FERRIGNO

Copyright © 2001 by Robert Ferrigno

All rights reserved under International and Pan-American
Copyright Conventions. Published in the United States by
Pantheon Books, a division of Random House, Inc., New York,
and simultaneously in Canada by Random House of Canada
Limited, Toronto.

Pantheon Books and colophon are registered trademarks
of Random House, Inc.

Library of Congress Cataloging-in-Publication Data

Ferrigno, Robert.
Flinch/Robert Ferrigno.
p. cm.
ISBN 0-375-40125-3
1. Los Angeles (Calif.)—Fiction.   2. Sibling rivalry—
Fiction.   3. Serial murders—Fiction.   4. Journalists—
Fiction.   5. Brothers—Fiction.   I. Title.

PS3556.E7259 V57 2001
813′.54—dc21   2001021576

www.pantheonbooks.com

Book design by Fritz Metsch

Printed in the United States of America
First Edition
9 8 7 6 5 4 3 2 1

To Richard Marconi

ACKNOWLEDGMENTS

I would like to thank Mary Evans, an agent who likes to read as much as she likes to sell, and my editor, Sonny Mehta, who asked all the right questions. Thanks to William Ungerman for his legal and ballistics expertise, Gregory Komenda, M.D., Orthopedics, for his advice on spinal-cord injuries, and Christopher Pawlik of the Lowry-James antique print gallery for showing me the Audubon folios. Special thanks to Jody, my first and last reader, who found the title among all the words.

FLINCH

Prologue

"Yeah, and I'm the fucking walrus." Jimmy Gage jammed the Egg-man's letter and everything else back into the manila envelope, balled it up, then made a long, arcing, half-court hook shot into the wastebasket down the aisle. He sucked his thumb where a staple from the envelope had caught him, tasted blood. Jimmy had gotten hate mail before, but this one was . . . different. He stared at the wastebasket, still seeing the words curling up from the paper like snakes, then tapped away on his keyboard, calling up his month-old *Dead Flowers* review on the computer:

```
After sitting through Tarantino's dancing hitmen
for the last ten years, couldn't Hollywood find
a better outlaw-hero for the new millennium than
the way-cool serial killer? I'm talking about
Dead Flowers, Damian Forth's latest $100 million
stiffy, starring former Calvin Klein model Chaz
Presley as yet another seductive überpredator
playing catch-me-if-you-can with the police.
    Bullshit. Serial killers are pimply losers,
ineffectual mama's boys hungry for the media tit,
not criminal masterminds or gourmet cooks who can
do wonders with fava beans. In real life, the
Nightstalker was caught by his neighbors in East
L.A. and beaten with baseball bats until he begged
to be turned over to the cops, and David Berkowitz
```

was a chubby postal clerk with bad teeth and a suitcase full of stroke books under his bed. Reality doesn't sell tickets, though; that's why we get Chaz Presley as the *Vanity Fair* psycho, complete with six-pack abs, a closet full of color-coded Hugo Boss threads, and a perpetually smoldering Gauloise on that sexy lower lip.

Dead Flowers is a petite rebellion for the platinum-Amex crowd, safe behind their gates and motion detectors, but the rest of us have to live with the consequences of killer kool, as teenage wannabes practice their bad-ass moves in the mirror, then take them to the schoolyard or the mall. Dig it: Anthony Hopkins and Chaz Presley ain't serial murderers, they just pretend for a few hours, then go home to Malibu. Where I live, the streets are mean and the dead stay dead.

—*Jimmy Gage, "Media Whore" column,* SLAP *magazine*

Jimmy read the review twice, then swiveled his chair toward the windows, refusing to be spooked. The *SLAP* editorial office overlooked the Newport Beach pier—from where he sat he could see bikini girls on rollerblades zipping past gaping tourists in madras Bermudas.

SLAP was an abrasive, upscale magazine, described by some asswipe at NPR as "a bikini-waxed version of the *National Enquirer*, mean-spirited and shallow, promoting stun-gun journalism." A consistent money loser, *SLAP* was kept afloat out of the deep pockets of its publisher, Antonin "Nino" Napitano, a slippery European media king who had moved to southern California one step ahead of an indictment by the Italian tax authorities. Delighted by L.A.'s blank sensuality and lubricious greed, Napitano had launched *SLAP*, a glossy homage to the city of his dreams. Jimmy had been one of his first hires, part critic, part investigative reporter, given free rein to explore whatever captured his interest: "Amuse me, dear boy" was his only directive.

Jimmy had profiled a rapacious, high-tech pirate with a Zen garden in his corporate jet and ridden with auto-repo men on midnight raids, showing off his own skills with a slim jim, popping a door lock in less than two seconds. He played war games in the Mojave with gun nuts and broke the story of a celebrity Sierra Club spokesman who had clear-cut five acres of his retreat outside Vail so he could land his Bell jet helicopter there. He got mail about everything he wrote, mash notes and death threats, but it was his film reviews that generated the most vicious responses.

Jimmy watched an elderly couple stroll along the pier, arm in arm, blinding in their yacht-club whites. They passed through the line of Vietnamese fishermen leaning against the side of the pier, the refugees bundled from head to toe in dark clothing, their long poles whipping through the air, as though saluting the commodore and his wife. The image was so beautiful Jimmy could hardly breathe, and he followed them with his gaze until they were out of sight. Then he got up, walked over to the wastebasket, and fished out the letter from the Eggman.

The envelope had arrived with no return address, just Jimmy's name and *SLAP*'s P.O. box number in black plastic letters punched out with a label maker. The mail room routinely ran everything through a scanner, checking for razor blades or dog shit, but he had held it up to the light before he opened it, just in case. Jimmy smoothed out the crumpled envelope on his desk, then shook out the contents: a flattened egg carton with the edges stapled together and a sheet of lined paper, the note written with a label maker, too, the raised letters giving the message an even more repellent texture.

Dear Mr. Gage:
    Here's the half-dozen eggs you ordered. Scrambled (ha-ha).
    You didn't order them? Think again. I read that Dead Flow-

ers review of yours and said to myself, this man is just asking for a delivery to set him straight. If you didn't like the movie, fine and dandy, but that's no reason to toss insults my way. Remember, Mr. Gage, the police only catch the mama's boys and jerk-offs who deep down want to get punished, not someone like me, who takes pride in his work. To prove my point, I spent this last month visiting the henhouse, picking out some grade A, extra-large beauties. Cops didn't notice anything out of the ordinary. Neither did you. So be careful what you write, because like they say, cheaper by the dozen.

Your faithful reader,
The Eggman

Jimmy still thought the Eggman should leave the melodrama to the professionals, but he started in on the egg carton anyway. He pried out the staples carefully, his thumb bleeding again as he popped open the carton. Saw-toothed news clippings were nestled in six of the egg cups, and he imagined a prim grandmother going through the paper with pinking shears, clipping recipes and Ann Landers, coupons for Polident and a "Garfield" comic strip. He unfolded the clippings, spread them out across his desk. No "Garfield," no recipes for Rice Crispies Squares. Instead there was a partial news report of a murder on a stretch of beach just south of Laguna. A gang killing in Santa Ana. A man gunned down while taking out the garbage. A high school track star shot during a dawn workout. A fry cook killed after work. A computer salesman found dead in the parking lot of an all-night supermarket. A half dozen murders in the last month, none of which had registered with Jimmy—just part of the background noise, unnoticed and unsolved. Like the note said.

A drop of blood landed on the porous cardboard of the egg carton, spreading out like a red starfish as Jimmy reread the Eggman's letter. Then he reached for the telephone.

Chapter 1

"Never take a woman on vacation to someplace where the cock-roaches are bigger than your dick," said Jimmy, scratching away at his reporter's notepad.

"We went to Costa Rica, man, land of enchantment," said Rollo.

"The land of enchantment is New Mexico," Jimmy corrected him, raising his voice over the cheers from the crowd. "Costa Rica is the land where your date rips off your bankroll and passport, then ditches you eighty miles from a phone."

Not that Jimmy was in any position to give advice. Rollo's brief vacation might have left him broke and desperate, but Jimmy himself had just gotten back after a ten-month absence that had been even more disastrous. He had quit his job at *SLAP* without giving notice, quit everything else, too, leaving Olivia with less notice than he gave his landlord. Most people thought he'd been reeling from the Eggman fiasco, burning bridges in his haste to get out of town, but Rollo knew better. Jimmy was surprised he hadn't asked to come with him.

"You still staying with the cop?" asked Rollo. "I don't think Desmond likes me, man. That one time I was over, he gave me a look like he wanted to frisk me."

"Desmond is a good judge of character," said Jimmy, watching Blaine the Robo-Surfer strut stiffly around the ring in a victory lap, the young wrestler grimacing in genuine pain, blood pouring down the side of his face. He was a blond behemoth in knee-length Aussie-print jams, silvery duct tape wrapped around his bulging biceps, power dials drawn crudely onto his shaved chest with orange Magic Marker. One hand held his ear in place from where the Kongo Kid had practically torn it off, trying to show off for the chubby ring girl. While the Robo-Surfer completed his glory circuit, the Kongo Kid was carried out on a stretcher to a chorus of boos. The ring girl adjusted her gold lamé bikini top in the far corner, oblivious to it all.

"Look at that ear." Rollo pushed back his black-framed glasses; he was a nervous nineteen-year-old with flyaway hair, a braided hemp necklace, and a scraggly soul patch under his lower lip. "Oh man, I am *so* fucked."

Jimmy and Rollo had met about three years before, after Rollo sent him a series of vicious but well-reasoned critiques of his movie reviews, plus a couple of petite mal–inducing animated shorts that he'd made for his tenth-grade media studies class. Rollo should have been studying filmmaking at USC by now, should have been churning out scripts or interning at Fox, but instead he chose to hustle hot electronic gear from the back of his VW van, using the profits to finance interminable documentaries on mall walkers and carpet installers that couldn't even get screened at Slamdance, let alone Sundance. Rollo was *always* overextended, always over budget, always in trouble. He was Jimmy's best friend.

"No way is Blaine going to talk to me with his ear thashed," complained Rollo. "All he's going to care about is Does it look infected and should he get a rabies shot and—"

"Stop sweating on me," said Jimmy, scribbling notes while watching the ring girl clomp around the ring in her high heels and baby fat, holding up an ARE WE HAVING FUN YET? sign. He was thirty-six years old, loose and lanky as a colt, wearing black jeans and a billowy gray checked shirt that resembled a TV test pattern circa 1955. The ring girl stepped around the spattered blood on the canvas, her smile faltering, and Jimmy stopped writing. There was nothing about her that was even vaguely reminiscent of Olivia, nothing but that uneasy smile, a brave smile, trying to tough it out. It was enough.

Olivia had been in the middle of a sweet dream the morning he left for the airport, a half smile on her face as she slept, one bare brown leg outside the sheets. The cab was already out front, but he had lingered in the doorway to the bedroom, watching her in the warm light, her hair spread out across the pillow, lips parted, as though about to say something, maybe ask him to stay. Ten months later and he still wondered what would have happened if she had awakened.

"You *listening* to me, Jimmy?"

The ring announcer climbed through the ropes, thumped the microphone, Testing, testing, one-two-three, but Jimmy's chest was pounding so loudly he barely heard it.

Club wrestling had come to southern California this Sunday afternoon, Retro Wrestling, an unapologetic blend of semipro contestants, unscripted violence, and net-stocking cocktail service. The cheap seats overflowed with accountants and frat boys, WWF cable potatoes looking for live-action body-slams. The plush ringside seats of the Big Orange Arena were reserved for richies slumming the latest trend: ash-blond yacht-club wives with smooth, bare arms and cigar-club morons with florid faces and thick fingers, mouths full of Stone Cold Steve Austin trivia and the exact height of the late, great Andre the Giant. Next month the nasty-cool thing could be cockfighting, and the richies would be name-dropping their favorite bird at the Monday-morning sales meeting, pontificating about titanium heel spurs over drinks and yellowfin at the Five Feet Café.

"*Jimmy?* Lose the fugue state, man." Rollo fumbled in his oversize black trench coat—a baby-faced brainiac who could play complete chess games in his head but couldn't use a self-serve gas pump without splashing his shoes. He finally pulled out a Palm Pilot speckled with pocket lint. "I was going to give this to Blaine as a peace offering, ask him to put in a good word for me with Pilar." He pulled off a Certs that was stuck to the case. "Now I don't know if—"

"Yeah, Blaine probably can't wait to E-mail his senator or access his on-line stock portfolio." Jimmy deftly caught the Palm Pilot as it slipped from Rollo's grasp, then tucked it back into his trench coat. "You'd do better with an autographed photo of the Rock and a lifetime subscription to *Muscle Mania*."

Rollo bundled the trench coat around himself. "I should never have come here tonight anyway. You shouldn't be here, either. I saw Great White when I first came in, that big fucker gliding around on the other side of the arena, and I half expected to hear the theme from *Jaws*. I don't think he spotted me, but—"

"If you saw him, he saw you."

Rollo shivered. "Sometimes when Great White looks at me . . . I think maybe he can read my mind."

"If that were true, you'd be dead already. We both would." Jimmy checked the crowd, barely moving his head. "Don't worry, the pure of heart have nothing to fear."

Rollo wiped his nose with the back of his hand. "What's that got to do with you or me?"

Jimmy grinned.

"Go ahead, make with the happy face—you got luck, what do you care?" Rollo burrowed deeper into the trench coat. "Me, I was born under the sign of fucked-up-and-fucked-over. Jimmy walks through a shitstorm and never gets wet. Meanwhile, back at the motorcade, Rollo takes a five-point-five-six-millimeter slug to the head, a hot shot from the grassy knoll."

"You're no JFK," said Jimmy. "I see you more like Jackie O, lunging for the rear bumper, making that percentage move out of the range of fire." He saw sweat rolling past Rollo's eyebrows. "If you're so worried about Great White, why are you here?"

"*You're* here, aren't you? I figure you know what you're doing."

"Since when?"

Rollo tugged at his lower lip as if he were pulling open a trap door. "Great White and Macklen, those two are last year's paranoia, over and done with. But Pilar, she's a right-here, right-now problem."

Jimmy looked up as crumpled dollar bills rained onto the canvas from the balcony. The ring girl bent down to scoop them up, and a party of drunken attorneys hooted and waved their neckties at her cleavage. "How much do you owe her?"

"More than I can borrow from you." Rollo pushed back his glasses again. "That's why I took a chance on coming here tonight. I figured I'd link up with Blaine in the dressing room afterward, ask him to talk to her for me—"

"Blaine is useless. You need to talk to Pilar direct."

"Pilar's been waiting for me to mess up longer than my guidance counselor. I go to see her . . ." Rollo shook his head. "It's like the roach motel, man: Rollo walks in, but he don't walk out. You've been gone, Jimmy. Things have changed."

"I hope so."

"No, man, things have changed for the *worse*. You remember that skateboarder Pilar had hawking tie-dyed yoga pants in Venice? He shorted her a few times, so she had Blaine cut off one of his pinkie fingers with pruning clippers. How bogus is that?"

"Pilar is just trying to scare you."

"I *seen* the finger, Jimmy. She keeps it in an olive jar on her coffee table, which is totally uncool." Rollo licked his lips. They both knew what was coming. "Can you help me? Pilar likes you."

"Pilar doesn't like anyone."

"Well . . . you're as close as she gets."

Jimmy checked the crowd, barely moving his head. He thought he had seen Great White before, too. "I'll talk to her."

Rollo sighed, looking even younger in his relief. The crowd hooted as the announcer introduced the Jackal, a beefy man in Kmart jungle-print briefs who sprinted down the aisle and awkwardly dove into the ring. "I'm out of here," Rollo said.

"Move slowly," said Jimmy, drowned out by the cheers for Blind Man Munz—Munz paunchy in baggy tights, dark glasses perched on his nose, tap-tap-tapping his way to the ring with a white cane. Jimmy waited until Rollo had disappeared into the crowd, then he eased over to the entrance to the VIP section and snagged an empty beer bottle from a passing waitress. He set the bottle on the very edge of a table and waited. When the security guard was momentarily distracted by the sound of breaking glass, Jimmy slipped past him and up the stairs to the VIP balcony.

The VIP balcony had been reserved by the Sunset Beach chapter of the Corvette Owners of America, tables full of Brylcreme buckos buying ten-dollar Coronas from the waitresses, trying to stuff bills down their tube tops. The air in the balcony was thick with cigarette smoke, the carpeting stained and threadbare, but the far right edge of the section offered a vantage point from which to observe everything going on below. Back when the Big Orange had been a punk dive, Jimmy had seen Baby Steve, half hidden behind his drum kit, loading up a sock full of glue before O.J.'s Knife started its set. When Baby Steve OD'ed a few months later, Jimmy already had his obit written. From this same spot during the Big O's brief country-and-western incarnation, as the Rhinestone Cowboy Club, Jimmy had seen George Jones sucker-punch a stagehand. Right now he could see Rollo hurrying into the lobby. *Slower*, Rollo.

Jimmy leaned over the balcony, his hands on the railing, trying not to check his watch more than once every five minutes. In a couple of hours Olivia was going to pick him up back at his place. He'd told her he needed a ride to Jonathan's party—it was a lie, but he wanted some time alone with her. Time to make amends. Time to convince her that *her* mistake had been as big as his mistake. If he was half as lucky as Rollo thought, the two of them would never get to the party.

The first time they'd met, he was interviewing her for SLAP—*he hadn't even wanted the assignment, said he wasn't interested in the washed-up-jock beat, but Napitano had insisted. Olivia was a professional golfer, a power player who could slam the ball 230 yards straight down the fairway but had failed to master the subtleties of the putting green. Three years on the circuit, and she'd never even covered her expenses. Now she was the teaching pro at Rolling Hills in Laguna, a new country club catering to a brash, easy-money*

*crowd, dot-com wannabes who raced their carts through the fresh
sod, tossing empty bottles of Corona in their wake.*

*Early one morning, he had waited outside the clubhouse for their
interview, seen Olivia walking toward him from the practice tee, and
forgotten why he was there, just stared at her striding across the grass
with this jaunty, confident gait, seemingly unaware that she had his
complete attention. Hard to believe you could fall in love with someone on the basis of her walk, but Jimmy trusted Olivia's sinewy grace
more than anything she could have said. People lied with words, but
a walk was straight from the heart. She had peeled off her golf glove
as she approached, and he imagined that the nape of her neck was
damp from the sun. He could still feel her handshake.*

Some paleo Queen anthem started up from the overhead speakers, and Jimmy headed toward the stairs, grabbing one of those ten-
dollar beers off a table as he passed. There were shouts behind him,
but he ignored them, taking a long, cool swallow as he glided past
the oblivious guard.

Blind Man Munz caught the Jackal across the face with his
cane, and the Jackal howled. The crowd booed its disapproval. A fat
man ringside tossed a lit cigar at Blind Man Munz, who batted the
soggy Cohiba back as if he were radar-equipped. Jimmy didn't
know the exact choreography, but he could guess the story line.
Blind Man had to have his glasses torn off and stomped on, maybe
even have his cane broken in half, before the Jackal pinned him to
set up the rematch.

The main floor of the arena was standing-room-only, but Jimmy
moved easily through the shifting mass of bodies with a series of
shoulder taps and hip checks, dipping instinctively into the gaps
and eddies of the crowd.

"Jaime!" A square-built homeboy in a cutoff "Selena Viva!"
sweatshirt banged fists with him. "Long time, *vato.* Where you
been?"

Instead of answering, Jimmy passed the homeboy the bottle of beer, unable to remember the man's name. He remembered the red teardrop tattoo, though, signifying a murder committed in defense of his set.

The homeboy draped a meaty arm across Jimmy's shoulder as he guzzled the beer down, then hurled the empty against the back wall. The bottle bounced off without breaking and clattered onto the concrete, and the homeboy's face hardened; he glared at Jimmy, then spit on the floor. *"Mala suerte,"* he muttered, walking away.

Maybe it *was* bad luck, Jimmy thought, as the Jackal loped clumsily around the canvas. Or maybe it had just been a bad throw. Blind Man flailed around with the cane while the crowd called out conflicting directions—"Right!" "Left!" "Not *that* way, Magoo!" The Jackal tore off Blind Man Munz's glasses and tossed them into the crowd.

Jimmy checked his watch. He wondered what Olivia was going to wear tonight, wondered if they would kiss each other on the lips when they first met; he was so intent on her, in fact, that he almost didn't pick up on what was happening behind him, sensing weight and movement only at the last moment. "Evening, Great White," he said, forcing himself not to turn around.

"Someday you're going to tell me how you do that, Jimmy," Great White said gently, his breath warm against Jimmy's neck. "I'd really like to know your secret."

Jimmy turned and looked up into those dead, black eyes. "I'll *never* tell."

Jimmy was tall, but Great White towered above him, a tidal wave in a lustrous black suit, his head shaved. A pair of lightning bolts were tattooed on either side of his neck—they looked like gills. "Been a while, Jimmy—almost a year. I remember because Macklen was still in the hospital. You came to his room and brought him a fifth of Wild Turkey, said you were leaving the next day. Doctor was mad at you for bringing that bottle. Mack still can't drink, but I guess it's the thought that counts."

"Yeah, but how would you know what I was thinking?"

Great White had the flat, unblinking gaze of his namesake. His brow ridges gleamed with sweat, his skull aglow from the red stage lights. "That Eggman thing was about a year ago, too. Did he ever write to you again?"

Jimmy shook his head. "Cops said it was a hoax anyway."

"Too bad."

"Too *bad?*"

"A serial killer—you have to admire the discipline." Great White ran a hand across his scalp, flung sweat onto the floor. "Cops are probably just covering their asses—I bet the Eggman's out there laughing at them right now."

"Could be."

"Why don't we go back to the office and surprise Macklen? He's out of the wheelchair now, whips around on these orthopedic canes like an acrobat—not like that phony fuck," Great White said, pointing at Blind Man tapping his way around the ring. "Come on, we'll pound some forties like old times. I got a bunch of new watercolors up on the walls, all framed and everything. I been taking lessons—"

"Not tonight."

"You have a date, Jimmy? *Love* connection?" Great White stretched his neck from side to side, seeming to grow even larger with every popping vertebra. "Anyone I know?"

Jimmy could see his reflection in Great White's eyes. "No."

"There was that one I saw you with at Ruby's, remember? You looked like you didn't want to introduce her to me," mused Great White. "Was she married?"

"I'm not sure if I remember her."

"Ladies' man. Must be nice." Great White snapped his fingers. "Olivia, that was her name."

"Oh, her."

Great White nodded. "That was right before you left town."

"She was OK." Jimmy sounded bored. "We only went out a couple of times."

"You're spoiled. That was a *fine* piece of woman, a regular fighter, you could just tell by the way she was digging into her burger, juice flying." Great White smacked his lips. "I would love to have a taste of that. You still have her phone number?"

Jimmy peered at Great White's skull. "I never noticed that big blue vein on the side of your head before. It reminds me of the Orinoco during rainy season."

Great White dabbed at his head, feeling for the vein. "The Oro . . . what?"

"It's a river in South America that twists and turns its way to the Atlantic." Jimmy squinted at Great White. "On the map it looks *just* like that vein of yours." He chuckled. "God, that's a filthy river. You wouldn't believe the ugly shit that floats down that thing: bags of rotting garbage, dead monkeys bloated from the sun. . . ."

Great White stared at him, the lightning tattoos on his neck twitching. "Well, I was never too good at geography, so I'll have to take your word on that."

Blind Man had the Jackal pinned. Jimmy hadn't even seen it happen. The referee smacked the canvas. One. Two. Three. It was all over, just like that.

Chapter 2

"You're going to get me in trouble, Jimmy."

"That never stopped you before," he said, opening the side window of the pool house with a squeak of warped wood. Jonathan had changed the lock on the door, but the window latch hadn't worked in twenty years. Halfway through he looked back and saw Olivia standing in the moonlight, her party dress the color of fresh-cut lilacs, goosebumps dappling her bare shoulders even though the night was warm. "Wait out here if you're afraid. I won't be long."

"I'm not afraid," she snapped, hiking up her skirt to follow. "I'm just not dressed for creeping around in the dark."

It was a low sill, but he saw a flash of white silk as she stepped over. He missed the red ones. Not that he was complaining. She had cut her hair since they broke up: where it used to hang past her shoulders, early Cher–style, emphasizing her narrow face and large eyes, this new, sophisticated bob was a helmet of tiny curls, the sides feathered across her cheeks. Her perfume was different, too. He hoped she still had the navel ring. They were standing very close together now, neither of them making any move to retreat.

"What is it?" said Olivia.

It wasn't just her clothes and hair that had changed; it was more important than that. The frisky, buoyant grace that had first attracted him had been replaced by caution and calculation. She used to like taking chances, driving too fast, making love where they didn't belong, the two of them locked and fearless and too crazy to care. It hadn't been that long ago . . . but it had been enough.

Jimmy had ostensibly left southern California to write a quickie book about the world tour of Yank, a local band that had gone triple platinum with a limp blend of white-bread hip-hop and techno. Jimmy didn't like the band or its music, but he had jumped at the invitation from the lead singer. He had told Olivia that he'd be back when the tour was over, but she'd made it clear that she wouldn't wait, her eyes so fierce it looked as if there were a fire raging inside her. He said he didn't expect her to, his smile faltering. Just don't fall in love with anybody, he added. Four months later she married his brother.

The breeze from the open window rippled through his tails-out rayon shirt, sent the black-and-white herringbone pattern fluttering around his lanky frame. The shirt had been perfect at the wrestling match, loose and casual, flagrantly self-assured. Now Jimmy imagined himself as a pirate ship hoisting a flag of surrender.

"What *is* it, Jimmy?"

"You look like such a lady. I feel like I should curtsy or something."

"Go ahead. Kiss my ass while you're at it."

Jimmy grinned. "That's my girl."

She didn't respond to that one. The drive to the pool house had been equally awkward, the two of them chattering away for the first few minutes, batting around perfunctory questions about mutual acquaintances. Olivia had quit her position at the country club since getting married—she said she was considering requalifying for the LPGA tour, but neither of them believed that, both falling silent then, listening to the road hum. Her new Mercedes had heated seats, airbags everywhere, and sideview mirrors that automatically adjusted to uneven terrain—a Panzer tank with glove-leather upholstery, hermetic and overinsulated. She turned on the radio, her face flickering in the oncoming headlights like in an old eight-millimeter home movie, and it was as if he had never left, as if nothing had changed. Jimmy leaned back in the seat, listening as she sang along with the music. A head-on collision and he would have died happy. Instead he asked her to stop by the pool house.

"Do you see it?" Olivia glanced around the room. "Whatever it was you *had* to find?"

"Not yet." Jimmy straightened one of his mother's paint-by-numbers masterpieces, her version of Mauna Loa erupting, blobs of dusty paint on canvas. His mother had decorated the place during her *Blue Hawaii* period—the Tiki Room, she called it, plastering the one-room cabana with peeling surf prints and movie posters of a bemused Elvis festooned with flower leis. Desiccated grass skirts served as curtains, and a fishnet studded with plastic ukuleles was draped across the ceiling. A worn leather sofa overlooked the swimming pool, and on the back wall two large wooden desks were butted against each other, sagging cardboard boxes stacked beside them. He left the lights off—the moonlight was enough. Faint pencil lines were scratched into one wall, growth marks, the lines faded now. Jimmy touched the spot where he had passed Jonathan. The last time his brother had allowed himself to be measured.

"I wish you had told me we were coming here," said Olivia.

"I told you I wanted to pick up something for Jonathan—"

"You didn't say you were going to pick it up *here*."

"I thought you'd like returning to the scene of the crime."

She walked toward him, annoyed, Manolo Blahniks going *clickety-clack* across the tile floor. Jimmy did a slow stutter dance for her in return, crouching, beckoning her toward the couch like a flight-deck engineer preparing an FA-18 for takeoff. Might as well piss her off royally. She laughed instead, and he knew that laugh, and for a moment he thought it was all going to work out.

They hadn't been dating long before Jimmy first brought her to the pool house, not telling her where he was taking her. He had parked a block away and led her through the gap in the back fence, the two of them giggling at their own haste. The television glowed in the main house, his parents watching *Nightline* in the upstairs bedroom. Stepping through the open window, Olivia had fallen silent and then, looking around at the Tiki decor, said she felt like she was in Disneyland. Jimmy had kissed her, whispered, "Welcome to the Magic Kingdom," and started undressing her.

Jimmy's father had almost caught them in the act. One in the morning, and Dr. Gage decided to skim the pool, walking the perimeter in his paisley pajamas, squinting at the surface for an errant leaf, a floundering yellowjacket. They weren't even aware of him until the yellow pool lights came on, highlighting them on the sofa, arms and legs glistening with sweat. Olivia tried to slide onto the floor, but Jimmy held her close, their slippery bodies shaking with laughter, until his father walked back to the main house, oblivious.

Olivia saw Jimmy staring at the couch and shook her head, reading his mind. "God, I thought your father was going to putter around all night. . . ." Her neck flushed. "Maybe my inviting you to Jonathan's party was a mistake."

"Maybe it was."

"I haven't told Jonathan you're coming. I wanted to surprise him. He . . . he's going to be happy to see you. This hasn't been easy on him, either, you know."

"I bet." Jimmy walked over to one of the cardboard boxes and roughly tore it open.

Olivia leaned against one of the desks. "It's hard to imagine that you and Jonathan once did your homework here."

"One of my father's brainstorms." Jimmy pushed aside the box and started in on another one. Jonathan's premed textbooks: anatomy, physiology, yellow highlighter on every page. He didn't know what he was looking for, but this wasn't it. "No distractions in the pool house. No TV, stereo, phone . . . just pure competition. He got off on the idea of our working head to head, scratching over our papers like scorpions in a bottle."

"Jonathan said you skipped a grade and could have skipped a couple more. He said you were smarter than he was."

"Don't believe anything Jonathan says about me." The next carton was filled with games and toys: Battleship, Monopoly, Risk, Magic 8-Ball.

"You didn't really need a ride to the party, did you? That was just an excuse to get me here." Olivia stepped on the deed to Baltic Avenue, her stiletto heel puncturing the low-rent property. "The scene of the crime. . . . Was I supposed to turn all gooey and nostalgic? Maybe throw a fast fuck your way for old times' sake?"

Jimmy walked over to her, put his hands on her hips, slowly kissed her.

She kissed him back, kissed him for a long time, long enough to get his hopes up, then pulled away. "Your brother's wife?" She arched an eyebrow, trying to maintain an air of cool indifference but breathing a little too hard to pull it off. "Isn't there a commandment against that?"

"There're a lot of commandments. I can't keep track of all of them."

Olivia fumbled a pack of cigarettes from her purse and tapped out a thick joint, a monster blunt. "Maybe *you* can't, but Jonathan"—the gold lighter flared as she took a deep hit—"he's got them all down."

"So maybe you have to get a little spanking afterward. That wouldn't be so bad."

Sweet smoke trickled from her nostrils. "Depends."

Jimmy couldn't take his eyes off her. "I've missed you."

"That's nice." Olivia offered him the joint, smoothly rolled it off her thumb onto his.

Jimmy held his temper and took a hit. He immediately felt the pot at the back of his skull, every synapse suddenly going *snap crackle pop,* a warm wave rolling down his spine. He took another hit and passed the joint back. He had to ask her. The question had been running around in his head since he first heard about the marriage. "You and Jonathan . . . it happened so fast. Were you seeing him when you and I were together?"

"No, there was just you."

"Until there was Jonathan."

"*You* were the one who left." Olivia dragged on the joint. "You know, when Jonathan first called to invite me out, I *actually* thought that he was going to pass on a message from you."

Jimmy picked up the Magic 8-Ball from the open box, gave it a shake.

"Ask the Eight-Ball why you left me," said Olivia. "I know we had problems, but I thought we had worked things out. One day things are fine, the next day you're packing your bags like you expect the door to be kicked down at any minute. Did you get yourself in trouble again?"

"A little."

" 'A little'? I'd like to think it took more than a misdemeanor to make you run away from me. I was hoping for a felony. I have my pride."

"I wasn't afraid of the cops; it was worse than that, if it makes you feel better. I didn't want you to get involved."

"Saint Jimmy."

Jimmy could hear a television set in one of the neighboring houses suddenly be turned up loud, then go silent, and he glanced out the window, half expecting to see Great White looking back at him.

"I was so hurt . . . so *furious* with you when you walked out." Olivia dragged on the joint, eyes narrowed. "You have no idea the things I thought about doing to you."

"Yeah, well, you came up with a real doozy."

"Blame yourself, Jimmy."

"I do."

Olivia took another long hit. It didn't seem to be affecting her. "I think about us sometimes. I used to love the way you could get us in anyplace. Off-Limits, No Admittance, it didn't matter to you. I'd take your arm and we'd cruise right past the bouncers and the velvet ropes just like we belonged there." She tapped the ash off the joint, watched it burst on the tile floor, then looked him in the eye. "You should have asked me to marry you when you had the chance."

"I'm sorry."

"Jimmy is sorry. There's a first." She exhaled a plume of smoke, offered him the joint again.

"No thanks."

"Did you turn into a lightweight while you were gone?" Olivia took a long, slow hit, then kissed him hard, forcing his mouth open, breathing the smoke deep into his lungs. She gripped his head in her hands, forcing him to hold the power-hit until she felt his erection against her, then grinding against him in return, Jimmy as intoxicated by the rough intimacy of her kiss as from the high-grade pot. She finally released him. "You didn't use to hesitate," she said, breathing hard. "You were always ready. *Now* who's scared?"

"Maybe I was thinking about that commandment." He could still feel the warmth of her lips.

Olivia shook her head. "I think what you're really scared of is the possibility that we would make love and I still wouldn't leave Jonathan, that I might actually be *happy* with him. Well, live with it: I *am* happy."

Jimmy spun the black ball in the palm of his hand, held it up. "Magic Eight-Ball says, 'No *fucking* way.' "

Olivia dropped the joint on the floor, ground it out. "I'm going to go to the party by myself. You can take a cab home."

Jimmy watched her stalk across the room. "If you knew why I was bringing you here, why did you come?" She stopped in the open doorway. "What did *you* want to have happen, Olivia?"

Olivia slammed the door behind her.

Jimmy listened to her footsteps hurrying away, then kicked the box of games, knocking it over and scattering the contents. The Visible Man clattered across the floor and came to rest faceup, a fourteen-inch-high, clear-plastic model of a man with all his vital organs placed in their proper positions. A human puzzle. He and Jonathan had each gotten one for Christmas one year, along with a copy of *Gray's Anatomy*. Jimmy had lost his almost immediately—he was always losing something—but Jonathan had kept his intact.

Jimmy picked up the Visible Man and smiled at the faint handlebar mustache he had scratched into the face so long ago, remembering Jonathan's anger when he saw what he'd done. He bobbled the model, dropped it, and accidentally kicked it under the desk. Jimmy cursed, bent down, stretched out his arm, and hit something sharp as he pulled out the Visible Man. A splinter from Jonathan's stash spot. Jimmy had forgotten all about it.

One afternoon when they were teenagers, Jimmy had spotted Jonathan building a secret compartment under his desk. After that, Jimmy would check out the cigar-box treasures every few weeks: tiny bottles of scotch his father had brought home from airplane trips, a switchblade, a parade of *Playboy* centerfolds, with Miss July 1983 holding the record for longest continuing appearance.

Now Jimmy reached under the desk, felt around, and pulled out the cigar box. He set it on the desk and opened it carefully, just enough to peek inside. Jonathan liked tricks and traps: soap that made you dirty, fake Valentines from girls who didn't know your name, mousetraps in your underwear drawer. Jimmy saw an envelope inside the box, bound by a couple of rubber bands. One of the bands broke and jumped across the room as he slid out a stack of color Polaroids.

Jimmy tilted the top Polaroid in the dim light to get a better view. There was Jonathan with his penis down the throat of some young woman, her face obscured by her blond curls. The next one showed him with a brunette in a similar pose, his back arched. Jimmy rifled quickly through the stack of Jonathan's Greatest Hits, imagining his brother visiting the Tiki Room after a hard day at the office, putting his feet up on the desk, and taking a stroll down lovers' lane. As he tossed the Polaroids back into the cigar box, one from the bottom of the stack popped out and fell onto the desk. Jimmy stared at the photo, then finally picked it up.

Steve DeGerra lay sprawled on the crushed-gravel running track of Dillard High School. He had been a muscular seventeen-year-old high hurdler, a B-minus student who wanted to be a travel agent when he graduated so he could fly for free. Now he lay there with his ear pressed to the ground, eyes wide, as though listening for something, something coming fast behind him, something that had caught up with him early that morning. The gunshot had come at close range, the exit wound blowing out the back of his skull, blood forming a dark corona around his head as it seeped into the fine gravel.

Jimmy picked up the stack of Polaroids and found the rest of the Eggman's half dozen at the bottom: Philip Kinneson, Denise Fredericks, William Hallberg, Carlos Mendoza, Elice Santos. Jimmy knew all their names, their birthdays, their favorite television shows. He laid them back in the cigar box and just stood there, time falling around him in the pool house, the room filled with ruined faces and bad memories.

Jonathan's Polaroids should have been no big deal. Street cops and morgue attendants had run an underground business for years peddling snapshots of their famous and infamous clientele, with celebrity suicides and Hollywood has-beens crashing their Harleys commanding top dollar. Jimmy had seen splatter shots passed around at parties where the guests' coolness quotient was measured by how they reacted to the gruesome images. Jaded insouciance scored max points. Jimmy always flunked.

Plenty of Eggman shots had been mailed to Jimmy at *SLAP*, crime-scene glossies and grainy Instamatic blow-ups, some sent by people pretending to be fans asking for his autograph and even more sent by screwheads pretending to *be* the Eggman. After a while Jimmy had dreaded opening the mail and let it stack up for days. He didn't remember getting any Polaroids, though—they seemed more personal somehow, more intimate, but then Jonathan had always known where his tender spots were.

Jimmy looked at the face of Steve DeGerra, the sprinkle of adolescent acne across his forehead. He imagined Jonathan going through his collection by flashlight, as much aroused by the Eggman photos as by his own frozen orgasms; imagined him slipping the Polaroids into an envelope with Jimmy's name on it, laughing as he licked the flap. Jimmy grabbed the cigar box off the desk and hurled it against the wall, the contents scattering, a blizzard of blow jobs and death.

He flipped open his cell phone, so angry that it took his fingers three tries to get Holt's office number right, needing to take it out on *someone*. "This is Detective Jane Holt," said the recording, "I am not available now. If you wish to speak to another detective, press one. If you wish to leave a message, wait for the beep."

"Jane, this is Jimmy. When I called last week you said the case was still 'ongoing,' which is a crock of shit, if you'll pardon my fucking French. Maybe if your uniforms hadn't been so busy freelancing splatter Polaroids they might have found something useful at the scene—you know, *evidence*—but what do I know, I'm just a civilian."

He broke the connection, then called for a cab, glancing around the room as he listened to the Muzak on hold. For a moment he was tempted to take some of the Polaroids with him, but then he picked up the Visible Man instead. After all, he couldn't go to Jonathan's party without taking his big brother *something*.

Chapter 3

Jimmy rode the service elevator of the Newport Tower to the top floor, a tray of jumbo prawns precariously balanced on one hand. Security had been tight in the lobby, but there had been plenty of confused action at the service bay behind the building, caterers unloading crates of champagne and iced canapés, no one really in charge.

He stepped out of the elevator, walked quickly through the small kitchen, set down the prawns, and kept going, ignoring the chef at the prep counter, who eyed his casual attire. A couple of busboys were sneaking a smoke in the hallway, their heads hung out an open window as though awaiting a guillotine. He held the door open for a waiter carrying a tray of empty glasses into the back, then stepped through into the world of Perfection Enhancements Inc.—a better and brighter world, the air chilled and electrostatically sanitized, the carpet thick and allergy-free.

P.E.I. took up the whole top floor of the building. Viewed through the full-length windows, the whole coast was dappled with lights: headlights and taillights strung along the PCH, Catalina Island glowing through the evening haze, the rhythmic red and green flashes of the offshore oil rigs pumping up crude off Long Beach. The reception area was spacious, its curved entryway feng-shui correct, welcoming to positive energy and success, the buttery yellow couches arranged into privacy alcoves, the carpet softer than a PGA putting green. A live band somewhere played Motown, but not loud enough.

Photographs lined the walls. There were the usual publicity shots of Jonathan shaking hands with various politicians and sports figures, but the ones that caught Jimmy's attention were a series of more informal photos taken on his brother's regular trips to South America and Africa: Jonathan beaming in his immaculate blue scrubs, surrounded by locals in their best clothes, awkward and serious before the camera. Jonathan spent three weeks out of every year doing reconstructive plastic surgery in impoverished countries, flying in complete surgical teams at his own expense. Jimmy stared at the children clutching Jonathan's hands and tried to align the image of the good doctor with the brother he had grown up with. The air smelled faintly of sandalwood, which was supposed to induce relaxation and harmony; it wasn't working on Jimmy.

An enormous saltwater aquarium flanked one interior wall, iridescent angelfish lazily drifting through the bubbles. A slender blonde strolled past the tank, and the angelfish followed her, lacy fins trailing like bridal gowns. The blonde wore a low-cut black dress that showed off her small breasts, her hair curling against her bare shoulders. She handed a waiter her empty champagne glass, took a fresh one, and walked over to Jimmy. "Practicing your Academy Award acceptance speech?" she asked. She saw his confusion and nodded at the Visible Man tucked under his arm.

Jimmy pumped the clear-plastic model over his head. "I'd like to thank all the little people," he said, annoyed that he had been so slow on the uptake. "My agent, my trainer—"

"Don't forget the Man Upstairs."

"He was evicted last month."

"Too many loud parties?" She watched him with Hockney-blue eyes.

Jimmy shook his head. "Nonpayment of rent. Poor old guy lost his job."

She smiled. Her teeth could have advertised chewing gum or soft drinks or anything minty-fresh. "I'm Michelle."

"Jimmy." He tore himself away from her eyes. "Have you seen Jonathan?"

"And I thought we were hitting it off."

Jimmy followed her through the well-dressed crowd—past the teenagers with fresh 90210 noses and vacuum-sucked midriffs, willowy matrons with drumhead faces and too many tennis bracelets, gray-haired executives whose skin was soft and laser-pink. There wasn't an ounce of fat or discomfort or embarrassment in the room: Jonathan's patients were perfect now, one step ahead of gravity and cellular fatigue, one step ahead of the vast thickening of all other living things.

Michelle grabbed a strawberry from a silver tray and looked around. She took a bite of the strawberry, grimaced, and tossed the rest into a potted plant. "I don't see him, Jimmy." He liked the way she said his name. "Here comes Kendall," she said. "Get ready to hear about her new tits."

Kendall was a tall, very thin brunette with addled eyes, a strapless red Versace, and a diamond pendant the size of a cocktail onion nestled between her buoyant breasts. She air-kissed Michelle, then told her, "You *really* should get your boobs upgraded, sweetie. You must be the last girl in California running on original equipment."

"Don't touch them," Jimmy advised Michelle. "They're classics."

Michelle toasted him with her champagne.

"There's no scar at all, Michelle, if that's what you're concerned about," said Kendall, irritated. "Jonathan went in through my belly button. The implant goes *under* the muscle, so it feels perfectly natural, and if you want to breast-feed—not that you'd *want* to waste your new beauties on a brat, but *if* you ever do—you can lactate away like some contented cow."

"What a lovely image," said Michelle.

"Madonna and calf," said Jimmy.

Kendall scrunched up her face, confused, and turned her attention to Jimmy. She toyed with her pendant, the diamond shimmering against her tan like a warm tear as she eyed him, taking in his untucked test-pattern shirt and black jeans. "Who's your new friend, Michelle, and how did he *ever* get past the rent-a-cops? All these gorgeous men walking around, and you're hooked up with one who looks like he's not even housebroken."

"Woof woof," said Jimmy.

Kendall tapped her front teeth with a fingernail, her head tilted back so that Jimmy could see the nostrils rimmed with cocaine. "This one has possibilities, Michelle. Short-term, not buy-and-hold," she cautioned, "but still . . . Oh look, there's Sarah." Kendall finger-waved at a stocky woman leaning against a pocked marble replica of the Venus de Milo. "Sarah used to be the top spackle diva in Hollywood. I don't know *how* Jonathan stole her away from Fox. Sarah switched me to a micropulverized lamb-placenta night masque that's *completely* changed my pH balance." She adjusted her breasts for maximum loft, then glided off to more promising company, but not before adding, "And me a strict vegetarian."

Jimmy saw Jonathan walk out of a door on the far side of the room. "I have to go, too, Michelle. It was nice meeting—"

"You really don't recognize me, do you?"

Jonathan was busy shaking hands with a local TV news anchor, Harrison Lee, a distinguished-looking white-haired gent with a twenty-something clinging to his arm. Jimmy turned back to Michelle, trying to place her, but finally shook his head.

Michelle grinned. "Then it was worth every dollar I spent."

Jimmy stared, intrigued. He still didn't remember her.

" 'Wilma Jean, the trailer queen,' " Michelle singsonged, then winced as if she had hurt herself.

Jimmy peered at her. "Wilma? Is that really you? You're . . . beautiful." He caught himself. "I didn't mean that . . . uh . . . what happened to your accent?"

"I done got rid of it," she drawled. "Got rid of my name, too, and that thirty pounds of ugly blubber them cool kids was always teasing me about." Her fingers moved across her face, pointing things out as if she were a spokesmodel. "I put braces on my teeth, bleached what I could and capped the rest," she said in her new, sophisticated voice, "switched to contact lenses, and had my hair lightened. Then Jonathan took over the heavy lifting. He shaved over half an inch from my chin, reset my jaw, lowered my brow line." She smiled. "The rest is all me."

Jimmy took her hands. "I'm happy to see you, Wilma."

"Michelle," she corrected him. "Well, aren't you going to ask me?"

"Ask you what?"

"Where I got the money. It always comes down to money, doesn't it?" She had a lovely laugh. He didn't know whether or not it was the same one she'd had in high school; he had never heard her laugh back then. "I worked two jobs all through college, lived on Kraft macaroni and cheese, took the bus everywhere. Jonathan let me run a tab. It took me years to pay it off, but he didn't even charge me interest—he said he was a doctor, not a bank. I'm an attorney now—family law." She smiled. "I handled Kendall's last two divorces."

"She's better than an annuity."

"Four years at Anaheim High," said Michelle, talking faster now, a hint of her accent coming back in her haste, "and in all that time you were the only boy, the *only* one, Jimmy, who ever held a door open for me, the only one to ask me how I was doing. I knew you were just being nice, but I was still grateful."

Jimmy remembered her sitting alone in the cafeteria, eyes downcast, her face hidden in a book.

"God, I had such a crush on you," said Michelle. "When you're homely, people tell you all the time about inner beauty, but *trust* me, Jimmy, inner beauty can't compete with the real thing."

"Well, now you have both."

Michelle blushed. "Look, Jimmy, I know I was the reason you got expelled in your senior year, and I want to thank you."

"I don't know what you mean."

Michelle stared at him until he thought he would melt. "I think you do."

"That was a long time ago."

"Not that long." Michelle fumbled in her purse. "I know you want to talk with Jonathan, but if you ever feel like getting together, having a drink or something. . . ." She pulled out a business card, wrote on it, and passed it to him. "This is my home number."

"Thanks." Jimmy tucked the card into his pocket. Jonathan was still busy with the news anchor. "I have to go now." He stopped as Olivia walked up to Jonathan and kissed him. It was the first time he had ever seen her do that. Olivia's laughter carried across the room. It felt like a slap in the face.

Michelle turned to see what Jimmy was looking at. "I'm sorry," she said quietly. "I heard about what happened with you two. That's why I was so surprised to see you here tonight. I thought maybe you were . . . over her."

Jimmy watched Olivia chattering away with Jonathan, touching his lapels, the two of them laughing it up for the other guests.

Michelle rested her hand on his arm. "Are you OK?"

"I have to go, Wilma—*Michelle*," Jimmy corrected himself.

"Of course."

"It was really good seeing you again." Across the room Olivia suddenly noticed him and tensed, and Jimmy remembered the way she'd looked standing in the doorway of the pool house, her composure shaken, afraid to answer him. He tossed the Visible Man on a passing tray headed for the kitchen, laid him in state among the shrimp remnants and empty champagne glasses. He didn't need to give Jonathan a gift; Jonathan already had everything he needed. Jimmy made his way easily through the crowd now, the waters parting as he headed straight for the happy couple.

Jonathan saw him approaching and stopped talking. He was thirty-seven, a year older than Jimmy, handsome, his features as smooth and unlined as a mannequin's, his skin so pale it appeared bleached. "James." He showed his large teeth.

"Jonathan." Jimmy flashed his own fangs.

"I didn't know you were back." Jonathan turned to Olivia. "Darling, did you know . . . ?"

"I wanted to surprise you," Olivia said, warning Jimmy with her eyes.

"Well, you certainly succeeded, and what a wonderful surprise it is." Jonathan wore a midnight-blue tuxedo that draped across his slender frame, a wafer-thin watch on his wrist, a study in casual elegance—if Jimmy hadn't known better, he would have believed the genteel, old-money look his brother cultivated. "Welcome, James." His handshake was cool and dry, lingering, more of an appraisal than a greeting, as if he were taking a patient's temperature. *"Welcome."*

"You're repeating yourself," said Jimmy. "Does one welcome cancel out the other?"

Jonathan chuckled. "Not at all. It's good to see you."

"How good is it?" asked Jimmy. "As good as a hot fudge sundae? Better than a blow job?"

Jonathan stared at him. "Coming here tonight—it can't have been easy for you."

Jimmy shrugged. "Who am I to stand in the way of love? That's what it was, wasn't it?"

"It was love." Jonathan glanced at Olivia. "True love."

"You're repeating yourself again," said Jimmy. "I'm starting to wonder about you."

"What's going on?" Harrison asked Olivia, the people nearby whispering among themselves. "Are they arguing?"

"Not at all," said Jonathan, "just a little verbal jousting." He inclined his head toward the news anchor. "Harrison, I'd like to introduce my—"

"We've already met," said Jimmy.

Jonathan raised an eyebrow. "Yes, of course."

The letter from the Eggman had driven the circulation of *SLAP* to its highest level ever and made Jimmy semifamous for a few weeks—Leno had mentioned him in a monologue, *USA Today* had run a photo in its "Newsmakers" section, and Harrison Lee had conducted a fawning interview for his top-rated broadcast, asking several times if Jimmy was concerned for his own safety, blustering on about the "fearsome responsibilities" of the press. Two weeks later Harrison Lee had been the first to accuse Jimmy of concocting the Eggman letter to advance his career; he had even called on the district attorney to investigate this "egregious violation of the public trust."

"Nice to see you again, Jimmy," said Harrison Lee, holding out his hand.

Jimmy ignored the hand, ignored Harrison Lee, too. "You get whiter every time I see you, Jonathan. You're almost a blank canvas now—is that the look you're going for?"

Jonathan patted the news anchor on the shoulder, watching Jimmy. "You'll have to excuse my brother."

"Don't make any excuses for me," Jimmy said, "and I won't make any for you, either."

"It's official, no excuses for anyone," said Olivia, her gaiety forced.

"Quite a place you have here," Jimmy said to Jonathan. "Perfection Enhancements Inc. I've finally seen the stuff that dreams are made of."

"Are you all right, James?"

"I particularly like the photos of you on your goodwill missions," said Jimmy. "The great white father standing there in your surgical scrubs surrounded by all those adoring faces. It brought a lump to my throat."

Jonathan's eyes were as cool as his handshake.

"Send me some postcards the next time you go off to save the world. You know how I like to get mail."

A hint of color blossomed across Jonathan's pale cheeks for an instant, then disappeared. "I hope you'll show Olivia some consideration, James. This has been very difficult for her. There were a lot of unpleasant comments when she and I first started dating. Even Mother and Father didn't think it quite appropriate."

"I had some comments myself. Want to hear them?"

"Please don't, Jimmy," said Olivia. *"Please."*

"It's very painful seeing you like this," said Jonathan. "Rambling, disheveled, accusatory. You used to have such a fine, incisive mind. I was quite in awe of you once upon a time."

"When exactly was that?" Jimmy felt lightheaded. "Help me out."

"Of *course* Jonathan will help you; he's your brother." Mrs. Gage squeezed out of the crowd and kissed him on the cheek. Their mother was a plump, apologetic woman who had once been thin. "Richard! Look who's here," she said, beckoning.

"I'm not blind," Dr. Gage said sourly. He caught sight of the news anchor's date and smoothed his fine gray hair—one hundred strokes a night—preening for her, the dandy in his dotage.

"Jimmy . . . it's so good to see you, so *very* good." Mrs. Gage dabbed her eyes with a tissue, then didn't know where to put it. "Was this your idea, Jonathan? What a wonderful, *wonderful* surprise. All of us together—"

"The credit goes to Olivia," said Jonathan, wrapping his arm around her waist.

"Isn't this wonderful, Richard?" gushed Mrs. Gage.

"Wonderful," said Dr. Gage.

"Are you back for good, Jimmy?" asked Mrs. Gage. "Please say you are."

Jimmy didn't answer.

"Your brother throws quite a shindig, doesn't he?" said Dr. Gage, affecting the faint British accent he put on when he was in social situations. "Baskets of orchids flown in from Brazil, black truffle pâté, *pounds* of it. . . ." A gold Harvard Medical School pin gleamed on his lapel: ashamed of his no-name alma mater, he had bought the tiny crest from a mail-order catalog. He saw Jimmy staring at the pin. "Jonathan knows quality when he sees it," he muttered, making it sound like a threat.

Jonathan still had an arm around Olivia's waist. She fitted herself into his embrace, and Jimmy turned away and hugged his mother. She had put on thirty pounds since he was a boy, but he could still feel her heartbeat when they held each other. "Good night, Mom."

"Don't go," said Mrs. Gage, clinging to him. "You're *always* leaving."

"Let him go," said Dr. Gage.

"Good night, Olivia," said Jimmy. She didn't answer.

"Don't be in such a hurry," said Jonathan. "The situation is difficult, I know that, but give it a chance. We're just getting started."

Jimmy smiled.

Chapter 4

The heavy-duty padlock on his double-wide storage locker was just the way he had left it, which meant that on this glorious Monday morning, with the sun coming up and birds making chirpity-chirp, Rollo was just as fucked as he had feared. On the drive over he had almost convinced himself that Nikki *really* hadn't cleaned out the locker, that he must have had a seizure last week when he looked inside. Malaria, maybe, or dengue fever—some weird bug he had picked up when he was in Costa Rica with her, a parasite that had eaten through his cerebral cortex. But no such luck.

Rollo shook the hair out of his eyes. The padlock was still in place, but he could see a thin gap on the shackle where it had been cut clean through. The commercials for the padlock showed the case withstanding a bullet, but nobody attacked a lock with a handgun anymore—nobody outside of old cowboy movies, at least, where the bad guy shattered the lock to the strongbox with one shot, money blowing in the wind. Nowadays the bad guy used a power saw with a diamond-carborundum blade that cut through hardened steel as if it were tofu.

Maybe getting ripped off by Nikki balanced things out for what he and Jimmy had pulled on Macklen and Great White, some kind of delayed yin-yang payback. Except that ripping off Macklen's high-speed memory chips had been all Jimmy's idea, and now Rollo was the one with the empty storage locker, Rollo was the one whose fingers and toes Pilar was about to snippety-snip. Jimmy's biggest worry was getting hooked up again with his old girlfriend. Where was the yin-yang bullshit balance in that?

Rollo was so scared of Pilar that he had done something stupid last week. Jimmy would have been pissed if he had known, but Rollo needed money, and after Nikki cleaned him out, the only thing he had left was the memory chips. Rollo didn't even get much for them—he got burned, was what he got. Selling the chips was risky, OK, but Pilar wanted her money *now,* and it wasn't like Great White and Macklen were still looking for the chips. It had been a whole year. Ancient history. Might as well expect *T. rex* to file a wrongful-death suit against the meteor that had smoked the dinosaurs.

The early-morning traffic crawled past the AAA-Best Storage Center, horns beeping, trucks noisily shifting gears—call it a Symphony for the Wage Ape. The air already stank of diesel fumes and grease from the Taco Bell on the corner. Fucking La Palma. Too far inland to smell the ocean, too far from L.A. to be part of the scene, a cramped suburb with more concrete than grass. No good movie theaters, either, just multiplexes with screens the size of Band-Aids and plush seats with Big Gulp cup holders. Just what Rollo needed, watching the latest Jet Li masterpiece while Debby and Donny La Palma sat behind him slurping their four-dollar Dr Peppers, Donny complaining that Debby didn't *tell* him it had subtitles.

Rollo hated La Palma and everyone in it. He had grown up here, had his skateboard confiscated by the cops for grabbing air at the Public Safety Building, been beaten up for having a stupid name, been suspended from La Palma Junior High for substituting *Evil Dead 2* for *Glory* in American history class. *Glory* blew, *Evil Dead 2* rocked, it was as simple as that. La Palma had plenty of storage facilities, though—double-wide lockers for families with too much crap to fit into their garages and units for mobile singles who needed to stash their beanbag chairs while they moved in with their latest dream date. Storage facilities for people like Rollo, too—entrepreneurs who needed a safe place for their inventory and a safe place to work. *Safe:* some joke.

Losing the inventory was bad enough—all those VCRs and laptops and the new Sharp portable DVD players (eleven hundred bucks apiece retail!)—but he'd also had the rough cut of his most recent film in the storage unit, along with a complete editing facility. He had brought Nikki here on their third date, let her look through his favorite camera, a Canon GL1 Mini-DV, an absolutely gorgeous hunk of technology. He had shown her the first two or three hours of the movie, *Coma Patient,* the two of them sitting on the love seat, eating microwave popcorn, going at it like a couple of maniacs.

Rollo had met her on the set of a porn shoot in the valley a couple of months ago. He had been second cameraman, shooting cutaways and facials, and Nikki had been one of the new girls, determined to get her face on the box. She had the body for it, hard and natural, but her complexion was a little broken out, and her nose was maybe a little too big. Rollo didn't care. He got performance acne himself, and he promised to find her best angle for her close-ups. She wore glasses when she wasn't being filmed, same prescription as his, too. It was amazing.

He'd been crazy about Nikki, but it wasn't like he was some trusting fanboy begging to be ripped off. He had blindfolded her on the drive over, which they both thought was pretty fucking hot. No way should she have been able to find the storage locker again. She had, though. She had found it and emptied it. The inventory was replaceable, but *Coma Patient*—that loss was going to go down in the history book of Lost Cinema Classics, along with the missing five reels from von Stroheim's *Greed.*

The only bright spot in the rolling disaster that was Rollo's life was that the rest of his films—fifty-one feature documentaries—were locked in the guarded, temperature-controlled vaults of Santa Monica Secure Deposit. They could survive a nuclear blast behind all that steel and concrete. He stared at the cut padlock on the door to the storage locker, chewing his lip. Nikki hadn't even liked *Coma Patient* all that much.

Rollo looked around. He should have crashed hours ago, but he was too amped up to go home, too nervous to close his eyes anyway. After leaving Jimmy at the wrestling match, he had hit some spots, trying to move product. He'd gotten bounced out of a couple of places when his fake ID didn't convince the bartender, but he'd managed to unload the last of his Palm Pilots to a table of auto mechanics at Cap'n Jack's in Sunset Beach.

Rollo had scoped the pod of Mr. Goodwrenches the moment he walked in, the four mechanics hunched over their beers, eyeing the babes. Probably nervous about their dirty fingernails. Rollo discounted the Palm Pilots way too cheap, but one of the mechanics threw in a full set of retreads for the van, and besides, Rollo's old man had been a grease monkey, a real sad case with raw knuckles and a bad back. The mechanics didn't even want a flight check on the Palm Pilots; they were just going to flash them at the bar and impress the honeys out of their thongs. When it came to women, men were idiots. Testosterone Nation, home of the brainless hard-on. And Rollo was their king.

He kicked the door of the locker, sending the padlock flying. Rollo swung the door of the locker open, flipped on the light. Nothing had changed. The storage locker was still empty except for a few trailing extension cords—Nikki had even taken the love seat. Probably going to use it in her next movie. He squinted, stepped inside, walked all the way to the back, still not believing what he was seeing. *Coma Patient* was stacked neatly on the bare concrete, forty-four half-hour digital film packs. He wiped his eyes, unable to help himself. Turning into a pussy, man. There was a heart scrawled on the bare wood of the back wall, a small red heart, a lipstick heart with the initials *RB + CT. RB* was for Rollo Boyce, but *CT,* that stood for Clara Thomas. Nikki had used her real name, not her professional one.

Rollo gingerly touched the heart, looked at the waxy smudge on his forefinger. It was her color. She hadn't needed to return his film. She hadn't needed to draw a Valentine. She hadn't needed to use her real name. He was fucked with Pilar, he was *beyond* fucked, and Nikki had done it to him—but in some weird-ass way, it was almost worth it to have met Clara, too.

Chapter 5

It was a little early for Desmond to have company, the sun just starting to come up through the palm trees, automatic sprinklers starting up on some of the lawns. A new pickup rumbled down the block, two Cambodian boys squatting in the bed, deep in conversation as they hurled fat copies of the *Times* onto the sidewalk. Jimmy had cruised around for hours after leaving Jonathan's office party and finally ended up drinking strawberry malts at the Harbor House Café while he finished the Retro Wrestling article on his laptop. At about four in the morning he used his cell phone to download it into the *Times*'s computer system, then drove home.

A blue Taurus was parked in Desmond's driveway—Jimmy saw a city garage bar-code sticker on the rear window as he pulled up to the curb. It must be some old buddy of Desmond's from the force.

About five years ago, long before Jimmy met him, Desmond Terrell had retired on half disability from the Newport Beach Police Department after being shot for the third time. He had put in for full benefits, but the brass had argued that even if he was no longer fit to ride a cruiser, he was certainly capable of riding a desk. Desmond had no interest in answering phones or booking the chief's squash game. "Three strikes and I'm out," he had insisted. You would have thought that after all the commendations and medals of valor, and with his being the first African American police officer on the NBPD, the department would have wanted to avoid any bad publicity, but Desmond refused to play the race card and eventually accepted his bosses' lowball offer. His last day on the job, he ticketed the assistant police chief three times before the man made it to the station—once for speeding, once for failure to yield, and once for resisting arrest. His retirement party was the largest in memory, with cops' coming from three counties away to drink whiskey and swap stories.

Jimmy dodged the spray from the sprinklers as he walked up the paving stones, felt the cool mist on his face. Desmond had them set to start up at 6:00 A.M., to give the grass a good drink before the morning heat evaporated it. "Waste not, want not" was one of Desmond's favorite mottos. Another one was "He who shits on the road will meet flies on his return," a South African proverb beloved of Nelson Mandela. Jimmy had started around the side of the house, toward the in-law apartment he was living in, when Desmond stepped out onto the porch.

"I've got someone inside who wants to talk with you," said Desmond, cradling a D.A.R.E. mug of coffee in his hand.

"Who is it?"

Desmond took a sip, peering at Jimmy over his gold wire rims, in no hurry to answer. He was a trim man in his early fifties, with a wide nose and a high forehead, wearing a crisp mint-green polo shirt, khaki shorts, and leather slippers, his short hair gray. He blotted his mouth with a paper napkin. "It's Jane Holt."

"Oh, *goody.*" Holt must have checked her messages at the office when she got up this morning—she had probably come by to warn him that it was a misdemeanor to use profanity on a department machine. Or to correct his grammar.

The Orange County Sheriff's Department had coordinated the task force set up to cover the Eggman homicides, but Holt had been the lead detective on the investigation, partially because she was the one he had called with the Eggman letter, but mostly because she was a tenacious bureaucratic infighter, unafraid to make enemies. She'd already had a law degree when she joined the Laguna Beach P.D. eleven years before; she had graduated second in her class from the academy and still hadn't forgiven herself. She had risen fast, breaking some decent cases, taking seminars at the FBI academy at Quantico like all the other hard chargers, pulling double shifts and never complaining. None of it had helped her with the Eggman case.

"Come in and pour yourself a glass of orange juice," Desmond offered. "Jane was kind enough to drop by before her shift, so the least you can do is be polite." Desmond's voice was carefully modulated, unhurried, as always avoiding street slang. He came down the steps to Jimmy, out of earshot from the living room. "What in *blazes* did you do now?"

"Not a thing."

"You're about as forthcoming as Holt is." Desmond took a swallow of coffee, his brown eyes alert over the rim of the cup. "Olivia picked you up last night, but you came home in a taxicab a couple of hours later to get your car. You should have called me if you needed a ride, instead of wasting your money like that. I wouldn't have rubbed it in." He took another swallow. "Of course, I *did* tell you she wasn't going to take you back."

"I never said I was smart, Desmond, I just said I was charming."

Desmond tossed the rest of his coffee onto the grass. "Jane Holt is an A-one cop. Charming won't get you anywhere with her." He walked across the lawn, picked up a plastic bottle cap, shaking his head. The world was riding to hell on a fast freight, and Desmond measured its progress by the amount of trash tossed into his yard.

"Why don't you tell her to come back later?" said Jimmy. "The market should be opening up any minute; I wouldn't want us to disturb you."

Desmond had started day trading stocks after his retirement—his living room had three computer screens, a high-speed DSL hookup, and Datek "real-time streaming quotes," whatever that meant. He was usually at his worktable every morning by 6:30 A.M.—9:30 on Wall Street—pounding out bids, buying and selling.

"Monday morning's always choppy," said Desmond. "I'm going to stay out of the water until I see where it's running. Protect your capital, that's the first rule. The only rule." He opened the door. "Come on in, get it over with."

Holt regarded Jimmy from a high-backed chair, legs crossed at the knees, a pretty woman in her late thirties, with high cheekbones and tired eyes. Even in southern California, where every media-savvy detective wore tailored suits and designer sunglasses, she was the best-dressed cop Jimmy had ever seen. This morning she wore a knee-length blue-gray cashmere skirt and a matching blazer that had probably cost her two months' pay. Not that she lived on her paycheck; the single strand of matched pearls around her neck had probably been in her family since the *Mayflower*. Only the top-siders on her feet revealed the practicalities of her profession. She glanced at her watch, raised an eyebrow. "I was expecting to find you in bed at this hour," she said, her voice flat and nasal. "I was prepared to apologize for stopping by so early."

"Sure you were," he replied. Holt specialized in that most re-fined of police tactics, the art of gracious intrusion. She liked to drop in unannounced, either late at night or at dawn, begging your pardon as she stood there, looking past you, hoping to find evidence that you'd been doing something illegal, cutting heroin or building an anthrax bomb or reusing postage stamps, it didn't matter—petty crimes weren't worth a bust, but they were leverage, and everyone was guilty of *something*. Jimmy gave her his best smile. "I'm the one who should apologize, Jane. Calling you last night—I was an ass-hole."

Holt recrossed her legs, not contradicting him. She believed his apology as much as he believed hers.

Desmond chuckled as he eased himself into his leather recliner, picking up the *Investor's Business Daily*. "By the way, Jane," he said, slipping on his bifocals, running a finger down the columns of small print, "tell your daddy I made sixty-seven percent on my port-folio last year. Ask him how well that hedge fund of his performed."

"I never discuss money with my father," said Holt.

"Me neither," Jimmy chimed in. "I guess we're more alike than you thought, Jane."

Desmond ruffled his newspaper.

Holt and Jimmy had spent a lot of time together during her initial investigation of the Eggman murders, when they were both hoping there would be a follow-up contact from the killer. He was living in a tiny house off Laguna Canyon Road back then—more of a shack, really. Holt would show up at all hours, always with an excuse for not calling first. She was friendly, gently asking the same question three or four different ways, coming back to his answers minutes later as though she had just thought of something—"I guess what I'm really confused by, Jimmy, is why this the Eggman character would contact *you* to get his message out. I never heard of a movie review's triggering a serial killer." Jimmy wasn't offended; he was a reporter, and he used some of the same techniques himself. He knew she had interviewed his coworkers, his neighbors, looked into his bank account. He had run a background check on her, too; he still laughed remembering the look on her face when he told her he was a little, well, *shocked* by her C-minus in statistics at Bryn Mawr.

With his approval, Holt had placed a pin trace on his home phone as well as his work number, the two of them sitting on his sofa two or three nights a week, playing Scrabble for five dollars a game and waiting for the phone to ring. Holt drank her own Darjeeling, bringing the loose tea and a sterling tea ball from home, and became increasingly annoyed as he won game after game. Once after he left the room he caught her examining the pieces, looking for rough edges on the high-value tiles, tiny imperfections that he might be using to cheat. She never found a thing.

Holt stood up. "Is there someplace we can talk?" It wasn't really a question.

Jimmy headed for the kitchen, heard her chair creak behind him. It was a small kitchen, and she leaned against the sink, so close he could smell her perfume—a subtle scent, clean, not floral. Holt had too many sharp angles for his taste; when he imagined the two of them making love, all he could think of was their elbows and knees banging together. Still, she smelled good. "How did you find me, Jane?"

"I was surprised to find that you were living with Desmond," said Holt, not answering the question. "I didn't think you had any friends on the *other* side of the lineup."

"Just Desmond . . . and now you," Jimmy said, taking the pitcher out of the refrigerator. "I guess we're both slipping, Jane."

Holt showed her teeth, giving him a glimpse of a slight overbite. You could always tell old money: rich people don't chase the cover-girl smile, wanting instead for their kids to resemble the oil portraits of their great-uncles and great-aunts hanging in the library or the conservatory or some other room not found in any floor plan outside of Agatha Christie. Jimmy liked the overbite and the way she stirred her Darjeeling without ever hitting the side of her cup with the spoon, and he particularly liked the way she was genuinely nonplussed when he laughed at her jokes—maybe the cops she worked with didn't appreciate her wry sense of humor.

A few weeks into her stakeout at his place, Holt had actually taken off her shoes, really off duty now, the two of them switching to dark Jamaican rum, matching each other shot for shot, playing Scrabble in pig Latin. That was the evening Olivia had chosen to drop in. After the introductions, there was a few minutes' worth of stilted conversation before Holt remembered some reports she had to file. After she left, Jimmy and Olivia bickered over everything *but* Holt, finally shutting each other up by making love. It worked. It usually had back then. Holt had continued coming by, but she never took her shoes off again. The Eggman had never called him at home. Never called him at work. Never sent him another letter. A year ago, Holt had written him a check for $285 in Scrabble losses, and that was the last he'd seen of her. Until now.

"Did you come by for a rematch?" Jimmy poured himself a glass of orange juice, then held up the pitcher, but she shook her head. She looked more stressed than he remembered, worry lines etched beside her mouth. "Come on, I'll play with half my vocabulary tied behind my back."

"You never cashed my check. Guilty conscience?"

"Maybe I was just being a gentleman." Jimmy took a gulp of

orange juice, gagged. "Jesus, Desmond," he croaked, emptying his glass into the sink. "You buying swap-meet O.J. *again?*"

"Kindly don't tell me how to shop," Desmond said from the living room.

Jimmy wiped his tongue with a paper towel. "If you need more money for my share of the groceries, Desmond, just say so."

"You mentioned some Polaroids in your call last night," said Holt. "I'd like to see them."

"I don't have them." Jimmy edged past her toward the living room. Jonathan was a creep, but that wasn't a crime. Neither was possession of splatter shots.

"These Polaroids," persisted Holt, "was there one of Philip Kinneson?"

"They were all there." Jimmy glanced over at Desmond. "In your professional opinion, Sergeant Terrell, does this constitute police harassment?"

Desmond didn't look up from his newspaper, his reading glasses perched on the end of his nose. "You don't know what harassment is."

"I'll bring them by the station tomorrow if it's so important to you," said Jimmy, opening the front door. "Right now I'm going to grab a shower and get some sleep."

"Go easy on my hot water," Desmond called after him.

Chapter 6

Jimmy could hear Desmond and Holt talking as he walked around to his apartment, an attached single room with a hard bed and a tiny bathroom. There were posters on the walls that Samuel, Desmond's son, had left when he moved out nine years ago—Eddie Murphy and Malcolm X, Chris Rock and Tyra Banks. Desmond hadn't removed them, and Jimmy wasn't about to, either. His first morning there, he had awakened, still half asleep, seen Malcolm glowering down at him, and jerked upright so fast he gave himself whiplash. Jimmy smiled at the memory. He wasn't planning on staying long anyway, maybe a few months, just long enough to save enough money for first, last, and a damage deposit someplace near the beach. Desmond refused to let him pay rent, just asked for half the groceries and utilities. He turned on the shower, stripped off his clothes, and stepped inside.

He gave in to the exhaustion, eyes closed, relaxing in the powerful spray—he was half asleep on his feet when he smelled Holt's perfume through the steam, just a faint wisp of her distinctive scent, an afterglow of her presence in the kitchen.

It had been a year since he had first called her from *SLAP*, holding the letter from the Eggman in his hand, unsure of what to make of it. She must have broken the speed limit all the way up from Laguna, breezing past the security guard, her jaw so rigid that Jimmy had wondered if her molars ached at the end of the day. She had just started her interview when a couple of local cops showed up, tipped off by someone at the magazine who must have overheard his call.

The Newport Beach detectives had tried to muscle the letter away from Holt, insisting that their department had jurisdiction. The senior officer, Cranston, had splayed his ass across Jimmy's desk and told her that they would take it from there, *"Miss,"* holding his hand out, barely restraining the impulse to snap his fingers. Holt coolly cited a section of the California Penal Code as she bagged the letter and tucked it into her purse. She looked at Jimmy, suggested that the two of them adjourn to a conference room so he could finish his statement, and turned on her heel before he could respond. Jimmy left the Newport cops fuming, followed her narrow hips.

Now, the warm water sluicing down his chest and back, he took a deep breath, stopped. Holt's smell was stronger now. He opened his eyes, pushed the hair away from his face. "Jane?" The shower curtain was patterned with bright tropical fish, through which he could see Holt standing there, her face distorted as though she were under water. "You sneaking a peek, Jane?"

"Don't flatter yourself."

Jimmy stepped back from the curtain and into the steam. "Why don't you go into the other room? I'll be done here in a few minutes."

"Modesty?" Holt stood her ground. "I'm surprised."

Jimmy poured shampoo on his head, lather cascading down his shoulders as he scrubbed, trying to ignore the sense that she was staring at him. "I don't like being pushed. I'm under no obligation to help you. I don't even have to talk to you."

"I just want to see the Polaroids. Do you think you can *manage* that?"

Jimmy turned around, let the water hit the back of his neck. Anytime a cop asked you for something and assured you that was all he or she wanted, you could be certain it was just the *beginning* of the demands. He did appreciate the way she'd coated the word *manage* with a sheen of contempt; that was a nice move. "What's the big deal?" he said, his voice echoing off the tile. "So what if some cop takes a few snapshots to pass around the local bar? Maybe he gives the blue groupies a thrill, maybe he makes a few bucks. What do you care?"

Holt moved closer, and for a moment Jimmy thought she was going to step into the shower with him. "Why are you being so difficult?" she asked.

"Why are you being so persistent?" Beads of moisture dappled the curtain between them. "Maybe it wasn't even a cop who took the Polaroids. I've been to crime scenes; you have all these forensic geeks coming and going—"

"The forensic techs shoot strictly digital."

"—news photographers snapping away from the far side of the tape—"

"These Polaroids, were they close-ups?"

"Yeah, *way* too close up."

"Then they weren't taken by anyone *outside* the tape, were they?"

"The captain of the debate team strikes again. All I'm saying is that there are lots of splatter photos out there, official and unofficial. So why are *these* so important?"

"With all due respect, Jimmy, I'm not at liberty to discuss the specifics of an ongoing investigation."

Jimmy turned off the water, the room suddenly quiet. "With all due respect, Jane, there *is* no ongoing investigation. The task force closed shop a long time ago."

"The Kinneson homicide is still an active case," Holt said tightly. "The task force doesn't make that decision; *I* do." She fingered her pearls, waiting for him to respond, the loudest sound in the room the water dripping from the showerhead, until even that slowed, then stopped. "Philip Kinneson was found in Laguna. That's *my* beach. *My* crime scene. I inventoried every photograph taken that morning, but the report wasn't called in until almost seven-thirty. By the time I arrived, the body was surrounded by a group of boogie boarders, junior high kids kicking up sand, the site totally compromised." She shook her head as though she were having an argument with herself. "If you saw a Polaroid of Kinneson, then it was taken by someone who got there *before* I did, when the site was still fresh—one of those kids, maybe, or a lookie-loo out for a morning stroll."

"Or a free-lancer who cruises around all day monitoring police calls. You've seen them, Jane; they're at every car crash and drive-by. Half the time they beat the uniforms to the scene. That's probably how the Polaroids ended up on the open market. If it yells, it sells. *Now* can I go back to my shower?"

Holt shook her head. "I'm not interested in the Polaroids per se; I'm interested in whoever *took* them. That person may have seen something, seen *some*one. He or she may have taken other shots, pictures of other people on the beach—witnesses, or suspects, even."

"Sounds pretty unlikely." Jimmy glimpsed her expression through the shower curtain. "You really don't have anything else, do you?"

Holt smoothed her skirt. "The task force may have moved on, but I haven't. Someone has Polaroids of my crime scene, and I want to find out where they came from."

"OK, Jane." Jimmy had decided without even knowing it. He put his hand on the shower curtain. "I'll take you there as soon as I change."

Holt turned away. Maybe she was the one who was modest.

Chapter 7

"Can you see them?" asked Holt.

Jimmy peered through the window of the Tiki Room, cupping his hands on the glass to cut the reflection, Holt beside him. The Polaroids were still strewn across the floor, the cigar box crushed in the corner where he had thrown it. Jimmy turned away from the window, the boards of the porch creaking as he stepped to the edge. A wooden glider hung from the roof beams by two lengths of rusted chain, most of the blue marine paint having flaked off. He looked across the drained swimming pool toward the main house, which the last earthquake had left uninhabitable, the foundation cracked, the roof sagging. One of the kitchen windows was broken.

The surrounding homes had been spared by the earthquake, but they looked equally shabby: paint peeling, lawns overgrown with dandelions. Dr. Gage had been a salaried general practitioner, embittered by having had to forgo the specialty training that would have brought in the big money, a man with grandiose visions and poor business judgment. The big house in Anaheim with the swimming pool and cabana was supposed to be a status statement and a canny investment, the real estate agent having assured him that the inland neighborhood was "upwardly transitional, a magnet for professionals with an eye for value." The real estate agent had lied. By the time Jimmy was in high school, there were regular smog alerts, and police helicopters flew over almost every night, searchlights glinting off the mirror surface of the meticulously maintained swimming pool.

"Is that *them*, Jimmy?"

Holt had no authority to enter the Tiki Room, no probable cause, no warrant. All he had to do was refuse, and she would have to turn around and leave, but once he opened the door . . . "Jonathan's my brother. I don't want to get him in trouble."

"I told you, I just want to know where he got the Polaroids."

It wasn't really Jonathan he was worried about; it was Olivia. Jimmy had told Holt that he had been alone in the Tiki Room last night, but once the detective got wound up, it was going to be hard to keep Olivia out of it. No telling how Jonathan would react to the news that they had been alone together.

"You don't have to come inside," said Holt. "This doesn't involve you."

Jimmy remembered his hate mail again, the red felt-pen scrawls blaming him for the murders, accusing him of profiting from the crimes; he could still see the kitty-cat stationery dripping with obscenities and fervent prayers for his loved ones to be eviscerated with a carpet knife.

Holt jabbed him with a finger. "Dammit, Jimmy, you said you were going to *help* me."

The intensity of her response surprised him. Holt prided herself on her self-control, but she was breathing hard now, her cheeks dappled with color. Jimmy slid into the porch swing, slumped against the smooth, worn wood. "Sit down and relax, Jane, the Polaroids aren't going anywhere." He scooted over to make room for her, but Holt didn't move. He hadn't really expected her to. He rocked gently, back and forth. The day had started off warm, but dark clouds were rolling in from offshore, edging over the sun, and the breeze was cooler now.

"Do you ever blame yourself?" Holt asked.

"I read the same press release from the task force as you: the Eggman was a hoax."

"You don't believe that, and neither do I."

"No, I don't blame myself." The swing creaked as Holt sat down beside him, and Jimmy smelled her perfume again, wondered where her pulse points were. She really wasn't his type, and he *knew* he wasn't hers—they had nothing in common except six dead people—but there was an attraction between them, unstated and unacted-upon. "I don't blame you, either."

"Philip Kinneson was murdered on his way home from the Paradise, a gay bar overlooking the water," murmured Holt, staring straight ahead as the chain creaked. "It was Monday-night football, special buffet, dollar well drinks, and Kinneson was a regular. The bartender said he liked walking home along the beach after the game, even though he'd been warned that it was dangerous, that skinheads hung around on the rocks. Kinneson said it cleared his head." She turned to Jimmy. "I didn't dismiss that scenario. I spent a lot of time those first couple of days running down leads. I talked to detectives in the gang unit, I was up all night accessing the hate site of the county database—"

"I know."

"Philip Kinneson's father used to call me every week to ask if I had made any progress," Holt said wearily. "Lately he calls only every month or so. He's an old man, and he's running down. I used to dread his calls, but now I'm afraid he's going to stop calling altogether, that he's going to die . . . or give up on me."

"He used to call me, too."

"I wasn't aware of that."

Jimmy wished he would learn to shut up around her. "I don't know if the Eggman letter was a hoax or not. I just know . . . sometimes I think about those six people, that's all."

"So do I," said Holt. "I don't know why I've become so . . . focused on this case. I've handled worse homicides, more violent assaults. The FBI profiler said the crimes were marked by an easy touch—clean, almost clinical—which actually contraindicated a serial killer. No sexual activity, no mutilation, just a single shot—"

"A single shot that blew out half their skulls. That FBI agent was a skank."

The Eggman's victims had all been shot with a .38 revolver. A

.38 didn't usually pack such a punch, but the killer had used Glaser safety slugs, highly frangible rounds that shattered on impact. Not only were the results devastating, but it was virtually impossible to make a ballistics match.

Holt pushed the swing back and forth. "Do you ever wonder why none of the victims exhibited any defensive postures? The shot came from close range, but none of them flinched, none of them threw up a hand." She kept rocking. "Lawrence Sacks said he thought Philip Kinneson was sleeping on the beach when he first stumbled over him, that was how peaceful he looked."

Larry Sacks was a beachcomber, a retired machinist with a belly the size of a beer keg, a ruddy man who'd been so intent on listening to his metal detector that morning that he'd almost tripped over Kinneson's body. It was the end of his regular route along the strand; he had almost cut up to grab breakfast at the Coffee Corral, but he'd kept going, eyes cast down, headphones on, the metal detector waving from side to side. A couple of years earlier he had found a gold class ring from a high school in Iowa right around there, just beyond the rocks. That morning he found Philip Kinneson.

"Mr. Sacks told me you showed up on his doorstep a few days after you got the letter," said Holt, looking out over the yard. "He didn't talk to any other reporters, at my suggestion, but he talked to you."

"I brought him a sixer of his favorite brew: Dixie beer, breakfast of people who think gravy is a food group. They don't ship much of it outside the Old South."

"How in the world did you find out what he drank?"

Jimmy shrugged. "Dixie beer still comes with pull tabs; I think it's kind of a good-ol'-boy thing, tearing off those tabs, tossing them over your shoulder."

"I'm not conversant in the semiotics of beer, but he said you were a good listener."

Jimmy remembered Sacks's cradling the six-pack in his lap,

popping the cans open one by one as he talked, inhaling the spray as though it were ambrosia. He had given Jimmy a sip—just a sip, not a swallow, dammit. Stuff tasted like boar piss.

"You never mentioned that you had visited him," said Holt, rocking slightly faster. "All that time we spent together, Jimmy, and you never said a word."

"Did you deputize me when I wasn't looking?"

"I didn't find out until after you left town that you had interviewed the families of all the victims. You chatted up the uniforms, too, even brought jelly donuts to the forensics lab."

"Did the M.E. tell you I threw up in his wastebasket?"

"Dr. Chakabarti said most reporters weren't nearly so considerate." Holt watched him. "On first impression you appear so . . . unstructured, but in fact you're quite diligent. People must underestimate you all the time."

"Don't, Jane."

" 'Don't' what?"

"Stop being a cop, just for a minute. Why don't we go out for breakfast and forget about the Polaroids? Call your sergeant, let him know you'll be an hour late. I'll tell you about the wrestling match I saw yesterday, and we'll both laugh and—"

Holt stood up. "I *am* a cop, Jimmy."

Jimmy stood up, too, then walked over and opened the door for her. It was unlocked, just as he had left it. "Go ahead, *Officer.*"

Holt pulled on a pair of surgical gloves, and the sight of her doing that made Jimmy's stomach lurch. The pool house was out of his control now. He stayed in the doorway as she walked slowly across the room, taking it all in, the palm fronds and net ceiling, the *Blue Hawaii* Elvis and paint-by-numbers volcanoes. She glanced back at Jimmy, raised one eyebrow, then walked to where the Polaroids lay scattered across the floor. She looked wildly incongruous with her pearls and surgical gloves in that dusty room.

"Ignore most of those," Jimmy called after her.

Holt scanned the photos, then bent down and nudged the Polaroids around with the tip of her pen, finally picking one up by the edges. She turned to him, staring, then put down the first Polaroid and picked up another, then another, her mouth tightening in disgust.

Jimmy understood her reaction. The celebrity slab photos he had seen at parties were bad enough, but stars sold their wedding pictures to the tabloids, hawked photos of their new babies to *People* magazine—dead or alive, their images were just another commodity. The Eggman Polaroids were different. Those six people were civilians, regular folks who'd never gotten their faces in the paper until they were murdered. They deserved better than to end up in some sick creep's cigar box. He watched Holt get angrier as she looked through them, and he moved closer, almost as though he wanted to protect her, which was ridiculous, but he did it anyway.

Holt tossed the Polaroids back onto the floor, glared at Jimmy. "Did someone at the task force put you up to this? Was this Imeki's idea of a joke?"

"Imeki?" Jimmy walked across the room and scanned the scattered Polaroids, seeing only Jonathan's Greatest Blow Jobs.

Holt pulled off her gloves, threw them into the wastebasket beside the desk. Her fingers sparkled with powder. "Was I supposed to faint when I saw these, Jimmy? Fan myself like some romance-novel heroine with an attack of the vapors?"

Jimmy looked under the desk for the Eggman shots, frantic now, and spotted a Polaroid that had fallen down between the desk and the wall. He worked his hand down the gap, pinched the photo between his thumb and index finger, and pulled it up. It was another fellatio shot, a woman in a white nurse's cap gazing coquettishly into the camera as she mouthed Jonathan.

"What was in it for you?" demanded Holt. "That's what I don't—"

"Do you really think I set you up?" Jimmy put his hand on her shoulder.

Holt slapped him so hard he almost hit her back. "Don't *touch* me!"

Jimmy tried to speak, but his face hurt too much.

"Go ahead and report me," said Holt, her eyes wide. "File assault charges if you like. You probably have grounds for a civil suit, too. If you want, I can refer you to a good plaintiff's attorney. I don't really care anymore."

"I hate to interrupt you two lovebirds. . . ." Jonathan stood in the doorway. "Ah, James, I should have known it would be you."

Chapter 8

A man stood in the doorway, wearing a suit the color of the sky on a perfect day, but Holt could see the wind whipping around him, tiny leaves scudding across the tile floor like insects. He would have been handsome except for the aura of arrogance that surrounded him; he reminded her of the risk arbitrageurs in her father's New York office, those sleek predators with their platinum dollar-sign cuff links and deadly, humorless laughter.

"I could have *loaned* you the money for a hotel room, James," the man said with a smirk, his skin so white and clear it was almost translucent. "The leather couch is cracked, and there's dust everywhere, but then, I guess there's nothing like the thrill of returning to the scene of the crime."

Jimmy jerked at that comment, more startled than when Holt had slapped him. Holt had never drawn her weapon in the line of duty, never wanted to, but she was suddenly aware now of the pistol clipped to the waistband of her skirt.

"James has a special fondness for this dismal place," the man explained to her. "He brings all his dates here, tells them stories of his childhood and shows off Mother's *exceptionally* grotesque decor. I've never really understood the appeal, but it seems to work for him."

"Where are they, Jonathan?" said Jimmy.

Jonathan ignored him, watching Holt instead. "Have we met?"

After she first made detective, Holt had flashed her badge reflexively, not to show off but to reassure herself that she belonged in charge of men years older than herself, men who resented her finishing-school accent and practiced manners. She didn't tip her badge anymore. "I'm Detective Jane Holt."

The man tried to cover his surprise. "I'm Jonathan Gage. *Dr. Jonathan Gage*," he said, as though sharing an ironic joke with her. His smile broadened. "Is my brother under arrest, Detective?" His smile collapsed as he saw the scattered Polaroids, his face flushing as he walked into the room, slowly at first, then faster. He scooped up the Polaroids and pressed them against his chest as if trying to cover them, but there were too many to hide. "This is *wrong*. You have no right to violate my privacy, no right at all." If his shock was faked, Holt thought he was doing a good job, but Jimmy wasn't buying it.

"Did you come by to gloat?" Jimmy pushed him, Polaroids fluttering from Jonathan's grasp. "This isn't funny."

Jonathan appraised him. "What are you . . . ?" He flinched as Jimmy cocked his fist.

"Stop it," Holt ordered.

"Thank you, Detective." Jonathan's face was flat and unemotional now, but color still bloomed in his cheeks. "My brother is a resentful man who blames me for his troubles. When his insults have no effect, he resorts to force, and when force fails . . ." He shook his head.

Holt watched Jonathan pick up the Polaroids again and then put them on the desk, not caring whether they were faceup or facedown in his haste. There was a faint family resemblance between the two brothers, but Jonathan had a more polished demeanor; he appeared more controlled, his smooth features seemingly untouched by pain or doubt, and less interesting because of it. Jimmy was more intense, more abrasive, but *poised* somehow. She remembered the way he'd been in the shower, caught off guard but refusing to be intimidated, trying to turn the situation into something playful. She admired that kind of composure and had ended up watching him through the curtain for longer than she'd intended.

"What exactly is going on here, Detective?" Jonathan moved away from the desk, putting some distance between himself and Jimmy. "Do I need to call my attorney?" he mocked.

"That's up to you. I'm just trying to find some Polaroids Jimmy said he discovered here last night."

"Last night?" Jonathan pursed his lips at Jimmy. "Aren't *you* the busy little bee?"

Holt brushed against the desk, surreptitiously slipping one of the Polaroids into her jacket as the two brothers faced off against each other.

"You didn't use to be a tattle-tale, James," chastised Jonathan. "Further evidence, I'm afraid, of the continuing degradation of your character." He turned to Holt. "While I must admit to a certain embarrassment, Detective, the women in the . . . sexual situations were fully aware that their pictures were being taken; in fact, they rather enjoyed that aspect. They were all of legal age, too, if that's your concern."

"We're here for the *Eggman* Polaroids," said Jimmy.

"Jimmy said he found some crime-scene Polaroids here last night," Holt said. "Possession of crime-scene photos is not a violation of the statutes, Doctor, if that's *your* concern. They may be useful in my investigation of the Eggman homicides, though, so if you have them, I'd like very much to see them."

"The Eggman." Jonathan nodded at Holt. "That's where I've seen you before. You're the police officer I saw on television last year, going on about James's serial killer. I thought that had been discredited." He glanced at Jimmy. "Is that how you got her over here? Telling her there were some photographs she wanted?"

"I saw them, Jonathan."

"Are you trying to humiliate me again?" Jonathan sounded more hurt than angry. "Making a scene at my party last night wasn't enough; now you bring in the police. Of course, Detective Holt is going to have to follow up on your accusation, so she'll have to interview Olivia about these supposed crime-scene photographs, and one question will lead to another, with perhaps a brief mention of the discovery of my little stash of . . . souvenirs."

"Olivia?" Holt felt a warmth at the back of her neck. The wife. Of course. She had read the marriage announcement in the society pages, but she hadn't connected the new Mrs. Jonathan Gage with the woman she had seen at Jimmy's house last year.

"Do you really think Olivia is going to run back to you because I kept certain . . . erotic mementos? I'm sorry to disappoint you, James, but it's not going to work." Jonathan picked a speck of dust off his lapel. "The Polaroids were taken before I got married. I plead guilty to a certain narcissism, Detective, but I hardly think that warrants—"

"Why are you here, Doctor?" asked Holt. "The house clearly isn't being lived in."

"No, it's not." Jonathan looked flustered. "I'm meeting with a contractor this morning; he's supposed to give me a bid for tearing the whole place down. The area has been rezoned for apartments, and I'm trying to convince my father—" Then his face tightened. "I don't think *I'm* the one who has to explain his presence here, Detective."

Holt spotted something on the floor, bent down, and picked up the remnant of the joint between her thumb and forefinger. Sniffed it. "Whom does this belong to?"

"It's mine," said Jimmy.

"I'm surprised you didn't try to incriminate me," said Jonathan. "You could have told the detective I was a drug trafficker, some narco kingpin flying it in on jumbo jets." His smile was halfhearted. "Perhaps there's hope for you yet."

"No, there isn't," said Jimmy.

Holt peered at the roach, then dropped it into a small clear-plastic evidence bag, which she sealed shut. "I'm sorry we disturbed you, Doctor. We'll be leaving now."

"What are you talking about?" said Jimmy. "You *believe* him?"

The door opened, and a beefy man in a corduroy sport coat stood there, hands on his hips. "Which one of you's Doc Gage?"

"Don't let him fool you," Jimmy said before Holt had even started her car. "He must have found out I was here last night. He must have come over, seen the mess, and taken the Eggman Polaroids."

Holt wrote down the license-plate number of the contractor's truck as she drove past. It started to rain; the wipers streaked the windshield. She should have replaced them weeks ago. She was letting everything slip. "The marijuana I found—it smelled potent."

"Yeah, that was it. I was tripping last night. You should have seen me standing in the middle of the four-oh-five directing traffic in the nude."

Holt pulled the evidence bag out of her jacket and jiggled it in front of him. "There're lipstick traces on this joint. You weren't alone last night; you were there with your brother's wife. Otherwise you wouldn't have felt the need to lie to me."

Jimmy didn't answer.

"Did Olivia see the Polaroids? The Eggman Polaroids, I mean, not those . . . other ones."

"No. She had already left."

Holt looked over at him.

"I said *no*."

Holt took the freeway on-ramp, weaving skillfully through the traffic, the roadway shimmering with rainbows of grease and gasoline.

"Jonathan took the Eggman photos. He came to the pool house after the party and—"

"How would he have known that you had been there? You didn't say anything. Would Olivia have told him?"

"Not a chance."

"Maybe she felt guilty? A married woman getting stoned with an ex-lover. . . ."

"Olivia didn't have anything to feel guilty about. I wish she did." Jimmy fiddled with the window, allowing the moist air to fill the car. "Jonathan might have seen something in our faces at the party, our body language."

"That still doesn't explain why he would have felt compelled to race to the pool house."

Jimmy hesitated. "Olivia and I . . . we used to make love in the pool house. It was a special place for us. Jonathan knew that. He might have suspected we would go there."

"I see." The rain was coming down harder now, Holt watching the wipers moving back and forth, back and forth. "At least now I understand why you were so resistant to bringing me there today. You were trying to protect her. That speaks well of you."

"Yeah, I'm a fucking hero."

Holt let it pass. She was aware of him slouched in the seat beside her, aware of the heat of his anger. She almost never rode with anyone. "I'm sorry I slapped you."

"I've been slapped before."

Holt cursed the Volvo station wagon in front of her, tailgating it until the driver moved into the right-hand lane. If she had been working traffic, she would have given herself a ticket. Lightning flashed in the distance. "After what happened between Jonathan and Olivia, the sense of betrayal you must have felt, then your finding all those . . . sexual Polaroids, no one would blame you for seeing what you wanted to see. I tried the lights; the power has been turned off in the pool house, so it was dark in there last night."

"The Eggman photos were *there*. Jonathan took them."

"Why?" Holt stomped on the accelerator. "Why take the Eggman Polaroids and leave the others? Why not just take *all* of them?"

"I don't know." Jimmy shook his head. "Jonathan . . . he likes playing games. You wouldn't believe some of the stuff he pulled when we were kids. He never got caught then, either."

"You're not children anymore."

"Yeah, but Jonathan is *still* playing games. You wait, as soon as I get another regular job at a newspaper or a magazine, someplace with a mailing address, I'll start getting love notes again—maybe a

Snoopy greeting card with a splatter photo tucked inside, inscribed, 'Still thinking of you, Your pal, The Eggman.' "

"Could you please . . ." Holt realized what he had said. " *'Again'?* You've received other correspondence from the Eggman?"

"Photos, letters, cards—but none of them really from the Eggman."

"That's for *me* to decide."

"I know the Eggman's style, Jane. I know the words and phrases he uses, the tone he adopts. None of the notes or photos was sent in a manila envelope or written with a label maker. It was junk mail. Sick—"

"You think Jonathan was responsible for this . . . junk mail?"

"Probably some of it. It's the kind of thing he would enjoy. Maybe when he ran out of Eggman Polaroids he'd start in with his greatest blow jobs, just to let me know what he'd done. Jonathan always makes sure he gets credit. You should see the photos of himself he has plastered all over his office."

"Did you get any Polaroids sent to you?"

"I don't think so." Jimmy stared out the window. "I stopped paying attention after getting an eight-by-ten color glossy of Denise Fredericks under an autopsy lamp, laid open like a deli counter with the words *DOES THIS BELONG TO YOU?* scrawled across her in green Magic Marker."

"You *still* should have told me."

Jimmy rested his head on the back of the seat, closed his eyes. "I should have done a lot of things."

Chapter 9

Jimmy was kicking Ray Cullen's butt, he really was—maybe it was a couple of lucky punches, or maybe Ray Cullen wasn't up to his own fearsome rep, but whatever it was, Jimmy was pounding him. Jimmy had just dodged another one of Ray Cullen's wild swings when Darryl Amaluca hit him from behind with an eighth-grade plane-geometry textbook, smacked him upside the head so hard his ears rang, hard enough that Jimmy didn't see Ray Cullen's next blow coming. The one that split his lip like a cherry tomato, spraying blood down the front of his Jetsons T-shirt.

Stunned by the pain, Jimmy stumbled backward and sprawled into the weeds of the vacant lot. He was rubbing sand out of his eyes when Ray Cullen tackled him, the bigger kid flailing away with his meaty fists, red hair flying as he sat on Jimmy's chest. Seeing that left eye swollen half shut like some crazed Cyclops's scared Jimmy even worse than when Ray Cullen had walked over to him in study hall and, for no reason at all, promised to beat the shit out of him after school. Not that Ray Cullen ever needed a reason.

Desperate to get away from that glaring eye, Jimmy drove a knee into Ray Cullen's back, knocked the wind out of him, then grabbed a handful of hair and yanked himself free. It sounded like he was surrounded by screams, and Jimmy couldn't tell if they were coming from Ray Cullen or from himself. He had almost made it to his feet when Darryl Amaluca slammed him again with the geometry book, using both hands this time, and Jimmy couldn't hear anything now, just the storm roaring through his cranium as he threw up.

Ray Cullen was curled up on the ground, bawling, while Darryl urged him to "Get up, you pussy, get up."

Jimmy didn't want to fight anymore; he just wanted to get out of there. He was picking up his red bicycle when he saw Jonathan half hidden in the grove of olive trees nearby, Jonathan astride his own blue Stingray bike, leaning over the high handlebars, watching him, his face all quiet like when he was looking through his microscope.

Jimmy started to call to him, and then slowly, like the slowest slow motion in the world, Jonathan smiled, and Jimmy knew he had been there the whole time, waiting there in the cool shadows since school got out, waiting for Ray Cullen to catch up with him on the shortcut home.

Jimmy jumped on his bike and rode off in the opposite direction, bouncing across the vacant lot, ears still ringing, crying now for the first time since the fight began, tears and snot streaming down his cheeks.

Chapter 10

Jimmy stood on the sidewalk, watching Holt drive away, ignoring the storm that blew around him, the warm tropical rain dripping off his hair. He and Holt had spent the last fifteen minutes driving in awkward silence, each of them waiting for the other to say something. Most women, if you told them you didn't want to talk, they took it as a challenge, but not *her;* you told Holt you didn't want to talk, and she treated it like it was *your* problem, not hers. The silence had been broken only by the steady slap of the windshield wipers. Holt needed new wiper blades, a lapse in maintenance as much out of character for her as a run in her stockings. He wondered what was keeping her so busy.

Holt turned left at the end of the block, and Jimmy saw an unfamiliar car parked on the corner, a bulky silver SUV with tinted windows, its engine idling, exhaust curling into the air. Jimmy glanced toward the house and saw Desmond observing him from the living-room window, hands behind his back, a worried look on his face. Jimmy waved, then turned back to the street. He should move out before he got Desmond hurt. Jimmy had come back from Europe without a job or a place to stay and with barely enough money to get his car out of storage. Rollo had given him a laptop and a cell phone, and Desmond had offered him Samuel's old room, insisting on his using it. Jimmy watched the SUV out of the corner of his eye. Nice to have friends. As long as you didn't get them killed.

Jimmy was going to move into his own apartment as soon as he'd saved enough for first and last plus a damage deposit. Desmond didn't owe him anything; he just felt guilty because Jimmy had done something about Samuel's murder and he himself hadn't. It was two years since the funeral, and Desmond still felt ashamed of himself for acting like a police officer instead of a father. But really, Jimmy was the one who should feel guilty. Not that he did.

I would like to thank Desmond Terrell for allowing me to speak today. I didn't know Samuel for very long, just a few days, hardly any time at all . . . but it was enough.

I'm curious by nature. If I see something out of place, I don't put it back where it belongs, or not at first, anyway; I turn it over in my hands and wonder who moved it, ask myself what he or she was up to. Sometimes I wish I'd leave well enough alone, but I can't help myself, and I'm glad about that, because if I were a different kind of person I would never have met Samuel. He got to me in those few days, he changed me . . . I guess he had a similar effect on the rest of you, or you wouldn't be here.

A couple of weeks ago I was coming home early one morning, just before sunrise, when I saw a man sleeping in his car. I had parked near my apartment, had just started across the street when I saw this man slumped over the steering wheel of a dented Toyota with mismatched doors. I watched him for a few minutes, trying to talk myself into minding my own business, and then finally I walked over to him, trying to make some noise, not wanting to startle him. Wake a man from a sound sleep, there's no telling what he might do. It isn't a bad neighborhood, but it isn't a good neighborhood, either, and people wake up to the sound of guns blazing even in the best of neighborhoods.

It had been a warm night, and the driver's-side window was down. I stood there watching him for a few moments, listening to him snore. Reassured that he wasn't dead, I was about to leave when he opened his eyes. He didn't jump up. Or cry out. He didn't even look startled. He just slowly straightened up, looked at me, completely calm, and said, "I'm not afraid to die."

"I am," I told him.

He smiled. He had bad teeth, junky teeth, neglected and rotten, but it was a beautiful smile. I don't know how to explain it. "Maybe you should read your Bible" he said, holding up the Good Book from his lap, a taped-together Gideon Bible from some motel nightstand.

"I'm OK." I was starting to wish I had gone directly up to my apartment.

"If you're OK with God, then you're not afraid to die."

"I don't think I'm that OK with God."

He smiled at me again. "You'll get there," he assured me, without any trace of the usual born-again smugness.

"Did you run out of gas or something?" I asked, wanting to get off the subject of my potential salvation. "I can give you a ride to a service station."

"I'm where I belong, thank you."

"Sorry to disturb you." I started to leave, but he called to me.

"Do you know my wife?"

He was a young black man, of course—I guess I should have said that up front. I live in Fountain Valley, which is pretty much equally divided among Latinos and whites and Asians. Not many blacks in Fountain Valley; not many anywhere in Orange County, as I'm sure you know. I don't think that was the main reason I thought he looked out of place sleeping in his car, but it was probably one of the reasons.

"Do you know my wife?" he asked me again. "Angela Marx. Blond lady. Not much meat on her bones, but pretty."

"I don't think so. I've only been living here a few months."

"We've got a little girl. Five years old."

"Right."

"Her name's Halley. Halley Terrell. Angela kept her own name, but I insisted that Halley get mine." He looked at me, the whites of his eyes road-mapped with broken capillaries. "My name is Samuel Terrell," he said, shaking hands through the open window.

His hands were like dry leaves in my grip. "I'm Jimmy."

"Just Jimmy, huh?" Samuel smiled again, even broader this time. "You don't give it away, do you?"

It was my turn to smile. "Jimmy Gage."

"That's all right, Jimmy Gage, I was the same way once."

"Are you . . . waiting for your wife?" I glanced at the blue clapboard house where I sometimes saw a little girl playing on the weedy lawn; suddenly I felt concerned about this scrawny man with the easy grin. "You aren't planning on doing anything crazy, are you?"

Samuel stared at the blue house. "No, I did my craziness some years ago."

"Your little girl . . . you wouldn't want to give her bad memories," I said carefully.

Samuel looked over at me. His cheeks were hollow and dusky, those of a shadow man barely hanging on to the world, but his eyes . . . he looked like he felt sorry for me. "It's not anything like that."

"I was just—"

"I thank you for your concern, though," said Samuel. "Kindness is a gift from God."

I waited, still not knowing what he was doing here. "You want to go get a cup of coffee? It's going to get pretty noisy around here in another hour, so you're not going to get much more sleep."

Samuel checked his watch, looked up at me, and nodded. "I can't stay gone long. I got to be here when he comes around."

I didn't ask him whom he was talking about. Sometimes you find out more by not asking, by letting people tell you what you want to know. There was a twenty-four-hour donut shop a few blocks away, but we went upstairs to my place for coffee. I don't usually invite strangers home, but I had a feeling about him that overrode my natural caution. Not a good feeling, particularly; there was a wasted quality to him, a sense of promise squandered that made me uncomfortable, reminded me of my own failings. Maybe it was his courage that drew me to him: Samuel was a leaky boat putting out to sea, knowing only that he was needed out there where the sun set, and willing to brave the storm. Let's just say I liked him, I don't know why.

I made a pot of strong coffee and watched him load four teaspoons of sugar into his mug—a junkie may give up junk, but he'll never lose his sweet tooth. We sat at my kitchen table overlooking the street, and I told him my story, and he told me his. He was probably more honest than I was. Like Samuel said, I don't give it away.

Samuel said he used to be a music producer. He had dropped out of college and sunk his student loans into an office in Studio City and a rented Mercedes, passing out his card to every opening act at every club in the city, schmoozing recording engineers, making the rounds. He was a smart guy with a good ear and a pregnant wife, and he actually did OK for a while. He got a couple of groups inked to small labels and landed one of his artists a semiregular gig on Moesha, and a hip-hop band he had put together himself was included on the soundtrack to Homeboys in Paradise II but got cut at the last minute. There was a lot of overhead, though—bar tabs and thousand-dollar monthly phone bills from the very beginning, and then later the heroin. Smack is a very expensive breakfast.

The office in Studio City became a P.O. box, and the Mercedes became a Buick Regal—"a loaner," he assured the parking valets. Then the Buick was gone, too. Before long he was your typical strung-out loser, skinny as a coat hanger, hair falling out. He didn't have the money or the connections to swing the Charlie Sheen Suite at the local detox spa, and he probably wouldn't have stayed there anyway. Begging money from his mother when his father wasn't home was more his style, and when the cookie jar was empty, he'd rip off her silverware, just like in the warning ads on television. The day of her funeral, he cleaned out the whole house while his father was at the memorial service.

Some time after that—he wasn't sure how long, exactly—Samuel took the cure. He got religion, and not the Sunday-morning variety but the real thing, the washed-in-the-blood-of-the-lamb, 24/7 kind. Samuel kicked, and he stayed kicked. He spent his days working in the Union Gospel Mission dispensing hot vegetable stew and testimony. After a while, when he thought he was strong enough, he looked up his wife and brought three years' worth of missed Christmas presents to his little girl.

It wasn't a Hallmark Special, though—his daughter didn't rec-
ognize him, and his wife was a still a junkie, doing the methadone
shuffle and going down on her dealer for a wake-up. Samuel's hand
was shaking so badly when he told me about it that he almost spilled
his coffee. He looked out the window of my kitchen, stared at the blue
house across the street. The sun was just coming up.

"My daughter sees everything; Angie doesn't even send her out to
play," said Samuel. "My wife used to be so beautiful. . . ." He lowered
his eyes. "I told her you couldn't get addicted if you stayed away
from the spike."

Samuel told me that a few days earlier he had parked in front of
Angie's place, and when the dealer came by at around ten for his
morning slice, he confronted him.

The dealer had put his hand inside his coat. "What's up, slick?"

Samuel had held up his Bible and told the man that he was a
born-again Christian and couldn't tolerate what was going on inside
the blue house.

The dealer, of course, had laughed in his face, pushed past him,
and walked inside, where he gave it to Angela, gave it to her good,
really made her put her lungs into it. When the dealer emerged half an
hour later, Samuel walked up to him again, and Samuel with his pipe-
cleaner arms and sunken chest threatened that dealer, told him he was
going to camp out in his car, live right there on the street, and the next
time the dealer came by, he was going to lean on the horn of his car
until the whole neighborhood came out to see what was happening.

The dealer just stood there, a chocolate-clove cigarette stuck in
the corner of his mouth, squinting through the fragrant smoke. "Bad
idea, slick."

Samuel told the dealer that he had two choices: either he was
going to have to stop coming around or he was going to have to kill
Samuel.

I told Samuel that he shouldn't have done that. He should call
the police, I said, but Samuel just smiled and said he knew what the
police could do and what they couldn't do. He told me that I didn't

need to try and save him, he was already saved, but he appreciated the thought. Then he got up, washed out his mug, put it in the dish drainer, and walked out the door.

I called the police myself, but the officer who took the call said there was nothing they could do. Other than cite Samuel for illegal parking.

Samuel stayed in the car for the next three days. He came by for coffee or to use the bathroom once in a while, but most of the time he took short breaks at the donut shop; I think he stopped by my place mostly so he could hear what CDs I was listening to, shaking his head sometimes, saying he couldn't tell whether I had bad taste or a hearing loss. He always said "May God bless you" when he left. I remember that because I knew he meant it. I think I was one of Samuel's little projects. I suspect there were plenty of us whom he took an interest in that way; some of you here today probably know just what I'm talking about.

Early on the fourth morning, I turned the corner on to my street, saw the blue lights flashing, and knew what had happened. I got close enough to see Samuel slumped over the steering wheel, his Bible open on the front seat beside him—he looked just like he had the first time I saw him, except now there was blood on the Bible's pages. A detective was walking out the door of the wife's house. I knew him.

The detective told me that Angela Marx was Samuel Terrell's ex-wife. She said that she'd been cleaning up her life when Samuel showed up the week before, strung out and demanding money. She hadn't heard anything this morning until the police knocked on her door. She told them Samuel had probably burned another junkie, said he was always ripping someone off. An autopsy found no alcohol or drugs in Samuel's system, but that didn't soften his ex-wife's insistence that she didn't know who had killed him.

I gave my own statement to the detective, told him what I thought had happened, but I didn't have anything specific that could help the investigation, since Samuel had never mentioned the dealer's name, and I didn't even know whether the man was young or old, white or black, or what. All I knew was that he smoked clove cigarettes. I *should have done more for Samuel; I apologize to his family for that. I wish Angela Marx were here today to see what she's lost. To see whom we've all lost. I wish their daughter were here, too, so she could see how many people cared about her father.*

I knew Samuel only for a few days, but I can't stop thinking about him. I like my apartment; the rent's cheap, and it's close to the freeway, but I'm moving to Laguna. I just can't stand looking out my kitchen window at that blue house anymore. I'm a film reviewer, so I see a lot of make-believe heroes in my job—buffed-out hunks, armed and dangerous and invulnerable, on-screen anyway—but Samuel Terrell was the only real hero I've ever met, and I'm going to miss him.

Lightning crashed in the distance, and Jimmy mentally counted off the seconds, calculating where it had struck. The SUV at the end of the block was gone now. It was probably innocent, but Jimmy hadn't seen it leave, and his lapse of awareness was more troubling to him than the strange vehicle itself.

The rain had turned colder; Jimmy's teeth were chattering now. He hunched his shoulders, thinking about the pool house this morning and how Jonathan had played him once again. Lightning crackled again, closer now, the air humming with electricity, and he could still see Holt sitting beside him on the drive home, her hands tight on the wheel. She had made a big deal of questioning Jimmy's version of what he'd found last night, doubting his motives, challenging his state of mind, but Jimmy knew better. If Jane was so sure that Jonathan was the injured party, if she was so sure there weren't any Eggman photos, why had she taken one of the blow-job Polaroids when she thought no one was looking? Jane, *stealing?* It had to mean something. Jimmy headed toward his room, eyes straight ahead, aware of Desmond still watching him through the rain-streaked window.

Where is everybody? *(deadboy69)*
Hey! Anybody here? *(deadboy69)*

> This site used to be happening. Now it's shit.
> Don't you people care? *(deadboy69)*
>   I hate ALL you fuckers!!!!!!!!!!!!!!!! *(dead-
> boy69)*

Jimmy yawned as he clicked off eggmanrules.com, leaving only the green cursor blinking on his screen. If he needed any confirmation that the Eggman case was comatose, he had found it on the Internet. Of the twenty-seven sites specifically dealing with the serial killer, ten were no longer operating, and the most recent visitor to the remaining seventeen had been two months ago, when deadboy69 logged on to eggmanrules.com and found himself all alone.

After changing out of his wet clothes, Jimmy had checked out dozens of murder sites on the Web, from thrillingmurder.com to PSYCHOKILLERSrUS.com. There were plenty of Eggman crime-scene photos for sale, but no Polaroids. None. Jonathan must have bought the ones Jimmy had found in the cigar box someplace else. Proving Jonathan a liar shouldn't be so important to him, but Jimmy liked playing games, too. He thought again of Holt behind the wheel, gently suggesting that Jimmy had been too stoned to know what he was seeing the night before, the Polaroid tucked away in her jacket all the while. He wasn't sure why she had taken it, but he knew it was a three-way game now.

Jimmy had left requests for Eggman Polaroids on every site he visited, specifying "price no object" and using the screen name mad4eggman. Within half an hour he had gotten three replies. No one had any photos for sale, but lustykillbitch was willing to sell "serial killer of your choice filmed reenactments, starring me and my boyfriend," and deadboy69 wanted to know if mad4eggman wanted to donate money to produce an Eggman comic book. Jimmy decided that when he got a chance, he would drive up to L.A. and check out Gallery Inferno, ask Cleo and Ian about Eggman Polaroids. If it involved death, murder, and mayhem, those two freaks were the experts. He didn't know how long he had been staring at the cursor blinking onscreen when his cell phone buzzed. "Hello?"

"I got your message," said Michelle. "I'm glad you called—after our encounter at Jonathan's party, I thought I had scared you off. I have a settlement meeting in about five minutes, and the rest of the afternoon is jammed, but perhaps we could have dinner?"

"This isn't a social call." Jimmy could sense her retreating an inch. "After I left the party, did you and Jonathan talk?"

"I wish we could have a conversation that didn't involve Jonathan. Just a moment."

Jimmy listened to her talk to her assistant, her voice steady and soothing, all the hard, trailer-park edges smoothed off. It must be reassuring to clients who were dealing with the pain and uncertainty of divorce, but he himself would have preferred it if she had kept a little of Wilma Jean's Tennessee twang. Maybe she let it slip out when she was by herself, or with a lover, feeling warm and happy and not caring who heard her backwoods past.

"Where were we?" said Michelle.

"I was asking you about the party. Do you remember that clear-plastic statue I was holding when we first met? The one with all the guts showing?"

"Your Oscar?"

"The Visible Man. Did you mention it to Jonathan?"

Michelle snorted. Evidently there were limits to Jonathan's skills. "Why would I do that?"

Holt had reasoned that Jonathan couldn't have taken the Egg-man Polaroids because he didn't know Jimmy had been to the pool house. But if Jonathan had heard that Jimmy was walking around with the Visible Man, he would have known where it'd come from. "You're *sure?*"

"What's going on?"

"I'm having an argument with a friend of mine."

"Maybe someday you'll tell me the rest of it."

"Maybe."

"I'll keep checking the weather report," Michelle said. "Sooner or later hell's just *got* to freeze over."

"We'll go skating when it does."

"I wish you had stayed at the party longer. Everything fell apart after you left. I could see your mother and father arguing, and Olivia was a total wreck. I walked in on her in the ladies' room, and she was frantic, searching all over the floor; she said she had lost one of her diamond earrings. I helped her look, but we couldn't find it. I think she was even more upset about you than about her earring. You ruined the party for *both* of them, Jimmy. I saw Jonathan slip out not more than an hour after you left; he didn't even say good-bye to his guests."

Jimmy almost dropped the phone. "Say that again?"

"He's got a private elevator that goes directly from the main operating room to the underground garage. Some patients don't like being seen after surgery because the bandages can be . . . unsightly." Michelle cleared her throat. "Jonathan is usually such a stickler for proper etiquette. For him to leave like that—well, you must really have gotten to him. I have to leave for my meeting, but I hope you two manage to smooth things over. You're *brothers,* Jimmy."

Jimmy said good-bye, then snapped the phone shut. Jonathan had left in the middle of his own party, ducked out without a word; he must have seen something between Olivia and Jimmy that had made him wonder. The pool house wasn't that far from the office, so he could have left and returned before he was even missed. Jimmy got up from his desk and stretched, trying to get the kinks out, exhausted. Jonathan would have been looking for evidence of love at the pool house, but he would have found only the Polaroids scattered across the floor. He wished he could have seen his brother's face.

Jimmy walked over to Samuel Terrell's graduation photograph on the wall, Samuel looking stiff and awkward in his cap and gown, his eyes restless, ready to take flight. He had been twenty pounds skinnier when Jimmy met him, with slack skin and bad teeth, but there had been a joy in his eyes, a sense of peace that was utterly absent in the graduation photo.

He could hear Desmond clattering around on the other side of the wall. Jimmy found the sounds comforting, but he wondered what Samuel had thought lying in this bed, what he had heard through the walls. Desmond had the eyes and ears of a beat cop, always on full alert; he knew when to ease off with Jimmy, when not to ask questions, but he would have been stricter with Samuel, more demanding. Samuel probably couldn't wait to get out of that room. It was too bad that he and Desmond hadn't reconnected before he was murdered, but it was equally good luck that had directed Jimmy to the man who'd killed him.

It was about a year after Samuel's murder, and Jimmy had landed the job at SLAP, writing film reviews, doing interviews. An assignment to do a piece on the latest resurgence of country music took him to an Orange County honky-tonk called the Rhinestone Cowboy, where he stood in the balcony watching lawyers in chaps doing the Texas two-step with beach bunnies in pink cowboy hats, feeling like he had taken some bad acid. Then he went to the back office to interview the new owner, Lee Macklen. He smelled chocolate and tobacco even before he opened the door.

"Call me Mack—Lee's a fag name," Macklen said, shaking hands like they were in a tough-man contest, Jimmy already thinking he looked familiar. Macklen sat down in his chair and threw his anteater cowboy boots up on the desk, a sandy-haired hard case with gnarled muscles and a thin, cruel mouth. "Hey, don't print that, slick, I'm a kidder."

"Slick." That was what Samuel had said the dealer called him. Jimmy stared as Macklen fired up a chocolate bidi, a flavored cigarette from India. The dealer had smoked the same brand: while Samuel had said that he didn't think the dealer was a junkie, since he had too much muscle on his bones, he had a junkie's sweet tooth.

"What's wrong?" Macklen asked, eyes narrowing, "You ain't one of those eco farts who're allergic to smoke, are you?"

"I'm not allergic to anything," said Jimmy, remembering Macklen from the old neighborhood, certain now. He had seen the man only once, swaggering down the street a few weeks before Samuel

turned up, and had never connected him to the crime. Jimmy tossed his notebook onto Macklen's desk and plopped down on the sofa, already knowing he was going to have to do something. "You got any beer, Mack? If a man's got to work, he should do it with a buzz on."

Jimmy jumped at the knock on his door and turned away from the photo of Samuel in cap and gown, thinking about the SUV idling at the end of the block and the terrible things that could happen when you didn't pay attention. Another knock. Jimmy flanked the door, wishing he had a gun, or at least a peephole. He flung open the door, fist cocked.

Desmond stood on the doorstep, holding a white mug in each hand. He stared disdainfully at Jimmy's fist.

Chapter 11

Olivia looked up as Jonathan's racing-green BMW came up the driveway and slid in next to her Mercedes. He was home early. Rain steamed as it hit the hood of the car, and she wondered again what his hurry was. He was an aggressive driver, his hands always in the perfect ten-to-two position on the wheel, taking maximum advantage of every curve in the freeway, every break in the traffic flow, rarely using his brakes, never using his horn. Jimmy liked driving fast, too, but he was more erratic, punching the accelerator as he wound out the gears, hitting the brakes when he miscalculated. Most of the time Jimmy was happy just cruising down the PCH with the windows rolled down, rubbernecking at the traffic lights, listening to other people's radio stations. No wonder he never got anywhere. She wondered how long it would take until she stopped comparing the two of them.

Jonathan got out of his car, peeling off his driving gloves. He waved. She didn't. He stood by his car, fingering his keys, his blue suit splattered with raindrops.

Miguel held the umbrella over her head as she lifted her golf bag out of the trunk of her car. "Let me carry them, señora, *por favor*," he pleaded quietly with her.

Olivia whipped the heavy bag onto her shoulder with a practiced movement. She and Miguel had the same conversation every day. She was still getting used to having his wife, Lupe, prepare meals, clean the house, and arrange the flowers that Miguel grew and cultivated in the backyard greenhouse. The two servants had their own quarters attached to the main house, but Olivia still felt they were as much of an intrusion as a convenience. She had talked about it with Jonathan, suggested cutting back their hours or at least moving them into an outside apartment, but he said it was out of the question. There were so many things that were out of the question with Jonathan.

"Why aren't you at the office?" Olivia asked her husband.

Jonathan glared at Miguel. "Why is the lady carrying her bag?"

"Because I insisted," snapped Olivia, already walking toward the house as Miguel kept pace, holding the umbrella high. "Don't blame Miguel."

"Of course, darling." Jonathan followed, almost slipping on the wet flagstones in his haste, the Italian marble not designed for wet weather.

Olivia set her clubs down in the foyer for Miguel to clean and polish—not that they needed much work, since she had gotten rained out after six holes, the storm cutting short a string of birdies, her best start in weeks, now wasted. "What's wrong?" she asked Jonathan.

He waited for Miguel to leave with the clubs. "I . . . I need to talk with you." His face was even paler than usual.

Olivia hung up her windbreaker where it could drip onto the terrazzo floor, then walked into the kitchen and beat Lupe to the refrigerator, getting herself a mineral water. The cuffs of her full-cut khakis were muddy. If it had been up to her, she would have waited out the rain, enjoying the soggy give of the turf, the smell of the fresh grass afterward, but the other women in her foursome had been worried about lightning, worried about their hair. She had planned on going home and firing up a joint in peace. Instead she was going to have to have a talk with Jonathan, a *needed* talk. She should have taken her chances with the lightning.

"Olivia? Can we speak privately? It's . . . *important.*"

Olivia headed into the living room, opened wide the sliding

glass doors, the sound of rain filling the room. The cold wind off the Pacific rippled the magazines on the coffee table, *Vanity Fair, Harper's Bazaar, House and Garden,* covers flapping in a welter of beautiful faces and beautifully decorated rooms. She loved storms, the electricity in the air, the crackle and hum of the elements, the raw power. She turned on the gas fireplace, shimmied off her wet pants, and tossed them in the corner, enjoying the distaste on Jonathan's face over her rough behavior. She had dated Jimmy for two years and never once seen that expression.

She sighed as she curled up on the couch in her panties, enjoying the heat from the fake logs on her bare legs. She could see the ocean through the open doors, the slate-green waves topped with whitecaps.

Jonathan closed the doors to the rest of the house, pacing the room before gingerly sitting down beside her at the end of the couch. He was waiting for some eye contact, but she was in no hurry. "You've been upset with me since you woke up this morning," he said. "I would imagine that you're miffed at the way I treated James last night—"

"I've never been 'miffed' in my life," said Olivia, watching the gas flames. "I've been angry, I've been pissed off, and I once wrapped an eight-iron around a poplar tree on the eleventh hole of the Doral Country Club, but I've *never* been miffed."

"James wanted to disrupt what should have been a wonderful evening for us, and he succeeded," said Jonathan. "I know you invited him because you wanted to surprise me, and I appreciate the impulse, but if you had asked, I would have suggested some other venue for our . . . family reunion."

"In the future, of course, I'll defer all questions regarding the guest list to my husband," said Olivia. "See, Jonathan? I can talk like a lady when I want to. So why aren't you at the office? I thought you had a full day of sucks and tucks and lifts scheduled."

Jonathan was crying. He was. He looked away, trying to hide the tears in his eyes.

Olivia sat up, cross-legged on the couch now.

"I apologize. I am *so* sorry, Olivia."

"What did you do?"

"I love my brother." Jonathan was trembling, his sky-blue suit fluttering around him. "I love James, and for him to do this . . . God, he must despise me."

"It wasn't like that—" started Olivia, about to explain, certain he had found out that she had been with Jimmy last night. She stopped as Jonathan pulled a large envelope out from his suit jacket and laid it on the coffee table. She reached for the envelope, but he put his hand on hers.

"Please, darling, not yet." Jonathan took a deep breath. "I'll show you everything, but we need to speak first." Gusts of wind blew rain through the open window, a wet mist that sizzled against the glass front of the fireplace. He glanced at the windows but made no move to close them. "This morning I went by my parents' house to meet with a contractor." He shook his head. "I still can't believe it."

"Quit blubbering and tell me what happened."

Jonathan dragged a hand across his eyes, embarrassed. "Our little secret: *you're* the strong one. I sometimes forget that."

Rain crackled and popped against the fireplace. It sounded like the real thing. There was a hesitant knocking on the door.

"Not now," barked Jonathan, still watching Olivia. "This morning I heard shouting in the pool house, walked in, and found James and this female detective having a lovers' quarrel. I don't know what he had said or done, but she had actually struck him."

Olivia tried to hide her shock. "Jane Holt?"

"Yes . . . I believe so." Jonathan edged closer. "Do you know her?"

"We've met." Olivia remembered walking into Jimmy's place in Laguna and seeing the two of them curled up on the couch, pretending to play Scrabble.

"I don't care if James wants to turn the pool house into a whorehouse, but I don't like his doing it at my expense." Jonathan nudged the manila envelope. "He had induced this Detective Holt to go with him there today by telling her he had found certain . . . photographs that she would be interested in. Evidently he was there last night, snooping around, going through my things."

Olivia watched him, her skin tingling with the heat.

"James told her he had found some crime-scene photos that belonged to me—grisly stuff, the handiwork of his serial killer. It was just a pretext to get her there, of course. There *were* no crime-scene photos, but there were . . . other photos for Detective Holt's amusement." Jonathan raked a hand through his perfectly groomed hair. "I'm afraid I've made a mess of things." He took her hands, clinging to her. "I love you. I always have. I remember the first time I saw you: James brought you to Mother's birthday party, and I couldn't take my eyes off you the whole evening. You were so . . . buoyant, and your laugh—no one ever has a good time at our family gatherings, but hearing you enjoy yourself, we were all charmed. I think I fell in love with you that evening." He released her hands, staring at the manila envelope. "I only hope you'll remember that."

"Get on with it."

"Am I that transparent?" Jonathan blushed as he reached into the envelope and extracted a stack of Polaroids. "James found these hidden in my desk. They're mine, I won't lie to you. I took them when I was single, long before . . . you and I began seeing each other. These are the photos that James really wanted Detective Holt to see."

Olivia took the Polaroids from him. The photo on top showed a chubby brunette in a low-cut cocktail dress swallowing Jonathan's penis.

"I should have gotten rid of them ages ago—it's my own fault for keeping them," stammered Jonathan. "Storing my bachelor antics in a cigar box like a child with his baseball-card collection—how pathetic. God, you should have seen the two of them poring over them, the looks on their faces."

The chubby brunette's lipstick was smeared. Olivia laid the

photo down on the coffee table. The next Polaroid showed a nude Asian woman, her lips tight around Jonathan's erection. Olivia tapped the woman's suspiciously large breasts with her fingernail. "A client?"

"I'm so ashamed—"

"Don't be ashamed," said Olivia. "Shame is so . . . middle-class, isn't that what you always say?"

"I'm ashamed that I didn't throw them away when we got married. I'm sorry to hurt you like this. I'll *never* forgive James for this. Never."

Olivia stared at another Polaroid of Jonathan bent backward, a woman in cutoff jeans on her knees in front of him. "I guess you and Jimmy are even now."

"I don't understand what—"

Olivia flipped the photo at him. "Embarrassing you was his payback for your marrying me. You humiliate him, he humiliates you. Jimmy's a competitor; he doesn't like to lose. I've always liked that about him." The next photo showed Jonathan under two identical blondes. Holt must have enjoyed that extravagance. Olivia imagined Jimmy and the detective examing the Polaroids, pretending a professional detachment that neither of them felt. She added the two blondes to the lineup on the coffee table. "Funny, I thought I was worth more than *this*."

"I'm just sorry you had to see these . . . things, but perhaps it's better that you found out from me than from someone else."

"Yes, having it come from you has made it ever so much easier to handle."

"If I hadn't walked in on James and the detective, she might have confiscated the photos," said Jonathan. "She probably would have interviewed you in a couple of days, asked if you had ever seen any of the crime-scene photos James told her about, and one way or the other, these Polaroids of mine would undoubtedly have made their way into the conversation. She would have found some excuse to show them to you. The police use whatever they can to unsettle people, to startle them into telling the truth."

"It worked with *you*, didn't it? That's why I'm getting this show-and-tell routine."

Jonathan didn't move, his face a porcelain mask, smooth and unlined. The sheer whiteness of him had both attracted and repelled her the first time she met him; her own skin was a deep olive color, made even darker by her long hours in the sun. More than once she had felt that making love with Jonathan was like making love to a ghost.

"You're only telling me the truth to head off the inevitable disclosure." Olivia wanted to knock him off balance, to shatter his fragile calm. "Honesty's got nothing to do with it."

"You're right." Jonathan said it so quietly she could barely hear him over the rain. "I would have preferred to let sleeping dogs lie, but James left me no choice."

Olivia nudged the lineup of Polaroids and smiled. "*Dogs* is precisely the right word." She ran her fingers through his silky brown hair. "Maybe this isn't so bad. They say confession is good for the soul. Maybe it's good for something else, too." She drew his head down into her lap, feeling him wrap his arms around her waist as she stared at the flames. "Jimmy must have brought the police in so he could turn it into a news story if he wanted to, something for the gossip columns, something to hold over you. A collection of sex and death photos. . . . You could come out seeming a little ghoulish, Jonathan. Not exactly a quality people are looking for in a plastic surgeon."

"There *weren't* any crime photos."

"It wouldn't matter. Jimmy knows where to find splatter shots if he wants them."

Jonathan gripped her hand. "That's what James called them at the pool house, when he demanded to know what I had done with them. He was out of control. I don't know about Detective Holt, but I almost believed him myself."

The wind beat against the windows, lifted the Polaroids, and sent them scudding across the coffee table. Olivia saw lips and hair and pink everywhere, Jonathan's face contorted in pain and pleasure.

"I know I didn't really confess to you," said Jonathan, "not a true confession from an open and willing heart, anyway, but I do beg your forgiveness." He squeezed her hand again, harder this time. "Forgive me?"

Olivia was thinking of Jimmy as she kissed him, and Jonathan responded eagerly, mistaking her anger for lust.

Chapter 12

Desmond stared at Jimmy's balled fist. "Can I come in, or do you want to hit me first?"

Jimmy stepped aside as the rain gusted around them. "I didn't know it was you."

Desmond wiped his feet on the mat and handed Jimmy one of the steaming mugs as he walked past him. "Thought you could use this. Any man who doesn't have sense enough to come in out of the rain needs all the help he can get."

Jimmy sniffed the cup, took a sip. It was gritty but warm.

"Instant hot chocolate, and instant marshmallows, too," said Desmond. "The secret is to use two packages per cup. That's the way Samuel used to like it." He looked around the room, checked out the posters and photographs. "I told you before, you can put your own things up on the wall, fix the place up the way you like."

Jimmy took another sip. "I like it this way."

Desmond took in Samuel's graduation photo. "So do I." He shook his head. "He was offered a baseball scholarship to UCLA. Full scholarship, but he turned it down. Said he had other plans."

"He wanted to be on his own. Make his own way."

"If I had told him to walk away from baseball, he would have jumped on the scholarship. That's the way it was between us."

Jimmy flopped onto the bed and pointed to the single desk chair. "Why don't you make yourself comfortable?"

Desmond pulled the desk chair closer to the bed and sat down, their knees almost brushing. He looked like a banker in his dark slacks and shirt, pearl buttons on his gray vest, but he watched Jimmy with unblinking cop eyes that didn't miss a thing. "I wanted to ask you how things turned out this morning with Detective Holt. She didn't look happy when she dropped you off, and you didn't look so chipper, either. You be careful with her. She's a good police officer."

"What's that supposed to mean?"

"You know what it means." Desmond warmed his hands around his mug. "Anything I can do to help?"

"Do I look like I'm in trouble?"

Desmond raised one eyebrow.

"I can take care of myself."

"That's what Samuel used to say."

Jimmy felt the weight of the murdered man in his chest, knew that the same grief filled Desmond, too. "I appreciate the offer—"

"Don't appreciate it, take me up on it. I want to help you."

"You don't owe me anything."

"Youngster, don't tell me what I owe or don't owe."

The bed creaked under him as Jimmy shifted his weight. He didn't talk, he didn't tell, but he trusted the older man. Desmond could keep a secret, too.

"You have the same lost look on your face that you did the first time we met," said Desmond, chuckling. "You came up to me at the memorial service and introduced yourself, asked if you could speak, and I thought, Who is this nervous white man wants to get up in front of a churchful of strangers and talk about my boy?"

"I *was* nervous."

"You had a right to be. Only people in the church were police officers and born-again dope fiends, everybody sitting there stiff as boards. Then you got up, and people started nodding and Amen-ing, and it was like Samuel was right there in the room. I'm not a religious man, but I felt his presence. We all did." Desmond inclined his head toward Jimmy. "I was grateful to you for that."

The two of them listened to the rain for a long minute.

"Something strange happened this morning with Holt," said

Jimmy. "We went to my parents' old pool house to pick up some photographs I found last night—Polaroids of the Eggman's victims. She wanted them for her investigation."

"Where did you get them?"

"They weren't mine, they were Jonathan's."

"What was *he* doing with them?"

"I'm not sure yet." Jimmy took another drink of hot chocolate, then put the mug down on the nightstand beside the bed. "What's important is that the Polaroids weren't there this morning. Jonathan removed them late last night. He left some other Polaroids behind, though—personal shots—just to confuse things. It worked, too. Holt couldn't decide whether I had made the whole thing up or was just delusional."

"That's her training coming into play. The first thing you learn at the academy is *never* to trust an eyewitness. It's not that eyewitnesses lie—"

"At the pool house this morning, Holt took one of Jonathan's personal Polaroids when she thought I wasn't looking."

Desmond stared at him.

"I saw her, Desmond. She palmed it."

Desmond dabbed at the corners of his mouth with a forefinger, fastidious as a great, grand cat. "Not only is that illegal, it's poor police work. Anything she took from the scene like that can't be used as evidence." He plucked at his lower lip. "Now why would someone as smart as Jane Holt do something as foolish as that?"

Jimmy shook his head.

"Why didn't you just ask her why she did it?" said Desmond.

"Would you have asked her?"

Desmond smiled. "No . . . I would have kept it to myself, too. For now."

"I thought maybe she was going to check the Polaroid for fingerprints," said Jimmy, "except she knew it belonged to Jonathan—he was in the photo—so what was the point?"

"Maybe she wanted to show it to someone, see if he or she could make an ID?"

Jimmy remembered the blow-job Polaroids, Jonathan's face contorted in pleasure. "There are more recognizable photographs of Jonathan available. The guy has his own publicity agent. All I know is that for Holt to violate procedure, she must have thought the Polaroid was important. She must have believed me, right?"

"It doesn't matter what a cop believes; evidence is the only thing that counts." Desmond finished his hot chocolate and slowly stood up. "Like I said, you be careful of her."

Chapter 13

Holt kicked off her topsiders just inside her front door and headed for the kitchen, her feet as tired as the rest of her. She laid her purse down on the serving counter in the usual spot, unclipped her nine-millimeter and placed it next to her purse, then took off her jacket and draped it over the back of a chair. The more exhausted she was, the more she relied on her routine to keep her from making mistakes. A cool mist brushed her cheek as she opened the freezer, saw the waiting martini glass, the Baccarat dusted with frost. She grabbed a can of Schweppes extra-dry gin martini from the refrigerator, gave it a quick shake, and popped the top. Her mother said that only James Bond and people who said "martoonies" ordered their drinks shaken rather than stirred, but then her mother couldn't imagine a world in which one could buy cocktails in a can.

Holt filled her glass and added a single large green olive, causing a few drops to overflow the rim, and she licked her knuckles reflexively, immediately feeling guilty. She used to take such pride in her self-control. But now . . . She closed her eyes to take the first swallow, opened them for the second. It was nothing like the perfect martinis her mother made—Martha merely swished the vermouth in the glass and then tossed it out—but as she reminded herself with a bleak smile, she *was* still using Grandmama's crystal.

She walked over to the picture window and deliberately looked past her reflection, not needing to be reminded how worn-down she appeared. The view from her oceanfront condo, usually so spectacular, was as bleak and overcast as her state of mind, the rain *still* coming down in sheets, the Pacific a dark, churning gray. Even on a sunny day, the ocean at this time of year was about sixty-two degrees, too cold to swim in without a wet suit. Snowbirds who came to Laguna Beach were always surprised, dabbing a toe into the water and then running back to shore. Like the bumper sticker said: WELCOME TO CALIFORNIA, NOW GO HOME. She had resented that sentiment when she first moved here from Rhode Island, but now she was as intolerant as any native of the tourists who crowded into the small beachside community, gawking at the bikinis and mispronouncing *chile rellenos*. She glimpsed her reflection and winced. She needed to start moisturizing.

Today had started out with such promise. She had checked her work messages as usual when the alarm went off, heard Jimmy's angry mention of Polaroids, and jumped out of bed already formulating her game plan. Her *game plan:* God, what was happening to her? She tried to remain above all the paramilitary slang and sports metaphors that the other detectives spoke in, but it was difficult. She knew Jimmy's address, of course—he had called her a few weeks ago to ask about the status of the Eggman investigation, and thanks to a federal grant, the department automatically logged in the time and initiating number of every incoming call. She was surprised when she found out that Jimmy had called from Desmond Terrell's house. She had been so hopeful on the drive over, which had only made the disappointment at the pool house even more bitter. She still didn't know what Jimmy had really seen last night, but she knew she couldn't afford to dismiss it.

Holt sipped her drink, watching the lights switch on up and down the coast. She imagined families sitting down to dinner, the husbands and wives asking each other how the day had gone, and maybe there were children . . . but she had no idea what the children would be saying. No idea at all. She fished out the olive from her drink, chewed it slowly. She didn't use to hate her job. She would arrive early and stay late, dictating notes while she drove, a consummate professional. The Philip Kinneson homicide had been just another case until three days after the body was discovered, when a little girl building sand castles on the beach found a Polaroid lodged between the rocks and ran crying to her mother. Who promptly called the police.

Holt tilted back the glass and felt the gin roll down her throat, the sensations of hot and cold as intricately wrapped as a DNA molecule. She looked out at the darkness, feeling old, waiting for the dull ache at the back of her head to ease off. She wasn't drinking any more since the task force had been disbanded, but she *was* drinking faster. She remembered her father's coming home from the office some nights after the market had been particularly brutal and pouring the martinis down his throat as though his insides were on fire.

Three days in the sun and salt air had faded the Polaroid, but Holt still recognized Philip Kinneson. She had assumed at first that one of her uniforms had taken the shot, mentally assessing who was the most likely to have violated her orders, but there was something odd about it: the teeth and exposed bone were in high contrast, the features flattened. It didn't look like the other Kinneson crime-scene photos. Most detectives would have written off the differences—if they had even noticed them—as the result of exposure to the sun, but not Holt. At the age when most girls were dancing by themselves in their bedrooms, she had set up her own darkroom and spent hours printing photographs under the red safelight. She had a good eye, and the Polaroid the kid had found on the beach looked to her like it had been taken with flash.

Kinneson had been killed shortly after midnight, and rigor had set his expression by the time his body was discovered the next morning. Every police photo and every CSI digital scan had been shot in daylight. The only reason for this Polaroid to have been taken with a flash was that it had been shot at *night.* Holt remembered the exact moment when she'd realized the implications of her fieldwork. She hadn't gasped. Her hand hadn't shaken. She remembered being suffused with a quiet joy. The impulse to document his own work was one of the identifying marks of a serial killer. Holt imagined the killer's first attempt being swept away by the wind, the

Polaroid carried off into the darkness. Maria Sinoa in Forensics had needed only a few minutes to confirm that the photo had been shot at night. It took the FBI lab almost three weeks to get to the Polaroid and run its own tests, but those results agreed with Sinoa's findings.

Lieutenant Diefenbacher, Holt's boss, had been skeptical, maintaining that even if the Polaroid had been taken by Kinneson's murderer, that didn't mean they had a serial killer at work. "Police work is all about hearing hoofbeats behind you and thinking it's horses," Diefenbacher had lectured her. "Hearing hoofbeats and thinking it's zebras, that's *grandstanding*, Detective, and the department doesn't need that kind of reputation. Neither do you." Holt knew he was just trying to protect her, but she didn't appreciate being talked to as if she were a rookie.

A month after the Polaroid was found, Jimmy Gage had called, introduced himself, and said he had just gotten a letter from someone claiming to have killed Philip Kinneson as part of a string of homicides. Holt had actually spilled her tea reaching for her notebook to take down the address of *SLAP.*

She finished the martini, walked back to the kitchen, and refilled her glass, then resumed her post at the window. Two was her limit, her absolute limit.

She'd been instrumental in forming the Eggman task force, but there had been resistance from the beginning, with the other jurisdictions insisting they needed a definitive link between the homicides, some solid forensic evidence. The ballistics were inconclusive, however, and no pattern was evident in the wide range of victims and locales. By the time the task force disbanded, she was the only one who didn't think Jimmy's letter had been a hoax. The existence of the Laguna Polaroid had remained under seal.

A former marine, Diefenbacher had thickened around the middle but retained the crew cut and steely posture of a combat veteran. He had initially been one of Holt's biggest supporters, leapfrogging her into a detective's slot, willingly taking the heat for his decision. She was smart and tough and *thorough*, with every hair in place but with no fear of getting her hands dirty, he had told the old-timers. But Holt's handling of the Kinneson homicide, her refusal to take direction, had made him question his judgment; he suspected her of trying to turn a simple gay-bashing into a serial killing for her own professional aggrandizement, of colluding with a questionable journalist to make her case in the media. He had lost faith in her, and they both knew it.

Maybe she *had* been grandstanding. Not at first; she had been sure of her motives at the beginning of the investigation, but as the case lay dormant month after month, and her contact at the FBI began to ignore her E-mails, she had started cutting corners, becoming more, well, procedurally creative. Diefenbacher had tried to rein her in, verbally at first, then later in writing, ordering her to not devote any further time or resources to the Eggman investigation, but she'd continued to work the case off the clock, had even paid a retired criminalist out of her own pocket to recheck her research.

The rain beat against the window so loudly that Holt stepped back, startled by the force of the storm. She had finished her second martini without even being aware of it.

There'd been a time, before the Eggman case, when Holt would have been disgusted with a police officer who let her personal feelings take precedence, a police officer who bent the law when it suited her. There'd been a time when she couldn't have imagined taking a photograph from an investigation, an uninventoried Polaroid; she might as well have been stealing it. Yet that was exactly what she had done this morning, and with hardly any hesitation. The photo might be useful, and that was all that counted. *Might* be useful. She had intended to sneak it to Maria Sinoa to be tested, but Diefenbacher had kept her too busy.

"Glad you could make it, Detective," Diefenbacher had said when she arrived late that morning, as he tossed the day's assignments on her desk, scattering her neatly arranged pencils. He had unwrapped yet another Power Bar as he watched her read through them, saying that if the caseload was too much for her, he would be happy to shift her to community relations. "You could give talks to the garden club, warn the old ladies to lock their doors and windows. It doesn't have the glamour of running down a thrill killer, but it's honest police work."

Most of her shift had been taken up with running down a series of car prowls at long-term local motels, interviewing drowsy single mothers and day-shift managers who scratched themselves in between answers. The rest of the afternoon had been spent taking the statement of a hyperventilating Main Street interior decorator who was convinced that a cigarette stubbed out on an atrocious seascape was an act of vandalism rather than the work of an itinerant art critic. By the time Holt got back to the station, Sinoa had punched out.

Holt slowly made her way back to the kitchen, walking carefully, proud that she never lurched or staggered. Even when she was past her limit, she could walk a straight line, recite the alphabet, touch a finger to her nose with her eyes closed. She had proved it in her living room about a week ago, happy for a moment, then overwhelmed by shame at having felt the need to test herself.

She stood in front of the refrigerator for several moments before opening it and taking out another canned martini. There was cold chicken and asparagus tips in the refrigerator. Fresh raspberries. She should have something to eat. Or maybe a little television. She had the complete BBC *Singing Detective* series on video. The treadmill was waiting in one corner of the living room, along with the ab machine and the StairMaster. She had cleared out her spare bedroom and shifted her library and fitness equipment out here to make room for her voluminous Eggman files and displays. The living room was cluttered now, but she didn't get many visitors. Correction: she didn't get *any* visitors, not since Eric had suggested one time too many that she was taking her work a little too seriously.

Holt poured herself a fresh drink but left it on the counter, untouched. She needed to maintain some self-control—slapping Jimmy this morning had marked a complete breakdown in her professional demeanor. He had a way of getting to her, unnerving her with a look or a remark; even his silences could seem insolent. She had checked his background carefully, the textbook approach with anyone who claimed to be in contact with a killer. His file was a jumble of conflicting entries: superior intelligence but a GED instead of a high school diploma, a financial history teetering on insolvency, and a rap sheet of petty arrests dating back to junior high school.

In ninth grade Jimmy had broken into the Griffith Observatory and taken his science class on an impromptu field trip. A string of car thefts had followed, each time with the vehicle being returned to its original parking spot, albeit with the tank so empty he must have driven the last few miles on fumes. The owners had never pressed charges. His only arrest as an adult came when he was nineteen, after he slipped into the Shrine Auditorium for the Academy Awards presentation, walked right past some of the tightest security in the country, and started seating movie stars, a genuine usher's badge clipped to his tuxedo. He got two months in county lockup for that one, but his article on the stunt was published in *GQ*, bringing him his first paycheck as a writer. Holt smiled. It was a good piece. She had read every article, every column, every word he had ever written.

She was glad there was no history of violence on Jimmy's sheet. None at all. He had alibis for only three of the Eggman killings: on two occasions witnesses had placed him at movie screenings, and while Carlos Medonza was being shot, Jimmy had been scouting locations with a young filmmaker named Rollo Boyce, a teenage dropout who'd sweated his way through the whole deposition. Holt trusted the two polygraph tests Jimmy had passed more than she did any witness, and she trusted her instincts about him most of all.

Holt walked over to her purse, snapped it open, and pulled out the fellatio Polaroid in its glassine evidence bag—a cop condom as one of her instructors at the academy had called the bags. The phrase had never been more accurate than now. She pressed the clear plastic flat to get a better look and saw Dr. Jonathan Gage in all his glory. The man fellated himself with every breath he took;

what did he need a woman for? The blonde's long hair was draped across his arched thighs, her hair silvery in the flash, caught at the very instant of passion. Holt would never, ever allow herself to be photographed like that—she smiled—not unless she retained possession of the photograph. Sex was one thing, and trust was quite another.

She didn't really know much about Jonathan Gage; her backgrounder on Jimmy had been extensive, but it had touched only briefly on his family members, and what she had found out had not aroused her interest or suspicion. Holt idly stroked her cheek as she continued to stare at the Polaroid, noting the cords in Jonathan's neck, the rapture evident in his strained posture. She squared off the Polaroid on the desk, touching it gingerly.

Sinoa had explained to her that Polaroids taken by the same camera could be matched up: the tiny bits of sand and grit in the camera mechanism and roller left microscopic scratches in the film emulsion, unique imperfections that were as reliable as fingerprints. Sinoa had tested dozens of Polaroids for Holt over the last year, every one that that dreadful woman from Gallery Inferno could come up with, every one that Holt found on her own. They had never found a match with the Laguna Polaroid. Even if they got lucky with this one, Holt couldn't use it in court—a good defense attorney would be all over her for breaking the evidentiary chain—but that wouldn't matter. If it was a match, Holt was going to close the case.

Holt picked up her martini and took a long drink for luck. Wait until Sinoa saw the Polaroid of Jonathan. Maria Sinoa was the only tech Holt could trust to evaluate the Polaroid without reporting it to Diefenbacher or to Dr. Chakabarti, the chief of Forensics. She would still log it in, of course—Sinoa wouldn't leave herself open to a reprimand—but she would see that the paperwork was misfiled. Sinoa was a stickler for proper procedures, but she was also a devout Catholic, a woman with faith in that which was real but not yet manifest.

Holt carefully replaced the fellatio photo in her purse. She didn't believe Jimmy would deliberately mislead her about the Egg-man Polaroids, which meant that either he had been too stoned to think straight, or he had really seen what he said he had. Lightning crashed right outside the window, but she barely reacted. Tomorrow, after giving the Polaroid to Maria Sinoa, she was going to start making inquiries about Dr. Gage.

Chapter 14

"You won't believe the call I just got, Mack." Great White walked out of the office of the Big Orange Arena, ducking his head to get through the door, his heavy footsteps echoing in the empty hall. There was no event scheduled for tonight. "Mack?" He spotted Macklen in front of the deserted bar, drinking fizzy water and watching Letterman on TV. Thunder shook the windows as he sidled over, shoulders hunched as though he were outside in the rain. He might have lightning bolts tattooed on his neck, but Great White hated storms. They made him feel small. He pointed to the screen, where Robin Williams was contorting his rubbery face for the camera. "Robin Williams is a Jew. Did you know that?"

Macklen didn't take his eyes off the TV. "Robin Williams isn't a Jew name."

"That's the way they work."

"Robin Williams cracks me up, I don't care what he is," said Macklen.

Great White wasn't about to argue the point. "I just got a call from Vorcek. Somebody's finally selling the memory chips."

Macklen jabbed the television over the bar with one of his canes, switching it off. "Why didn't you *tell* me that instead of going on about who's a Jew and who isn't?"

"No need to hurry; Vorcek made the deal last week. He said he bought fifty of them, which was all the guy had."

"Damn Red bastard took his own sweet time calling," said Macklen, swinging himself over toward the office, moving faster than most men could walk. "Maybe he's like you, too busy debating whether Oprah is a dyke or if Mr. Rogers is a fucking Martian to take care of business."

"Oprah's not a dyke, she's a nigger."

"Who was selling my chips?" snarled Macklen.

"You know Vorcek: he wants his reward first."

Macklen was panting, not from exertion but from excitement, his narrow eyes bright and hard. He'd had the build of a coal miner before he was shot, with knotted arms and thick, whipcord wrists. Now he was even stronger. Great White might have to hold his legs up straight for him, but Macklen could do two hundred upside-down push-ups without breaking a sweat. He stood there before Great White now, the tips of his boots dragging on the floor as he swayed on his canes, a dangerous bundle of compressed violence.

Great White towered over him. "What do you want to do, Mack?"

"What do you think?" said Macklen. Lightning crashed, and he had to wait a moment so he could be heard. "Pull your head out of your ass and call Vorcek back. Tell him we got his money."

Chapter 15

Fisher looked up from his bare desk in the Roseate-Plum Alcove (positive energy, prosperity), his hands folded on the blotter. The last time Rollo had seen him, it must have been over a month ago now, Fisher was sitting in the exact same position. "Rollo, what a pleasant surprise. Any news about the movie?"

Rollo stood just inside the door of ChromoGenesis, rain dripping off his jacket onto the burnt-umber carpet (cleansing, fresh beginnings). "Not yet. I'm having, like, distribution problems."

Fisher nodded, a slumping, middle-aged man with a weak chin and droopy eyes—the face of an intellectual basset hound. "I appreciate your trying to help me spread the word about ChromoGenesis, but sometimes the world is not ready for the innovators."

"Yeah, well, fuck 'em, right?"

"Indeed," Fisher said, his words like cotton balls.

After inheriting a modest stock portfolio on his mother's death the year before, Fisher had quit his job as a dog groomer, liquidated the portfolio, and put all the proceeds into a chain of psychospiritual spas—ChromoGenesis—whose bare rooms were designed to induce various emotional states strictly through the use of specific colors. The Lava-Red Room stimulated the lethargic, the Blush-Pink Room calmed those with violent natures, the Pure-White Room fostered intellectual clarity.

The idea for ChromoGenesis had come to Fisher while he was attempting to show-clip a sexually aggressive standard poodle. After he slipped his own rose-colored sunglasses onto the animal, it immediately lost all interest in humping his leg and became quite docile. To this day, Fisher could not explain what had made him put the sunglasses on the poodle—he considered it one of those serendipitous breakthroughs that dot the history of science.

Rollo had shot a seven-hour feature about Fisher and Chromo-Genesis as part of his Don Quixote series on hopeless visionaries. He had submitted it to fourteen different film festivals and gotten it accepted by Omaha and Little Rock, but so far there had been no awards, no press, no call from Miramax. Bite me, Harvey.

Fisher sighed, a spray of fine droplets misting the air. "Is this a . . . social visit, or are you going to shoot some more film?"

"I need a place to stay."

"Ah."

"I'm in trouble. The large-economy-size trouble."

"Well, perhaps the Azure-Blue Room, then," said Fisher, steepling his fingers. "Harmony and relaxation. Pure, timeless bliss is all that exists within the heavenly blue."

"I want to move into that timeless bliss, man. I want to take out a ninety-nine-year lease."

Fisher nodded. "I've been spending a great deal of time in the Azure-Blue Room myself."

"Hey, man, I don't want to evict you from your crib—"

"No, I should move into the Pure-White Room for a while anyway. I need to make some decisions." Fisher stared at his hands. "You're the first person to walk in the door since—well, since you left. I'm starting to wonder if I've made an error in judgment."

Ten months ago, Fisher had launched ChromoGenesis, opening four outlets in Orange County. No expense had been spared—getting the exact color tonalities had taken sometimes ten or fifteen paint jobs, the carpeting was hypoallergenic, the air triple-filtered. The public had no interest in ChromoGenesis's Spartan, unfurnished rooms however. People wanted hot tubs and Jacuzzis, sofas and love seats, seaweed wraps and salt massages and herbal colonics. Three of the spas had already closed; this one, just off Main Street in Seal Beach, was the last remaining.

"Perhaps I was overly ambitious," murmured Fisher. "I was doing good work at the salon, useful work; the dogs respected me. . . . Perhaps I let my ego run wild. Too much vermilion, that was my mistake."

"Hey, Fisher, any asshole can spend his life flea-dipping the lower phyla. You gave it your best shot, man. I respect you for that."

"That means a great deal to me," Fisher said softly. "Many film-makers would have approached my work with a certain . . . bemused contempt, a freak-show mentality. I appreciate your lack of conde-scension."

"I may switch price tags at Kmart, man, but I don't cheat when it comes to my work."

Fisher lowered his eyes. "You might have achieved more com-mercial success if you did."

"I make the movies I want to make, no excuses. Artists and en-trepreneurs, man, we boldly go, that's our nature."

"You are a very rare individual." Fisher stood up, smoothed his purple suit, and led Rollo through the spa, silently stepping through zones of color, the big, ultimo pack of Crayolas, finally coming to the open door of the Azure-Blue Room.

"Whoa." Rollo looked around. The walls, ceiling, and carpet were all the same rich cerulean blue, a totality of blue as far as the eye could see. He couldn't hear the storm from here. No lightning. No thunder.

"Is this better?" asked Fisher.

Rollo sat on the carpet, slowly breathing in that deep blue, feel-ing a calmness lapping at him like an incoming tide, inching past the horror-show images of Blaine standing over him with pruning shears, of Great White staring at him with those flat, black eyes, a tag team of his deepest fears. Rollo stayed focused on the blue, let-ting the color still the voices in his head, allowing the cool blue si-lence to roll through him.

"Stay as long as you like," said Fisher, closing the door behind him.

Rollo lay down and looked up at the blue ceiling, floating, to-tally at peace now. It was like falling into a Librium.

Chapter 16

Jimmy's bare feet sank into the soft, damp sand as he walked toward the water, holding his shoes in one hand as he struggled through the first light of morning. He had thought to surprise Jonathan while he was still in bed, give him a taste of what that was like, but the housekeeper who'd answered the intercom had said Jonathan was out. The woman hadn't been willing to disturb Olivia, but she had told him that Jonathan was on the beach.

Jonathan's oceanfront property was just south of Newport; the beach below the expensive homes would be teeming with locals by midmorning, but it was still deserted now. Last night's storm had littered the sand with plastic bottles, broken pieces of Styrofoam, and clumps of brown seaweed. A single tennis shoe flopped back and forth at the tide line, performing a silent tap dance to drowned boys everywhere. Far down the strand, Jimmy could see Jonathan standing in the surf, the sunrise creeping over the high rises inland making him appear to be made out of gold.

Jimmy moved closer, his feet splashing in the shallows, but the ocean was freezing and he quickly retreated out of reach, wondering how Jonathan could tolerate the cold.

Wearing a snow-white bathing suit for his morning yoga exercises, Jonathan was standing on one foot, with his other leg pulled back behind him with one hand, and the other hand stretched to the sky. He stood there perfectly balanced as the waves lapped around his thighs.

Jimmy shivered just looking at him. He should be back home having a cup of lousy coffee with Desmond, the two of them reading the paper while Desmond waited for the stock market to open and Jimmy got ready to call around trying to snag some free-lance assignments. That was going to have to wait, though. Jimmy hadn't had a good night's sleep since he found the Eggman Polaroids in the pool house, the gory images fluttering through his dreams as though dropped from a great height, and waking didn't put an end to it. There were too many ugly possibilities running around in his head now, and Jonathan was the only one with the answers.

Moving smoothly from the king pose, Jonathan sank to his knees, the frigid water at his chin now as he faced the horizon, eyes closed, as serene as if he were sitting in a warm bath.

"Hold that pose until the tide comes in," said Jimmy.

Jonathan opened his eyes, then slowly stood up and turned around toward Jimmy, his tight, compact body as white as his bathing suit, and virtually hairless. His eyes sparkled with the reflection off the water, only his hard, tiny nipples and the reddened tips of his ears betraying the cold. "How did you find me? Did Olivia tell you I was here?"

"Would that bother you?"

"It would surprise me. She's rather annoyed at you after your boorish behavior at the party." A gull screamed, and Jonathan watched it dive into the water, his face expressionless as he followed its progress back into the air with a fish in its mouth. "What exactly do you want, James?"

Jimmy moved to the edge of the water. He could see the small, curved scar alongside Jonathan's navel.

Jonathan touched the scar, as if reading his mind. "One of your many gifts to me."

"You moved."

"I *breathed.*"

"You weren't supposed to breathe."

Jonathan had been thirteen at the time, Jimmy just twelve, the two of them playing flinch, one of their private games, a blend of misdirection and fearlessness. Jonathan had lost a mental contest—a math puzzle, maybe, or naming every other president—and losing required him to stand there while Jimmy flailed away at him with a linoleum knife, Jimmy dodging and feinting and making phantom thrusts while Jonathan stared indifferently into space. That morning Jimmy had charged in and pretended to stumble, his knife hand outstretched, and Jonathan had flinched. He hadn't cried out when he was cut, had merely sucked in his breath. It had taken fifteen stitches to close him up, but the game had continued, in various, evolving forms.

"What do you want?" Jonathan repeated.

"I wondered if we were still playing flinch. You're supposed to tell me, you know. It's not fair to start without me."

"Ah . . . *fair.*" Jonathan touched another scar, a smaller one on his shoulder. "I have all these marks, but you were untouched, James. What does that tell you about fairness?"

"It tells me that you flinched and I didn't."

"Perhaps you just trusted me more than I trusted you." Jonathan stroked his flat, knotted belly. "I can still remember that one time we played right at the end of summer before high school. It was my turn, and I was swinging Mother's meat cleaver at your throat. The cleaver was so heavy I had to use two hands, whipping it back and forth across your windpipe while you stood there sweating, absolutely still. Both of us had such perfect self-control at that moment, our lives hanging in the balance. . . . It was one of the most beautiful moments of our youth. You were so glorious. What happened to you, James?"

Jimmy stared at him. "You're afraid of me. I don't know why, but you are."

Jonathan clasped his hands in front of him and slowly leaned backward until the top of his head touched the water, holding the position as the tide lapped against his face, then just as slowly straightening up again. "I'm drawn to the precision and self-control that yoga demands, the discipline of mind and body, the transcendence of the physical. You should try it."

"I like the physical. I like it hot and juicy, with a double order of fries. I wouldn't want to transcend it."

"A pity." Jonathan exhaled, bowed to the new day, then walked out of the water, sunlight gleaming on his wet skin, his face a mask. "Perfection, James, that's what eludes you—perfection in yoga, as in surgery, is achieved through self-control and endless repetition."

"Fuck perfection. I had a dream last night: you were in my room, standing over me."

Jonathan cocked his head, curious. "Is that why you're here? You had a bad dream?"

"It was so real—even after I woke up, I kept expecting to see you in the shadows."

"I don't even know where you live." Jonathan shook his head, the water beaded along his shoulders shimmering like pearls. "Earlier this week you accused me of spiriting away Polaroids that I didn't even know about. Today I'm accused of floating through a locked door—you *do* lock your door, don't you? Why do you invest me with such power?"

"Are we playing a game, Jonathan? Just tell me. I'll play anything, you know that."

"Yes, I do." Jonathan walked up onto the sand, where his towel and robe lay folded. "It's really one of your most appealing qualities."

"Where did you get the Eggman Polaroids?" Jimmy followed. "I've been looking into it, and they're hard to come by."

Jonathan put on his hooded robe and faced him. "How is the delightful Detective Holt these days?" he said, swaddled in the thick white terry cloth. "I'm a little disappointed that you didn't bring her along this morning, but then again, she may be feeling less than charitable toward you after your performance Monday morning."

"I'm not going to quit until I find out."

Jonathan shoved his hands into the deep pockets of the robe. "I certainly hope not. I hadn't realized how much I'd missed our times together, James—the insights you have, the challenge you present. No one else can really keep up."

"Holt isn't giving up, either. She's smart, Jonathan."

Jonathan sighed. "You look exhausted. You really *must* take better care of yourself. Mother even commented on it."

Jimmy moved in on him, but the sand gave way beneath his feet, and he stumbled.

"Watch your step," Jonathan warned. "You're not at all in the position you think you're in." He ducked as a seagull dive-bombed them, screeching and beating at them with its wings. "She must have a nest nearby," he said, watching the gull circle. "Instinct is such a powerful force, as overwhelming and elemental as gravity. Which one of us could resist the call?"

"Did you do it?"

"Do what?"

"*Did* you?"

"You're repeating yourself," said Jonathan. "That's what you told me at the party—and quite pleased with yourself, I might add. You said repetition canceled out the original statement. So what did *you* do, James?"

"Me?"

"I always associate you with blood—that's odd, isn't it?" mused Jonathan. "Perhaps because you've cut me so many times, or perhaps it's just a metaphor: blood ties, blood kin."

Jimmy felt Jonathan leading him in deeper and deeper, waiting for him to make a fool of himself. Jonathan would be telling the story for years to come—concerned, of course, shaking his head at the deterioration of Jimmy's faculties, the once-sharp intellect now given to fantasy and paranoia.

Jonathan had been a twisted fuck all his life, even as a boy creating vile nicknames that stuck with kids forever, starting rumors that were never traced back to him. Once, in high school, Jimmy had found his physics research final missing from his notebook the morning it was due; he'd spent the next two months bicycling to summer school, seeing pages from his paper nailed to trees along his route. Jimmy had never told his parents, never told anyone. It wouldn't have changed anything. There was the good son and the bad son, the good brother and the bad brother, and they both knew which was which.

"I'm sorry to hear that you're still troubled by nightmares," Jonathan said sympathetically. "You had such bad dreams when we were children, screaming in your sleep. I had hoped you had outgrown that."

"Me, too."

Jonathan smiled. "I used to wonder what you saw when you closed your eyes, but you never told me."

"You knew what I saw."

Jonathan shrugged. "You really should try yoga. There are so many benefits, mental and physical, but for me its greatest attribute is the way it smooths the chaos within. All those jagged thoughts, the ceaseless striving, the *futility* of self. . . ." He closed his eyes as he inhaled through his nostrils, then slowly breathed out through his mouth. His eyes were open again, brighter now. "Yoga calms the spirit and allows one to see one's true face."

"Do you actually look? You must be a brave man."

Jonathan didn't rise to the bait. " 'Brave'? I wouldn't describe myself that way. A focused man, disciplined, and perhaps given to feeling a little guilty, too, about the pain I've caused you—inadvertently, of course, but painful nonetheless. If Olivia and I hadn't gotten married—"

"Don't blame Olivia."

"If you say so."

"I know you left your party early," said Jimmy, wanting to wipe that smirk off his brother's face. "It must have been something important for you to leave your guests like that."

Jonathan watched him, his face expressionless. "Is that what they call a *scoop* in your profession?" he said at last, laughing now. He clapped his hands, genuinely delighted. "I *have* missed you. You were away far too long."

"I'm back now, Jonathan."

"Wonderful." Jonathan cocked his head. "I've got to get ready for work now, but the Opera Guild is having a benefit ball on Saturday evening, and I'd like you to be my guest. We can continue our conversation then."

"I don't know."

"Please come. I bought a whole table." Jonathan turned up the collar of his robe. "I'll save you a spot next to me." The sun was behind Jonathan now, and try as he might, Jimmy couldn't see his eyes.

Chapter 17

The two gardeners glanced up as the wrought iron gate buzzed, then went back to weeding Pilar's flower beds as they argued in Spanish, their hands expertly plucking out the clover from the bright-red zinnias and yellow marigolds. The surrounding houses were badly kept, their driveways cluttered with dirt bikes, the yards brown and weedy. Pilar's double lot was a lush, groomed oasis with neat borders and fruit trees in the back, the whole place surrounded by an eight-foot fence topped by coils of razor wire, security cameras tracking movement on the street.

The gardeners continued their argument as Jimmy walked up the winding path, the two men debating the relative pussy-magnet merits of the Camaro versus the Buick Crown Royal. It was the basic philosophic divide that questions of love always come down to: thrills or ease of handling. The Camaro had a gritty, raffish charm, but the Crown Royal was a roomier, more comfortable ride. Jimmy was about to tell the Camaro man that he had his vote when the front door opened.

"Dude!" Blaine the Robo-Surfer filled the doorway, a blond, sweet-faced bruiser wearing skull-and-crossbones jams that grazed his kneecaps, his bare chest still decorated with the orange Magic Marker power dials from Saturday night.

Jimmy held up one hand. *"Gort, klaatu barata nikto."*

Blaine scrunched his face, confused, then embraced Jimmy eagerly, smothering him in his python arms, lifting him off his feet. "That story you wrote in the *Times* this morning was *lethal* cool. I didn't even know you were at the match." He gently set Jimmy down. "When I saw you on the minicam, I told Pilar you were probably here to interview me about my career plans, but she just laughed. I think she's jealous of me being famous now."

"Yeah, fame's a bitch." Jimmy could see dark stitches zigzagging across Blaine's right ear where the Kongo Kid had taken a bite. Blaine had howled into the spotlight, then snapped the Kid's leg like a toothpick, the crowd going silent for a moment before roaring its approval. "How's the ear?"

"Itches," Blaine said, pulling on his lobe. "You know Mr. Macklen, don't you? He told the wrestlers that we were each going to get a video of our match, but I never got one. I asked Great White, but he said it wasn't his department, like he could give a shit. I thought maybe you could talk to Mr. Macklen. . . . Jimmy? Hey, wait for me."

Jimmy walked past Blaine and into the house, strolling past the Aztec velvet paintings and phony Dalí prints stacked twenty deep against the walls, through rooms so filled with cartons of Cuisinarts and espresso makers, CD players and Apple computers, that the two of them had to walk sideways. He found Pilar in the family room, sitting cross-legged on the sofa watching television, a Lean Cuisine chicken teriyaki microwave dinner in her lap. She was a short, bull-necked Latina in her late forties, wearing silver-studded leather pants and a matching vest that showed off her powerful arms. Her glossy black hair was swept back into a ducktail, the tips frosted. A large paper bag filled with oranges from her own trees was on the floor.

Pilar glanced over at Jimmy, then turned back to her TV. Which was a bad sign. Pilar had greeted him with a can of iced tea tossed at his head, had welcomed him with curses and insults, and once, when high on Special K at Club Marengo, had actually kissed him on the cheek, then laughed at the bright-red lipstick smear for the rest of the evening. She had never pretended to be uninterested. Jimmy was tempted to make some excuse and head for the door, but he had promised Rollo.

"You want to go in back to do my interview?" Blaine's soft round eyes made him look even younger. "I have a lot to talk about. My philosophy, my triceps routine—stuff like that."

"Some other time." Jimmy patted Blaine on the back—the kid was as solid as a Clydesdale—and then sauntered over to the couch and sat down beside Pilar. *"Hola, chica."*

Pilar held up an orange. "You want one?"

"Maybe later."

Pilar tossed the orange back into the bag. "Maybe later I don't offer you one."

"I'll take my chances."

Pilar nodded. "So it seems." Her features were broad, her dark-brown cheeks finely pitted. "You have waited a long time to come for your money, Jimmy," she said, her voice faintly accented, so that she pronounced his name "Shimmy." "You must have been in a great hurry to leave California."

"Maybe I just like having you owe me." Jimmy put his feet up on the hatch-cover coffee table, the teakwood littered with orange peels, a Keds shoe box, a Mossberg pump shotgun, a TV remote, a thirty-two-ounce bottle of Diet Pepsi, and the olive jar that Rollo had told him about. A half-completed Charlie's Angels jigsaw puzzle took up half the table. He nudged the Mossberg. "What happened to the Uzi?"

Pilar grimaced. *"Esstúpido* fell asleep in a movie theater and left it behind afterward. The Mossberg is twice as big. Let him try to forget *that.*"

"Wasn't my fault," grumbled Blaine. "I was at a *Rocky* marathon."

"It was Mr. T's gold medallion in *Rocky Two,*" said Jimmy. *"Never* stare at the medallion."

"Wow." Blaine's Adam's apple bobbed, and Jimmy imagined the dials inked on his bare chest going into overload as he tried to process the information.

Pilar reached into the shoe box, took out a stack of hundreds, flicked off ten bills, and laid them on the table. "Now we are even.

That was a foolish bet, by the way. No way you should have been able to name all the members of the Dirty Dozen."

"Everyone forgets Jiménez." Jimmy didn't touch the money.

Pilar poked the bills. "You want to arm wrestle for it? Double or nothing?"

Jimmy felt her bicep, shook his head.

"Maricón." A bracelet of tiny purple flowers was tattooed around each of her wrists, an innocent, girlish touch. Pilar must have gotten them a long time ago. She jabbed at her microwave dinner. "You want some breakfast?"

"No, thanks. I can't stay long."

"Jimmy cannot stay long. Jimmy is a busy man." Pilar looked at him, and her eyes belonged in the reptile house at the L.A. Zoo. "You probably have time to talk about Rollo, though. Yes?"

"That's right."

"An honest answer, but then, Jimmy is always truthful when the truth does not matter."

"Rollo is pretty shaken up. He calls me two or three times a day to ask if I've talked to you yet. You've got him scared."

Pilar shifted on the couch, her leather pants crackling. "Rollo *should* be scared." She scraped the bottom of the Styrofoam tray, then licked her fork. *"Esstúpido,* get me another one. Lasagna this time." She watched Blaine lumber into the kitchen, his surf jams flapping around his knees. "Do you know how long it took to train that one? Now he is ruined. That article of yours has taken away his concentration, his ferocity . . . his *bite.* All he talks about is this WWF and did he get a call from Vince McMahon and do I think he could be in a Texas Death Match even though he is from California?"

Jimmy was laughing now. He hoped Pilar would join him, but she wasn't that easy.

"He was up late last night emptying every *L.A. Times* rack within five miles. . . . Blaine!" Pilar called to the kitchen. "How many copies of Jimmy's article did you get?"

Blaine poked his head out of the kitchen. "Three hundred and eight." He licked his lips. "You probably . . . you should try to remember to call me Robo-Surfer, OK?" He nodded at Jimmy. "Especially . . . you know, in front of the press."

Pilar reached out as Jimmy started to fit a puzzle piece into Farrah's tanned body, grabbing his wrist and twisting, making him drop it. "I do not care if you help with the other Angels, but do *not* touch Farrah." She gently laid the piece into Farrah's hip, smoothed it into place. "You really want to help, tell me where I can find Rollo."

"I don't know. He moves around a lot."

"He calls you up, he begs you to talk to me"—Pilar chugged Diet Pepsi, smacked her lips—"yet you do not know where he is?"

"That's right."

"Such loyalty! You should be a saint on the shelf of a church, Jimmy. Women with black shawls could light candles to you and pray that their husbands would be so faithful. It is too bad you get so little loyalty in return." Pilar checked her manicure. "I heard that your girlfriend married your brother." Laughing, she whacked the table, knocking over the olive jar. "Your *brother?*"

"We're going on Jerry Springer next week," said Jimmy as the olive jar rolled slowly toward him. "You might want to tape it."

"Brave talk, but I know it must hurt."

Jimmy caught the olive jar as it rolled off the table, and glimpsed a human finger through the murk—a wrinkled, white finger, slightly curled, beckoning. He looked at Pilar.

"Beep-beep!" Blaine came in from the kitchen, walking herky-jerky, practicing his robot moves, a microwave dinner in one hand. He set it down on the coffee table.

Pilar peeled back the clear-plastic lid of her lasagna and watched steam rise from it like mist. "Take your money, Jimmy. I do not like to owe you."

"Keep it as a down payment on Rollo's debt. He just wants to be able to go home without getting grabbed. If he can't do business, he can't pay you back—"

Pilar poked Jimmy in the arm with her fork. "Don't tell me what to do." She jabbed him again, harder this time, leaving indentations in his skin. *"Comprende?"*

"I got an idea, Pilar," said Blaine. "Maybe I could send the Kongo Kid some flowers in the hospital, and Jimmy could be there with a photographer, show the fans that there's no hard feelings about what he done to my ear."

"Are you proud of yourself?" Pilar hissed at Jimmy. "You and your article have convinced Blaine that he can think." She grabbed the thousand dollars from the table, shoved the bills into his shirt pocket. "I pay my debts. Tell Rollo to pay his."

Jimmy rubbed his arm where she had stabbed him, sensing a minute shift in Pilar's mood. He stood up, trying not to hurry.

"Walk Jimmy to the door, Blaine." Pilar scooped up a forkful of lasagna. "Before he goes, though, show him some of those moves that you are always practicing."

"He's not a trained professional, Pilar. I could hurt him."

Pilar smiled, took a bite.

Blaine blocked the doorway as Jimmy tried to go around him. "Pilar?" he said, unsure of what he was supposed to do. "There's no give to the floor here. Jimmy could break something—you know, something important."

"Pobrecito," clucked Pilar.

Jimmy punched Blaine in the face, then hit him again as hard as he could. Blaine, looking more disappointed than hurt, suddenly grabbed him and threw him against the far wall. As he bounced off, Blaine drop-kicked him in the chest, and his head snapped back against the wall, cracking the plaster.

Pilar watched, chewing with her mouth open.

"I told you," groaned Jimmy, "I don't know where Rollo is."

Pilar was busy with her Charlie's Angels puzzle again. "This isn't about Rollo." She rolled a puzzle piece over in her fingers. "Show Jimmy your special move, Blaine. What is it called? The Big Kahuna Drop?"

Blaine hoisted Jimmy over his head, making roar-of-the-crowd noises as he held him aloft, then—"Kowa . . . BONGA!"—dropped him over his bent knee.

Jimmy lay on the floor, twitching, trying to breathe.

"Pretty cool, huh?" said Blaine.

"You hit like a girl," gasped Jimmy.

Blaine acted like he hadn't heard. "I'll be right back. Don't go away."

Pilar pounded a puzzle piece into place with the flat of her hand as Blaine hurried off. "Blaine is by nature much too sweet for his own good, so from time to time it is necessary to blood the boy, to put him through his paces. He is so fond of you—it was a perfect test of his training. I think he will be all right now."

"Glad . . . glad I could be of service."

Pilar smiled at the puzzle. "Tell Rollo to call me and we will make arrangements."

"Just like that, all is forgiven?"

Pilar shrugged. "Rollo is a moneymaker."

Blaine rushed back into the room with a newspaper and knelt down next to Jimmy. "Sign this for me, OK?" He held out a pen. "How about 'To Robo-Surfer, future champion'?" He blushed.

The paper trembled in Jimmy's hand. The *Times* had run his article with a photo of the Robo-Surfer breaking the Kongo Kid's leg, Blaine giddy and triumphant in the spotlight. Jimmy scrawled his name.

"I can't wait to show this to my mom," said Blaine, carefully folding the newspaper. He leaned closer. "You were right before—I didn't really hit you that hard," he whispered. "But don't tell Pilar, OK?"

"Be quiet, Blaine," Pilar ordered. "I have some advice for Jimmy."

"No advice," said Jimmy.

"Consider it a gift then, a Mexican proverb to soothe your wounded heart," said Pilar. "You have had a woman stolen away from you, a woman you think is like no other, a queen you can never replace, but Jimmy"—she wagged her index finger at him—"*todas son reinas en la oscuridad*—'in the dark, they are *all* queens.' Every one of them."

Chapter 18

"Good morning, Donna," said Holt, more perkily than she'd intended. She resisted the impulse to look over her shoulder at the door to Forensics. "I wanted to get a status report on the prints CSI pulled at my car prowl yesterday."

Donna glanced up from the current issue of *Cosmo,* a lumpy peroxide blonde, her peacock-blue shadow troweled on so thick it was a wonder she could keep her eyes open. "There's a long line ahead of you, Detective. We don't play favorites here."

Holt forced a smile. "Of course not, I understand that." (You lying bitch, she thought, tell that to Bartoli with his mustache and his muscles the next time he asks you to give his folder a nudge.) "I was just trying to get a heads-up. You can't blame a girl for trying." She could see two techs working at the light table, while Maria Sinoa sat at her desk across the room, peering through a thick magnifier.

"Anything else?" said Donna. "I'm busy here."

"Is that coffee fresh?" Holt asked sweetly.

" 'Coffee taster' isn't part of my job description," said Donna, going back to her magazine.

"Well, it's got to be better than the sludge we have upstairs," Holt said to the top of her head.

"Don't forget to leave a quarter in the can," Donna mumbled as Holt crossed the room. "You detectives are always coming down here and drinking our coffee and not paying for it."

Holt kept walking, pleased that Sinoa had looked up to see what was causing the commotion in the quiet of the forensics office. Holt took her time fixing her coffee, then theatrically stuffed a dollar bill in the empty coffee can that was used to collect payment. Dr. Chakabarti was visible through the glass wall of his office, busy at the computer, probably working on another densely reasoned piece for the professional journals he regularly submitted articles to.

Holt blew on her coffee. She had arrived early, hoping to beat Lieutenant Diefenbacher in, and had cursed out loud when she saw his brightly polished red Ford Explorer in the parking lot. She was convinced that he was keeping track of her movements, probably building a file on her. Diefenbacher had issued a standing order for her not to request any Eggman-related research from Forensics without prior approval. She sipped her coffee, which really was a lot better than what they had upstairs, and checked the door again.

Sinoa adjusted the magnifier, pretending to be working as she watched Holt, nervous now. Sinoa, a short, soft-bellied older woman with a placid face and the slender fingers of a concert pianist, had been a forensics tech for almost thirty-three years. Over lunch one afternoon, she had revealed to Holt that at the start of her career she had applied to take the detective's exam, drawn by the intellectual challenges of the job, but back then women, and particularly Hispanic women, were steered to the technical areas of law enforcement rather than fieldwork. Sinoa was a stickler for proper procedures, a rigorous scientist who had never padded her overtime or taken a sick day she didn't deserve, but if Holt asked for her help, she would oblige.

"Looks like you have another Dodger ball, Maria," Holt said, walking over to her desk. She picked up the baseball and pretended to read the autographs.

"My cousin Ernesto caught it last week," said Maria, a little too loudly.

Donna looked up from her magazine, then went back to her reading.

Holt checked the door again, then slipped the fellatio Polaroid in its glassine envelope onto Sinoa's desk.

Sinoa held the Polaroid in her hands, not staring, simply looking, allowing her dark eyes to take in the image. She showed no reaction except in raising one thick eyebrow. She put the Polaroid under the magnifier and leaned forward, a tiny gold crucifix swinging down from her lovely brown neck as she examined the photo, and Holt wondered what Dr. Jonathan Gage would have thought of her smooth skin. Sinoa pushed back her gray hair, unconsciously reacting to the disarray of the woman in the photo. "I cannot test this now. Harrison is using the scanning microscope all morning."

Holt replaced the baseball.

The Polaroid disappeared into Sinoa's desk as she bent over the magnifier again.

"Thank you," whispered Holt, eager to get out of there. She had cleared time to drop in on Olivia Gage later this morning; she wanted to find out just what had happened at the party last Sunday, and whether Olivia had given her husband any indication that she had been with Jimmy earlier that evening.

Holt had just left the forensics lab when she saw Lieutenant Diefenbacher's black lace-ups coming down the stairs. *Damn.* She walked faster, almost managing to duck into the ladies' room before he spotted her.

"There you are, Jane. I wondered where you'd disappeared to."

Jane stood there, holding the door to the ladies' room half open.

Diefenbacher strode toward her, his crew cut at a perfect ninety-degree angle. "I wanted to apologize for my bad humor lately. I've been getting a lot of heat about the unit from the chief of detectives—too much overtime, and we're looking at serious budget cuts."

"You . . . you don't have to apologize, sir."

"I know; that's part of the fun of being in command." Diefenbacher grinned, then got serious. "I still think you could be the best in the department, Jane. If I've been riding you lately it's only because I thought you were jeopardizing your career with that Eggman nonsense. I've seen other bright stars burn out over one botched investigation, and I don't want it to happen to you."

"I appreciate that," said Holt, taken aback by his candor.

"Good." Diefenbacher started to walk past her, then stopped. "What were you doing down here, anyway?"

"I was checking on the car-prowl case I ran down yesterday. I wanted to see if Forensics had blocked out any of the prints they pulled."

"Jesus H. Christ, Jane, that's exactly what I mean," sputtered Diefenbacher. "You saw the memo—Forensics is backed up a week at least. You expect these guys to drop everything for a penny-ante car prowl?"

"I'm trying to keep my out-basket ahead of my in-basket, Lieutenant, just as you requested."

"Don't be cute. I won't have one of my detectives upsetting Chakabarti's schedule. The last thing I need is another E-mail from him complaining about unreasonable demands, with a c.c. sent to the chief and another to the budget director. Jane, you're going to have to stop thinking of yourself as an independent agent and realize you're part of a team."

"Yes, sir," said Holt, trying to cut off the lecture before someone came out of Forensics. It was a bad move; her deference made his eyes narrow, suspicious now. "Did you find the report I left on your desk about the Bel-Air burglary?" she asked.

Diefenbacher was still chewing on his suspicions. "Yeah, I got the report." He straightened his necktie with the nautical-flags pattern. He didn't sail, but the chief did. "You get started on that Clothestime shoplifting assignment?"

"The store doesn't open until eleven."

Diefenbacher made a show of checking his stainless steel diving chronograph; the reddish blond hair on his thick wrists, curling around the band, made Holt queasy. "Maybe it would be a good idea for you to show up a little early, meet the manager when she arrives, let her know you're on the job."

Holt stood her ground, her posture as erect and squared as Diefenbacher's. "I'll get right on it."

Diefenbacher's expression softened, and he pushed wide the door to the ladies' room, held it open for her. "Go on about your business, Jane. First things first."

Chapter 19

"I just talked to Pilar," Jimmy said into the phone. "You're OK."

"What's wrong with your voice?" asked Rollo.

"Blaine and I were wrestling."

"Oh." Rollo processed that bit of information for a nanosecond, then got back to business. "You're sure Pilar's cool? She's not mad at me anymore?"

"She just wants her money. You should call her." Jimmy hung up and stepped out of the phone booth. He shook out six aspirins from the cracked childproof container and crunched them between his teeth, washing down their bitterness with a long, cold swallow of beer as he limped slowly toward his car, shambling like Karloff's mummy.

A young mother leaving the minimart with her son in tow gave Jimmy a wide berth, trying to shield the kid from the sight of him.

Jimmy glimpsed himself in the glass storefront: hair wild, collar crooked, a can of beer in his hand at ten in the morning . . . his reflection scared him, too. He took another drink. Don't feel sorry for yourself, Jimmy. You're living in southern California, home of Disneyland and the decorative offshore oil rig, the birthplace of McDonald's, Jell-O shots, and the leatherette auto bra. You've got a part-time job, a no-rent room, and your very own concussion. Time to buy a lottery ticket, Jimmy; this is your lucky day. He would have smiled, but he had learned his lesson.

He fumbled for his keys. A block away he could see Blaine's car parked, one wheel up on the curb—hard to be invisible in a metallic-gold Corvette convertible, but Blaine had faith. At least that was one explanation. He took another swallow of beer, feeling a little better. He didn't mind Blaine's following him—this way, at least, if he passed out, Blaine could take him home. Probably apologizing the whole way. Blaine had helped him to his car back at Pilar's, half carrying him, telling him if he pissed blood for a few days not to worry, it happened to him all the time. Something else to look forward to.

Blaine got out of the Corvette, bare-chested, and hurried toward him, carrying a tire iron.

Jimmy dropped the beer can and pulled open his car door.

Blaine stopped at an *L.A. Times* newspaper box, popped it open with the tire iron, then walked over to Jimmy with a stack of papers under his arm, his flip-flops beating against the pavement. "You dropped your beer, dude."

Jimmy picked the can up. There was still a little left.

"Pilar said I should make sure you got home safe, but you're taking your own sweet time, and I kind of want to practice some more of my ring moves. I got to be ready in case I get a call from the WWF."

Jimmy rubbed the back of his head. "I think you're ready."

Two teenagers glided out of the 7-Eleven, wearing baggy pants and baggy shirts buttoned to the neck. They warily approached Blaine, circling. "You're *him*, ain't you?" asked the skinny white kid with the buzzed hair.

"You the Robo-Surfer, right?" said the skinny black kid.

Blaine crouched in his shooting-the-curl pose, newspapers spilling from under his arm.

"Kowa-BONGA!" shouted the teenagers in unison, high-fiving each other.

Blaine beamed at Jimmy, but Jimmy was staring at the white kid and the small wine-stain birthmark behind his ear that made him look like Steve DeGerra, lying dead on the running track with a hole in his skull. Jimmy remembered holding the Polaroid in the pool house, its shiny surface catching the moonlight, and he wondered now if Jonathan had seen his own reflection in the photo, the true face that he insisted yoga had revealed to him.

"When you gonna be on TV, man?" asked the black one as the white one picked up the papers for Blaine. "You gonna be on *Slapdown*?"

"Waiting on the call," confirmed Blaine, autographing a paper for each of them. "Stay in school," he counseled as they retreated, newspapers clutched to their chests.

Jimmy's cell phone beeped as he watched Blaine lumber off. Five minutes ago it hadn't been working, the case cracked from the Kahuna body-slam, but now it was back in action. He didn't recognize the number on the phone's caller ID. "Hello?"

"Have you had lunch yet, dear boy?" The voice was a buttery coo.

"Nino?" Jimmy rubbed his neck, groaned, pain shooting down his spine.

The publisher of *SLAP* magazine chuckled at Jimmy's groan, a short, dirty laugh from a short, dirty man. "I hope I have not interrupted anything of a carnal nature."

Jimmy massaged his neck. "No such—" He gasped.

"Give her a stroke or two for me," urged Napitano. "Greet the dawn with an adamantine erection, dear boy, but never ejaculate before the workday begins. *Never.* You lose the killer instinct with the first spasm, and then what good are you?"

"I always feel like I should disinfect the phone after I talk to you, Nino." Jimmy actually liked Napitano, admiring his brains and tenacity, his willingness to burn bridges, his unrepentant carnality. After liquidating his European media holdings one step ahead of the Italian tax authorities, Napitano had moved to Los Angeles, chastened but determined to reestablish himself as a grander and more important presence than ever—"just like Aphrodite waking each morning with a new, unbroken hymen," as Nino put it.

SLAP had been launched six months later with a sumptuous party at the Hollywood Bowl, the amphitheater transformed for the evening into the Roman Coliseum, complete with Vegas-showgirl gladiators and the U.S. Olympic water polo team dressed as wild animals. High-profile guests in their complimentary cashmere togas had applauded wildly as Pavarotti stepped onstage, the big man sweating through *"E lucevan le stelle"* from *Tosca* while the Fuji blimp floated overhead flashing *"SLAP!* Love Hurts!" The society critic for the *Times* had pronounced it the "debut of the season," and for months afterward Napitano had been feted at every A-list event in L.A. He had donated lavishly to the right charities, been appointed to the mayor's Excellence Ahora! Committee, and hosted a post-Oscar party at his hilltop estate that drew more Academy Award–winners than the *Vanity Fair* bash at Morton's.

Napitano had been infatuated with L.A., but as in all of his love affairs, he'd grown bored quickly, directing the staff at *SLAP* to target the very people he had so recently cultivated. Celebrities used to fawning coverage of their most vapid pronouncements about the homeless found truckloads of panhandlers dropped off in front of their Malibu mansions. Television rent-an-experts had their college transcripts published. Politicians demagoguing institutional sexism were photographed leaving strip clubs, faces half covered, caught in the paparazzi strobe. *SLAP*'s advertising dwindled, and there were no more party invitations, but Napitano seemed to thrive on the hostility, blooming like a lily on a sludge pond.

"What can I do for you, Nino?"

"I'm offering you a fine lunch. Vitamins and minerals, trace elements to replenish that which you have splashed so carelessly—"

"You fired me. Did you forget?"

"You wanted a leave of absence," sniffed Napitano. "What did you expect me to do?"

"I had a book contract."

"Ah, yes . . . but alas, no book was forthcoming." Napitano made slurping sounds. A little man with a gargantuan appetite, he had a dozen raw oysters and four ounces of black beluga caviar every morning and afternoon. "Eat with me, Jimmy." More slurping, and Jimmy imagined the bivalves sliding down his gullet. "I saw your piece in the *Times* this morning, that monstrosity."

"Is that what this call is about? You're pissed that I'm working for someone else?"

"The *Times* butchered your work," said Napitano. "Simplistic photography, inept layout . . . and *below* the fold?" He clucked his disapproval. "Have breakfast with me, and we'll discuss your future."

Jimmy watched the two teenagers saunter off with their autographed newspapers. The white kid, the one with the birthmark, turned around, feeling Jimmy's eyes on him, and flipped him the finger. "Not today," he told Napitano.

"Tomorrow, then, and bring your appetite, dear boy."

Chapter 20

"May I call you *Jane,* Detective?" Jonathan smiled. "Since this is after hours, I hoped we could dispense with the formalities."

"What was so important that you had to speak with me now, Doctor?"

"Please, call me Jonathan," he said softly, his lips barely moving, his velvety tone that of a man who never needed to raise his voice. "I know we got off to a bad start at the pool house. . . ." His pale skin flushed, and Holt saw none of the arrogance that had been so evident Monday morning. "I do apologize for any embarrassment I may have caused you."

"I wasn't embarrassed."

They were seated on the veranda of l'Hermitage, a fine French restaurant located in a historic beach cottage in Newport. Jonathan's regular table had a spectacular view of the sunset and the harbor, while being protected from direct sun. The doctor was casually dressed in a pale-blue suit with a vanilla-cream silk polo shirt, the sea breeze rippling his soft hair. There was a boyish elegance to him that was lost on Holt, but he was doing just fine with the table of yacht-club wives at the other end of the veranda, three blondes sneaking glances, whispering among themselves, fiddling with their jewelry.

"I'm glad to hear that. Sometimes James's idea of a joke is remarkably tasteless. Not that I'm any better: I've played some tricks on him in the past that were equally unfair." Jonathan reached out, clinked his glass to her untouched one, and sipped his martini, a small jalapeño pepper where the olive should be. "Are you sure you wouldn't like a cocktail? Fernando makes an excellent Cajun martini."

"I don't drink." Holt took a small swallow of her tonic water.

"Laudable self-control, but I believe the stress-reduction aspects of alcohol more than make up for its slightly drying effect upon the skin." Jonathan smiled again. "Listen to me lecturing you. It *is* hard to leave the office, *n'est-ce pas?* People like us, we take our jobs with us wherever we go." He pushed back his tousled light-brown hair. "I do appreciate your returning my call. When I tried you at the department, the woman at the switchboard said you were unavailable for the next two weeks. I didn't know—"

"My lieutenant insisted that I take some vacation days, otherwise he said I was going to rupture his overtime budget." Holt swirled the ice in her drink. One look at Lieutenant Diefenbacher's face when he summoned her into his office, and she had known what was coming. He said it was bad enough that she'd disregarded his orders by taking yet another one of her "damn Polaroids" to Forensics, but her *lying* to him about it, that was intolerable. He said he was placing her on paid leave pending an investigation to determine whether she would be suspended. He didn't look angry when he told her; he looked disappointed. She knew the feeling. To make things utterly perfect, Maria Sinoa had been too busy to find out if there was a match between Jonathan's fellatio Polaroid and the one the Eggman had left on the beach. Now Sinoa was being watched so closely it would probably be a few days before she was able to slip past her boss. Damn, damn, and double-damn. Holt sipped her tonic water and wished it were gin. "You said you had something important to discuss with me?"

"Yes . . . all right, I see that the social amenities are over." Jonathan traced the rim of his glass with a fingertip, turning serious now. "I'm concerned about James. I know you have more than just a professional interest in each other—"

"I think you're overstating the situation, Doctor."

Jonathan looked as if he were about to correct her form of address, but then he stopped himself. "Perhaps I misunderstood. I saw you slap his face in the pool house and assumed there was a certain . . . emotional involvement."

"What you saw was my overreaction to not finding the Polaroids Jimmy had described to me," said Holt. The wind danced across the white sand beach, sending clouds of grit flying around them. "I apologized to him and informed him of his right to file a formal complaint with the department."

"Oh, James would never do that. *Never.*" Jonathan savored his martini. "Even as a child, Jimmy never tattled. I personally think there's a time and a place for telling the truth, but he was always adamant about keeping silent no matter what the personal consequences. No, I don't think you have anything to fear from James."

"I never said I was afraid."

"No, of course. . . . But now I've offended you." Jonathan shook his head, crestfallen.

"Are *you* scared of Jimmy, Doctor?" said Holt, interested now.

"You're very astute, or else I'm very transparent." Jonathan's eyes were such a light, watery blue that it was if the color had been diluted to the absolute minimum. "In answer to your question, yes."

Holt hid her surprise. "Has Jimmy ever threatened you?"

Jonathan hesitated.

"If you think Jimmy might physically harm you, then you should contact your *local* police. Not me."

"It's not that simple." Jonathan bristled. "I told you James had an aversion to betraying a confidence, yet he brought you to the pool house, he exposed my most private possession to scrutiny—"

"He didn't do it willingly. I was quite insistent."

"James doesn't do anything he doesn't want to. The two of you pawing through my things, that whole wild story about my having other photographs . . ." Jonathan looked away, out toward the sunset that was turning the sailboats to flame, the color in his cheeks matching their heat. He turned back to her. "James and I have a history of playing pranks on each other; I thought afterward that the incident in the pool house was simply a particularly bad joke, his way of letting me know that the usual boundaries were no longer in effect."

"I don't think Jimmy was joking."

"Neither do I." Jonathan moistened his lips. "Have you read Freud? According to the good doctor, humor is merely violence in disguise. I'd be the first to admit that I'm as guilty as James in that regard."

The waiter appeared with a fresh round of drinks, indicating the table of yacht-club wives at the end of the veranda. The blondes raised their glasses in salute, and Jonathan waved back. He had lovely hands.

"It seems you have a fan club, Doctor."

"Merely aficionados of my work." Jonathan turned away from the blondes. "I expected James to be bitter about my marriage, that's understandable. But I hoped that after the shock wore off he would come to accept the fact that Olivia and I are married. I'm not so sure now." He leaned toward her. "This morning James confronted me on the beach, making wild accusations, shouting at me, just talking crazy."

"Short of getting a restraining order, I'm really not sure what to suggest."

"I feel like his behavior is escalating. Sunday he made a scene at my office party, and then this morning he rails at me on the beach." Jonathan cleared his throat. "One of the clubhouse stewards says James was there last week, sitting at a window table in the lounge, just watching Olivia on the practice tee." He grimaced. "James isn't even a member."

Holt laughed. It was the kind of remark her father might have made—she remembered his reaction the time their cabin in the Berkshires was burglarized, her father annoyed at the thief as much for failing to wipe his shoes as for stealing the hundred-year-old quilts off the beds.

Jonathan's mouth tightened. "I don't know how well you know James—" He stopped, then forced himself to continue. "When we were growing up, there were some . . . problems. I wasn't privy to the details, we were both too young, but I do know we moved at least once to get away from trouble in the neighborhood. I remember my parents arguing . . . my mother crying."

Holt watched him, knowing that he wasn't finished yet.

"There was one incident when he was in high school, a violent confrontation with some fellow students. I heard that a young woman James was interested in had started dating a football player. The player ended up in the hospital, and James was expelled for the remainder of his senior year."

"I've read through your brother's file, Doctor. I wasn't aware of any incident like that."

"My father spent a great deal of money getting the original police report suppressed. Our attorney exerted pressure on the injured boy's family and the high school administration to get them to cooperate. That does happen with juvenile records, doesn't it?"

"Sometimes."

"James was supposed to get counseling, but I don't think he ever did. My father never had any respect for psychiatrists." Jonathan lowered his eyes. "I tried to talk to James about it, but I didn't try very hard." He looked up at Holt. "I feel like the whole family let James down, but myself most of all. He's my brother, and I . . . I let him slip away."

Holt looked out across the water, pretending to be only marginally interested in Jonathan's story, watching a forty-foot party boat rumble out to catch the last of the sunset, loud music echoing across the waves. She had checked Jimmy's background carefully; she knew all about his arrests for car theft and trespassing, but there was no record of any violent incident in high school. No record of any violence at all.

"James seems convinced that I had tricked him Monday morning at the pool house, and that's what scares me. He has always been a poor loser; if he thinks I made a fool of him, and in front of you, no less . . . well, you can understand my concern."

Holt didn't answer.

"I'd like you to talk with him . . . as a friend," said Jonathan. "Let him know I mean him no harm. Perhaps he'll listen to you."

"I really doubt that Jimmy will—" But then she cried out.

"What is it?"

She clutched at her right eye. It felt like someone had stuck an icepick through her cornea.

Jonathan pulled her hand away from her eye. "You're making it worse," he said firmly. "I'll take care of it." He dipped the end of his cloth napkin in his water glass and moved his chair closer "Easy, *easy* now," he said, his voice cottony as he gently tilted her head back. She blinked furiously, fighting back panic, tears flooding down her cheek. He stroked the skin under her eye, and she felt herself relax involuntarily, then he separated her eyelids with one hand and gently swept the moist edge of the napkin across her eye, sliding the grit toward the inside edge. "Almost got it, Jane. Hang on. Almost . . . *there*." He showed her the grain of sand caught on the napkin. "It probably felt like a boulder," he said, still holding her face in his hands. "Close your eyes for a second, we'll make sure I got it all. Go on, I won't hurt you."

Holt closed her eyes and felt his fingertips moving lightly across the lid. She had never been kissed that delicately.

"You can open them now, Jane."

Holt blinked her eyes open.

Jonathan looked concerned. "Better?"

Holt nodded, still blinking. "Thank you . . . Doctor." They were awkward again, even more awkward than before. "Where were we?"

"You were thinking that I was overreacting to James's violation of my privacy, to his stalking my wife—that's where we were."

"I don't blame you for being upset, but yes, I do think you're overreacting."

"James always gets the benefit of the doubt." Jonathan sighed. "That must be marvelous, to have people instinctively trust you and like you. I don't even think he's aware of it." He fiddled with his drink. "Do you have any siblings?"

"No."

"Then you have no idea what it's like between James and me." Jonathan plucked the jalapeño out of his martini and gobbled it down with barely restrained ferocity. "Between brothers it's never a democracy, never share and share alike. Family is Darwinism in its rawest form. I don't know who started it, but James and I have been at each other's throat since the day he was born. I may be the elder brother, but for most of that time *I've* been the one playing catch-up."

"I find that difficult to believe, Jonathan."

"Do you?" Jonathan glared at her. "Of course you do. The board-certified surgeon honored by his peers, and the fly-by-night writer scrambling to make his rent money—is that how you see it?"

"I just don't see you allowing yourself to fall behind anyone."

"Don't be fooled by the trappings of success—you need to look closer." Jonathan reached for her. "May I?" He barely waited for Holt's acquiescence before lightly stroking the tiny fat pads under her eyes. "The skin here is thinner here than almost anywhere else on the body; that's why fatigue manifests itself under the eyes first, makes a home for itself in our dark circles." His fingers caressed her forehead, and to her shock, she allowed it. "Worry lines, they call these. You have fine, patrician features, classic bone structure, but on a woman in your line of work, living on stress and suspicion, the lines etch themselves in deeper every day."

"I wasn't expecting a medical evaluation," said Holt, pulling away, annoyed at herself for letting his words bother her.

"You're missing my point," said Jonathan. "Keats equated beauty with truth, but he was wrong. Beauty is *surface*, Jane; it's anything but truth. Beauty is a nest of wrinkles lasered out, a breast augmented with a saline sac, a thigh sucked and smoothed. Beauty is skin-deep, and that's quite deep enough for most people, but not for you. Don't be fooled by my house and car, the plaques on my office walls. It's all for show. If I tell you I've felt defeated by James my whole life, believe it. If I tell you I'm concerned that he's going to do something, believe that, too."

Holt watched him.

"Jane . . . I have a confession." Jonathan shifted in his chair, seemed to shrink, his pale-blue eyes brimming over. He turned his chair so that his back was to the rest of the patrons, from which position he stared back at Holt. "I'm not as noble as I pretend. My fear of James . . . it's not just physical. If I'm very, *very* honest with myself, I'm also worried that Olivia may change her mind about our marriage." His smile was sad. "Who could blame her?"

"Are you and she having problems?"

"Not until James came back. But I . . . I didn't mean that the way it sounded."

Holt put a hand on his arm. She usually avoided physical contact in professional settings, but the way he had touched her face, the sensitivity of it . . .

Jonathan straightened up. "I apologize for my behavior. Please forgive me. I was wrong to drag you into it. This is between James and myself." He tried to laugh, but it was a failure. "Perhaps I'm the one who needs therapy."

Chapter 21

"I thought I'd find you here." Jimmy sat down beside Desmond in the shaggy grass of center field, the two of them alone in the night.

"It's been one of those kinds of days," said Desmond, his elbows resting on his knees, staring at home plate. It was overcast, the stars hidden, the dugouts in shadow.

"Market take a dive?"

"No, that's not it."

Jimmy understood now. "You want me to leave?"

Desmond shook his head. "I wish you could have seen Samuel suited up," he said. "He wasn't a power hitter, but he was consistent, batted over three-fifty year in and year out, and *fast.*" He shook his head again. "Stole twenty-seven bases his first year on varsity, stole home three times. *Three times.* Still a record at Fountain Valley High. I used to watch him try to stand still, coiling and uncoiling like he just couldn't wait to let it rip." He smiled as the breeze rippled through his short, iron-gray hair. "God, he was beautiful."

Jimmy nodded.

"He should have come to me for help with that dope dealer." Desmond tugged at a blade of grass. "I was his father. He should have come to me. Not you."

"He didn't come to me for help; we just had coffee together a couple of times. Samuel was determined to handle the situation in his own way."

"Yes, that was Samuel, all right."

"I got a call from my old publisher today. I think he's going to offer me my job back at the magazine."

Desmond wasn't listening. He ran his hands through the lush green grass, feeling the softness of the earth, the ripe, clean smell floating around the two of them like the memory of a perfect summer.

The Samuel Terrell Memorial Baseball Field was open to boys and girls of all ages, with league and pickup games scheduled out into infinity. No charge. The property had been bought by Desmond a few weeks after the funeral, almost three acres near a middle-income neighborhood, the field sodded and landscaped, bleachers built by an endowment he had set up. The kids who used the field kept it mowed, working with their parents and coaches. The land alone had cost more than two million dollars, but Desmond had bought Amazon at the IPO, loaded up on eBay at less than four bucks a share, split-adjusted, and dumped it all before the big tech crash. He still bought marked-down chicken at the supermarket and kept his coupons neatly organized.

Desmond did a slow scan of the field. "They do a nice job of maintaining the place, don't they? Graffiti painted over, baselines straight, pitcher's mound strictly regulation."

"I should move out, Desmond. It's not fair—"

"There's no hurry, I told you that when you moved in. Besides, I need the rent money."

"I don't pay rent."

"That's right, I forgot." Desmond plucked a blade of grass, chewed it thoughtfully. "You wouldn't want to leave an old man with memory lapses all alone, would you? I might forget to turn off the oven or lock myself in the bathroom." He was focused on home plate again. "Did you ever find out why Detective Holt took your brother's Polaroid?"

"Not yet."

"I was just curious as to why you're suddenly so eager to pack your bags again," said Desmond. "I thought she might be closing in on that business you pulled with Lee Macklen. Her jurisdiction might be questionable, but a good cop can always—"

"I thought we weren't going to discuss that anymore."

"I think about it sometimes, that's all." Desmond inhaled, drinking in the sweetness of the grass, eyes half closed in the darkness, probably seeing Samuel rounding the bases, arms pumping, racing for home. "First thing you learn as a police officer is not to be surprised, because people are capable of anything. Yet I look at you sometimes, all loose and easy, and I think about what you did . . . and I still can't hardly believe it."

"You don't know what I did, Desmond."

"That's true. You've never admitted anything, and I appreciate that. If I knew for certain, retired or not, I'd have to arrest you."

"Sure you would."

Desmond sat up, knees popping. "You want to rake the infield with me? The last team left it fine, but I enjoy the work." Jimmy followed him over to the field-equipment locker and watched him twirl the combination with practiced ease. "There's an early game tomorrow. Girls' Little League, Cheetahs and Tigers."

Jimmy glanced around while Desmond busied himself, but they were alone on the field. He was looking over his shoulder even more than usual these days.

Desmond checked out the open locker, noted with satisfaction the neatly organized rakes and shovels and lime spreaders, plumb lines and umpires' masks. He handed Jimmy a bamboo rake and kept one for himself, then the two of them walked onto the infield. "Did you ever think of going into police work?"

Jimmy just laughed.

"You have a knack for it," said Desmond. "I was retired when we buried Samuel, but I called in every street IOU I had, even canvassed the neighborhood myself, and still couldn't get a whisper on this dope dealer. The detective assigned to the case didn't do any better." He brushed off home plate with the palm of his hand. "Even after I managed to locate Angela in Florida, living with a cousin, and I flew back there to talk with her, it didn't help. I still send her a check every month, and she sends me photos of my granddaughter whenever she feels like it, but she won't tell me anything. Never saw anyone so scared in my life."

Jimmy followed Desmond's lead, moving in concentric arcs out from home plate, the two of them working close to each other. Their rakes scraped lightly across the reddish dirt, smoothing out the tiny bumps and hollows, the tines floating over the surface, leaving long, even lines on the field.

"I couldn't find the dealer who murdered my boy, but *you* did," said Desmond. "What was it, a year after the funeral that you called me up with a name? Lee Macklen."

Jimmy leaned into the rake. "It was just dumb luck, I told you that."

"I don't believe in luck," said Desmond. "I was shot three times—was I unlucky because I got shot, or lucky because I survived? Your running into Macklen after all that time, recognizing him, that wasn't luck."

"Not for him, anyway."

Desmond picked up a gum wrapper off the ground, slipped it into his pocket. "I ran Macklen's sheet after you gave me his name, and he looked right for Samuel's murder. Arrested twice for distribution of heroin some years earlier, but no convictions. Witnesses seemed to disappear right before trial, just vanish off the face of the earth. But in those days he was just another struggling businessman with a liquor license and bills to pay." He laid a hand on Jimmy's shoulder. "You're raking too hard," he chided, demonstrating the proper technique. "Always in a rush. Just like with Macklen: I would have found something to hang on him eventually. You wait long enough, *everybody* makes a mistake."

"He made his mistake when he murdered Samuel."

"That he did, and he made another mistake the night he opened his door to those three gangsters. Chickens coming home to roost, that's what I remember thinking when I saw his picture in the paper that morning, reading about the botched robbery at the Rhinestone Cowboy the night before—a massacre, they called it. The three punks who tried to steal the night's receipts were DOA when the police arrived, and poor Macklen with four nine-millimeter rounds in his guts. Interesting timing, though, you have to admit: one day I tell you there's no way to arrest the man, and a few weeks later he's in the intensive care unit and can't feel his legs."

"He's out of the wheelchair now."

"You think you're the only one who keeps track? He's out of the wheelchair, but he's still not right."

The gangsters had been a trio of Vietnamese psychos who called themselves the VC Boyz, a regular rolling felony crew, suspects in a couple of dozen violent robberies and at least four homicides. Great White had killed them all with his bare hands, breaking their bones, crushing their skulls. A week after the attack, the mayor had presented Macklen with a California Citizen Hero plaque in the hospital, Great White standing beside the bed, arms crossed, skull gleaming in the light of the video cameras.

"Jimmy? You listening to me? I *said*, the VC Boyz were home-invasion specialists, preying on their own community. So what were they doing taking down a honky-tonk?"

"It's over and done with, Desmond."

"A buddy of mine on the Garden Grove P.D. said he heard afterward that the VC Boyz fenced their goods to Macklen, so maybe they were arguing over prices and percentages." Desmond waited for Jimmy to lie to him, but Jimmy didn't say a thing. "You ever hear of a restaurant in Little Saigon called the Nha Trang Café?"

Jimmy kept raking.

"Nice little place—good food, good people," said Desmond. "My buddy told me the VC Boyz used to hang out there, almost ruined it before they got themselves killed. I went there about a month after the shoot-out and passed around your photograph—just curious, you understand. . . ."

Jimmy waited.

Desmond leaned on his rake. "Nobody there had ever seen you before. They hardly looked at your picture, just turned away, shaking their heads. Lost all their English, too."

Tran crossed himself as he laid down the bowl of crab and asparagus soup, ducking his head slightly, and Jimmy thought at first he was just being a good Catholic. "Don't look, Jimmy," Tran hissed.

So of course Jimmy turned toward the door of the Nha Trang Café, saw three young Asian dudes saunter in, black-leather boys swinging their shoulders like Mildred Pierce, faces lean as razor blades, long hair oiled back, shaved along the sides. The other customers in the café all took a sudden interest in their plates, conversation stopping like somebody had pulled the plug.

Jimmy had cultivated Macklen after making him as Samuel's killer, dropping by the club regularly, drinking beer with him. He had seen these same three leather boys walk out of Macklen's office at the Rhinestone Cowboy the week before, and had thought at the time that they didn't look like country-music lovers. But then, neither was he.

The smallest of the VC Boyz saw Jimmy, the only round-eye in the Nha Trang, looking at him. He walked toward Jimmy's booth, his high-heeled boots tapping time.

Tran held both hands up as the dude approached, begging in Vietnamese.

The dude smacked him aside with the back of his hand, eyes locked on Jimmy. Jimmy started to get up, but the dude was quicker, snatching the pair of unused chopsticks off the table and shoving them up Jimmy's nose, one in each nostril, up, up, up. Jimmy gasped in pain, tears rolling down his cheeks; he tried to fight, but the dude just shoved the sticks higher, forcing him to half stand. He could see a pistol tucked into the waistband of the dude's black trousers.

"You want fuck me, Joe?" the dude said lightly. He smelled of airplane glue and Brut.

"No," Jimmy said, trying not to move, feeling the tips of the chopsticks press even farther against his sinus cavity. Blood trickled from his nostrils.

"You don't want fuck me, Joe, why you look at me?"

Jimmy didn't answer. Talking made his face move.

"Claude! Leave that ghost alone. Food's getting cold."

Claude slowly, slowly, ever so slowly withdrew the chopsticks from

Jimmy's nose, used them to pluck a morsel of crabmeat from the soup bowl, and popped it into Jimmy's open mouth. He walked back through the utter silence to the table where his mates were already being served.

Jimmy stood there, blood dripping steadily onto the Formica tabletop, until Tran bustled over and handed him a wad of paper napkins. Jimmy spit the crab out, holding the napkins against his nose. He sat down but didn't look at the tableful of VC Boyz. "Who . . . who are those guys?"

"You don't want to know," whispered Tran, swiping at the table with a damp rag, smearing it.

"Yes, I do."

"They're bad, Jimmy."

"No shit."

"VC Boyz are crazy fuckers. They break into houses, take what they want, and burn the rest. They'll kill you for nothing."

Now Jimmy knew what the VC Boyz had been doing in Macklen's office. They'd been there either to buy dope or to move what they'd stolen the night before. Jimmy smiled, forced himself not to look at Claude. Desmond had said the law couldn't touch Macklen, but those VC Boyz, they were crazy fuckers.

The rake shot out from Desmond's hands, and he lightly drew it back, repeating the process over and over. "There's not a cop alive who hasn't been tempted to take out the trash," he said, keeping up the same steady pace, "but once you start down that road, where do you stop? The law is slow and erratic, but without the law we'd have mob justice, and that leads to some folks swinging from tree limbs while other folks cheer and clap themselves on the back." He looked at Jimmy, his eyes shiny in the twilight. "At least that's what I always believed, Jimmy. Now I don't know anymore."

"If it makes you feel any better, what happened in Macklen's office . . . it wasn't supposed to turn out that way."

"Samuel wasn't supposed to die the way he did, either. He was my child, my *only* child, and there was nothing I could do for him, not while he was alive, not when he was dead. But you—"

"Whatever I did, it wasn't for Samuel. I thought it was, but . . ." Jimmy shook his head. "There's so much shit in the world that the only way to stay sane is to go on about your business and let somebody else handle it—the cops, the courts, God himself when all else fails—but sometimes, Desmond, sometimes . . ." He shook his head again.

"I hope you get away with it."

Jimmy bent down and ran his fingers through the grass, still feeling the warmth of the day, the last of it. "Nobody gets away with anything."

"Yeah, the wheel just keeps on turning, and you're right at the center of it, with no place to hide. That's why you ran away to Europe, isn't it?"

"I'm not complaining." Jimmy stood up. "I never thanked you for getting me out of trouble in Italy, Desmond. I don't know how you found out—"

"What are you talking about?"

"Rome—I don't know what it cost you, but I'm grateful."

"I don't know anything about Rome except what I saw in that *Gladiator* movie you took me to. Doesn't seem like my kind of town."

Jimmy nodded. "Whatever."

Desmond laid his hand on Jimmy's shoulder. "If Samuel was the way you described him at the end, he wouldn't have been happy with what you did to Macklen. Turn the other cheek, that's what the Good Book says."

"I'm behind in my reading."

Desmond smiled, and Jimmy saw Samuel's face, older and wiser, but Samuel's face nonetheless. "I guess I am, too," Desmond replied.

Chapter 22

Vorcek glanced at his watch, a Rolex studded with gold nuggets. "I have not much time," he said in heavily accented English.

"For a man in a hurry, you took your own sweet time telling me about the memory chips," barked Macklen.

"It is I who am doing you the favor," glowered Vorcek, a beefy, white-haired Chechen with a face the color of blood pudding, the tattoos so thick on his hands that it looked as if he were wearing black lace gloves. He snapped his fingers. "First you pay me five thousand dollar."

"You were supposed to call me as soon as you got offered the chips," said Macklen, pounding the ground with one of his canes. "That's the word I've been putting out for the last year. You get offered Dyak one-twenty-eight RAM chips, you call me pronto. You understand 'pronto,' you fucking Commie drunk?"

"Guys, I don't think we need to get personal," said Great White.

"You think I have nothing better to do than call you?" Vorcek sneered at Macklen. "I do you favor taking your money. You say my information is too late? Fine, I get in my car, drive away now. You can stay here in fresh air and wave good-bye."

The three of them stood in the middle of the stink of an oil field in Huntington Beach, one of the last working fields in Orange County, eighteen acres' worth of small grasshopper derricks creaking away day and night, pumping up low-sulfur crude. Vorcek's black Lincoln Town Car was parked on the narrow access road that wound through the site, with Stanislav, his bodyguard, leaning against the grillework, cleaning his fingernails with the end of a wooden match. Macklen's full-size Dodge Ram truck, special-ordered with all the controls on the steering wheel, was backed up against one of the greasy derricks. The flat landscape was speckled with pools of oil and rusted fifty-gallon drums, and in spite of the gates and barbed wire, there were graffiti and empty beer cans everywhere.

Macklen glared at Vorcek, swaying on his canes, the tips crushing the stunted dandelions that grew wild everywhere. His legs were weak, almost useless, but he still wore ostrich-skin or anteater cowboy boots every day, the boots clipped to his denim jeans, the toes dragging the weeds now as he rocked back and forth.

"Make decision," said Vorcek. "Stanislav and I have woman to see. Blond woman, big ass like Victoria Secret. We give her your money, she suck us until we say 'Stop, no more.' " He turned around to his bodyguard.

"Victoria *Secret*," Stanislav repeated, beaming, a big, rawboned bruiser with yellow teeth and a cheap brown suit identical to the one his boss wore.

"Pay him," said Macklen.

Great White stepped forward.

"Pay *him*," snarled Vorcek. "I do not touch your stinking dollars."

Great White walked over to the Lincoln Town Car, handed Stanislav an envelope full of hundreds, and waited while the bodyguard slowly counted it out, lips moving, the wooden match doing a do-si-do from one side of his mouth to the other.

"Was *boy* who sold me the chips," Vorcek said to Macklen. "Clever boy, always talking about movies, all the time movies, like I give a good goddamn. Rollo is his name. You know him, yes?"

"I know him," said Macklen. "Who was he fronting them for? The chips couldn't have been his; no way that jitterbug could sit on something that valuable for a year without selling it."

"The chips are not so valuable now," said Vorcek. "A year ago yes, much money, but today they are outdated, hardly worth my trouble. Rollo, like a fool, takes my first offer, says the man who owns the chips is desperate, so it is *double* my luck, Macklen. First I fuck him, then I fuck you." He turned to the bodyguard and laughed. "Then I fuck Victoria Secret."

"That's three times the luck," Great White corrected him.

Vorcek scratched his full belly, slid his hand down his pants, and shifted his hefty balls from one side to the other, watching Great White. He had been a full colonel during the civil war against the Russians, had led the house-by-house retreat from Grozny and personally killed forty-three enemy soldiers. Some of them he'd shot, some of them he'd blown up with grenades, and some he'd tortured to death for information that he was not even interested in, making them hold hot coals from the cookstove, smelling the ripe stink of them as their bowels emptied. Losing the war had been terrible, but killing Russians—there was nothing sweeter. California was a new world, an amazingly different world, but there were pleasures here, too.

Macklen's canes sank slightly into the sandy ground in front of Vorcek, and Macklen shifted, making sure he was locked in position. The canes were high-tech wonders, titanium alloy, shaped like upside-down Ls, but he had improved them, adding twelve pounds of lead to each of the hand grips. He had practiced with the canes two hours a day for the last year with a Japanese stick-fighting master. A month ago he had shattered the man's collarbone and stoved in three of his ribs. Macklen figured it was time he graduated anyway.

"Do you know where Rollo is now?" Macklen demanded. "You ever think of getting a phone number for Rollo, someplace where he can be reached?"

"I am not secretary calling on the phone," snorted Vorcek. "People come to *me* with deals, I do not come to *them.*"

"You should have asked him for his number," said Macklen.

"You should have asked who the chips belonged to. This is the U.S. of A., we *earn* our money here."

"Come work for me," Vorcek said to Great White. "I give you twice what this pitiful creature pays you."

"Gosharootie, think of all the paints and colored pencils I could buy," said Great White. "I'm getting tempted here, Mack."

"Ask Stanislav how he likes to work for me," persisted Vorcek. "We have fuck, we have fun—"

"Rollo ain't worth five thousand dollars," said Macklen, fuming. "Not if I can't find him to ask him who he got the chips from."

"Why you work for this man wears a diaper?" Vorcek said to Great White. "He does not need you, he needs nurse to powder his ass."

Stanislav laughed behind him.

"Give me back the reward money," Macklen said to Vorcek. "You want to get paid, you find Rollo and bring him—"

Vorcek spit at Macklen's splayed feet, hitting one of his boots. "Check watch, you crippled turd. Your time is over. You no longer inspire fear, or respect, or—"

Macklen flipped his right cane, caught it near the tip, then whipped it high and brought it down with full force onto Vorcek's head, staggering him. Macklen braced himself on the other cane, swung again with the right one, caught Vorcek in the temple, and sent him sprawling. The cane crashed down onto the Chechen's head again as he started to rise, driving him face-first into the dirt, blood pouring from his ears. "My time is over?" Macklen hopped closer. "You *sure* about that?"

Stanislav had his nine-millimeter Glock drawn and aimed at Macklen when Great White stepped into his line of fire. The bodyguard didn't hesitate, firing as he advanced, hitting Great White in the upper chest once, twice, three, four times, the impact rocking the big man back on his feet.

Stanislav's eyes widened as Great White reached out and grabbed his gun hand, slowly bending the gun back.

Great White smiled as the bodyguard struggled against him, their faces inches apart, the two of them almost dancing, the surprise on Stanislav's face giving way to fear. Like all strong men, Stanislav was used to being dominant in any physical confrontation. Great White could smell the onions on the hamburger the man had had for dinner as he bent Stanislav's hand back until his pistol was pointing at his own face. Great White watched the bodyguard's eyes as he forced him to pull the trigger, searching for something, waiting to see what would rise to the surface.

Stanislav tried to duck, and the first shot grazed his cheek, tearing a bright-red furrow along the bone. The second shot caught him full in the mouth and blew out some of those yellow teeth. The third one hit him squarely in the forehead. Stanislav went limp, but Great White tightened his grip, emptying the rest of the clip into the man's face. Then Great White tossed him aside. He had never even touched the gun himself.

It was a small thing, but Great White took pride in such details, the same way he took pride in the ceramic-composite body armor he wore his every waking moment. The armor was available only to federal law agencies—the vest would stop a high-velo military round, but it hadn't stopped Great White from taking it from the DEA agent it had belonged to, after he snapped his neck like a stalk of crisp celery.

The moist, crunching sound Great White heard coming from behind him now—there was really nothing else like it. He turned and saw Macklen finishing up, balanced on one cane, the other one covered in brain matter. The titanium was actually dented. Vorcek lay on the ground, his head looking like a Halloween pumpkin that had been thrown off a ten-story building. "Whew," said Macklen, giving Vorcek one last whack, a little out of breath but happy.

Great White nudged Vorcek's shoe. "This could be trouble, Mack."

"Cost of doing business," said Macklen. A patch of white hair had ended up stuck to his cheek. "Load them both into the trunk of the Lincoln. We'll drop it off at the chop shop in Santa Ana, let the beaners take care of the bodies in exchange for the wagon." He jabbed Vorcek's shattered Rolex with a cane, gave the man's ruined noggin a final whack. "What time is it now, asshole?"

Jimmy checked his watch. It had taken him thirty-one minutes to drive from Perfection Enhancement in Newport to his parents' old house in Anaheim. He had kept it just above the speed limit, not fast enough to risk a ticket. Traffic on the freeway was light at this point in the evening, but it would have been equally so around the time Michelle said Jonathan had left the party. Thirty-one minutes. Plenty of time to drive to the pool house and get back before too many people missed him.

Jimmy tried to imagine Jonathan's face when he saw his precious Polaroids strewn around the room. He wished he had been there to see it. Jonathan's first impulse would have been to scoop them up, every one of them, but his brain would have been in high gear—that ice-cold yoga calm—so he would have stopped himself and considered the possibilities. Jonathan would have known that Jimmy had been disgusted by the Eggman photos, but he also would have known that sooner or later he would come back for them. What did Jonathan say on the beach? "No one presents the challenge you do, James." Leaving just the blow-job Polaroids had been a way of sending a message to Jimmy, issuing a direct challenge. Jimmy headed home, singing to himself as he drove.

"You're pretty chipper," said Great White, wedging Vorcek in beside the spare tire. He pushed down Stanislav's legs and slammed the trunk of the Lincoln Town Car.

"I always told you this day would come. I never gave up hope." Macklen spun on his crutches, doing an awkward pirouette to the squeaking accompaniment of the oil rigs. "First we're going to find

Rollo—I don't care what it takes, we're going to find him. That boy's going to tell us who fronted him my chips; he's going to fall all over himself giving up the name of the man who stole my legs." Silhouetted against the bobbing oil rigs, Macklen capered across the filthy ground, head thrown back, canes whirling, the foulness of his imagination boiling inside him.

Chapter 23

Olivia drove golf balls from the practice tee, slamming them out past the 230-yard marker, a regular athletic machine, hitting straight and true. There were plenty of other golfers working on their games, flailing away, the best of them looking clumsy and awkward compared to her; they seemed to know it, too, and gave her plenty of room.

The large bucket of balls beside Olivia was half empty now, but she continued her steady pace. She had kept to the same routine for as long as Jimmy had known her: a bucket for woods, another bucket for irons, a frustrating hour on the putting green, then a round of eighteen. Her dark hair gleamed in the morning light. She wore a cream-colored cashmere sweater against the damp, full-cut khakis with the cuffs rolled, and spiked saddle shoes—stylish and practical, not even aware of how perfect she was.

"Olivia?"

Olivia glanced over at him, teed up another ball, set her feet. The ball sailed straight down the fairway and kept rolling, and she followed it all the way.

"We need to talk."

Olivia bent for another ball, and he could see a sheen of sweat on her upper lip. Her next drive didn't go quite so far or quite so straight. She turned to him finally. "I almost made a big mistake with you Sunday night. I'd like to blame it on the pot—you know how horny I get when I'm loaded—but that's no excuse."

"The only mistake you made on Sunday night was walking out the door." Jimmy tried to take her hand, but she shook him off.

"I thought I knew you, but that . . . stunt you pulled Monday morning, bringing in the police—I gave you more credit than that."

"What did Jonathan tell you?"

"Everything."

"That'll be the day. I gave *you* more credit than that."

"Jane Holt questioned me yesterday." Olivia's dark eyes flashed. "She looks tired—have you been keeping her up past her bedtime?" She shoved the driver into her golf bag and pulled out a four-wood. "You told her we were at the Tiki Room together."

"I didn't tell her. She figured it out by herself."

" 'I apologize for having to ask you this, Mrs. Gage,' " Olivia said, mimicking Holt's Yankee nasality, " 'but at the office party, did you mention to your husband that you had just come from an . . . assignation at the pool house with Jimmy?' An *'assignation'?* Who talks like that?"

"I didn't know she was going to question you—"

"Jonathan knew." Olivia brushed her hair back. "He told me that your favorite detective would be coming by to make some ugly innuendos, and that's just what she did." She stepped closer now, but Jimmy held his ground. "I know all about the Polaroids, if that's what you're here to tell me about. Jonathan already showed them to me. He's got nothing to hide now."

"He showed you the Eggman photos?"

"Don't be cute. You know the ones I'm talking about."

"Oh."

"Yes, *oh.*"

"You're mad at me because Jonathan keeps a stash of his favorite blow jobs?"

"Your discovering the Polaroids Sunday night was very convenient. Did I spoil things by running out before you expected? Seeing Jonathan with those other women—was I supposed to fall into your arms, tell you all was forgiven?"

"That's not how it was. I didn't care about the blow-job photos. I brought Holt to the pool house to see the Eggman Polaroids because she said they might help with her investigation."

"There *is* no investigation anymore, everyone knows that. You used to be a better liar." Olivia made a pretense of teeing up another ball. "Trying to win me back is one thing, I may have even found it flattering, but getting Jane Holt involved . . ." She kept her eyes on the ball, took a half-swing. "Did you expect her to confiscate the Polaroids, make an official report? Jonathan has a reputation to maintain; do you hate him so much that you'd try to ruin him?"

"I didn't start this."

"It's not a contest, Jimmy. You need to grow up and see that." Olivia swung wildly, topping the ball and sending it dribbling thirty yards.

"Nice shot."

Olivia laughed in spite of herself.

"That's better."

"No, it isn't," said Olivia. "You *wounded* him, Jimmy. He was so worried about what I was going to do that he was crying."

"Jonathan crying? I hope you got it on videotape."

"He thinks you're trying to destroy our marriage, and I have to admit that seeing the photos of him with those other women, knowing he had kept them—that was upsetting." Olivia tapped the sod off her spikes with the head of the club. "It pissed me off, if you want to know . . . but being married changes people."

"I know. I liked you better before."

"You think *you* haven't changed?" Olivia snapped, not caring who heard. "Take a look at yourself: you sound so bitter and small."

"Should I be crying? Would that help? Should I hang my head and blubber, maybe leave a stuffed teddy bear on your doorstep, or hire a skywriter? That brokenhearted-little-boy routine might work for Jonathan, but I don't think I could pull it off without wanting to punch myself in the fucking teeth."

"No, begging wouldn't suit you," Olivia said, and both of them were surprised by the sadness in her voice. "Why are you here, Jimmy?"

"I miss you."

"I'm glad." Olivia grimaced. "I remember when you left, your mother said that you were going because you were distraught about the Eggman, that you blamed yourself for what had happened. Your father said a woman my age was ready for marriage, and you were afraid of responsibility, always had been."

"What did Jonathan say?"

"You shouldn't have left me, Jimmy."

"I told you I was worried that you—"

"That's right: you *had* to run off because something you had done was catching up with you, and you wanted to protect me." Olivia slowly shook her head. "Bullshit."

"It's true."

"Why didn't you ask me to go with you, then? If you loved me, you would have at least asked. Were you afraid I would say yes?"

Jimmy didn't answer. This wasn't going at all the way he'd planned.

"It's all right."

Jimmy missed her even more now: she was right beside him, close enough for him to feel her heat, but he was never going to reach her now.

"Those last few months before you left, it seemed like all we did was fight." The breeze lifted her hair, the strands dancing around her cheeks. "Your friends, my friends—it seemed like the only time we were happy was when it was just the two of us."

"I'll settle for that."

Olivia shook her head again. "You don't want me back. You just want to take me away from Jonathan."

"That's not—"

"It *is* true." Olivia silenced him with a finger over his lips. "I'm not insulted. Really. I'm over you, Jimmy."

"OK."

"It wasn't easy. Even when I could feel things starting up between Jonathan and me, I tried to get in touch with you—"

"I said, OK."

"I don't know if I was trying to give you one last chance or if I just wanted to tell you what was happening," said Olivia, ignoring him. "I left messages in Berlin, Stockholm, Tokyo. . . . I don't know how many times I called before the band manager got back to me. He said you had jumped the tour back in Rome. You never even bothered to let me know."

"I couldn't." Jimmy hesitated. "I was in jail. My lawyer kept telling me every week that I was going to get released any day, and before it was over I'd been in for almost three months."

"What did you do?"

"I was on my way *home*—pretty funny, huh? I had checked my luggage at the Rome airport and was waiting for my flight to be called when I was arrested. They found a gun in my luggage. It wasn't mine. There were no fingerprints on it."

"Why didn't you call me? I would have been on the next plane over."

"I kept thinking it was going to be straightened out fast, but the Italian legal system is as bad as ours, and things just kept—"

"You still should have called me."

"Would it have made a difference?"

Olivia held his gaze until he had to turn away.

"Yeah, that's what I thought, too."

"Don't look so sad," said Olivia. "You got what you wanted. We both did."

"Yeah, it feels like fucking Christmas."

Olivia laughed, a full-throated laugh, clean as the morning. "I *do* miss you sometimes, too. No one makes me laugh like you do."

Jimmy kissed her, their lips lingering, then slowly pulled away. "I don't want to make you laugh anymore." He saw tears shimmer in her eyes, or maybe it was his eyes that were shimmering. "I don't want to be friends, either."

"Don't say that."

"That's what I want. I couldn't stand it otherwise."

Olivia nodded, then turned away.

Chapter 24

"I appreciate your seeing me on such short notice," said Holt. "I know you must be busy."

"Fridays are always frantic, but I'm happy to help in any way I can, Detective." Michelle came around from behind her antique white-pine desk.

"Call me Jane, please."

Michelle beckoned to the flowered sofa in her law office, and the two of them sat down beside each other. "You look like you could use a cup of coffee."

"No thanks." Holt crossed her legs. Michelle Fairfield's legal office was lush and friendly, the warm room filled with plants and macramé, with Persian carpets on the floor and photos of children everywhere. Holt tried not to stare. She was used to the high-tech sterility of corporate law offices, but this seemed like a good place to do family law, a snug refuge from which to work through the dissolution of a marriage, a reminder of what the warring parties were leaving behind.

Michelle fluffed up a small embroidered pillow and settled back. "Is Jimmy in trouble?"

Holt assumed an expression of bemused curiosity. "I said I wanted to speak with you about Jimmy and Jonathan Gage. What makes you wonder if Jimmy is the one in trouble?"

"What exactly is this about . . . Jane?"

"I'm just trying to understand the two of them a little better," said Holt, taken aback by her unwillingness to be drawn out. The cozy surroundings were deceptive. "They've both been very helpful in an investigation I'm working on. I thought any insights you might have about them would be useful."

Michelle looked coolly down her perfect nose at Holt. She was a lovely woman, but her intense, bright eyes didn't match her flawless features. A cover-girl face and a mane of tawny hair might open doors and get you the best table; a face like that made everything easy. But you didn't develop a fearless gaze like hers unless you'd had to fight for everything you had.

"I hope you don't mind," said Holt.

Michelle didn't blink. "Why me?"

"I got the guest list for Jonathan's party from the security service earlier this week," said Holt. "I understand that there was a confrontation between the two brothers at the party, but I'm not interested in that now. I talked to Olivia Gage, and she said that you'd gone to school with the two of them. That's what I want to ask you about."

Michelle had an earthy chuckle, as incongruous as her sophisticated appearance. "You want to ask me about high school? Are you *sure* you're a police officer, Jane?"

"Quite sure." Holt smiled back at her. "I'm just trying to understand the two of them. Jonathan and Jimmy, they both put up smoke screens—different kinds of smoke screens, but smoke screens all the same. It's been my experience that we're never more ourselves than we are in high school, before we learn to hide our true personalities."

"That's an interesting theory," said Michelle.

"How would you describe Jonathan and Jimmy when you knew them back then?"

"I wasn't friends with either of them. I didn't have many friends in those days."

Holt nodded, surprised. "Anything you can tell me would help." She moved closer to Michelle. "It's important."

Michelle watched her, one manicured fingernail idly tracing the embroidered pattern of the pillow. "Well," she said at last, "Jonathan was always the quiet, studious type. He kept himself apart from everyone—I did, too, but then I didn't have a choice." A smile tugged at the corners of her mouth. "With Jonathan it was more his sense of being, I don't know, a little better than the rest of us, a little smarter, certainly a lot more motivated. Jonathan always knew what he wanted to be when he grew up." She looked away, and her hand moved up to her face, ran along her jawline.

"And Jimmy?" prompted Holt. "What was he like?"

"Jimmy . . ." Michelle shook her head. "He was more . . . out there. You just had to see him walking down the hall, see the way he carried himself, taking it all in, to *know* there was something different about him. Jimmy was popular without having to work at it, and smart enough that the teachers let him alone. Girls liked him . . . I know *I* was crazy about him."

"I can see that," said Holt.

Michelle blushed.

"Did Jimmy have problems with anger in high school?"

"I don't know what you mean by that," Michelle said evenly.

"High school can be a very stressful time," said Holt. "All those hormones running wild. . . ." She waited in vain for Michelle to respond. "I spoke with Jonathan yesterday, and he mentioned that Jimmy had been involved in some sort of violent confrontation during his senior year. It must have been serious, considering that he got expelled."

Michelle's eyes hardened.

"I tried to track down the expulsion records this morning, but they're sealed," said Holt. "I thought you might be able to fill me in. There are no secrets in high school."

"Is that really why you wanted to talk to me?"

"Yes." Holt had found that in dealing with some people, honesty was not only the best policy but the *only* policy.

"Jimmy is a friend of mine," said Michelle.

"I like to think he's a friend of mine, too," said Holt.

Michelle nodded, as though she'd made a decision. "Last year, if you had asked me, I wouldn't have been able to tell you anything about it except that Jimmy had gotten into a fight with three football players. But a few months ago I got a phone call from one of the boys, Greg. He works at an auto dealership now, says he's their top salesman. I hadn't talked to him since high school. Actually, I don't remember *ever* having talked to him."

"Why did he call *you?*"

"He wanted to make amends."

"I don't understand."

"Greg had recently joined Alcoholics Anonymous and started the twelve-step program," said Michelle, smoothing her skirt flat, smoothing it again and again. "Step nine is to make amends with anyone you caused an injury to in the past."

"So in high school this . . . Greg hurt you? Was that why Jimmy beat him up?"

"He never hurt me. Jimmy stopped him before he could." Michelle took a deep breath, then slowly let it out, trying to regain her composure. "Greg said the three of them had made a pact to rape me after school. He started crying when he told me about it. He said they used to watch me cut across the athletic field on my way home from school—that was what gave them the idea. You see, it was homecoming week, and we were playing our crosstown rivals, the Bulldogs. That was why they picked me." She tore a hand through her hair. "I was a bowwow," she said quietly.

Holt could only stare at her.

"Somehow Jimmy must have found out what they were planning. That afternoon, he surprised them where they were waiting for me behind the handball court." Michelle shook her head. "I wasn't even there—I'd gone home early that day because I felt sick. I didn't even hear about the fight until I got to school on Monday." She recrossed her legs and leaned toward Holt. "I tried to bring it up when I ran into Jimmy at the party last week, but he acted like he didn't know what I was talking about. Can you believe that?"

"Jimmy attacked them? All three of them?"

"Oh, yeah." Michelle grinned. "He *kicked* their asses."

Chapter 25

The door to the limousine closed with the muffled *thunk* of a bank vault, and Jimmy settled into the black-leather bench seat beside Antonin Napitano as the driver walked around to the front. He'd had Napitano pick him up in Belmont Shore, a swank yet seedy beachfront town just south of Long Beach, the kind of place where the coke dealers kept blue Burmese cats instead of pit bulls, and girls in string bikinis waited in line at the bank cracking their gum and reading *Marie Claire*. They drove slowly through the traffic on Second Street, and he watched a tattooed teenager roll past on a skateboard, boom box blaring on his shoulder, the sound muted through the thick, smoked glass of the limo.

"I hope you brought your appetite." Napitano showed his tiny white teeth, watching Jimmy with barely concealed delight. As always, he was dressed in black silk pajamas, his feet in silk slippers. He was a small man, barely five foot four, with an oversize head and dirty eyes, the face of a rapacious infant. "You haven't commented on my new vehicle; I feel slighted."

Jimmy looked around. The spacious passenger compartment was lined with soft rolled black leather, deeply padded. Two television sets faced them; a bar, a refrigerator, a computer console, and three telephones were fitted into various nooks within the interior. "It looks just like your other limo, maybe a little bigger—lousy pickup, though," he said, wishing he had called off his meeting with his former publisher, still annoyed at being dismissed by Olivia. She wasn't going to believe anything he told her about Jonathan.

Neither was anyone else. He leaned forward, pointing at something near the right jumpseat. "Nino, what *is* that?"

Napitano picked up a small fluffy dog from the satin pillow. "This is Tina. Say hello to Jimmy, Tina." Tina panted at Jimmy, her tongue hanging out. "Say hello, Jimmy. *Please?* You don't want to hurt her feelings."

"You sure that's a dog? It looks like an Ewok."

Napitano nuzzled the dog's face. "Tina is a Yorkshire terrier, aren't you, Tina? Yes, you are." They rubbed noses, the dog's gray whiskers tickling Napitano's pink cheeks.

"Careful, Nino, I think those things were originally bred to hunt rats."

"I see you've lost none of your cleverness." Napitano gave the dog a kiss on the lips, then tossed her back onto the pillow. He touched a button on the console. *"Avanti!"* The limo accelerated up the ramp and onto the 701 freeway.

Napitano pulled a bottle of Dom Perignon out of the ice bucket, filled a couple of champagne flutes that were as delicate as soap bubbles, and handed one to Jimmy. "To the return of the prodigal," he toasted Jimmy, taking a long drink, gargling noisily before swallowing. He smiled with those milk teeth, and Jimmy wondered if he had an infinite supply of incisors and bicuspids stacked in his skull, since he must wear them away every few months with that voracious appetite of his—never satisfied, forever hungry.

The first time they met, Napitano had sat behind his enormous desk at *SLAP*, bare feet up, a one-kilo tin of caviar in his lap, watching Jimmy from between his wriggling toes. Neither of them had spoken. After a while Jimmy had taken off his own shoes and socks and put his feet up on the desk, too, still not speaking. It was the weirdest job interview he ever had, but Nino hired him on the spot, said he could write about anything he wanted, and offered him a spoonful of beluga to seal the deal.

One of the cell phones beeped, and Napitano picked it up without answering, just listened.

While Napitano talked on the phone, Jimmy finished his champagne, which was even better than the stuff Jonathan had served at his office party. The limo gently swayed as the driver accelerated, and Jimmy felt drowsy, ensconced in the heated leather seat. He yawned.

"It is rather womblike in here, isn't it?" Napitano said, putting down the phone. "Warm and soft and self-contained, the two of us like a pair of fraternal twins floating peacefully in our mobile amniotic sac, clutching our penises—our *respective* penises, I hasten to—"

"There's an image I'd like to have surgically removed from my memory banks."

"Americans are such prudes," clucked Napitano. "You look exhausted, dear boy. Close your eyes and rest. We'll be there soon."

Jimmy yawned again. "I'm not sleepy." The noon sunshine glanced off the cars they passed, but the interior of the limo basked in a serene twilight as Jimmy drifted along to the hum of the engine.

"Wake up, Jimmy." Napitano shook his shoulder, dark eyes glinting.

Jimmy stretched carefully, mindful of his ribs. He didn't think Blaine had cracked any of them, but it hurt every time he took a deep breath.

"Prepare yourself to dine like an emperor," said Napitano.

Jimmy looked out the window and saw the glitter of broken glass. At the end of the block, a high cyclone fence surrounded an auto junkyard, but abandoned cars were parked all along the street, windshields shattered, tires stripped, as though they had tried to reach the scrapyard but hadn't had the strength to make it. A rusted clothes washer lay turned on its side in a vacant lot, next to a sofa whose stuffing was leaking onto the weeds. A few yards away stood Lorraine's Bar BQ, a squat concrete-block structure with barred windows and two wooden picnic tables set on a cracked patio. Three young Hispanic men in white shirts and ties sat at one of the tables, bent over their takeout, watching the limo between careful bites.

There was a rap on the window, and Napitano rolled it down and took an armload of paper bags from his driver, a large, powerfully built black man wearing a tuxedo. Jimmy could see the man's shoulder holster as he leaned inside.

"Did you take care of yourself, Carlton?" asked Napitano.

"As you know, Mr. Napitano, I'm a vegetarian."

Napitano rolled up the window as the driver took up a position at the front of the vehicle, arms folded, glowering behind mirror shades. Napitano tore open the bags, set out baskets of baby-back ribs, baked beans, chicken wings, biscuits and gravy, hot links, sweet-potato pie, and cornbread dotted with jalapeño peppers. "*Eat*, Jimmy," he urged. The dog bounded into Napitano's lap as he dug into the bags, grease flying, the limousine filling with the redolent smell of smoked meat and honeyed barbecue sauce. He dug out a large pork rib for himself and handed one to the Yorkie, who dragged it back to her pillow.

Jimmy started in on a chicken wing, juice running down his chin as he nibbled away. "I like the fact that only four months after a triple bypass you're back on a damn-the-cholesterol-full-speed-ahead diet. It shows a certain insouciant idiocy on your part."

"You heard about my little surgery, did you?" Napitano noisily sucked the meat off the curved rib bone. "Wandering around Europe, the vagabond prince, and still you had an interest in Nino. I knew you'd miss me."

"The news of your operation was unavoidable. Every newspaper in Rome had your face on the cover. I saw an old man go into a toilet with a copy of *La Stampa*, and when he came out, the front page with your picture was gone."

Nino's tiny teeth tap-danced across the pig bone. "Was that when you were in jail?"

Jimmy stopped chewing, the chicken bone halfway to his mouth. "How did you find out about that?"

Napitano polished off the rib, tossed it aside. "Who do you think got you released?"

"I thought . . . I thought it was someone else."

"How lovely to have so many friends that you don't even know whom to thank. Why didn't you call upon me as soon as you got into trouble? I found out about your situation quite by accident."

"I had one of the best defense attorneys in the city. I didn't think there was anything else that could be done."

"There is *always* something else that can be done. Your pride cost you three months of your life."

"It cost me a lot more than that."

After three months of frustration and pasta twice a day, Jimmy's attorney had shown up outside his cell one afternoon, speaking rapidly in Italian and waving a decree plastered with gold seals. The guard had farted, taking his time reading through the paperwork, then unlocked the door. Jimmy had checked into a hotel, made plane reservations for the next day, and called Olivia. Taking into account the ten-hour time difference, he called her at the country club. The pro-shop steward said she had gotten married the day before and was on her honeymoon. Jimmy thought they must have a bad connection and asked the man to repeat the message. He held the telephone receiver in his hand long after the steward had hung up, wondering if there was any time zone in the world where it was still yesterday, where he could have called and gotten to talk to Olivia before it was too late.

Napitano took a piece of well-chewed meat out of his mouth and tossed it to the Yorkie. "I *am* disappointed in you for being apprehended so foolishly. All luggage is checked at Italian airports, not just carry-on pieces; I thought everyone knew that. Why would you travel with a loaded pistol anyway? Europe is not the Wild West— the *polizia* take such things very seriously, particularly after the recent terrorist bombings."

"It wasn't my gun."

"Of course."

"I was set up. Someone must have bribed one of the hotel porters to slip the gun into my bag. Luggage locks aren't worth shit. I tried telling that to the police—"

"The police are very poor listeners." Napitano waved a fresh rib bone like an orchestra conductor. "Do you have any idea who did this to you?"

"I had a fight with the lead singer of the band I was traveling with, that's why I was coming back home. He might have done it— he could have smuggled a gun in the equipment easily enough— but I'm not sure. He was pissed off at me, but I didn't think he was angry enough to do something like that."

"The world is filled with pygmies." Napitano stripped the bone with a practiced scrape of his teeth and reached for his champagne glass. "Giants like us, we create enemies with every stride we take."

"How much did it cost you to get the charges dropped?"

"It wasn't a matter of money, though of course money did change hands. There are still people there who owe me favors, and truth be told, crimes against the state are relatively easy to excuse; it is the taxman who is unforgiving. Once he has his fangs in your buttocks, abandon all hope."

"I owe you, Nino."

"Of *course* you do, dear boy. Oh, look!"

The young men sitting at the picnic table stood up, knocked their food over, and scattered as a group of homeboys sauntered out from a burned-out building across the street, bandannas draped low across their foreheads.

Nino licked his fingers. "Carlton," he said into the microphone.

"I see them, Mr. Napitano," said Carlton, speaking into his lapel.

"Carlton used to be with your Secret Service," said Napitano. "I've offered him a blank check if he will tell me some of the sordid little secrets of your American presidents, but he refuses. I will *never* understand you people."

The five homeboys separated, closer now, moving fast.

Carlton pushed away from the hood of the limo and stood in front of Jimmy's window, legs spread, pistol drawn—a real cannon, too, a forty-four mag with a six-inch barrel. He assumed the two-handed Weaver stance and pointed the gun right at Jimmy's head, then pulled back the hammer.

Jimmy shouted to Napitano and hit the floor, cowering, trying to bury his face in the carpet. Even inside the hermetic interior of the limo, the gunshots reverberated. Three shots in quick succession: *POP POP POP.* He could hear Nino laughing, a full belly laugh. Jimmy slowly sat up. He could see the five homeboys backing away as Carlton watched them, waiting until they had disappeared back into the building before he holstered his revolver. Jimmy stared at his window. Carlton hadn't fired blanks. Jimmy could see the bullets, caught in the glass somehow, like flies in honey.

"Amazing, yes?" Napitano pounded on the glass. "The latest in armor technology, developed by NASA—some sort of viscous epoxy that's three inches thick and completely shatterproof. A fine joke, don't you think? Your expression, Jimmy! I wish you could have seen it. Did you see your life flashing before you? All the parts you thought you had forgotten, from your mother's teat to your first kiss?" He scooped a spoonful of baked beans into his mouth, a few errant legumes falling into his lap.

Someday Jimmy would look back on this moment and laugh. Someday . . . about an hour after the sun went nova.

"How soon can you start back to work?"

"The sooner the better," said Jimmy, his heart still racing. "I need to borrow ten thousand dollars—you can take it out of my salary over the next year. I wouldn't ask, but a friend of mine is in trouble."

"Ah, the joy of a friend in need." Napitano flicked crumbs off his belly. "I will have a check waiting on your desk."

"Thanks." Jimmy tapped the thick armored window. "What's with the war wagon? Who are you worried about?"

"*Everyone,* dear boy—everyone." Napitano plucked a juicy morsel from his lap and plopped it into his mouth. "Accident or intentionality, the tragedy of death was too much to bear or to tolerate. But no longer. Nino has no worries, no cares or woes. Sex is lovely, food and drink are divine, but *security* is the ultimate indulgence."

He patted the sides of the limo. "Reinforced Kevlar up and down, over and under. Carlton could drive over an antitank mine, and it would do no more damage than a firecracker."

"There's just one problem, Nino: this thing is designed for direct assaults—carjackings, bombs, gunfire—but the bad guys, the really smart ones, don't follow the script laid out by the salesman who sold the limo to you, or by the engineers who built it. They come at you from your blind side, from someplace you would never expect. There is no safe place."

"We shall see." Napitano jabbed at him with a wedge of sweet-potato pie, then took a bite. "I want you to take on some different assignments at the magazine. It would be a mistake for us to try to duplicate your past success." He chewed with his mouth open. "The Eggman created such exquisite buzz for *SLAP*, such glorious . . . *friction*," he mused. "Even after the task force came out with its final report, we still got play. While you sat in a Roman jail, I did *Geraldo* for three nights in a row, discussing the police cover-up with the usual screamers." He wrinkled his nose. "That shrill woman from CNN has the foulest body odor, but I got thirty minutes on Larry King with her help. Alas, such opportunities are rare, and I think it is time to put our Eggman to bed. Perhaps a series of profiles would be the best use of your talent—"

" 'Our' Eggman?"

"The scent of death that clings to you has only added to your cachet; *anyone* will sit down with you now." Napitano wiggled his toes with delight, then caught sight of Jimmy's expression. "What's wrong?"

Jimmy watched Napitano's legs swing back and forth, his own thoughts chaotic. "Nino . . ." He didn't know where to begin to address his sudden doubts. "I can understand your using the Eggman letter, I'm a big boy, but you need to tell me whether you *wrote* that letter. I need to know. Tell me the truth, because if I find out that you've lied to me, you're going to need more protection than this tin can."

Napitano took another bite of pie, then belched. It smelled like cinnamon. "I fear nothing and no one in my armored chariot. I ride the freeways, safer than the pope himself."

"The pope was shot blessing a crowd in Saint Peter's Square." Jimmy formed his right hand into a gun and pressed his finger against Napitano's temple. "*Bang*. It could happen just like that. *Bang*, and we've got brains all over this nice leather upholstery."

Napitano squirmed away like a pudgy raccoon. "I am not amused."

"Did you send me that letter?" Jimmy placed his cocked index finger between Napitano's eyes. "The *truth*, Nino. This thing could go off."

"Mr. Napitano?" Carlton's voice was deep and resonant over the intercom.

Napitano broke free. "I'm quite all right, Carlton." He smoothed his black silk pajamas, watching Jimmy. "I don't create monsters, Jimmy; I merely take advantage of them. But your point is well taken. There is no safe place, just as you said."

Chapter 26

"New location," said Jimmy.

"Melrose was a toilet," sniffed Ian, slouching against a black Lucite slab the size and shape of a sarcophagus. A sallow, emaciated dandy with a pencil mustache, dressed in a billowy black jumpsuit with zippers on the sleeves, chest, and thighs, he looked like an astronaut who couldn't make the weight.

Gallery Inferno had come up in the world since Jimmy wrote about it a few years earlier. It was just a dingy former Laundromat when he went to the grand opening, at which the usual poseurs and street creeps swarmed the buffet of beer and Velveeta cubes impaled on toothpicks. That first show had included the shooting script for the original *Psycho,* signed by Tony Perkins, a collection of cockpit recordings from airliners that had crashed, and some Christmas cards from serial killers. Jimmy's review was scathing, but the show sold out anyway. So much for the power of the press. This new location was in Santa Monica, a few blocks from the beach, upscale and elegant, with high ceilings and museum lighting.

Jimmy stopped in front of a large acrylic by John Wayne Gacy, a vibrant painting of Pogo the Clown standing between Ian and his wife, Cleo, a tall, brittle woman in a black strapless. Ian wore a black suit and a red bow tie. Pogo had on a white ruff, a pointed red hat, and a striped suit. They all had the same painted-on smile.

"I'm afraid that one's not for sale—it's from our personal collection," said Ian. "John finished the portrait only two days before his execution. It was a veritable race against the clock. Cleo and I commissioned it before we even had the gallery—we just *knew*."

"You, Cleo, and Gacy." Jimmy clapped his hands. " 'Table for three in hell. Something with a view of the piss factory, monsieur?' "

"Ian?" Cleo walked out from one of the many alcoves, trailing a fresh-faced young couple who were holding hands. Cleo wore a black polka-dot dress that swirled around her knees, her metallic-orange pageboy shaped like a helmet, her bangs cut straight across her forehead. "The Andersons wish to purchase the large Ramirez drawing. I told them they could take it home."

"We're having a dinner party tonight," explained Mr. Anderson shyly, a dot-com geek wearing chinos and a denim work shirt, his wife gauzy and luminous as a moth beside him. "Cleo said you wanted to keep it until the show closed, but—"

"Nonsense, Christopher," burbled Ian. "For you two, anything." He waved his fingers and waited until an assistant brought over a gilt-framed pencil drawing of a giant rat feasting on an eviscerated body. "See where he signed it Richard Ramirez, and wrote 'The Night Stalker' in parentheses?" he said, tapping the lower right-hand corner. "Richard does that only with very special pieces."

The Andersons bent over the drawing.

Jimmy wandered into the rear of the gallery, moving carefully, his back still sore from where Blaine had knee-dropped him. A display of metal lunch boxes was arranged atop a nineteenth-century embalming table; the Donald Duck lunch box, signed by Jeffrey Dahmer and accompanied by a letter of authenticity, was only six thousand dollars. One side room was devoted to items from Jonestown, with a beatific photo of Jim Jones overlooking the moldy Bibles and woven palm hats. A pitcher of grape Kool-Aid rested on a pedestal. Jimmy ducked into another alcove, but there was no relief there. This one featured official eight-by-ten photographs from California's gas chamber. The Caryl Chessman was priced at fifteen thousand dollars.

"Gas-chamber photos are a splendid investment," Cleo said,

coming up behind him, her skirt rustling against his leg as she stood beside him. The polka dots were youthful and exuberant, but her face was stiff with makeup, a mummy mask of indeterminate age. "Supply and demand—they don't give the gas anymore, and lethal injection is *so* much less dramatic. Very little sell-through on lethal injection, but gas is blue-chip."

"What about hanging?"

"Hanging appeals to the historical collector rather than the aberrant-art connoisseur, which is a different market, much less momentum-driven," Cleo lectured, her charm bracelet of tiny gold skulls jingling. "Unless, of course, you can see the erection. That happens, you know. When someone's hanged, his thing . . . it gets like a crowbar." She leaned closer to him. "If you can see the erection, you can just about name your price."

"Makes you wonder why people waste their time investing in real estate or the stock market," said Jimmy.

"We've been waiting for you to come by. Ian didn't recognize you, but I did."

Jimmy had no idea what she was talking about. "I want to ask you about some photographs you may have sold. The Eggman—"

"They're in the back room, silly," said Cleo, taking his arm with a hand that she must have kept in a Deepfreeze when she wasn't strangling kittens with it. "You love to play games, don't you? I bet no one ever knows what you're up to."

Jimmy hesitated, then followed her through the black velvet curtains into the rear office.

"Over here." Cleo beckoned him over to a long wooden work-table covered with Eggman photographs, dozens of them in neat rows, each with a gold skull embossed on its ragboard mat. "Do you have a pen that you prefer to sign with?" She waited. "I'll pay you thirty dollars for every one," she prompted. "We've got ninety-four shots—let's make it an even three k."

Jimmy just stared at the dead. Crime photos all looked alike—from black-and-white tabloid shots of Paul Castellano lying with his head in the gutter to the Weegee portfolio at the Museum of Modern Art—so what made Cleo's display so much worse? The difference was that Jimmy knew every face in the photos before him, knew all their children, their parents, had sat in their living rooms talking to the people who'd loved them. He knew that Denise Fredericks had rented a Britney Spears costume for a Halloween party she never got to go to. He knew that William Hallberg had been halfway through a Stephen King novel when he was murdered; it was on his nightstand where he had left it, the page he was on dog-eared down.

"Our Eggman retrospective opens in three weeks." Cleo laughed. "I planned it to coincide with National Dairy Month."

Jimmy resisted the impulse to knock that laugh down her throat.

"You're a naughty boy," chided Cleo, hovering beside him, "making me wait until the last minute. I thought we were going to have to launch our exhibit without the Eggman's favorite writer. I sent two or three certified letters to *SLAP*, but they all came back. I called, I left messages. You never responded."

Most of the photos were eight-by-ten color prints, outside-the-police-tape long shots blown up grainy, and small thirty-five-millimeter snaps of cops with rubber gloves prodding the victim with pencils. There were a few close-ups, but not many Polaroids, and no Polaroids at all from the Laguna homicide. Not one. Like Holt had said, she ran a tight crime scene.

"Play hard-to-get," warned Cleo, "but don't overplay it."

Jimmy noticed a digital print of William Hallberg in the alley where they had found him the next morning. It was clearly an official photo, taken by one of the forensic techs, the image sharply focused. The paper bag of garbage Hallberg had been carrying lay by his side, its contents spilled, half a grapefruit covered with coffee grounds beside what was left of his head. Every particle of coffee was in high relief.

"That's a lovely piece," said Cleo.

Jimmy stared at her. Anyone who didn't think aliens walked among us had never met Cleo. He picked up a Polaroid of Carlos

Mendoza slumped beside his car, one hand resting on the whitewall as though he were about to pull himself to his feet. It looked like the one he had found in Jonathan's cigar box—same angle, same pose. Jimmy felt his face grow hot.

"That's a very popular shot," said Cleo. "We've sold probably three or four Mendozas in the last year. When a photographer has access, he'll shoot five or ten identical Polaroids if he can. We try to discourage multiple images, but you can't blame the photographer; paying off the police can be expensive. That's the last one we have."

Jimmy waved at the table. "Are these all the Polaroids you've got?"

"This is the most extensive selection you'll find anywhere," said Cleo, annoyed. "Polaroids are *very* hard to come by."

Jimmy handed her a small photograph. "This is my brother, Jonathan Gage. Have you ever done business with him?"

"Jimmy has a brother." Cleo eyed the photo.

"He's a plastic surgeon, if that helps. Extremely white skin, whiter than milk—the photo's not very good, but it's the only one I have."

Cleo shook her head. "No, I don't recognize him, but then, some of our clients use intermediaries to maintain their anonymity. I think they enjoy the sense of shame." She looked at Jimmy. "Surgeons call scalpels blades, did you know that? I find that very erotic."

Jimmy took the photo of Jonathan back from her. "I'd like the name of the photographer who took this shot of Carlos Mendoza. Maybe Jonathan bought the Polaroid from him directly."

"That's proprietary information. Out of the question."

Jimmy tapped a blow-up of Holt with Kinneson's body. "This woman is a police officer. If I call her up, she'll subpoena you for the name of the photographer."

Cleo's eyes sparkled. "I love a man who makes threats, but you're going to have to do better than that. Jane Holt has already been here."

Jimmy stared at her. Holt had acted surprised when he told her about the market for splatter photos. "Was this in the last couple of days?"

"No, Detective Holt came in shortly after your story appeared," said Cleo. "At first I thought she was a serious spender—she looked like money, and the buttoned-up types have the kinkiest tastes and the portfolios to satisfy them." She sighed, her charm bracelet jingling. "I was *so* disappointed when she said her interest was strictly official."

"Yeah, me too," said Jimmy, not really paying attention, trying to figure out what Holt had to gain by lying to him. "What did she want?"

"Polaroids."

"You mean close-ups," Jimmy corrected her. "She was interested in close-ups that might show something the police photographers had missed."

Cleo shook her head. "Polaroids were all she cared about. I lent her every one I had at the time, and she brought them back a few days later and asked for any more I could get my hands on."

Now Jimmy was truly confused. "Why only Polaroids?"

"Well, they're more collectible since there's no negative, and they have a certain rough, found-art quality, but I don't think she was concerned with that." Cleo held up two pens. "I'll make it thirty-two hundred. Red or black?"

"What did she do with the Polaroids you lent her?"

"Who knows? I told her she couldn't make copies; I made it clear I'd sue for copyright violation if she did."

Jimmy looked back at the table. "Why don't you have any Polaroids from the Laguna Beach crime scene?"

"None of the photographers could get access to the body," complained Cleo. "I asked Jane if she could . . . appropriate a few Kinnesons from the crime lab in appreciation for my help. You would have thought I had asked for her ovaries."

"So you've *never* offered a Polaroid of Philip Kinneson for sale?"

"I wish. There are collectors who would pay *huge* to complete their Eggman collections." Cleo's voice softened. "Jimmy, do you have access to a Kinneson Polaroid?"

Jimmy stared at an eight-by-ten color print that had been tossed aside onto a shelf. It looked like an abstract composition, with a rough circle of blue dots at the center of a white background, a wavering yellow line circling the blue dots, and more white and brown dots on the edges of the frame. It took him a moment to realize that it was the Laguna Beach site viewed from the surrounding bluffs. The blue dots were uniforms, the yellow line was crime-scene ribbon, and the brown and white dots were lookie-loos. It looked like a target. He picked it up. "This is interesting."

"To you, maybe, but not to me. Besides, I thought you were interested in Polaroids. Just like Detective Holt." Cleo smoothed her lipstick with a forefinger. "Sign the photos and I'll make it thirty-five hundred. My best offer."

The other photos were more graphic, but there was something uniquely disturbing about this one, a sort of arrogance—maybe it was the angle or the elevation, but it gave the impression that the photographer had a perspective that no one on the ground had, not even the police. Jimmy held up the photo. "Who took this?"

"That just came in, but it's not even worth framing. It doesn't show . . . *enough*," Cleo said contemptuously. "I've bought several other Eggman shots from the photographer, he's a real go-getter, but it looks like he's scraping the bottom of his files now."

"What's his name? It's important, Cleo."

"Aren't we the alpha male, beating our chest, making demands." Cleo waved the pens. "I don't *do* favors."

The killer's returning to the scene of the crime was the oldest cliché in police work, but there was an element of truth to it. Most smart detectives had the crowd at a homicide scene photographed, and sometimes they even found the killer savoring his work among the bystanders. Jimmy stared at the photo. Maybe the photographer hadn't been alone up at that vantage point, looking down on the cops scurrying about the body; maybe he had had company, someone with an emotional investment in the proceedings.

Jimmy tucked the eight-by-ten print into a manila envelope and took the pen from Cleo. "Keep the money; just give me the photographer's name, address, and telephone number." He started writing, scrawling "You sick fuck" and his signature as fast as he could.

Cleo read over his shoulder. "Oh, that's *wonderful*," she said, clapping her hands with delight, setting the gold skulls jingling against her wrist like tiny bells.

Chapter 27

Jimmy rechecked the address Cleo had given him for the photographer who'd shot the panoramic Laguna Beach photo ("His name is ATM, like the cash machine," she'd said). He had driven over to the guy's apartment yesterday after leaving Gallery Inferno and waited around for a few hours without success. His phone messages had remained unreturned by the time he left the house today, but he still hoped to get lucky. The duplex at 1705 Pierson Street was in a run-for-your-life part of Long Beach, a one-story, cider-block structure painted army-surplus green, with tire-tread marks on the lawn. The two front doors of the duplex shared a common porch, a common wall, and a common neglected look, paint peeling and smudged with years of handprints. A kid's tricycle was chained to the wrought iron porch railing.

Music blasted from the apartment building next door as Jimmy stepped out of the car—Limp Bizkit demanding nookie. He walked onto the porch and stood there trying to decide between the two doors. The tricycle was chained to the left-side railing, so he knocked on the right-side door. ATM wasn't a dad's name. Or maybe Jimmy was just getting old.

After he'd been knocking for a long time, the door opened and an obese man poked his head out, his face obscured by a mass of braids.

"ATM?"

"Depends." The man sucked noisily on a milkshake, hitting bottom but not deterred. "You got wheels, pilgrim?"

Twenty minutes later they were racing down the emergency lane of the number 5 freeway, a narrow ribbon between the backed-up, bumper-to-bumper Saturday-afternoon traffic on their right and the concrete divider on their left.

"Princess Di! Princess Di!" ATM shrieked as Jimmy sped under the overpass in his rusty black Saab, the man laughing now, the same way he had shrieked and laughed for the last five overpasses as they chased the red and blue lights flashing far ahead of them.

"Shut *up*." Jimmy wished he and ATM could have just had a talk back at the apartment, but nothing was simple anymore. Everyone had a price, and it went up when you showed any interest. "You do that again, you're walking home."

"Hey, *you're* the one who knocked on *my* door." ATM scratched himself, an unshaven lout with a nest of braids, a fast-food gut, and three cameras draped around his neck. "You don't want to give a fellow journalist a lift, that's fine and dandy." He made a zipping movement across his lips.

"Look, I'm driving you, aren't I? Just no more screaming."

ATM belched. "Well, try driving *faster*, they're getting away."

Jimmy accelerated, yellowed newspapers and road trash billowing in the Saab's wake. Heads turned in the line of stopped cars as they roared past, inches from the concrete wall. They were doing over eighty-five, the steering wheel vibrating so hard that Jimmy thought it was going to snap off in his hands. Now he knew why ATM's car was in the shop with a blown engine. "I just wanted to know if you were alone on the bluffs when you took the crime-scene photograph. Why is that such a hard question?"

"Questions are easy; answers cost money. ATM accepts cash only, no personal checks."

Jimmy could see the blue and red lights of the ambulance fading in the distance. The Laguna homicide had been the first of the Eggman murders, and if the killer was ever going to admire the results of his handiwork, watch the scene swarming with police, the bluffs there offered the perfect, lofty perspective. Cleo might think that ATM's long-shot photograph didn't show enough, but Jimmy thought it showed plenty. The only question left was, did the Eggman like to watch?

ATM unwrapped a roll of antacids, popped a couple into his mouth, and offered the roll to Jimmy.

Jimmy shook his head, afraid to take his eyes off the road.

ATM thumbed a couple more antacids into his mouth, his "Ron Jeremy for President!" T-shirt spotted with ketchup and special sauce, the remnants of Big Macs and Jumbo Jacks past. "This job is killing me. All these celebrity stakeouts and car crashes have flat out ruined my digestion. I got gas you wouldn't believe."

Jimmy rolled down his window a little more, the wind howling through the Saab now. Deciding to try another tack, he reached into his jacket and pulled out the small photo of Jonathan. "Twenty bucks just to tell me if you ever sold this guy any Eggman Polaroids. Twenty bucks for a simple yes or no."

ATM rubbed his fingers together. "Money, honey."

Jimmy fished a twenty-dollar bill out of his jeans, still trying to keep his eyes on the road.

ATM took the money and the photograph. "Weird lighting."

"It's not the lighting; he's just the whitest man you ever saw. Do you recognize him?"

"I sold lots of Eggman photos—don't tell Cleo, though, 'cause she likes to keep me exclusive."

"Yes or no, did you ever sell *him* any Eggman Polaroids?"

"Maybe . . . he looks familiar."

Jimmy let it go; he didn't really care about Jonathan anymore. "That photo you shot from the bluffs was beautifully composed. I really liked the omniscient perspective; it was like being in the sky-box at the Super Bowl, the players all laid out before you. Most shooters would have gone for something close up—"

"I tried, but this lady cop put a stop to that," said ATM. "Bitch threatened to arrest me. Cops always say that, but I believed *her*." He sniffed. "She didn't want me on her beach, fine—ATM took the high ground."

"Must have been pretty crowded up there, a good spot like that."

"Nice try." ATM pressed a portable police-band radio against his ear, listening.

"I don't have much cash left, but I can pay you whatever's fair tomorrow."

"Instinct, pilgrim, that's what's made me the man I am today. You want to know if I had company up there so bad that even I can taste it, and that's going to cost you. Not tomorrow, *today*." ATM waved the radio in Jimmy's face. "Goddammit, there's already another meat wagon at the scene. We lose the pickup, I lose the money shot."

Jimmy leaned on the horn as a four-by-four just ahead of them started to pull into the emergency lane, the Saab veering left and coming so close to the wall rail that Jimmy's sideview mirror was torn off.

ATM cheered, pumping his fist in the air. "I'm going to turn you into a gore-chaser yet. You could probably use a career change. I used to read your stuff all the time in *SLAP*, but then you disappeared. I hear Napitano's crazy as a shithouse rat."

"I'm back on staff."

"You serious?"

"Just got rehired."

ATM raised his camera and snapped Jimmy's photo, the flash momentarily blinding him.

"Don't do that."

ATM took another shot. "First rule of the business: Don't listen to anything anyone tells you." Another flash. "I'll print you up a—"

Jimmy grabbed the camera and jerked on it hard, the strap pulling ATM forward, cracking his head against the dash, sending his braids flying like a runaway mop.

ATM rubbed his head. "That was unnecessary. I was going to make you a souvenir portrait. That really hurt. You might have chipped a disk or something. I could sue your ass for everything you got." He checked his cameras for the tenth time. "A *SLAP* paycheck, that must be nice. I been trying to get my stuff in that deep-pockets rag since the beginning, but the art editor has it in for me.

He wouldn't even look at my portfolio. I don't make such a good first impression because of my slow metabolism, but that's no reason to blackball me." He self-consciously tugged his sweat-stained T-shirt over his belly. "You try standing outside the Lizard Lounge for seven hours waiting for Leo DiCaprio to show up, living on junk food, see what happens."

"The art director isn't such a bad guy," Jimmy said idly. "I could crack the code for you."

ATM fingered his camera, trying to hide his eagerness. "Yeah . . . maybe you could set up an interview for me. I could fit that into my schedule."

Jimmy kept driving.

ATM licked his lips. "OK, you guessed right about the bluffs. I wasn't alone up there."

"Don't tell me what you think I want to hear. Just tell me the truth."

"We had a regular party going on—must have been seven or eight of us fighting for a spot on the railing. How soon can you talk to the art director?"

The steering wheel was vibrating again, the Saab about to shake itself apart, but Jimmy stomped on the accelerator even harder, the wind shrieking around them. "Could you describe any of them? Maybe sit down with an Identi-Kit artist and—"

ATM picked up the photo of Jonathan. "He was up there. I think so, anyway. I thought you were fucking with me before, trying to get an answer for cheap." He squinted at the photo. "It was a year ago, and I've seen a lot of faces since then, but he definitely looks familiar. If it really matters to you, I could check my files."

"What does that mean?"

ATM jiggled his cameras. "Hey, these ain't love beads. I got *photographs* of everybody up there with me. I shoot spec portraits all the time. Ten bucks a print, which barely covers my cost, even shooting thirty-five-millimeter bulk loads. None of those cheap bastards on the bluffs were interested, though. No sale. All they wanted to do was watch the show with the cops down below and—"

"So why did you keep the photos?"

"I never throw anything away—you never know who you're snapping, so you keep it all. Like that Zapruder guy. He was just taking home movies on his vacation when he caught Kennedy getting popped. You know how much he got for that footage?"

"Jonathan—the man in this photo—you're sure he was on the bluffs that day? His picture has been in the papers plenty of times. Maybe that's where you saw him."

"Maybe." ATM looked at the photograph again. "I think he was the one who didn't want me to take his picture. He made a big deal about it, turning his back on me."

"So you *don't* have a photograph of him?"

ATM cackled. "I didn't say that. I just said he didn't want me taking his picture." He drummed his fingers on the dash. "*SLAP* does these double-truck photo spreads every month: up-and-coming movie stars, hotshot politicians, Eurobabes. . . . It must be nice to get an assignment like that."

"Just get me the snaps you took that morning on the bluffs. I want to see everyone you shot."

"It'll take me a few days. I don't throw anything away, but I'm not much for housekeeping." ATM jabbed the radio. "Damn! The first meat wagon is leaving with a full load. Goose it, will you, pilgrim? We got hamburger all over the highway, and you're driving like my grandmother."

Chapter 28

Jimmy dumped off his car at valet parking and sprinted up the long pink-marble staircase to the Gold Coast Opera House, still not sure that he wasn't making a mistake. ATM had said he recognized Jonathan from the Laguna bluffs; if Jimmy were smart he would wait for ATM to find the photo, then show up at Jonathan's house and slap him across the face with it. If Jimmy were smart, he would give Holt the photo and let *her* ask Jonathan what he'd been doing up there that morning. Jimmy took the stairs two at a time now, hurrying. Smart guys didn't know how to have fun.

"Your invitation, sir?" A slender man stepped out from an alcove, a snooty cockatoo in sequined tights, a cape, and a feathered hat. He took in Jimmy's jeans and white tuxedo shirt with the cuffs rolled. "Your invitation?" He had lost the "sir" pretty quickly.

"Jimmy Gage. I'm supposed to be on a guest list."

The cockatoo ran a finger down his list as though he were doing Jimmy a favor. He looked up from the list, perplexed. "It seems that you're at setting A-Seven, the premier spot in the house. Perfection Enhancements Inc. bought the whole table." He swung open the double doors, letting the music out, a great, grand, symphonic sound. "Fifty thousand dollars for the table, and you don't even get to steal the silverware. It doesn't seem fair, does it?"

A young woman met Jimmy in the lobby. She was dressed like a fawn, her arms and face dappled in umber and yellow. "May I help you, sir?"

"Table A-Seven."

"Well, aren't you the lucky one?" said Bambi, taking his arm and leading him down the frescoed hall.

The grand ballroom was large and softly lit, the orchestra in the wings, a young woman onstage singing, barely audible over the din of conversation. The pale-pink walls were lavishly decorated with murals illustrating great moments from Verdi, Puccini, Bizet, Wagner, Mozart, and the rest of those guys. Ultrabutch women in horned helmets loomed over bewigged Italian aristocrats while a waifish French girl fended off a chubby clown with red-rouged cheeks. Jimmy knew just enough about opera to know that he liked it best with his eyes closed.

Men and women in elaborate costumes sat around the long rectangular tables, most of them dressed in bright medieval finery, the women in frilly, low-cut gowns, hair pinned up high as Spanish galleons, the men in tights and frock coats, while the wait staff, dressed as animals, ferried drinks and hors d'oeuvres. The soprano onstage was working through a selection of Puccini highlights; she had a lovely voice, but no one paid her any attention—the art lovers were too busy gobbling and gorging, cell phones beeping as they argued over real estate and who had the worst commute and who had the best Japanese horticulturist ("Sato is an absolute genius with dichondra!"). A few body-slams and a ring announcer with a bad toupee, and it would have looked like the Big Orange Arena last Sunday night.

"I'll find my way from here," said Jimmy, spotting Jonathan at the front-row table. His brother faced the soprano, giving her his full attention, his food untouched, and the singer returned his gaze, singing directly to him, her voice aching and high and clear. Olivia sat beside Jonathan in a patchwork Gypsy dress, gold hoops through her ears, gold bracelets on her wrists, pretending to listen to what was being said by a debonair man in a velvet frock coat. At the far end of the table, Michelle held court in a black wig and red flamenco skirt, chatting with a handsome French cavalier, the man touching her on the wrist as she spoke. Michelle noticed Jimmy and waved.

"James." Jonathan stood up. He was dressed in a white, stiff-necked officer's dress uniform, gold buttons and epaulets flashing, a white cap resting on the table by his plate. "What a pleasant surprise."

"You invited me."

"Yes, but I didn't think you would actually come." Jonathan pulled out an empty chair beside him. "Darling?" he called, raising his voice over the music. "Look who's here."

Olivia gave Jimmy a blank smile, then turned back to the frock-coated courtier next to her. Jimmy sat down beside Jonathan. He was aware of the conversation all around them, aware of the orchestra and the soprano, but the sounds were muted somehow—it was as though he and Jonathan existed in some cocoon of tangled DNA, just the two of them with their secrets.

"I really should have mentioned that costumes were de rigueur tonight," said Jonathan. "I hope you don't feel too uncomfortable."

"I just came from a three-car meat grinder on the number five—it's going to take more than this to make me uncomfortable."

Jonathan draped his arm over the back of Olivia's chair.

"A woman in a Honda had hit the windshield, spiderwebbed it, but she didn't go through. I stood there watching the firefighters pull her out, and in the darkness it looked like she was sleeping, but then the flashers from the ambulance caught her, and I could see shards of glass embedded in her face. . . . She looked like a mosaic glistening in the lights." He shook his head. "How can something so terrible be so beautiful? Why can't things be one or the other?"

Jonathan watched him, then slowly removed his arm from the chair and leaned closer so he wouldn't have to raise his voice. "What is it you want to say, James? That's why you're here, isn't it? To tell me something."

"What's your hurry? You usually have such wonderful manners."

Jonathan looked amused. "I hope you don't intend to spoil another evening for me."

"Oh, I'm going to spoil a lot more than your evening." Jimmy flicked one of Jonathan's gold buttons. "Who are you supposed to be, anyway? You look like you should be driving an ice cream truck."

Jonathan didn't react. "I'm Lieutenant Pinkerton from *Madame Butterfly*. It's a rather famous opera."

"Oh yeah. Pinkerton was a real bastard, though, wasn't he? He knocked up Butterfly and ran away, then came back a couple of years later with an American wife. A lowlife in a snow-white uniform—that's an interesting choice for you tonight."

"It's not a matter of *morality*," Jonathan said smoothly, making the word sound distasteful. "Pinkerton and Butterfly were simply playing different games."

"What game are you and I playing?"

"Why, the same one we've always played: flinch." Jonathan smiled. "So swing away, but don't forget, I get a turn, too."

Jimmy felt the blood boil in his cheeks as the music swelled around them. "Does it ever bother you?"

"Nothing bothers me, you know that. It's one of my best qualities."

"Losing bothers you." Jimmy saw that he had hit a nerve with that one. "I remember the look you used to get on your face when I beat you at something—crossword puzzles, racing, *anything*. You didn't complain or make excuses, I have to give you that, but the look in your eyes—it was if your heart were caving in. When we got older, you got better at hiding it, but I suspect I'm going to see that look again pretty soon."

"I hate to disappoint you, but that's simply *not* going to happen." Jonathan nodded at the soprano, who had just launched into another aria. "Why don't you have some lobster and a drink and just enjoy the show? I don't know if you're familiar with this selection; it's 'Si, mi chiamano Mimi,' from *La Boheme*. Mimi is meeting Rodolfo, a young, impoverished poet who lives next door to her in Paris—"

"She dies at the end."

"Yes, but it's a gloriously moving experience." Jonathan sat there, his eyes half closed. "Don't you think that's the most that any of us could hope for?"

"You made a mistake, Jonathan."

Jonathan idly conducted the orchestra with his hand. "Nothing permanent, I trust."

Jimmy leaned closer. "Those people tonight, being loaded into ambulances . . . I heard them moaning and crying, the ones who were still alive, I heard them, and all I could think of was that five seconds before it happened, all they cared about was what they were going to have for dinner, or what was going to be on TV, or how their kid did on his spelling test, all the mundane things that occupy our attention, and now . . . now, in an instant, everything was different, everything had changed."

Jonathan opened his eyes. "You're so melodramatic—you should be writing operas, not listening to them."

"Is that the appeal for you? The Eggman killings were emotionally blank, just over and done with—one moment they were alive, the next they were dead. Is that what you got off on, the power of life and death?"

Jonathan picked up his white officer's cap from the table, spun it around his finger. "Oh, my, this sounds serious. I feel a night sweat coming on."

"Totally random, no discernible pattern—that's one of the reasons the task force dismissed your letter, but we know better. The rush wasn't the killing, it was the choosing—*this* one not that one, *here* not there, *now* not later. The very randomness, that was the part you loved the best."

Jonathan smiled more broadly now, spinning the cap around his finger faster and faster.

"Is everything all right?" asked Olivia.

"James is just free associating, darling." Jonathan kept his eyes on Jimmy.

Jimmy smiled back at him. "Give me your hand."

"I beg your pardon?"

Jimmy held his own hand out. "What's the matter, are you afraid?"

Jonathan hesitated, then laid his right hand in Jimmy's. "You're still doing the fingertip push-ups, aren't you? I could feel your strength when we shook hands at the office party." His flesh was cool and inert in Jimmy's palm. "I bet you can still do a hundred at a time."

"There are twenty-seven bones in the human hand." Jimmy's eyes met Jonathan's as he slowly closed his fingers around his brother's hand. "I used to read your anatomy textbooks when I was alone in the pool house . . . funny the things that stay with you."

Jonathan's hand stayed where it was, resting in Jimmy's steadily closing grip. "Strength is good, but you sacrifice fine motor control." Jonathan nodded toward Michelle. "Lovely, isn't she? Some of my best work."

"She was beautiful *before* you got to her."

Jonathan laughed. "Ask *her* if she thinks that's true." He shook his head. "We all seek perfection, James—witness you and your endless rewrites—but I get to work at a more elemental level than you; I get to rewrite Mother Nature herself, and she can be *such* a sloppy bitch."

Jimmy continued to apply pressure. "Twenty-seven bones, neatly arranged, precisely aligned—distal phalanx, middle phalanx, proximal phalanx, fifth metacarpal . . . and that's just your pinkie."

The soprano had launched into Turandot's opening aria, in which she challenges her suitors to answer three riddles. If one answers correctly, he will win her hand and become emperor of China. Those who fail will be executed. The singer's high, clear voice made it seem like an offer no man could refuse.

Jimmy squeezed the base of Jonathan's hand, saw beads of sweat break out along his hairline as he steadily increased the pressure. "Capitate, triquetral, lunate, scaphoid, trapezoid, trapezium, pisiform, hamate—they look like broken teeth on an X ray, don't they?"

Jonathan relaxed even deeper into Jimmy's grasp, breathing through his nose.

"You have beautiful hands," said Jimmy, grinding the bones against one another. "Supple and smooth, capable of the most minute sensitivities. . . ."

Jonathan's mouth tightened as Jimmy increased the pressure, but he didn't pull away. "I can tie knots in number-three silk with two fingers, left hand or right. Shall I show you?"

"All those delicate nerve endings—they're what make the hands so sensitive, aren't they? Hands like yours, they must have *lots* of nerve endings."

Jonathan gasped, but he kept looking into Jimmy's eyes, offering no resistance. "These hands of mine have the power of life and death, James, so be aware of what you're doing. My work isn't all vanity, you know that. That was your big scoop, remember? I ducked out of my party last weekend because I was paged to go to the hospital. There had been—" He cocked his head, sensing Jimmy's shock as the soprano's voice rose higher around them. "You spoke of a meat grinder tonight? Well, that's just what I faced on Sunday night: a pileup on the Santa Ana Freeway, a van full of children returning from a church-choir performance, none of them wearing seat belts."

"You're lying."

Jonathan pretended not to understand.

"You left the party to go to the pool house."

"Ah, yes, Jimmy and his precious Polaroids." Jonathan shook his head. "Sorry, but I was in the operating room all night. I thought you knew."

"I . . . I don't believe you." Jimmy released his hand.

Jonathan's shoulders relaxed slightly, but his hand stayed immobile on the white linen tablecloth for a few moments until the feeling returned. "I think you're placing too much faith in these Polaroids of yours." He brushed at his jacket, plucked something invisible off his epaulets and released it.

For the first time, Jimmy considered the possibility that the Eggman Polaroids didn't really exist, that Holt had been right in suggesting that he had simply seen what he wanted to that night in the pool house. "I don't need the Polaroids, because you've given me all the necessary evidence," he said, so cold now that he was shivering. "You had to watch from the bluffs—well, *smile*, motherfucker, you're on *Candid Camera*."

"What *are* you talking about?"

"It's not just a game, Jonathan."

"I'm concerned about you." Jonathan spun his officer's cap around his finger again, around and around. "Most older brothers have time to grow, time to have a separate life before the new arrival in the happy home, but you and I, we're barely a year apart. I can't remember when you didn't exist. You were *always* there, sharing my room, sitting across from me at the table . . . we might as well have been twins." The white cap was spinning faster now. "Detective Holt asked me out for cocktails earlier this week, and she was just *full* of questions about you. I'd check my alibi twice if I were you." He set his cap on Jimmy's head.

Jimmy snatched the cap off and smacked Jonathan across the face with it.

"I thought you were eager to be cast as the dashing young officer," Jonathan said airily, unconcerned. He beckoned Jimmy closer. "It was nice holding hands with you before, skin to skin. I don't permit such intimacy very often, but then, you and I, we have no secrets." He was taking his turn now, his eyes bright in the dimness of the hall. "There have been times these last months when I was making love with Olivia and I could sense that she was thinking about you, and James, it didn't bother me at all."

"Gee, that's nice."

"She's very athletic," Jonathan continued. "A bit more muscular than I like, but quite a healthy animal, musky and wild. I *still* haven't quite tamed her, but give me time."

Jimmy tried to concentrate on the soprano's voice, Turandot's challenge echoing throughout the perfect acoustics.

Jonathan fingered his gold buttons. "Last night was really . . . quite special. Olivia and I were making love, and I could tell she was fantasizing about you, closing her eyes, her head thrown back in a certain way, truly lost in her senses. There were three of us in our bed last night, but you were just a ghost, James, and I was the one driving into her, making her groan."

Jimmy held himself back. He was aware that Olivia was watching them, trying to overhear what was being said.

"You know," purred Jonathan, "when the time finally comes when she's stopped thinking about you, when it's just the two of us alone in our marital bed, that's when I'll have to get rid of her." He showed his teeth. "I *will*, James. I'll do it."

Jimmy grabbed him by the collar, and Jonathan's chair tipped over, throwing them both onto the floor. He heard Olivia cry out.

Jonathan smiled up at him, their faces close enough to share a kiss. "You lose, *again*," Jonathan gloated, disentangling himself. "Well, at least you're consistent."

Chapter 29

"How's your head, bud?" Blaine asked for the third time, the Robo-Surfer in green spandex lifting shorts and a WWF tank top this Monday morning. He looked around, lowered his voice. "I'm really sorry about tossing you around last week, but I can't second-guess Pilar. She's the boss. She likes you, though, Jimmy."

"That's what everybody tells me."

"There you go." Blaine beamed. "It must be true, then."

Pilar wandered in from the back room, speaking Spanish rapidly into a cell phone, her voice girlish, her eyes hard. She wore flared jeans with silver studs down the sides and an intricately embroidered denim cowboy shirt, red and yellow parrots on the yoke. She pivoted on her high-heeled boots as she talked, her voice dropping seductively. She looked at Jimmy and winked.

As soon as he got home from the opera gala on Saturday night, still seething, Jimmy had called ATM. There was no answer, but he left a message for a callback as soon as ATM found the photos from the Laguna bluffs. He spent the next few hours trying to sleep before finally giving up and reaching for the phone.

The night desk of the *Times* confirmed that there had been a four-car accident on the Santa Ana Freeway Sunday night, the victims taken to Newport Hills Hospital. A Newport Hills ER nurse with a bad cough said that Jonathan had performed surgery that night, but she had no idea when he'd arrived or when he'd left—she hacked away into the receiver, sniffed something about confidential information, and hung up. Jimmy listened to the dial tone, wondering if Jonathan still might have had time to drive to the pool house before he and Holt got there the next morning. He lay there in bed, staring up at the meandering cracks and tributaries in the ceiling as dawn slowly lightened the room, smiling at the memory of Great White's expression when he'd told him about the Orinoco River. The morning paper thumped onto the lawn, but Jimmy didn't react; he had already decided to check into Jonathan's South American travels.

"If your back is still sore from the Kahuna Drop, I've got this ointment stuff from China called tiger balm that really helps," said Blaine. "It's like Ben Gay, only lots stronger. Or we got Percodan."

Jimmy shook his head, watching Pilar pace, the telephone cupped against her ear. His Spanish was spotty, but he knew what she was saying. She was asking someone at the police department in Cervaca, Venezuela, if there had been any unsolved homicides between June 4 and June 18 of last year. She had cajoled and pleaded her way from one officer to the next for the last twenty minutes, playing the role of an American college student studying Latin American police procedures. The way the woman said *"por favor"* could melt a stone.

The period from June 4 to June 18 was when Jonathan had set up his reconstructive-surgery clinic in Cervaca—Jimmy had called Jonathan's publicity agent this morning and requested that a summary of Jonathan's charitable work for the last five years be faxed to him at *SLAP*. Pilar hadn't said anything when Jimmy showed up just before noon and handed her the itinerary, with all references to Jonathan removed. Pilar didn't ask who had traveled to these small towns or why Jimmy wanted to know about any killings there. She didn't mention Rollo, didn't mention money or payback. No quid pro quo. She just told Blaine to make them some fresh coffee, sat down, and studied the paperwork.

"She's really something, isn't she?" Blaine said as Pilar walked past. "She's not just smart, most girls are smart, but Pilar—I seen her bench-press twice her body weight."

"Yeah, she's something."

Jimmy had read everything he could about serial killers after getting the Eggman letter. Mass murderers fell into two broad categories: spree killers and serial killers. Spree killers were screwups like Charles Whitman, the Texas Tower sniper, losers who suddenly snapped, their victims chosen at random, just *bang, bang, bang* until they were killed or captured. Serial killers, such as Ted Bundy, were much more dangerous; methodical and cautious, they were social chameleons who were able to escape capture for years at a time. The typical serial killer was a sexual psychopath who chose his victims carefully, categorizing them by gender, profession, general appearance, or even, in the case of the Son of Sam, the way they parted their hair. Unlike the spree killer's, the serial killer's crimes were marked by a cooling-off period between murders, a time-out that might last for weeks or years, until the hunger asserted itself again—and the hunger *always* did.

Blaine picked up the Mossberg and tried balancing the barrel of the pump shotgun on one finger. "I still haven't gotten the videotape of my match from Mr. Macklen," he said, walking around unsteadily, the shotgun wobbling on the tip of his finger. "You think you could talk to him for me?"

Jimmy looked around for Pilar. "Do you really think that's a good idea?"

Blaine tilted his head back as he walked slowly across the room, the shotgun balanced on one finger. "I know what I'm doing."

The problem with the Eggman killings—and one of the reasons the task force had decided that Jimmy's letter was a hoax—was that they exhibited characteristics of *both* types of mass murderer. Like a spree killer's, the Eggman's victims were randomly chosen, with no sexual mutilation or interval between the crimes, but like a serial killer, the Eggman had taken great care to cover his actions, leaving no forensic evidence. Spree killers were incapable of stopping themselves, but the Eggman had quit abruptly after only a few weeks, with only his letter to Jimmy marking his territory.

Jimmy knew that if Jonathan was really the Eggman, he wouldn't have started killing in Orange County. He would have honed his skills someplace else, perfected them on his overseas trips; and those regular excursions to South America and Africa would have provided a welcome release after a cooling-off period in southern California. So why had Jonathan broken his pattern and started killing close to home? It had to be because of Jimmy. *Look at me, look at me.* Well, Jimmy was still looking, and he still wasn't sure. He'd feel better when ATM came up with a photo of Jonathan at the Laguna Beach crime scene. He'd feel better when Pilar came up with a series of unexplained murders that coincided with Jonathan's outreach work. He'd feel better when he *knew.*

Blaine was moving faster now, trying to maintain position as the shotgun tilted further and further off vertical.

Jimmy dove for the floor as the shotgun went off. He lifted his head and saw a fist-sized hole in the far wall, plaster drifting down.

Blaine picked up the shotgun, mouthing "Sorry" to Pilar, who glared at him from across the room.

Jimmy stood up, took the shotgun from Blaine, and laid it on the coffee table. There wasn't much on television, but he kept flipping through the channels anyway, finally finding a Bugs Bunny cartoon. Blaine sat beside him on the couch, hunched forward, laughing at that wascally wabbit as he ran from the voracious Tasmanian devil, keeping one step ahead of him all the time.

Pilar snapped shut her phone as Jimmy stood up. "The Cervaca police do not keep such good records, but Sergeant Enriquez said if I called him tomorrow he might know more." She smiled. "He wants me to tell him what I am wearing the next time we speak."

"Cervaca is a glorified fishing village," said Jimmy. "How many unsolved murders could there be there?"

Pilar shook her head. "You betray your ignorance, my spoiled gringo. The police station in Cervaca probably has no air conditioning, no computer, no medical examiner, no microscope, no ballistics lab, not even any fingerprint powder. In all likelihood the officers supply their own pistols and bullets. I made it clear to Sergeant

Enriquez that I was not interested in crimes of love or theft or vengeance; I told him that the man we are looking for is someone who kills in more . . . *gentle* ways."

Jimmy swallowed. He hadn't told her about the Eggman connection.

"I asked the sergeant to see if there had been any such killings during those two weeks," said Pilar. "After I am done with my own business, I will make more calls for you."

"Thanks, Pilar."

"You gonna stick around, Jimmy?" asked Blaine, still glued to the television.

"I have a screening this afternoon," said Jimmy, taking in the Roadrunner cartoon Blaine was watching. *"Beep-beep."*

"Beep-beep, dude."

Chapter 30

Gene and Hector, the two clerks behind the counter at Scarecrow Video, stopped their arguing as soon as Macklen appeared in the doorway of the small shop.

"Treasure Island." said Hector, scoring first.

"I'm looking for the manager," said Macklen, swinging forward on his crutches.

The place was stacked with obscure videos, laser disks, and DVDs, the aisles organized into sections like "Nazi Zombies," "Beach Blanket Babe-O-Rama," "Psycho Killers," "Mythic Cowboys," "Children with Strange Powers," and "Lawyers in Love." Every inch of wall space was covered with movie posters—war movies with guns bristling, cheesy fifties sci-fi classics, Victor Mature gladiator epics, and, at the very center, like the Virgin of Guadeloupe, Marilyn Monroe in *The Seven Year Itch,* skirts flying.

"Rear Window," responded Gene, a bored, scrawny teenager in shorts and a Ren & Stimpy T-shirt, his glasses so thick he could start a forest fire just walking outside into the sunshine. No danger of that, though.

"My Left Foot," said Hector, a chubby, tie-dyed fifty-year-old, his long hair streaked with gray.

"Dr. Strangelove," said Gene.

Macklen pivoted closer. "You both deaf or retarded, which one is it?"

"People versus Larry Flynt," said Hector.

Gene yawned. *"Sunrise at Campobello."*

". . . Witness for the Prosecution," said Hector.

Gene caught the hesitation in Hector's voice and pounced. *"Whatever Happened to Baby Jane?"*

Macklen stood in front of them now, muscles bulging against his bright-orange bowling shirt, the pins stitched on the yoke jumping as though he had just rolled a strike. There was a time when he had used that move to amuse the ladies, make them laugh, loosen up their panties. Nowadays he couldn't even get two morons like these guys to pay attention to him. Well, it still cracked up Great White.

"The Man Who Came to Dinner," said Hector.

"It's a Wonderful Life," said Gene.

Hector chewed his lip. "Challenge that."

Gene laconically cleaned his glasses with the tail of his T-shirt. "Mr. Potter, dipshit."

Hector smacked himself in the forehead.

"Winner and *still* champion," said Gene as Hector waddled over to the candy machine to pay up.

"Yeah, hippie, you look like a winner," said Macklen. "You know a kid named Rollo?"

Gene took the roll of Starbursts from Hector, unwrapped the end.

"I'm looking for Rollo," said Macklen.

"Welcome to the club," said Gene, chewing with his mouth open, showing off his braces. "Dude's got six overdue DVDs."

Macklen reached into his jacket and tossed the six DVDs onto the counter. "I found these at Rollo's place with your sticker on them. Looked like he was a regular customer."

Gene stacked the DVDs. "We loan Rollo tapes and whatever else he wants. He's going to make a film about us. Like *Clerks,* only better."

"Like *High Fidelity,* only better," countered Hector. "It's gonna be called *Please Rewind.*"

"Please Rewind, Asshole," corrected Gene.

"You have any idea where I might find Rollo?" said Macklen, trying to sound cheerful.

Gene leaned across the counter. "Does he owe you money? Because if he does, that don't make you special."

"Being overextended is an artistic prerogative," offered Hector. "Sam Peckinpah never carried cash, either."

"Francis Ford Coppola went bankrupt on *One from the Heart*," said Gene.

"Don't start that shit up again," warned Macklen, swinging gently back and forth, trying to restrain himself from turning these two idiots into hamburger. "Rollo came to me with a business proposition for this film he wanted to make, and I want to give him the go-ahead. Got the cashier's check right here in my wallet."

"Rollo got a go-ahead?" said Gene. "Awesome."

Hector nodded at Macklen. "Festus here is trippin'," he said to Gene. "Rollo is brilliant, but there's no commercial potential in documentaries."

"I don't know brilliant from bullshit, *slick*," growled Macklen. "I'm just looking for a tax deduction."

"Told you Rollo would hit it big someday," Gene said to Hector. "*Man of La Mancha*."

"*Rocky*," responded Hector.

Macklen whacked his cane on the counter, smashing a stack of DVDs. "Speak English, goddammit!"

The two clerks backed up against the poster of the Hammer version of *The Mummy*, the mummy catching a gunshot through the midsection in a shower of bandages.

"I need to find Rollo." The bowling pins were dancing on Macklen's shirt again.

Hector sniffed. "I guess you already tried his place in Huntington Beach."

"Good guess." Macklen leaned on one cane, twirling the other one. "Maybe you two geniuses should put on your thinking caps, screw them on good and tight, and see what you come up with."

"He had a place somewhere out in the boonies, didn't he, Gene?" asked Hector, watching the cane. "Some ratty-assed trailer park. I thought you gave him a ride one day when his car broke down."

"Maybe I did, maybe I didn't." Gene showed Macklen his braces. "If you're looking for a tax deduction, I got a few scripts of my own you might be interested in, mister."

Macklen moved closer. "Where exactly was this trailer park?"

Chapter 31

"This *already* sucks donkey dicks," whispered Rollo, barely waiting for the credits to roll.

"There's my lead," said Jimmy, settling back into the cushiony seats of the executive screening room. " 'Chaz Presley's *The Last Caper* sucks donkey dicks.' Now I can relax and enjoy the rest of the movie."

"Shhhh," hissed Carlotti, the reviewer from the *L.A. Weekly,* who was bent over a few rows away, scribbling notes with his light pen in the dark, a junket whore in a red nylon Planet Hollywood jacket.

Rollo bounced a Milk Dud off Carlotti's head. "We should bag this and scoop up some Jet Li vids at Scarecrow, Jimmy. There's a player at ChromoGenesis we can use—I'll show you the Azure-Blue Room."

"Can't do it. I've got an interview with Chaz this week, and I have to say something about his new movie."

"*Chaz?* What are you, buddies now?"

Jimmy watched the action onscreen, not really paying attention. He had placed another call to the surgical unit at Newport Hills Hospital but still hadn't gotten any specifics on when Jonathan had finished operating that Sunday night. ATM hadn't called him, either. The power of the press was a wonder to behold.

Chaz Presley slithered along a narrow air duct in a tight leather bodysuit, his sculpted pectorals popping. An unexplained key light limned his cheekbones, making the sweat beads shine.

"Ten minutes before we see him in his underwear," said Rollo. "Ten minutes and he flashes the six-pack."

Chaz Presley worked his way through the high-tech security systems of the Getty Museum, inching his way toward the Ellison Diamond, "the world's largest blue flawless." Over the next 144 minutes the diamond would be stolen, fought over, and recovered, and a fake substituted, in a series of razzle-dazzle moves so complicated that even the players wouldn't be sure where the real gem was. The movie would gross 150 million domestic, minimum.

"You *sure* Pilar told you she was going to leave me alone?" said Rollo.

"That's what she said."

"Yeah, well I called my place in Huntington this morning, and somebody was there." Rollo turned around, glanced at the exit, reassuring himself. "I got my answering machine set up to monitor the place, and I heard noises."

"Pilar is probably just being careful. I'll cash Napitano's check and pay her a visit tomorrow."

"Why don't you pick up a new cell phone, too? I tried you four or five times this morning before getting through."

"Any other requests?"

"Yeah, I'd like Madonna to stop making movies." Rollo shook the last of the Milk Duds into his open mouth. "You want to go by Scarecrow *later?* After sitting through this epic of modern cinema, I'm going to need something good to watch. Gene and Hector said they had some *Citizen Kane* outtakes coming in."

"Can't do it. I need to check in on a guy I met on Saturday, a photographer."

Rollo shifted in his seat. "Jimmy, I just want to say, about Pilar . . ."

"I know. If I ever need a kidney—"

"I'll steal you one, man, no kidding."

Jimmy watched Chaz Presley slip on a pair of goggles that allowed him to see the gridwork laser security system in the room below. No wonder everyone loved techno-thrillers. Every plan was as complicated as possible, allowing an infinite variety of cool poses and computer-generated effects, yet in the end, all you really needed to succeed was the right hardware and the right haircut. Jimmy knew better. In reality, the two most important requirements in committing a crime were a simple plan and a lack of concern with the consequences of failure. Jimmy had taken down Macklen and the VC Boyz with two military-surplus flash-bang grenades and a fuck-it attitude.

Chaz Presley removed the grille of the air duct and dropped a thin nylon cord to the case where the diamond rested. He had just squeezed himself through the duct when a drop of sweat rolled off his nose and fell in slow motion, just missing one of the infrared laser beams below. Chaz Presley pulled himself back into the air shaft, wiped his brow, then peeled off the stifling black leather jumpsuit and gracefully lowered himself down the nylon cord to the diamond, wearing only his skimpy white underwear.

Rollo threw a hand up into the air. "Six-pack!"

"Do you *mind?*" hissed Carlotti.

Chaz Presley hovered upside down over the diamond, totally controlled, fearless. Must be what they called star power. The night Jimmy had ripped off Macklen, Johnny Cash's greatest hits were pounding out from the sound system—even today he couldn't hear "Ring of Fire" without feeling his knees shake.

Jimmy and Rollo had waited in Rollo's van, parked down the street from the Rhinestone Cowboy, as the Big Orange Arena was called then. Jimmy watched from the passenger seat while Rollo fidgeted, asking over and over if Jimmy was really sure he wanted to do this dumb-ass thing. It was a good question.

Tran, the waiter at the Nha Trang Café, had told Jimmy that every time the VC Boyz made a score, they celebrated at the café, demanding the best of everything, threatening the staff and customers. They would pull wads of cash out of their pockets and play cards until three or four in the morning while the cooks waited. Sometimes the VC Boyz would just barge through the door and start giving or-

ders, but when Claude wanted imperial duck, a dish that took eight hours to prepare properly, he would call Tran earlier in the day. So that was when Tran called Jimmy, his voice so hushed that Jimmy could barely hear him. Jimmy had staked out the Rhinestone Cowboy twice after the calls, and both times the VC Boyz had shown up and been ushered into Macklen's office. The third time Tran called him, Jimmy tagged Rollo, told him it was show time.

"You sure?" said Rollo. "Maybe they're not—"

Jimmy held up a hand as he spotted the three VC Boyz turning the corner—he was out of the van, walking fast, as they strutted toward the front entrance, taking their time, black hair lacquered high and wide as winged war helmets. One of them carried a briefcase. They pushed their way past the bouncers as if they owned the joint, Claude, the kid who had cleaned out Jimmy's sinuses with the chopsticks, slapping aside a moonlighting UC Fullerton football player twice his size.

Jimmy turned into the alley beside the Rhinestone Cowboy, popped off the window grating he had unscrewed earlier that day, and slipped inside. He made his way toward the office in the semi-darkness, the country band on stage sawing away about a woman in tight blue jeans.

Jimmy stood in the shadows watching Claude slouch outside the door to Macklen's office, imagining that at any minute he would feel Great White grab him by the throat, or Claude, jacked up on glue and with all kinds of sharp objects at his disposal. Jimmy shivered, his fingers so cold they felt carved from ice. Still time to back out, but he knew he wasn't leaving. Not yet.

Macklen had killed Samuel Terrell and gotten away with it. The law couldn't touch him, but Jimmy could. If he was willing to take the risks, that is—and there were all kinds of risks, some you could see and some you couldn't. Jimmy had run over the same argument with himself ever since Desmond had told him there was nothing the police could do. Sometimes he wished he had never met Samuel Terrell. He wished he had passed by that parked car, gone upstairs, and *slid into bed. He would have looked out his window a few days later, seen all the cop cars, and wondered what had happened.*

The Johnny Cash cover band was still going down, down, down in a burning ring of fire, but Jimmy wasn't paying attention to any-thing but Claude smoking a cigarette, holding it between his thumb and forefinger, Continental-style, checking out the cowgirls. Claude always stayed outside, on guard, while the other two conducted busi-ness inside. Always. He watched Claude reach into his jacket, adjust the gun in his waistband. Still time to back out, Jimmy.

Jimmy slowly exhaled. You could come up with a plan, work it all out, even do a couple of dry runs, but the reality was that at some point you either did the deed or went home and made excuses for yourself. Jimmy called Rollo on his cell phone. Rollo was already in position, waiting for the call, probably still hoping Jimmy would say "Game called on account of coming to my senses." Instead what he heard was "Let's do it."

"Yeah, you and Gary Gilmore," said Rollo. "You sure?"

Jimmy snapped the phone shut, put his hands in his jacket, felt the two flash-bang grenades, five-inch white cylinders made of com-pressed paper and loaded with black powder. Rollo had gotten the grenades from a customer in the National Guard, traded him a video camera for them—they were strictly limited to military and police use, 145 decibels loud and blinding, but nonlethal, designed only to stun and disorient. He slipped past the crowd and moved closer.

Every light in the Rhinestone Cowboy suddenly went out as Rollo cut the power, the speakers dying in a flare of static. The crowd stirred behind him in the sudden silence, complaining but not panicking. That was good. Jimmy already had his gloves on. In the darkness he put in his earplugs, then pulled the fuse cord on the grenade, count-ing to himself. He had four and a half seconds.

Claude flicked his lighter and held it aloft, pounding on the office door. His cigarette had fallen from his mouth, the tip glowing on the floor.

The door swung open, and Jimmy glimpsed Great White filling the doorway. He tossed the grenade, trying it throw it into the office, but it bounced off Great White's shoulder and landed at his feet. Which was just as well. Jimmy shielded his eyes as the grenade exploded in a burst of white light, knocking Great White backward into the office. He could hear Claude stumbling in the dark, cursing loudly as tiny bits of burning paper from the grenade floated down around him like fireflies.

There were screams coming from the auditorium now in response to the explosion, people shouting and the sound of tables being over-turned. One of the fire doors was thrown open, then another, the crowd surging toward the luminescent Exit signs.

Jimmy pulled on a ski mask. His heart was pounding so loudly he thought his chest was going to burst. Fuck it. He flicked on the flash-light, ran forward, and tossed the second grenade into the office, then slammed the door. The blast buckled the heavy wood. Still stunned from the blast, Claude slumped against the wall, struggling to get up. Jimmy sucker-punched him, grabbed the pistol from his belt, and kicked the office door off its one remaining hinge.

One look inside and Jimmy realized he didn't need the mask—no one in that room could see or hear a thing. Macklen and the two other VC Boyz were sprawled on the floor, dazed, white smoke and specks of flaming confetti drifting on the air currents. Great White was bent over gagging, blood pouring from his ears and nose, his eyebrows singed off.

Jimmy took a deep breath and walked right past Great White, the flashlight barely illuminating the smoke, the pistol in his hand. No fear now, no trembling; he knew what he was doing. The briefcase was open on the desk, stacked high with small metallic rectangles. Jimmy had no idea what they were. He didn't care. He pointed the gun at Macklen's chest while Macklen coughed, still blind.

Shoot, Jimmy. This is what you came for. Three quick shots to the chest and back out the door. Three shots for Macklen, then toss the pistol on the floor and slip away. Let the cops sort it out.

One of the VC Boyz was on his hands and knees feeling around on the floor for his gun, and getting close, too. The flash grenade had set Great White's circus drawings on fire, lions and tigers burning in the night. Macklen swayed, ribbons of snot running down his face, helpless, caught in the beam of Jimmy's flashlight.

Kill him, Jimmy. Do it. What are you here for if not to kill him? The pistol trembled in his hand. Jimmy heard a noise behind him, turned, and saw Claude in the door frame, calling out in Vietnamese. The only word Jimmy recognized was Macklen's name being shouted over and over. Jimmy turned back to Macklen. *Do it!* Jimmy dropped the pistol instead. He had never been so disappointed in himself. He stared at Macklen, then stepped to the desk, snapped the briefcase shut, and started for the door, imagining what the VC Boyz would say when the smoke cleared and their goods were gone.

Claude was screaming, a high-pitched, angry shriek, as he fumbled his way into the room. He had a gun now—a guy like him would always have a backup, just like in the movies. His gun hand swiveled back and forth, random movements searching for a target, and Jimmy thought of the waving antennae of the live lobsters in the tank at the Nha Trang Café.

One of the other VC Boyz suddenly answered in Vietnamese, and Claude stepped forward, blinking, inches from Jimmy. He fired several shots rapid-fire from his semiauto, spraying the room. Jimmy's ears rang even with the earplugs, but he wasn't hit. One of the other VC Boyz stood very still for a moment, lips moving silently as blood gushed from a hole in his throat. Macklen cursed, banging into his desk in his haste. Great White had gotten to his feet and was rubbing at his eyes. Jimmy's flashlight made the smoke in the room glow, eddies of light in the darkness swirling around them all. Macklen had managed to get one of his desk drawers open, and he pulled out a gun; he held it close to him, shouting for Great White.

Jimmy edged past Claude, being careful not to touch him, but Claude must have sensed his presence, and turned toward him. Jimmy hit him with the briefcase. Bullets slammed into the wall nearby, and Jimmy could see Macklen peering at them, still half blind. Jimmy shined the flashlight in Macklen's face, made him squint, and Claude saw the light and advanced toward it, firing with

every step. Jimmy saw Macklen get hit at least twice, the bullets mak-
ing a dull thud, Macklen grunting at the impact. Jimmy kept the
light on him as Macklen leaned back against the desk, a movement
that looked more casual than pained. Then Great White launched
himself at Claude, fists flailing, and Jimmy backed into the doorway,
turned, and ran toward the Exit sign. He heard more gunshots be-
hind him.

The machine gun–fire onscreen jolted Jimmy back to the screening room, automatic weapons opening up in full Dolby, even louder
than the real thing. He looked over and saw that Rollo was sound
asleep, Chaz Presley reflected in the kid's glasses, our hero driving a
red Ferrari convertible through a series of explosions, not a hair out
of place.

Jimmy checked his watch. When *The Last Caper* was over he
would drive to ATM's place, hoping to find out the truth about Jonathan, while at the same time hoping that no one would ever find out
the truth about *him*. So he wasn't going to get the Moral Consistency
merit badge. Tough. He looked over, heard Rollo gently snoring. If
Jimmy had had a blanket, he would have covered the kid with it.
That had to count for something.

Chapter 32

"What are you doing here, pilgrim?" ATM slouched in the doorway of his apartment.

"You were supposed to call me when you found Jonathan's photo."

ATM sucked on a McDonald's milkshake. "Who's Jonathan?"

"The man on the Laguna bluffs."

"That's his name?" ATM held up the milkshake. "You want some?"

"I'm in a hurry."

"Yeah, I've been busy myself. I staked out the Viper Lounge last night and nailed everyone that walked out. Stars puking, that's big money—*tabloid* money."

"Why don't we get started? I'll help you look through your negatives."

"I already printed them up, but you should relax, pilgrim, you're going to give yourself an ulcer." ATM burped into his fist, his greasy braids flying like ropes around a maypole as he ushered Jimmy inside. "You sure you don't want some milkshake?" He sucked noisily on the straw. "Chocolate shake with three spoonfuls of milk of magnesia. Give you a dump make you feel like you died and went to heaven."

"We have very different visions of the afterlife," said Jimmy, stepping over the piles of dirty clothes and open-mouthed pizza cartons that littered the living room.

"I got a call from the art director at *SLAP* this morning. You move fast."

"I told you I'd take care of it."

"People tell me they're going to do things all the time." ATM tossed the milkshake toward a garbage bag and missed, ice cream spraying the wall. He parted the heavy blackout curtains where the bedroom door used to be, held them open for Jimmy. "Most of them don't do anything but talk."

Jimmy looked around ATM's bedroom, amazed at the sense of order. Stainless steel tables ran along the walls, with photographs arranged in neat grids on top and file cabinets underneath. Clotheslines crisscrossed the room at regular intervals, holding dozens of color and black-and-white prints dangling from clips. A fluorescent light table glowed with color slides and transparencies, while an air filter hummed away in the far corner. Every surface was immaculate, the floor scrubbed to a high gloss. The lightproof door to the bathroom was open, a state-of-the-art developer and enlarger filling the small room.

"I got to move my developing trays to use the crapper," said ATM, nodding at the bathroom. "That's what you were asking yourself, right?"

Jimmy walked over to one of the clotheslines and plucked off a black-and-white print. It was one of the photos ATM had taken on Saturday evening, shot through the cracked windshield of the Honda, the woman's face embossed with jagged lines.

"That was some ride," said ATM. "You drive pretty good, but I thought you were going to blow your lunch when you saw this chick—they don't make enough thread to stitch something like that back together."

Jimmy clipped the photo back.

They had come onto the accident site suddenly, a three-car pileup just around a curve, Jimmy slamming on the brakes, the Saab fishtailing as he fought for control, one of the cops jumping behind his cruiser for cover. The cop had come at them as soon as Jimmy turned off the ignition, his weapon drawn, but ATM had just leapt out, waving his press pass from the Golden Globes, and started taking pictures, keeping up a running banter with the cop, taking his photo with the wreckage in the background, promising him a copy for his wife. The cop said he wasn't married, but ATM just flopped down on the pavement for another shot, right there in the broken glass and road grease, and said he'd make it a half dozen prints for the cop's girlfriends.

It had been quite a performance, ATM chatting up the ambulance drivers, talking trash about movie stars he had caught with their pants and their panties down, pushing himself closer and closer to the action. At one point he'd leaned his head into the window of a burning Volkswagen, and one of his braids had caught fire, but he'd just stuck his smoldering hair in his mouth and kept shooting. ATM was fearless and professional, but all Jimmy could think of was the woman in the Honda, and the sound of a kid screaming from somewhere.

"Where're the photos you took at Laguna?" asked Jimmy.

"Hang on," said ATM, squatting down beside the file cabinets, opening drawers. "I've got them here somewhere." He slid one drawer back in, pulled out another.

Jimmy ignored most of the color prints; the images of the victims were too real for him, but there were other photos ATM had taken, black-and-white shots that worked as pure composition rather than horror show: a pool of black blood shimmering in the road flares, a close-up of a broken taillight that was a maw of jagged plastic, a dented hubcap that evoked a ruined dream.

"No commercial potential," said ATM, nodding at the black-and-whites as he walked over with a folder in his hand, "but I got to do *something* for myself." He pushed his braids back, beckoned Jimmy to where he had fanned out a stack of color prints on one of the tables.

Jimmy had to restrain himself from tearing into them and instead content himself with crowding the table. It had been beautiful that morning in Laguna when they found Philip Kinneson on the beach, the sky a cloudless blue, the ocean a dark green—the perfect backdrop to the lookie-loos watching the murder scene from the bluffs.

"Check the happy couple here." ATM flicked the top photo—two gorgeous, golden Californians posing for the camera, the wind blowing the woman's long hair around her shoulder, the man with the brainless, angular features of a model in a fuck-'em-and-forget-'em perfume ad. "These two didn't stay long. The girl said she couldn't see the blood from so far away."

The next photo showed an enormous woman in a paisley print dress leaning over the railing, looking annoyed at the skinny man standing next to her.

"That lady was pissed off because her husband kept saying they were going to be late for his doctor's appointment, and she wanted to stay longer." ATM sucked on his teeth. "Can't blame her—she wasn't the one coughing up green sludge."

Jimmy spread the photos around, but he didn't see Jonathan. "Where is he?"

ATM tapped one of the photos. "You blind or something?"

A pale, slender man stared directly into the camera, his eyes wide, a serious expression on his face. "That's not Jonathan." There was a resemblance, but Jimmy was sure.

"Look at him, that's the whitest man I ever seen."

"That's a fucking tourist. Jonathan is *white*. You said you recognized him from the photograph I showed you."

"I said I thought he looked familiar. Hey, it was a year ago, and I've been busy."

Jimmy remembered his own behavior at the opera on Saturday, loud and cocky, so eager to believe the worst about Jonathan that he hadn't even waited for the evidence. All he had done was convict himself of being the jealous loser that Jonathan said he was.

"I wasn't ripping you off," said ATM. "I really thought this was your guy."

"You said he didn't want his picture taken." Jimmy waved the photo of the tourist in ATM's face. "This guy is looking right at the camera."

ATM rifled through the rest of the photos from the bluff. "*This* is the one I was thinking of." He held out a photo of a muscular young skinhead in a tank top and cammie pants, his arms tattooed from wrist to elbow. "This is the asshole who didn't want to be photographed. I got him and the tourist mixed up. Sorry."

Jimmy took the photo. The skinhead rested his hands on a low chain-link fence, staring at something below the frame, and though his face was in profile, it was clear that he was enjoying whatever it was he was watching.

"He threatened to throw me over the side if I took his picture," said ATM. "Kept asking me if I was a faggot and if I wanted to join my faggot buddy on the beach."

"He said the guy on the beach was a faggot?"

"Yeah. He had a real thing about gays."

"Do you know his name?"

"Sure. He gave me his shoe size, too."

Great White probably knew the skinhead by name, rank, and serial number, but Jimmy was in no hurry to see *him*. Maybe Holt would have better luck. She wasn't going to like what the photo suggested—a skinhead's enjoying the view of the crime scene jibed with her lieutenant's gay-bashing scenario—but she would follow up on it anyway. If it turned out that the Eggman letter really had been a hoax, then so be it. She and Jimmy could be disappointed together. "Can I take this?"

"Go ahead, but I got my copyright stamp on the back of it. It sees print, I see green." ATM looked at Jimmy. "What's wrong, pilgrim? You still pissed off that I don't have a glossy of this Jonathan you're looking for?"

"A little." Jimmy shrugged. "I should be happy you don't."

"You don't *look* happy."

"I've got a dirty mind, ATM."

ATM burped. "Heck, as long as it don't show, who cares?"

Chapter 33

Holt eyed Jonathan's penis—what she could see of it, anyway. Most of it was in the blonde's mouth. Jonathan's head was thrown back, his face contorted, and she found herself wondering what he was saying. If he was saying anything at all.

During her mercifully brief stint in Sex Crimes, she had learned that the vast majority of men who frequented prostitutes were interested in oral sex rather than intercourse. When her sergeant had asked her why she thought this was so, she had answered that it was probably a matter of convenience, since oral sex could be performed in the front seat of a car, without the john's even having to remove his pants. The sergeant had laughed and shared her answer with a couple of other vice cops, who found it equally hilarious. "You haven't ever been married, have you, Jane?" he had asked. She hadn't, of course. "Well, Jane," said the sergeant, draping a burly arm around her shoulders, "most married men haven't had a good-to-the-last-drop blow job since their honeymoons. They pick up a working girl . . . well, you do the math."

Yet Jonathan had kept a stack of secret Polaroids, photos of himself being fellated by dozens of different women, and he had been married less than one year. What did that do to the sergeant's theory? Holt reached for her glass, but she had already finished her martini. Her fourth. Or was it her fifth? Oh, well, it wasn't as if she had to get up and go to work in the morning. Suspended. Interesting nomenclature—she saw herself dangling over a precipice with rocks far below, hanging there by a rapidly unraveling rope . . . which was her career. Easy on the self-pity, Jane.

Holt hunched over the worktable in her converted second bedroom, the windows blacked out to prohibit the distraction of her million-dollar view. One whole wall was cork-boarded, covered with dozens of photographs neatly lined up—Philip Kinneson, Denise Fredericks, William Hallberg, Carlos Mendoza, Elice Santos, Steve DeGerra—crime-scene and autopsy photos, the images duplicated and arranged into different patterns: chronological, geographical, ballistic, forensic. In her file cabinets she had complete background workups on the victims and a series of photographs taken, at her insistence, from the epicenter of every crime scene, a complete 360-degree view, so she could see everything the victim and the killer had seen. Every detective kept a murder book of each homicide he or she was working, complete with photos and diagrams, witness statements and autopsy reports; Holt just had the luxury of floor space.

She peered again at the blonde's full lips, then brought the Polaroid closer, trying to gauge the size of Jonathan's equipment. Men were so concerned about size. Holt giggled, thinking, They should be. The Polaroid blurred, and she blinked the image back into focus, saw Jonathan's face, his smile twisted in some sort of terrible pleasure, and she remembered him last week at the French restaurant, confessing that he had always felt overshadowed and intimidated by his brother, and she marveled at all the coexisting aspects of a human being: dominance and submission, arrogance and humility. It was a wonder that any of us could walk around without bumping into our own contradictions.

The fellatio Polaroid shook in her hand. Thanks to Holt, Maria Sinoa had gotten her first reprimand in thirty-two years on the job, but Sinoa had examined the Polaroid anyway, examined it in direct violation of Dr. Chakabarti's orders, trying to match it against the microscopic striations of the Laguna Polaroid found on the beach. Holt laid the fellatio Polaroid back on the table, embarrassed at her own interest now that there was no longer even the veneer of evidentiary potential to justify her staring. No need to keep it in a plastic envelope anymore. No need to keep it at all. Maria Sinoa had called from the forensics lab this morning to tell her the results. "I am sorry, Jane, there is no match," Maria had said. So am I, Maria, Holt thought.

She flipped through the dossier she had started on Jonthan Gage. It wasn't much—crammed with professional accomplishments but thin on personal details. Serial killers were formed in childhood, the signs apparent in retrospect, but Holt had been too busy over the last few days to interview the neighbors who had watched Jonathan grow up, the elementary school teachers and Little League coaches who might have seen something telling. If there had been a match with the Laguna Polaroid, she would have eagerly put aside everything else to follow it up, but with no match, what was the point?

Holt tossed down Jonathan's folder, and it landed beside Jimmy's own, thicker file, that one filled with arrest reports, financial documents, and phone records. She had reread the whole thing after talking with Jonathan, troubled by his suggestions of jealousy and violence in Jimmy's background, wondering what else she had missed in her initial investigation. She had read it again after talking with Michelle Fairfield on Friday morning.

She started for the kitchen and stumbled against a chair, felt annoyed at her clumsiness. She sat down, the room spinning around her. Maybe she would just stay here for a little while longer. She spent most of her time in here anyway. Eric had called it the chamber of horrors, which was remarkably narrow-minded of him, and dismissive of her work. She didn't miss him—hardly ever, anyway, just on Sunday mornings when she woke up alone and didn't have anyone to read the paper or argue politics with. In spite of what her mother said, her standards were *not* too high. All she wanted in a man was a good kisser who would massage her feet once in a while and not ask her what she was thinking, not ever. Was that too much to ask for? She rubbed her eyes. Evidently it was.

Holt scanned the notes and crime-scene photographs that covered her walls, and admitted to herself that sometimes the room *did* look like a chamber of horrors. The Eggman task force had looked for connections between the separate homicides, commonalities that would indicate something about the killer—a consistent victim profile, a favorite locale or identical method of homicide, some kind of *signature*. If the Eggman had a signature, though, it had been written in disappearing ink.

The victims were of all races and genders and ranged in age and life-style from a seventeen-year-old track star to a sixty-three-year-old retired short-order cook. The crime scenes included a public beach, a barrio sidewalk, and the alley of a yuppie suburb. The homicides were all committed after dark, but the time of death varied from early evening to just before dawn. There were no footprints or fingerprints, no traces of fiber evidence, no tire tracks, no signs of sexual assault or mutilation, no personal items taken.

In short, there was no common thread linking the murders other than the fact that the victims had all been shot once in the head with a thirty-eight-caliber revolver. At last count there were 23,455 registered thirty-eight revolvers in Orange and Los Angeles counties, and probably twice that many unregistered. If it hadn't been for the letter Jimmy Gage received from the Eggman, the police would never have even thought the crimes were connected.

The other five detectives on the task force had been skeptical of the Eggman letter, their joint investigation driven more by Holt's enthusiasm and the prodding of the media than by anything else. The letter sounded right—the braggadocio, the wounded pride, and the implicit threat that the writer would start killing again were all typical of the breed—but as the FBI profiler had pointed out, serial killers had become a mainstay of the film and book industries. Anyone with a library card and a sick sense of humor could have written the letter.

Even if they dismissed the letter, Holt had argued, there was still ballistic evidence: each of the six victims had been shot with Glaser safety slugs, a brand of what was commonly called explosive bullets, highly frangible rounds that shattered on impact. A ballistics match was impossible with Glasers because there was simply never enough of them left to match with other slugs from similar crimes, but their use itself was a definite signature, Holt had said. Frangible rounds cost two to three times more than hollow points and were not widely used in street crimes. Six different homicides committed within a couple of weeks, all with frangibles, all with a single shot—there had to be a connection.

It was Imeki who had sunk her theory. Holt had assumed operational command of the task force, but Lieutenant Carolyn Imeki, representing the Sheriff's Department, had final authority. Imeki had held back during the first month, letting Holt stick her neck out, waiting to see if there was credit to be claimed before making her move. But then, on a sunny, perfect California day, Imeki had shut down the task force, and she had loved doing it.

Holt had walked in to the weekly meeting five minutes late, apologizing for having been caught in traffic on her way from Laguna. Imeki sat in her usual seat at the head of the table—a huge woman, half Samoan, moonfaced and aggressive, her big hands folded in her lap now—but when Holt saw that she was smiling, she knew she was in trouble. The other detectives avoided looking at her, confirming her suspicion.

In front of each of the detectives was an issue of Handgun Fanatic *magazine, the cover showing a busty, half-naked woman cradling a forty-four magnum with both hands. Holt had never seen the magazine, never even heard of it. She sat down, picked up her copy, and opened to where it had been marked with a paper clip. "Killer Rounds: The Ultimate Terminator," was the headline, the article detailing the one-shot stopping power of Glaser safety slugs.*

"Notice the date of issue, Jane." Imeki didn't even wait for Holt to look. "Two months before your Eggman killings started. I did a little research—that's what we're paid for, you know—and there were two thousand four hundred and fifty-five copies of this particular issue of Handgun Fanatic *sold in Orange County. That's newsstand sales; subscription sales were three hundred twelve." She was twiddling her*

thumbs now. "There is no Eggman, people—what we have here is a sales spike, not a serial killer. A few thousand gun studs read the article, pass it around, and then run out and buy a box of Glasers. Over the course of the next couple of months, anybody who wants to waste somebody uses the bullet du jour. The Eggman's half dozen was just the tip of the spike, until the bad boys moved back to their reliable, cheaper hollow points and copper jackets—"

"There wasn't any surge in sales for Glasers prior to the Eggman homicides," Holt interrupted. "I ran the figures myself."

"Gun shows and swap meets, Jane." Imeki yawned. "Completely unregulated and unreported."

"That's bullshit!"

"Let's keep this professional, shall we, Detective?" Imeki tapped her pencil on the desk, gaveling the room quiet. "I think we can now discount the use of Glasers in the six homicides under review as nothing more than a short-lived consumer preference. And as for the letter sent to Jimmy Gage, let's just call it a stunt by persons unknown."

"What about the Polaroid found near the Laguna crime scene?" Holt asked, too quickly, knowing it was already too late. "The FBI confirmed that it was shot with a flash—"

"Ah, yes, Detective Holt's wonderful Polaroid, the photograph that started this whole magical mystery tour." Imeki shared a chuckle with the lads. "I have no reason to doubt your conclusion that the individual who murdered Mr. Kinneson took that photograph, but Jane, you don't have to be a serial killer to document your work." She glanced around the table. "Kinneson was a homosexual, undoubtedly with many lovers, some of them quite jealous, I would imagine. Perhaps one of them killed Kinneson and took a last photo for a souvenir, or paid to have him killed and demanded the photo as proof of a job well done. If you want to find out who murdered Kinneson, Detective, you need to lay off the psychics and do some old-fashioned police work." She rapped the table. "Let's grab some lunch on the county."

Holt tore the copy of *Handgun Fanatic* off the wall, threw it against the opposite wall, and raked her hands across the photographs, ripping them off the corkboard, breaking a nail, not caring. She ran out of steam fast, breathing hard, her head throbbing. No more alcohol. She had told Jonathan that she didn't drink, and maybe that was a good idea. For a while, anyway. She bent down and picked up a color photo that had fallen to the floor, an eight-by-ten of Jimmy that she'd torn roughly down the center in her frustration, half his face hanging down, the other half visible. It was a *SLAP* publicity photo, Jimmy's smile crooked and knowing.

Holt's head ached so badly she could hear sirens. Jimmy's photo fell from her fingers and dropped back onto the floor. It wasn't sirens she was hearing, it was her doorbell. And not the security buzzer to the downstairs entrance, either: there was someone at her *apartment* door. No one had a key to her building. She had never even given one to Eric.

Holt walked carefully out of her murder room, gathering speed as the doorbell continued to ring. Her head felt like it was going to fall over her shoulders and roll down the hall, with her chasing after it. She glanced at her nine-millimeter semiauto in its clip-on holster lying on the kitchen counter, hesitated, then checked the peephole. Jimmy waved back at her.

Chapter 34

Holt stared at Jimmy through the peephole, still not sure he was really there. She glanced over at her purse, primped her hair in the mirror instead. Her eyes were bloodshot, but there was nothing she could do about that now. She opened the door. "How did you find out where I live?"

"Are you the lady of the house? I'm on a work-release program selling sides of range-fed beef. Could I put you down for a hundred pounds of T-bone, ma'am?"

"How did you get past the lobby?" demanded Holt, still feeling lightheaded.

"Can I come in?"

"It's late."

"I won't tell."

Holt reluctantly stepped back and ushered him inside, glancing up and down the hall before closing the door again. She caught Jimmy checking out the remnants of her dinner on the table, the barely touched chicken breast and broccoli with congealed cheese sauce.

"I always wondered what your place would look like." Jimmy strolled around the cluttered living room, checked out the view from the panoramic windows, and noted the fitness equipment crammed into the corner with a raised eyebrow.

"What can I do for you, Jimmy?"

Jimmy walked farther into the living room, stopping in front of the engraving of a wolverine that hung over the sofa, a plate from

John James Audubon's imperial folio *Viviparous Quadrupeds of North America*. The wolverine was exquisitely rendered in blacks and browns, its back arched, its teeth bared, the aggressive posture suggesting its tenacious, territorial nature. The Audubon engraving was the only thing she had asked for when she moved out of her parents' home. Jimmy jabbed a thumb at the beast. "One of your relatives?"

Under other circumstances Holt would have laughed, but right now she just wanted to sit down and drape a cool cloth over the back of her neck.

"I was at Gallery Inferno a few days ago—Cleo says hello." If Jimmy was anticipating a response, he didn't get one. "Why did you rush over to my place to see the Polaroids when you knew there were plenty of them on the market? You got me all worked up for nothing. I made a real asshole out of myself—twice."

"Are you going for three in a row?"

"Be nice, I brought you a present. Don't get excited, though, you're not going to like it."

That got Holt's attention, but Jimmy looked as if he were willing to wait her out. "Would you like a cup of coffee?" she offered.

Jimmy followed her into the kitchen and stood around while she ground beans and filled the coffeemaker with water. She was grateful to him for busying himself in the white-pine cabinets, checking out the spice rack, pretending not to notice while she gathered the empty extra-dry-martini cans and dropped them into the garbage under the sink.

It felt nice in that small kitchen, listening to the coffeemaker sputter and drip—domestic, somehow, without being like a Hallmark commercial. Holt wished they could just sit around drinking coffee and waiting for the sun to come up. Maybe play a little Scrabble. A pajama party between . . . friends. Blame it on the martinis, but she felt comfortable with him. She filled a couple of stoneware mugs, not asking if he wanted cream or sugar. She knew the way he liked it. She took a sip, winced, and saw him wince, too. "You said you brought me a present."

Jimmy put his coffee down, reached into his jacket, and handed her a color snapshot.

Holt held the photo. A skinhead leaned against a chain-link fence, staring off into the distance, his forearms so heavily tattooed that they looked blue. "Who's this?"

"It may be the man who murdered Philip Kinneson."

Holt leaned back against the counter, covering her sudden dizziness.

"I don't know if he did the deed, but I thought you should see it. The picture was taken from the bluffs overlooking the Laguna crime scene. There were a group of people up there watching you work, but the skinhead seemed particularly interested. He was also the only one who didn't want to have his picture taken."

"A lot of people don't like having their picture—"

"He was the first one there. The photographer wasn't even aware of the vantage point until he saw the skinhead watching. The other lookie-loos showed up later, but the skinhead knew right where he wanted to be."

Holt noted the man's casual posture in the photograph, the scars on his knuckles. Even with his face in profile, there was no mistaking the fact that he was enjoying himself.

"He knew Philip Kinneson was gay, and he wasn't a big fan of alternative life-styles, according to the guy who took the photo."

Holt hadn't known about Philip Kinneson's sexual orientation until she started her interviews later that morning, and the fact hadn't been publicized until the afternoon papers came out. Maybe the skinhead had just made a lucky guess about Philip Kinneson. Or maybe it *was* a gay-bashing, and Lieutenant Diefenbacher had been right all along.

"I'm still not ready to call the Eggman letter a hoax, but I figured you'd want to investigate. The photographer's name and phone number are on the back. He didn't have an ID on the skinhead."

"I wouldn't be surprised if this individual had been in the system before," Holt said, frowning at the photograph. "I'll fax this to a friend of mine in the OC gang unit tomorrow morning; they have a computerized tattoo registry that can pop a match in under a minute."

"You should be happy, then. If you get lucky, you'll have your killer."

"You should be happy, too. If this is our killer, it'll be a big story for you. Not as big as the Eggman, but you'll probably get your old job back."

"I already *have* my old job back." Jimmy watched her, and she watched him back, the kitchen getting smaller around them. "Do you have any more of those canned cocktails? We could toast our triumph."

Holt opened the refrigerator. "Dry martini, Manhattan, or Rob Roy?"

"Wow, a liquor cabinet straight out of *The Thin Man.*"

"I'm waiting."

"Rob Roy."

Holt started to pour the cocktail into a highball glass, but he gently took the can from her. Mr. Macho. She told herself she had already had more than enough, but she opened another extra-dry martini anyway. "Would you like to sit in the living room?" she asked.

"I like standing here better." Jimmy took a tentative sip, then a real swallow. "Feels like we're camping—a little cramped, but intimate, like being in an Airstream."

"Airstream?"

"An aluminum trailer. Classic Americana."

"Where you came from, perhaps." Holt bit her tongue. "I didn't mean it that way."

"No offense taken, Jane. I like me just fine."

"So do I." Holt looked away. She was *definitely* over her limit.

"Cleo said you borrowed every Eggman Polaroid she had, then returned them all a few days later—what were you looking for?"

"Don't spoil the moment."

"Are we *having* a moment, Jane?"

Holt's fingernail tapped out an answer on the crystal martini glass; she felt certain that he didn't know Morse code.

"Sorry, it's hard for me to let go," said Jimmy. "You should have seen me that night at the pool house, digging around in Jonathan's treasure box—curiosity, Jane, it may have killed the cat, but it didn't do me any good, either." He took another swallow of the Rob Roy. "I went overboard at the pool house, but *Saturday* night I really made an ass of myself. I showed up at this charity ball and essentially accused Jonathan of being the Eggman." He finished his drink and tossed the can across the room; Holt heard it clatter into the wastebasket. "You should have seen Olivia's face as the security guards escorted me out of the Opera House." He shook his head.

"Olivia wasn't right for you. I thought that the moment I met her at your old place in the Laguna hills." Holt caught herself, too late. "Not that it's any of my business."

"Anything else you want to get off your chest?"

Holt sipped her martini, let the cold alcohol burn its way down her throat, then set her glass down. She was done now. "I was put on administrative leave. I may be suspended. That's why I'm not going to be in the office tomorrow."

"What did you do?"

"It was my own fault. Lieutenant Diefenbacher ordered me to discontinue the Eggman investigation, and I didn't. What was worse, I lied to him about it. It falls under the general category of insubordination."

"Did Diefenbacher take away your badge and gun and put them in his desk? That's what they always do to Dirty Harry."

"No, I got to keep my badge and weapon."

"I'm sorry."

Holt nodded.

"Sorry you got caught."

Holt laughed first, then Jimmy laughed, and neither of them wanted to stop, but they had to come up for air eventually.

"You were right about the pool house, if that's any consolation,"

Jimmy said. "The Eggman Polaroids . . . I must have been seeing things. Jonathan was called into surgery the night before—"

"I know," said Holt. "There was an accident, a van full of kids rolled over. . . . It was terrible, from what I heard. I talked to the surgeons who assisted him: Jonathan didn't leave the table for over nine hours. He barely had time to change clothes before he got to the pool house the next morning. The Eggman photos never existed. It was dark . . . and you saw ghosts."

"I guess." Jimmy hesitated. "You talked to the surgeons directly?"

"Yes." Holt touched his shoulder. "If it makes you feel any better, Jonathan was wrong about you, too. He tried to warn me about you, said that you were dangerous, that you'd been expelled from high school for landing another student in the hospital. A football player."

"High school was a long time ago."

"Jonathan said he'd heard the football player was dating a girl who threw you over. He suggested that you were jealous and out of control . . . but I know what really happened. I talked to Michelle."

Jimmy tried to hide his surprise. "Michelle? She doesn't know anything."

Holt shook her head. "She found out last year. One of the football players confessed. She said she asked you about it at Jonathan's party, but you pretended not to know what she was talking about. Why would you do that?"

"It was a long time ago. Maybe I forgot."

Holt moved closer to him. He didn't step back. "Why didn't you go to the authorities when you heard Michelle was going to be attacked? Or to the principal?"

"The *principal?* The jock who ended up in the hospital was the first-string quarterback."

"You should have done something."

"I *did* do something," Jimmy snapped, his face flushed, and Holt realized why Jonathan thought he was dangerous: there was violence all around him. "I overheard them in the locker room," he said, quietly now. "One guy said they should put a paper bag over her head so they wouldn't have to look at her, but the quarterback said a flag would be better—they could fuck her for the land of the free and the home of the brave." He looked at Holt, and she couldn't have turned away even if she'd wanted to. "I couldn't let that happen."

"Three against one. Who did you think you were, Superman?"

"Yeah, well, I don't fight fair, Jane."

"I can see that. Did Jonathan know what the fight was really about?"

"I don't think so. My father and his attorney kept it quiet."

"I'm asking if Jonathan deliberately lied to me."

"I never talked to him about what happened. I never talked to anybody."

"It's nice to meet a man who can keep a secret." Holt said, maintaining eye contact. She had forgotten how long they had been standing there, inches apart. She took a deep breath. "Would you like to spend the night?"

Jimmy blinked.

"If you have to think about it—"

"I wouldn't want to take advantage of you, that's all."

Holt's laugh was clear and clean as a waterfall. "You couldn't if you tried."

Jimmy smiled. "Yes, Jane, I would like to spend the night."

"Good."

"Good," Jimmy agreed. He put his arms around her, not clutching at her, thank God, just resting his hands on her hips.

Holt kissed him. He tasted sweet from the Rob Roy, but the sadness that they shared, their private lost cause, that was the sweetest taste of all.

"That was . . . interesting," said Jimmy, candlelight flickering on his face.

" 'Interesting'?"

Jimmy kissed her again, caressed her throat with his fingertips, and she shivered. "I think we're both a little out of practice."

Holt threw her leg across his belly, enjoying the animal heat of him. "Are you still in love with Olivia?" She felt him pull back slightly. "The truth, Jimmy."

Jimmy propped himself up on one elbow. "It's over."

"That's not what I asked."

"I still love the woman I walked out on a year ago . . . but I don't know this new Olivia."

"If she left Jonathan, though, you'd want to see if there was still something there between you. You'd have to find out, wouldn't you?"

"That's right, I'd have to find out."

Holt straddled him. "I'm glad we can still be honest with each other. Sometimes that gets lost when people . . ." She felt him rise against her. "I just don't want there to be any misunderstandings."

Chapter 35

Rollo licked harder, but the guava frozen yogurt ran down his wrist, dripped onto his Desert Storm surplus cammie shorts. He glanced up, then suddenly downshifted, the VW van chugging as he pumped the brakes, trying to slow down, pumping harder now, the tires squealing as the van finally came to a stop halfway through the intersection.

Horns blared from all sides, and some fat bastard leaned out of his Volvo, screamed something, and gave Rollo the finger.

As Rollo gave it back to him, with a *twist,* the frozen-yogurt cone slipped out of his grasp and landed on his bare ankle, the cold yogurt dribbling down into his hightops. Rollo didn't care about the mess; he had the rough cut of *Coma Patient* stashed in the back of the van, every hour of it, along with a short he had completely forgotten about, an animated cartoon he had done in seventh grade, *Bipolar Disneyland.* That one had gotten him suspended. Like it had mattered: he'd spent the time attending a Kurosawa festival in Little Tokyo.

He had gone by Scarecrow Video yesterday after the screening, but it was closed and there was no sign of Gene and Hector. The store was supposed to be open until nine unless those two had something better to do, which meant that if Rollo hadn't been wasting his time watching Chaz Presley, he would have gotten there in time to tag along with Gene and Hector. Typical rotten luck. They had left in a hurry, too, leaving videos strewn across the counter— probably gotten a lead on some whack screening at somebody's house and just dropped what they were doing, the two of them fucked up on weed, watching Mexican biker flicks while Rollo hung out in the Azure-Blue Room bored out of his brain stem. A person could stand only so much serenity.

The VW rattled like a coffee grinder as Rollo accelerated, double-clutching to slip it into second. The van was a classic, but it needed a valve job and brakes, and the oil manifold was leaking. Still, it would get him to the Shady Rest and back.

It was too early for Rollo to be making with the king-of-the-open-road thing, but Fisher had surprised him first thing this morning, turning on the light in the Azure-Blue Room, not even knocking first. Rollo had been asleep only a couple of hours, but he knew right away there was trouble, because Fisher hadn't brought him his double-tall mocha wake-up. Fisher said he was sorry, but Rollo had to move out. *Now.* Rollo played his music too loud, left take-out food cartons everywhere, and dried his hands on whatever was around. The guy sounded like his mother. More time in the Mint-Green Room, Fisher.

Rollo had spent most of last night looking for Clara—or Nikki Sexxx, to be exact. He had driven all over the San Fernando Valley, going to five different shoots to ask for her, getting redirected from one secluded split level to the next. Just before dawn, Mavis, the second cameraman on *Bend Over and Pray #5,* had told him that Nikki moved to Hawaii a couple of days ago. "I heard she inherited some money," Mavis said, changing reels, "or maybe it was one too many Bukkake vids." Mavis asked him if he was looking for work, said they could always use a camera jockey, but Rollo passed.

He rapped out a drum solo on the steering wheel as the van lurched over potholes. Rollo missed her, but not every love story was a June-and-Ward-Cleaver suburban hookup, and besides, Clara had returned his films to the storage locker, and that said something. Getting evicted by Fisher was no biggie, either—Rollo still had a trailer permanently parked at the Shady Rest Mobile Home Haven. And best of all, Jimmy had bought him some time with Pilar.

Leave it to Jimmy—he had the touch, the easy moves and perfect timing that opened doors. All the high-tech equipment Rollo had access to, and Jimmy had gotten into the Rhinestone Cowboy by himself, sliding past Macklen's security like the fucking Invisible Man. Rollo had sat parked in his van across the street, the power grid to the country-and-western joint already wired, waiting for Jimmy to call with the go-ahead. Country tunes had echoed through the night, and Rollo had kept thinking that he didn't want Jimmy to die with that shitkicker music stuck in his head.

No one had been more surprised than Rollo when Jimmy hurried up to the pickup point with a briefcase full of memory chips —must have been a thousand of them, full-lattice chips, more valuable than gold. Rollo could have turned them over in a couple of days, but Jimmy had insisted that they throw them off the Huntington Beach pier that same night, the two of them scattering them into the surf, the chips glittering like stars. If Rollo had been a better person, he would have tossed them *all* in; he wouldn't have tucked a couple of handfuls into his cargo pants as insurance for a rainy day. Jimmy was smart, but somebody needed to tell him that there was *always* a rainy day coming.

Jimmy listened to Holt's steady breathing for about five minutes, making certain she was asleep before he carefully slipped out of bed. She was sleeping with one long, bare leg on top of the sheets; even through the thick curtains, the late-morning sunlight was warm and buttery on her skin, and he couldn't help but stand there and enjoy the sight of her.

They had made love for most of the night, and then, just before dawn, Holt had gotten up and told him she'd be right back. He thought maybe she was going to fix them breakfast, but a few moments later he heard a fax machine running. So much for Betty Crocker fantasies. Holt eased back into bed a few minutes later, and Jimmy thanked her for fitting him into her busy day, asked if she had collated her documents. She pinched his nipple, told him she had sent the skinhead photo to the gang unit. She pinched him harder, climbed on top of his chest, looked down at him, and said he looked sexy when he was feeling threatened. Jimmy was about to disagree, but his mouth was full.

Jimmy smiled to himself at the memory, then crept out the door and down the hall to the second bedroom. Like most interior doors, this one had a simple push-button lock that it took him just seconds to open with a bent paper clip. Jane had walked ahead of him on the way to her room last night, closing this door as she made conversation, telling him she didn't want him to see what a poor housekeeper she was. Jimmy had caressed her hip and said he wouldn't grade her if she wouldn't grade him, already knowing that he was going to find out what was in that room when he got the chance.

Seagulls screamed outside as he opened the door, and Jimmy jerked. He was *way* too jumpy. A map of Orange County covered one wall of the room, with small red push pins clustered around the six Eggman murder sites; another wall was given over to crime-scene photos, rows and rows of them. A worktable dominated the space, notes and photographs scattered across its surface.

Jimmy walked inside and went over to the table, feeling more uncomfortable than he had anticipated about violating her privacy. He stopped and turned toward the hallway, listening, then started lifting up the manila folders, noting exactly where to replace them. A Polaroid peeked out from one of the piles of paper, and he slid it out, saw the photo of Jonathan getting a blow job that Jane had swiped from the pool house. Jimmy should have been looking at the woman, but his attention was all on Jonathan, with his bared teeth and triumphant expression. He still didn't know what Jane was doing with the Polaroid, and was glad to put it back where he'd found it.

Later today he was going to stop by Pilar's. He would cash Napitano's check first, then show up at her front door with a stack of hundreds and an autographed photo of Farrah Fawcett. That should get Rollo off the hook. Then he'd ask Pilar if Sergeant Enriquez had called back with news of any strange killings in Cervaca. It wouldn't make any sense, not now, but Jimmy would ask her anyway.

He worked faster now, concerned that Holt would wake up and

find him gone. He started in on another folder and saw another Polaroid, this one inside a small glassine evidence envelope, a crime-scene photo of Philip Kinneson lying on the beach. He opened the bag and removed the photo, holding it by the edges. It was pretty thrashed, creased and water-spotted. He checked the nearby wall and saw at least a dozen similar Polaroids and prints of the Laguna crime scene pinned there, but they were all in pristine condition. He stared at the beaten-up Polaroid, checked the back. There was no date or signature from the on-site forensic tech, which was odd but not unprecedented. He opened the blinds, brought the photo closer to the light, wondering why this one merited special protection. He glanced behind him.

Holt stood in the doorway, a cell phone against her ear. She wore a sheer white nightgown. Which was more than Jimmy was wearing. "That's wonderful news, Edgar, and I really appreciate your getting back to me so quickly." She listened, still watching Jimmy. "I'll contact the San Diego sheriff's office myself. Yes. I'll let you know. Good-bye." She snapped the phone shut. "Good morning, Jimmy."

"I was . . . snooping."

"A naked burglar . . . that's a distinctive M.O."

"I'm sorry," said Jimmy. Holt didn't look nearly as angry as he had expected. "Closed doors always make me wonder what's behind them. I shouldn't have done it."

"You're a lucky man, because at this particular moment, I'd find it easy to forgive you anything." Holt shook her head at Jimmy's smile. "I wasn't talking about *that*." She held up the phone. "The skinhead in the photograph just got ID'ed."

Jimmy moved closer. "The tattoos do it?"

Holt nodded. "His name is Vaughn Sparks."

"Are you going to pick him up?"

"That's already been taken care of." Holt's smile was blinding. "Mr. Sparks is currently residing in the San Diego County Jail on an attempted murder charge, while the D.A. considers whether to file an additional hate-crime charge. Two weeks ago, celebrating his eighteenth birthday, he and three buddies were drinking their way to Tijuana when they stopped for gas in Del Mar. On the way back to the freeway, they passed a gay bar and became so enraged by the crowd of men standing around outside that they decided to start shooting. Two men were wounded, but the bystanders got the license-plate number. Mr. Sparks and his buddies were arrested at the border. Mr. Sparks kept repeating that it was his birthday, as if that constituted a mitigating circumstance."

"Sounds . . . promising." Jimmy kissed her. "Congratulations."

"More than promising. Congratulations to you, too, Jimmy—I owe you."

Jimmy's face fell. "I wish it *had* been Jonathan."

"Because then you'd have a chance with Olivia?"

"No, Jane. *No.* It's just that . . . in some way, I think he's guilty."

"The Eggman was a hoax," said Holt. "I got carried away with the idea of a serial killer, too—a diabolical monster seems so much more interesting than an angry loser like Vaughn Sparks. But it was Sparks who murdered Philip Kinneson, not the Eggman."

"You don't know that."

"It's all over except for the indictment," said Holt, almost giddy. "When the cops searched Sparks's house, they found a photo album filled with fight-club Polaroids—skinheads showing their fists for the camera and flashing guns and knives, even a few victims with blood gushing from their broken noses. I'm putting in a request to have the album sent to Maria Sinoa in Forensics immediately."

"What's that going to do?"

Holt shrugged and walked over to the desk, looking for something. "It can't hurt to tell you now." She found the faded Polaroid of Philip Kinneson, held it up. "You see this?"

In the distance Rollo could see the Shady Rest Mobile Home Haven set out in the flatlands beyond La Palma, rusting Road Buddies and Travelmates arranged in interlocking rings like a benzene molecule. Rollo adjusted the wing window, directing the warm breeze onto his face. It was barely nine in the morning and already sweltering, yesterday's downpour rushing down the storm drains toward the Pacific, carrying a flotsam of dead cats, used motor oil, and plastic Slurpee cups. What the asphalt didn't shrug off was sucked down into the sands and forgotten. Southern California was still a desert, no matter how much water they imported or stole or trucked in. You could divert the whole Colorado River and it wouldn't help, though Rollo wished they'd try.

Sweat ringed the nape of Rollo's neck. There was no air conditioning in the VW, of course—he kept it strictly factory-compliant —and no air conditioning in his trailer, either, not since the window-rattler broke down a couple months ago, and that was a real drag. Without air conditioning the trailer was just a twenty-five-foot aluminum hotbox; he might as well be Alec Guinness in *The Bridge on the River Kwai*. Except Rollo would have done whatever Sessue Hayakawa wanted and avoided the hotbox in the first place.

Rollo took the turnoff, the van bouncing over the potholes. He was going to have to leave the windows open in the trailer, so forget any REM sleep. Between the brats hollering, the dogs barking, and the rednecks in space #23 with Limp Bizkit cranked on a shitty J. C. Penney's sound system, it was a stone lock there was going to be no rest at the Shady Rest. But it would have to do until Jimmy gave Pilar the down payment on what Rollo owed her.

The trailer sagged in the middle and couldn't be moved without falling apart; it was narrow and cramped and smelled like stale Honey Nut Cheerios, but it had a stocked refrigerator and clean clothes in the closet, a Trinitron beside the bed, and a couple of boxes of John Ford and Coen brothers DVDs. He could handle it there for a few days until Jimmy took Pilar's temperature.

Rollo pulled into the trailer park: forty-six spaces jammed into an acre of scabby hardpack, bordered by a concrete-block wall covered in graffiti. He drove past the clump of vending machines outside the showers, saw Mrs. Haggerty walking back to her trailer, her head a nest of pink curlers. She had been in the park forever, her trailer ringed with flowers, *real* flowers, with a "Have a Nice Day!" bumper sticker in her front window. One of the redneck kids was playing in the sandbox with his Tonka trucks, a filthy little boy with a mouthful of crooked teeth—he looked up as Rollo drove past, tugged at his overalls, bright-blue eyes staring after the van.

Rollo could use a shower himself, and he hadn't shaved in a couple of days because his skin was still sensitive from the sunburn. Two weeks and he was still raw—who knew the sun in Costa Rica would be way hotter than in L.A., even? They should warn you at the airport, maybe give you some sunscreen to welcome you to their fair, fucked-up country. The Costa Rica board of tourism was missing a real opportunity.

His sunburn made him think about Clara again, and there went any hope of relaxing. Actually it wasn't Clara he was thinking of— Clara was kind of an intellectual, always asking him his opinion about Bosnia and Rwanda, all these places that didn't even have film festivals—it was her screen persona, Nikki Sexxx, who went round and round in his brain. Nikki Sexxx was hot and nasty and totally cinematic. *She* was the one responsible for all the trouble he was in, not Clara. If it hadn't been for Nikki Sexxx and those tiny tits of hers, he would never have invited Clara to go to Costa Rica with him.

The VW kicked up dust from the gravel road, the grit billowing through the screen doors of the trailers like fog. There was a five-mile-an-hour speed limit in the park, but Rollo was lost in a private fantasy. No speed limits there.

Most porno queens had silicon zeppelins, but Nikki Sexxx's were small and natural, just the way he liked them. Rollo had thought it pure luck that he met her that day on the set a couple of months ago—his first day shooting porn, picking up some extra coin behind the camera, and *her* first day, too, she had told him, lowering her eyes. He'd known it was bullshit, but he wanted to believe her, seeing her through the lens as he slowly zoomed in for her close-up. Major pink. The other guys on the crew had laughed at his hard-on, said he would lose wood soon enough. You crew for porno, they told him, all the Viagra in the world wouldn't help after a few weeks. Morons.

Rollo remembered the lipstick Valentine Clara had drawn on the storage locker when she returned his films. That was her way of telling him that it was Nikki Sexxx who had ripped him off, not her. Clara was the one who'd told him about growing up on a farm in Georgia, who'd explained crop rotation to him while he pretended to care. The one who'd liked his work and said he should go to film school to get even better. Clara was the one he had fallen for, but it was her flashy, porn-queen, tongue-stud self, Nikki Sexxx, that Rollo had taken to Costa Rica. His seventh-grade teacher said Rollo had tested out at 163 on the IQ test. The school wanted him to take it again, just to be sure, but Rollo couldn't be bothered. He already knew he was smart. It was amazing how someone so smart could be so stupid.

A new rig was parked across from his trailer, a forty-foot Roadmaster with Vermont plates and a satellite dish on top—snowbirds on their way to Palm Desert, probably. Anyone who could afford a Roadmaster would stay at the Shady Rest only long enough to pump out his sewage tanks and hit the nearby Costco. Rollo pulled into his space and backed in so that the van was facing out, still trying to sort it out between Clara, who wanted to fuck him, and Nikki Sexxx, who wanted to fuck him *over.*

The front door to the trailer squeaked as he unlocked it. He headed right for the refrigerator, opened a can of Inca Cola, and took a long swallow. It was fizzier than Coke, and sweeter, too. Rollo took another swig, the soda bubbling over onto his shirt. He looked around for something to wipe himself off with, then went to High Alert! The cupboard doors were open, his clothes on the floor.

Rollo darted for the door, then stopped. He had made plenty of noise. If one of Pilar's boys were still here, he'd have already come out from the bedroom, fists swinging. He couldn't figure out how Pilar had found this place. His CD player was still where he'd left it, but somebody had punched in both the speakers. The TV was upended, his tapes and DVDs scattered. It had to have been Blaine or some other of Pilar's boys, rather than a ripoff artist. He crossed to the storage locker and removed the false front at the top. The digital security camera was still there, still plugged in. He popped out the video, saw that it was at the end of the tape—he had a record of whoever had tossed his trailer. He was starting to put it into the VCR when he saw movement out of the corner of his eye.

Enoch, the biggest and dumbest of the redneck brothers, was edging toward his trailer, crouched over, trying to hide his beefy tonnage behind Mrs. Haggerty's decorative Dutch windmill—"Souvenir of Solvang!" Through the opposite window, Rollo could see Enoch's brother Esau sauntering down the road, hands in his overalls, Dallas Cowboys cap on backward, whistling, looking everywhere but at Rollo's trailer. Pilar must have asked around after she had the trailer trashed, found those two fuckwads, and put a bounty on him. Signed, sealed, and delivered.

Rollo stepped toward the door, went back for the security tape, and sprinted out the trailer, almost tearing the door off the hinges on his way. He saw Esau running toward him now, all muscle and bone, his cap blown off, blond hair blowing behind him like a dirty mop. Rollo jumped into the van and locked it.

Enoch tripped over the decorative Dutch windmill as Rollo jammed his key in the ignition, the engine grinding while he cursed it and promised to buy the piece of shit only unleaded extra from now on if it would just start. Please-please-please! The engine died. Enoch charged the van, his face split into a triumphant grin.

Rollo turned the ignition again as he gently fed it gas; he heard it sputter, then start with a roar.

Esau reached the van before his brother and jerked at the driver's-side door handle. It came off in his hand, and he fell backward onto the dirt.

Rollo waved bye-bye, flooring it, the tires churning rocks and dust.

Enoch dove for the van from the opposite side and actually cracked the windshield with his hard head, clawing at the wipers, trying to hang on as the van picked up speed down the gravel road. Rollo leaned on the horn, Enoch's mouth flying open, showing off his stumpy teeth. Rollo hit the brakes, sent the redneck tumbling, and then accelerated the VW, rolling right over him. In the rearview he saw Enoch lying in the road, clutching his bare foot.

But now Esau was coming up fast behind the van, arms pumping, hair whipping from side to side with his exertions.

Rollo shoved the van into second gear, took the speed bump without slowing, the van going airborne for a moment, groaning as it landed, skidding as he fought to maintain control. He checked the rearview again: Esau had lost ground, but he was still running hard. As Rollo neared the front entrance he saw the redneck kid still squatting in the sandbox, one of his toy trucks clutched to his chest. Their eyes locked as Rollo roared past, and it was like falling into an abandoned well.

Rollo fumbled out his cell phone, steering with one hand, and thumbed Jimmy's number on the speed dialer. Jimmy had told him that things were cool with Pilar; he had *promised*. Answer your phone, Jimmy! It's another rainy day, dude.

Chapter 36

Blaine buzzed the street-side security gate and opened the front door, stumbling down the front steps in his haste to meet Macklen and Great White as they came up the walkway.

Macklen pivoted on one crutch, spinning the other with his right hand like a drum major leading a parade. Great White just stood there in a black leather trench coat, his shaved head gleaming in the afternoon heat, watching Blaine with the same little smile he had worn into the dressing room at the wrestling match that Sunday night, checking out the contestants tugging on their costumes like he was better than anyone else.

Great White wasn't even that big, maybe 360 pounds, but it was hard to tell how buffed out he was with the trench coat on. Probably hiding a gut and a complete lack of muscle tone. Blaine was only 247 pounds, but he had less than 6 percent body fat and knew the Montana Death Lock besides. He decided to ignore Great White. "Mr. Macklen." He stuck his hand out to shake, then took it back, confused by the crutches. "Gosh, sir, you didn't have to deliver the tape personally."

Macklen peered at Blaine, then looked over at Great White. "You know what the fuck he's talking about?"

Great White wiped a hand across his skull and flung the sweat onto the ground—Blaine felt it spatter his bare feet, warm and disgusting. "We didn't bring the videotape of you and the Kongo Kid," Great White said to him. "It's still being edited. We're putting in some special effects." He still had that I-could-kick-your-ass smile on his face.

Blaine looked at Macklen. "So what are you doing here?"

"How about we come inside, slick?" Macklen leaned on one crutch, wiped his arm across his forehead. He wore jeans and a sleeveless T-shirt that showed off his hard, knotted muscles. "The sun's baking my brains."

"I'm not supposed to . . . Pilar doesn't allow . . ." Blaine pondered the situation, then grinned. "I get it. You saw the write-up on me in the paper and want to sign me up fast. I sure am grateful for the opportunity you gave me, but I don't think I should sign a long-term contract. I'm still waiting to hear from Mr. Vince McMahon at the WWF."

"Yeah, right," said Macklen. "Maybe we could go inside and talk about a special bout, a one-shot deal that wouldn't get in the way of your big career."

"*Cool,*" said Blaine. "I mean, I don't even have a manager yet, but if Pilar says it's OK, then I'm ready for anything. She's out back."

Macklen nudged him with the tip of his cane. "Time's a-wasting. Let's run it past the bitch, and then you can sign on the dotted line."

Blaine led them back up the sidewalk, his steps slowing as they neared the front door, until he finally turned. "Mr. Macklen . . . Pilar, she don't like being talked to like that."

"Lookee here, Mack," said Great White. "It's Miss Manners."

Blaine looked at Great White, thinking maybe he should hammer-slap him across his bald head, but thinking, too, that he didn't want to lose out on the special bout that Mr. Macklen was offering. While he was trying to decide, Great White walked right past him into the house, knocking him aside. It was Blaine's own fault for not having his feet planted—you had to always be in position, that's what the Rock wrote in his autobiography. Blaine was going to have to double-underline it. He glanced at Great White's retreating back, wishing he would try that move again, then turned to Macklen. "Watch your step, sir."

Macklen easily hoisted himself up onto the porch, biceps popping—he was gnarly, not huge but with great vascularization, his veins standing out like linguini. He patted Blaine on the shoulder. "I'm going to make you a star, kid. Let's go break the good news to Pilar."

Blaine led the way through the house, Macklen keeping up with him. They found Great White in the TV room with Blaine's Mossberg slung casually over his shoulder. Seeing him with the shotgun, Blaine got this shivery feeling in his stomach and thought maybe he had made a mistake in letting the two of them into the house without asking Pilar.

Great White nodded at a velvet painting on the wall, a bare-chested Aztec warrior wearing a leopard-skin cape. "That there's a masterpiece. I'm an artist myself, so I know what I'm talking about."

Blaine squinted at the velvet painting. "If you say so."

Great White racked the slide, pointed the shotgun at him. "You like circus pictures?"

Blaine glanced at Macklen, then turned back to Great White. "I don't know—"

"Circus pictures are my specialty," said Great White, his finger wrapped around the trigger. "Circus drawings, circus paintings, circus watercolors. . . ."

"Like the bearded lady and the hippo that sweats blood?" asked Blaine.

"That's freak-show stuff, you dumb fuck." Great White held the shotgun one-handed, as if it were a pistol, and slowly moved it up from Blaine's midsection until it was level with his face. "You think you're funny?"

Blaine stared into the barrel of the Mossberg. It was really dark in there.

Great White's finger tightened on the trigger. *"Bang!"* he said.

Blaine jumped.

Macklen laughed. "Don't frighten the boy."

"I wasn't scared." Blaine wished he had his full Robo-Surfer outfit on instead of just his jams, wished he had his dials freshly inked on his chest, power gauges reading full-on.

"Let's do a jockey-shorts check," Great White said to Blaine, still training the shotgun on him. "I bet you're carrying a load of chocolate pudding."

"I told you, I *wasn't*—"

"Catch." Great White tossed Blaine the shotgun, laughing as he bobbled it. "If you need a shotgun to take care of business, I wouldn't want to deprive you. Me, I never felt the lack of firepower."

"We're just playing with you." Macklen grinned at Blaine. His eyes reminded Blaine of a dog that had bitten him once. "No hard feelings, huh?"

Blaine checked the Mossberg, so angry his hands shook. The shotgun was loaded, the safety off.

"He's thinking about it, Great White," cawed Macklen. "You're in trouble now."

Great White stared at Blaine. "I doubt it."

"Fun's over, kid," Macklen said. "How about you take us to Pilar?"

Blaine led them out the back door. He waved the Mossberg with one hand, but it was too heavy for him to hold steady. Great White caught him trying and smirked.

Macklen looked around the yard, taking it all in—the manicured lawn, the fruit trees heavy with oranges and lemons and tangerines, some of the trees butted right up against the eight-foot iron security fence, tangerines brushing the coils of razor wire. Pilar was doing bench presses, the weight-training area a concrete slab surrounded by grass. She had promised to put in a wrestling ring, had already ordered it, but it hadn't arrived yet. Blaine wished the ring were set up—he'd invite Great White to have a go with him, show him what fun really was.

Pilar saw them and stopped what she was doing, holding the weight bar in midair. She slowly lifted the bar back into place and sat up. "What is this, Blaine?"

"This is Mr. Macklen," said Blaine.

"I know who he is," said Pilar. "I know the other one, too." She stood up and wiped her hands on a towel. She wore red Lycra lifting shorts and a matching sports bra. "What I want to know is, what're they doing *inside?*"

"I thought they were bringing me my videotape," said Blaine. He hefted the Mossberg to show her he was still in charge. "There's no tape yet, they're still adding the special effects, but Mr. Macklen is going to give me another match. The main bout, too."

Pilar watched Macklen scoot over to one of the orange trees and pluck off a ripe one. "You still should have asked me before you let them in, Blaine."

"I didn't mean to get the boy in trouble," said Macklen. He bit into the orange, spat the skin onto the grass, and started sucking the juice out. "This is real sweet back here, Pilar, a regular Garden of Eden." He tossed the husk aside, bouncing it into a row of flowers, then scooted over to the bench and checked the Olympic plates with the tip of one cane. "How much you benching, Pilar? Two twenty?"

"Two sixty," Blaine said proudly.

"Shut up, Blaine," said Pilar, holding her shoulders so tense that Blaine wanted to give her a rubdown. She nodded at Great White and his black leather trench coat. "You're overdressed for the weather."

"I'm delicate," said Great White. "I'm what you call a hothouse flower."

Macklen lay down on the bench, gripped the bar, and snapped off ten fast repetitions. "Why don't you slide a couple of forty-fives on for me, Pilar?"

"I'll get them." Great White ambled over to the weight racks, slid off a couple of forty-five-pound plates, and carried them over as if they were tea-set dishes.

Macklen started his reps with the 350 pounds, taking it slow, keeping his breathing regular. "I've been asking around," he said on one of the upstrokes. "They say you're the one who fronts Rollo his high-tech goodies. If he sells it, it's got your name on it, that's what they say."

"Rollo who?" said Pilar.

" 'Rollo who?' " Macklen laughed and then carefully laid the barbell back onto the rack, the ends bowing slightly from all that weight. He sat up, reached for his canes.

Blaine noticed two shaggy teenagers from next door peering through the bars of the fence, a couple of junior-high punks half hidden by the surrounding foliage. Great White must have spotted them, too, because he suddenly picked up a ten-pound plate and whipped it at the kids. The plate slammed into the fence just above their heads, sending them stumbling away.

"Time for you and your ugly friend to go," Pilar said to Macklen.

"Rollo moved some memory chips last week," said Macklen, his canes digging into Pilar's perfect turf. "I figure he was moving them for you."

"What's a memory chip?" asked Blaine.

Macklen leaned into her face. "You fucked up, lady."

"I am no lady," said Pilar.

"Was it me you were after or the VC Boyz?" said Macklen. "It don't make no never mind, I'm just curious. Were they your chips to begin with? Did those gooks rip you off first? I can understand you being pissed off, but that don't excuse what—"

"You bore me," said Pilar. *"Adiós, pendejo."*

"I been waiting a *long* time to find out who ripped me off," said Macklen, rocking gently now. "Great White told me to give it up, but I knew if I waited long enough Christmas was bound to arrive." He grinned at her. "Look around you, lady, it's fucking snowing."

"Blaine?" Pilar said carefully, keeping her eyes on Macklen. "I want you to kill Great White if he does not start walking toward the side gate right now. Empty the magazine. Then call the police, say we have shot an intruder."

"What about me?" said Macklen. "Ain't I worth shooting?"

"You I will take care of myself," said Pilar.

"I don't need no shotgun to take care of Great White," said Blaine.

"Sure you do, boy." Great White sneered.

"Do what I say," said Pilar.

Blaine reluctantly leveled the shotgun at Great White, braced it against his hip. "Yes, Pilar."

" 'Yes, Pilar'," mimicked Great White. He moved closer to Blaine, leather trench coat rustling, and spread his arms wide to give him an easy target. "Does this help?"

Macklen sniffed. "You smell something, Great White?"

Great White leaned toward Blaine and sniffed. "It's not chocolate pudding, Mack."

Blaine slowly shook his head, then laid the shotgun down. "I'm not afraid of you."

"Blaine!" cried Pilar. "No!"

"Have some faith in me, Pilar. I know what I'm doing." Blaine stretched, loosening up, ready to rumble. "You're going to be so proud when you see what I do to him."

"That's quite a boy you got there," Macklen said to Pilar, rocking faster now. "He's going to go quick, but *you?* Just stealing my goods would have got you dead"—his face twisted into something unrecognizable—"but stealing what you took from me, you fucking *cunt* . . . we're way beyond dead now."

Chapter 37

Air conditioning was the second-greatest human invention, better than the wheel or fire, even better than the Yamaha 330-X editing console. Rollo stood in the Warehouse Electronics Superstore, feeling the sweat cooling on his forehead, the whole back of his shirt clammy in the air-conditioned bliss of the store. It was a blast furnace outside, the asphalt sweltering in the late afternoon, and driving the freeways felt like being stuck in the La Brea tar pits. Inside, though . . . inside it was a constant sixty-seven degrees, day and night, winter and summer. He shivered with pleasure, just breathing out and in, still seeing the redneck crew chasing him in the hot sun, barefoot and stupid in the rearview mirror, like Gila monsters, oblivious to the heat.

"Can I help you?"

Rollo looked at the salesman with the pointy Captain Kirk sideburns and the name tag on his wrinkled white shirt that read Terrence. "Doubtful, dude," he said, blowing right past him, homing in on Big Mom and Barbie arguing about compact stereo systems over in aisle 12. Rollo played with price tags, slowly moving closer. The debate centered around a Sony with a three-CD changer versus a JVC with a stackable CD tray that would hold ten discs. Barbie wanted the JVC so she could play dance party until her protocerebrum exploded. Big Mom wanted the cheaper Sony.

"Can I help you?" asked Rollo.

"Yeah, we want the JVC," said Barbie, defiant in lime-green

hip-huggers and halter top, her belly button knotted tighter than a heart suture.

"We certainly do not." Big Mom clutched her purse, wearing a pink acrylic pantsuit, an outfit seen only in strip malls and *Cagney and Lacey* reruns. "We'll take this lovely Sony."

Barbie stamped her foot. She had a pierced nose, roseate acne, and a bleached shag.

Rollo leaned closer to Big Mom. "Actually, lady, the JVC is a better value. More power, cleaner sound, plus Dolby B and C. I know it's a little more money—"

"A *lot* more money, junior," grumped Big Mom.

Rollo pushed back his glasses. "No problem," he said, not liking that "junior" crack, not at all. "Can you wait until tomorrow to save some money?"

"Oh, is there a sale starting?" asked Big Mom.

"More of a special offer," said Rollo. "Let me take down your name and phone number, and I'll guarantee you the JVC for the price of the Sony. I'll even throw in free delivery."

"That would be very nice . . ." Big Mom searched Rollo's chest for a name tag.

"Rollo," he said, handing her one of Fisher's ChromoGenesis business cards. "Just write your name and number on the back."

Barbie grabbed the card from her mother, scrawled her name and phone number, then gave it back to Rollo, batting her mascara. "How about tossing in a few CDs?"

"I could do that," said Rollo, lingering on Barbie before turning to the mother. "Free delivery, like I said, but we have to insist on cash. It's policy."

"It's policy, Mother," echoed Barbie. "Does the special offer include headphones?"

"Ah . . . sure," said Rollo.

"I don't see why I can't use my Discover card," said Big Mom.

"Cash payment allows us to pass the savings on to you," said Rollo.

Barbie led Big Mom away. "Phone me when you're coming," she called to Rollo.

Rollo waved. He was nineteen, she was maybe fifteen . . . if you added up their ages and divided by two, it would be legal. In Arkansas, maybe.

"What's doin', man?" someone said in his ear.

Rollo jumped. "Don't sneak up on me like that."

"You ain't rustling my customers, are you?" leered Dickson, an ex-jock gone to fat and middle management. As the assistant manager at Warehouse Electronics, he was entitled to wear a clip-on black tie embroidered with the company logo in simulated gold threads.

"Roping and branding, but you'll get your regular fee," said Rollo. "I want this JVC system here. Slip it in the trunk of your Toyota after work, and I'll pick it up tonight."

"No can do," said Dickson, looking around like a contestant on *World's Dumbest Criminals*. "Corporate just installed these new wide-angle security cameras on the loading dock. They can see the blind spot by the Dumpster now."

"That's unconstitutional, dude."

"Inventory control is one of the seven keys to profitability," recited Dickson, sweating even in that cool, crisp sixty-seven-degree air conditioning.

"What's that, page one of the company handbook? Get some self-respect, will you?" A behemoth SUV rolled past the front window; Barbie waved to Rollo, and he waved back. "You got a digital minirecorder? I have an eight-millimeter tape I want to check out."

"This isn't going to take long, is it?" Dickson said a few minutes later, as he patched the digital recorder into the bank of televisions in the viewing room.

"I just want to see who trashed my trailer," said Rollo. "If it was that idiot Blaine, he can forget about me descrambling the next pay-per-view Wrestlemania."

"Can you do that?" Dickson popped in the last connection, looked up. "How about the Playboy channel?"

Rollo pushed Play on the unit and watched the wall of forty-eight televisions roll over at the same time, showing the inside of his trailer, flickering, flickering. It was hypnotic to see the same low-light image replicated over and over, the TV sets stacked up like the blocks in Tetris, a fly's-eye view of the door to his trailer, the knob turning.

"This isn't going to be some porno movie, is it?" Dickson straightened his tie.

Rollo kept his eyes on the video array as all forty-eight doors swung open, perfectly synchronized, a Busby Berkeley wet dream—

"What the *hell* is that?" said Dickson.

Rollo couldn't talk. He couldn't move. He couldn't do anything but watch.

"That is the ugliest thing I have ever seen," said Dickson.

Forty-eight images of Great White standing in the doorway, his shaved head bent forward so as not to hit the ceiling; forty-eight Great Whites surveying the trailer, small eyes like sinkholes in the vast, bland expanse of his face.

Behind him Rollo could hear a little girl crying, but he didn't turn around to see what it was that was scaring her. He knew.

Great White banged his head on the trailer's ceiling fan, then tore it down with a swat of his hand, no trace of anger on his face as he did it, merely an implacable forward motion.

Rollo pulled out his cell phone as Great White filled the frame.

Chapter 38

Jimmy saw kids running from Pilar's backyard carrying armloads of oranges as he drove up, and more loose oranges rolling down the sidewalk in the soft evening light. He parked the car, knowing it was already too late. Pilar was never going to spend the money he had brought for her.

Men and women streamed from the house lugging velvet paintings and stacks of VCRs, the front gate propped open with a Cuisinart. A gray-haired woman in a long dress staggered down the steps with a TV set, huffing and puffing; she tripped on a paving stone, and the TV fell, its screen imploding with a loud *POP.* She got back up, gave Jimmy a toothless grin, and raced back into the house, her dress flapping.

The security gate to the backyard was wide open, too, and Jimmy decided to go in that way, walking slowly, forcing himself. He looked around. The trees had been stripped, the branches torn down to give up the higher fruit, oranges and tangerines lying flattened in the grass, stepped on, their insides crushed. He sagged, seeing Pilar on the far side of the bench press, her head thrown back, her body twisted.

Jimmy bent down over her and gently touched her face. She was gone. There was a deep circular imprint in her bare midsection, a purple bruise radiating from it, but that wasn't what had killed her. One side of her head was crushed, bits of blood and hair rimming the edge of the weight stack where she had fallen. Or more likely, been thrown. Jimmy stood up, wobbly now, then sat down on the bench, taking deep breaths.

Pilar had enemies, business rivals . . . or maybe it was a wrecking crew that'd heard she kept cash in the house, some take-no-prisoners outfit like the VC Boyz. Jimmy looked around for Blaine. Where *was* he? There were noises coming from the house, of drawers being flung to the floor, cardboard boxes being torn open. Jimmy got up, still queasy, and started toward the stairs to see if he could find Blaine.

"*Jimmy.*"

Jimmy stopped, looking around, not sure he had really heard his name.

"Here."

Jimmy saw a hand poking out from the underside of the house. He walked over quickly and saw Blaine lying in the crawl space, holding up a section of siding. The siding had been cut so that when it slid down, it lined up perfectly with the skirting around the foundation. Jimmy went to pull him free, but Blaine cried out at his touch, shook his head. Blaine was wearing just a pair of shorts, so Jimmy could see that there wasn't a cut or a scrape or a wound of any kind on him, but it was obvious that something . . . enormous had happened to him. His skin was clammy and purplish, exploded blood vessels mottling the surface. He looked like he'd been carved out of blue marble.

"Everything . . . everything's broke inside me," whispered Blaine.

"Don't move." Jimmy pulled out his phone but couldn't get a dial tone. "Hang on. I'll go inside and call nine-one-one."

Blaine grabbed his wrist.

"I'll be right back."

Blaine clamped down harder, whimpering at the pain the movement caused him but not letting go. "Don't leave me. *Please.*"

"You need help."

Blaine's teeth were chattering. "I don't want to die alone, Jimmy."

"You're not going to die."

Blaine slowly shook his head. "I'm not smart . . . but I'm not stupid, either." His eyelids fluttered. "I was just lying under here listening to the footsteps. Boy, the neighbors are having a real party." His eyes were open wide now. "Pilar's dead, isn't she?"

"Yes."

"Pilar was always getting ready for bad things to happen. . . ." Blaine waved at the crawl space. "She had places rigged up all over the house where we could hide, fake closets and secret doors. When I got broken . . . when I couldn't hardly breathe, that's what I did. They were busy with her, and I crawled in here and closed myself in." He looked away. "I *left* her, Jimmy. I put my hands over my ears, but I could still hear what was going on."

"You couldn't have helped—"

"Don't tell anybody I chickened out."

"Do you know who killed her?"

"Promise you won't tell anyone," pleaded Blaine.

"You did what you could. No one could blame you for trying to save yourself."

"I *did* try to protect her. . . ." A drop of blood hung from Blaine's nose. "I drop-kicked him, should have stoved in his ribs, but he was wearing something, Jimmy—it was like an armored suit."

"Do you know who did this to you? Did you recognize them?"

"That's cheating, isn't it? I mean, you can't wear armor in the ring."

"Yeah, sure, Blaine. It's cheating."

"I hurt him, though." Blood ran down from Blaine's smile. "I snapped a couple of his fingers. I heard them pop." His smile faded. "He didn't even make a sound when I did it. Not even an *ouch*. Then he picked me up in his arms . . . I felt like a little baby." His eyes filled with tears. "He *squeezed* me, Jimmy."

Jimmy stared at Blaine and felt cold, too. There was only one person he knew who could toss Blaine around like a baby. "Blaine," he said carefully, "did Great White do this to you?"

"I let Pilar down," blubbered Blaine. "The Robo-Surfer—what a joke."

"Blaine, talk to me. Was it Great White?"

Blaine looked past Jimmy. "Pilar didn't take his stupid chips. Why didn't she just *tell* him that? Maybe they would have left. Mr. Macklen . . . he's not a bad guy."

Jimmy sat down beside Blaine, too weak to move. It felt like someone had opened his heart, and his life had poured out. He had suspected Great White and Macklen as soon as he saw that none of Pilar's security gates had been knocked down, no guns had been fired. The Mexican mafia or a wrecking crew would have driven a moving van through the fence and poured out, assault rifles blazing. It would have been a spray-and-pray takedown, not this . . . cruel and quiet killing.

"I still don't even know what a memory chip is," complained Blaine.

Jimmy sat beside him, holding his hand, watching his body darken as he drowned in his own blood, the kid's blond buzz cut purple at the roots now. "This was my fault, not yours," he told Blaine.

"No way. It was Rollo they wanted."

"I'm sorry, Blaine."

"Pilar wouldn't tell them where Rollo was, she wouldn't tell them anything, and Mr. Macklen kept getting madder and madder, hitting her with one of his canes . . . he's fast, Jimmy. Then Great White pushed her and Pilar fell and hit her head and Mr. Macklen got *totally* snapped out when he saw she was dead. I could see him through a tiny gap in the siding."

"I'm sorry," said Jimmy. "I'm so—"

"Mr. Macklen was screaming at Great White, smacking him with his cane, and Great White just hung his head and took it. I kind of . . . I liked that part."

Jimmy's phone rang. He tried it, and the connection was clear.

"It's me." Rollo sounded like he had just run a marathon. "I fucked up."

"I know."

"No, I *really* fucked up. I didn't throw away all the memory chips that night. I kept some of them, and . . . I sold them about a week ago. Macklen must have found out—"

"I *know.*" Jimmy watched Blaine settle back into the crawl space, lying on his back now. His nose had stopped bleeding. He looked almost peaceful.

"I needed money, and I thought it was safe, and . . . what do you mean, you know?"

"Can we do my interview now?" Blaine mumbled.

Jimmy smoothed Blaine's hair. "You need to go underground for a while, Rollo. Macklen's looking for you."

"No shit, Sherlock. Great White already trashed my trailer. I'm sorry about the chips, Jimmy."

"No, it wasn't you. I got you into this."

"Yeah . . . that's true."

"You'd better find someplace to hide for a while." Jimmy looked over to where Pilar lay sprawled in the ruins of her backyard, saw blood splashed on the grass, and had to turn away. Pilar had plenty of her own crimes on her conscience, but she had never done anything to Macklen. That one belonged to Jimmy Gage, the man who could walk through a shitstorm and not get wet, even while everyone around him drowned. "You hide *deep,* Rollo," he said, talking around the stone in his throat. "I'll clean up the mess I made."

"What are you going to do?"

Jimmy shook his head. "I have no idea."

"Where am I supposed to hide?" Rollo's voice crackled, the signal breaking up. "Can I stay with you?"

"Bad idea."

"What did you say?" Rollo's voice was fading.

"Call nine-one-one," Jimmy said loudly. "Have them send an ambulance to Pilar's house. I'll call you back soon on another line. I know where you can hole up. Can you hear me?"

"I'm not deaf," said Rollo, sounding like he was right next to Jimmy.

Jimmy snapped the phone shut and took Blaine's hand again. "The EMTs are going to be here soon. They'll take care of you."

"Can we do my interview first?"

Jimmy stared at him. "Sure."

"OK . . . OK, first off, I'm totally into natural strength training, no steroids or anything, except sometimes maybe a little crystal meth. My favorite . . ." Blaine was shivering again, his eyes closed now, his hand clutching Jimmy's. "My favorite surf spot is Trestles, but I've never been out of the USA. I heard the waves in Fiji are awesome, so maybe . . ."

Blaine's mouth was still moving, but Jimmy couldn't hear what he was saying. He leaned closer, until Blaine's lips were brushing his ear.

"I want all you little wrestlers," breathed Blaine, "you little guys, to listen to your mom and dad. Don't put them down, they're raising you up. And, oh yeah, don't forget to . . ."

Jimmy waited for the rest of it, but it was too late.

Chapter 39

It was dark by the time Jimmy got home from Pilar's. He had waited with Blaine for as long as he could, sitting beside his body, listening to the neighbors ransack the house. It had been total chaos when the aid car and a police unit arrived, people scrambling out windows and over fences, carrying what they could and dropping the rest. Jimmy had strolled out the side gate, head down, and circled the block before coming around to join the crowd of gawkers asking the uniforms what had happened.

Jimmy had gotten Pilar and Blaine killed, that was what had happened—it was called the Law of Unintended Consequences, or the fuckup's guide to the universe. In the 1980s, for example, the CIA gave Stinger missiles to the Afghani mujahideen, enabling them to shoot down Russian attack helicopters and hasten the fall of the Evil Empire. Then the mujahideen turned their Stinger missiles on the Great Satan. Jimmy had wanted to punish Macklen for murdering Samuel Terrell, determined to balance the scales, and he didn't much like the V C Boyz, either. It had seemed like a good idea even after it went bad, and Jimmy had never regretted what he'd tried to do, not until today, when the wrong people had started dying.

There was a light on in Desmond's living room, but he was long gone; his regular Thursday-night cops-only poker game started promptly at 6:00 P.M., and the punishment for tardiness was to get stuck with the rickety chair. Jimmy rested his head against the steering wheel. He was more than just tired; he was beaten up and beaten down, a smart guy who had outsmarted himself and still managed to escape the repercussions. Pilar and Blaine were dead, Rollo was on the run, but nobody was looking for Jimmy. Lucky man.

Jimmy got out of the car, walked heavily toward his apartment around the back, and opened the door. Before he even switched on the light, he knew he wasn't alone. Once, on a flight to Las Vegas, Jimmy's plane had hit extreme turbulence, shaking so badly that the overhead bins opened up, spilling carry-ons into the aisle, the plane plummeting over a thousand feet before the pilot finally regained control. This felt worse. "Great White . . . what are you doing here?"

"You *are* good, Jimmy." Great White closed the door, the wood floor groaning with the weight of him, the room still in semidarkness. "Didn't I tell you he was good, Mack?"

Macklen stood in the shadows, his face hidden, the moonlight coming through the window glinting off his metal canes. "Hope you don't mind us dropping by like this, slick. Your door was unlocked, so we figured we'd come in and wait."

"I didn't leave the door unlocked."

"Well, I'm extra glad we came by, then," replied Macklen. "Somebody must have broken in and gotten scared off when he saw Great White coming." He pivoted over to Jimmy and held out his hand, and they shook. "I heard you were at the wrestling match last Sunday night. You should have stopped by the office to say hello."

"Next time," said Jimmy, still feeling Macklen's horny, calloused grip. They didn't *know*—not yet, anyway.

"Can I turn on the lights now?" Great White asked Macklen.

Jimmy moved first, switching on the three-way table lamp at its dimmest setting, leaving the room as softly lit as an aquarium. He could make out the rap posters on the wall, Eddie Murphy and Ice Cube and Dr. Dré, but Samuel's framed graduation photo was murky. He didn't know if Macklen would recognize the confident young man in the cap and gown as the scrawny ex-junkie he had murdered, but Jimmy didn't want to chance it.

Macklen braced himself on his canes, neck bulging as he looked around the tiny room, even more powerfully built than Jimmy remembered. "This is real cozy."

"Glad to see you out of the wheelchair," said Jimmy.

"Yeah, well, I still feel like one of Jerry's kids, but what the hell, that's life, right?"

There was a welt along Macklen's jaw, and one of his eyes was swollen half shut. "What happened to your face?" Jimmy asked, pleased to see that Pilar had gone down fighting.

Macklen rubbed his jaw. "Female trouble."

Jimmy could see Great White looming by the door in his black leather coat, vast and threatening, three of his fingers wrapped together with adhesive tape. "Nice coat. Was the S.S. having a garage sale?"

"I *told* you, Great White." Macklen roared with laughter and ended up coughing. "I told him the exact same thing, Jimmy," he said, hacking away while Great White stood immobile. "You and me must be on the same wavelength."

"There's a terrifying thought," said Jimmy. "How did you find out where I live?"

"Wasn't hard at all." Macklen sucked on a tooth. "Your buddy Rollo gave it to us."

"Yeah?" Jimmy locked his knees to keep his legs from shaking.

"Yeah." Macklen rocked back and forth so that his face moved into and out of the shadows. "We stopped by this rusted-out trailer Rollo has out in the boonies. That little chancre wasn't there, but he had your name and phone number written down, so we just took it from there."

"You must have wanted to see me pretty bad."

Macklen shrugged. "This isn't about you. It's Rollo we're looking for. I thought you could help us."

"Don't loan him any money, that's the only help I can give you," said Jimmy. "Does he owe you, too?"

"*Big-time,*" said Macklen.

"Too bad," said Jimmy. "He hit me up at the wrestling match, cleaned out my ready cash."

"How come you got all these mud people on your wall?" Great White tapped a photo of Malcolm X. "You one of them wiggers I seen on Jerry Springer, talking trash, wishing you were black?"

"I don't watch Springer," said Jimmy. "That show's strictly for morons."

The lightning-bolt tattoos on Great White's neck flared, but he didn't say anything.

"You'll have to excuse Great White," said Macklen. "He's Aryan Brotherhood. Me, I got an arena to fill, and the only color I care about is green. Heck, I met some good jiggs and some bad ones, same as white folks, gooks, or beaners. You got to have an open mind when you're in the hospitality business."

Jimmy laughed. He couldn't help it.

"You laugh, Jimmy, but I got no prejudice," insisted Macklen. "Remember that doctor I had, Great White? Best orthopedic surgeon in L.A., and black as the ace of spades."

"If the nigger was so good, how come you ain't dancing?" said Great White.

Macklen glared at him, and Great White looked away.

"I don't have any idea where Rollo is," said Jimmy. "He bounces all over the place. But if he calls, I'll let him know you're looking for him."

"Don't you tell him a fucking thing." Macklen jabbed Jimmy in the chest with one of his crutches, jabbed him hard, then caught himself and tried to make light of it. He tapped Jimmy on each shoulder with the crutch. "I dub you Sir Slick . . ." His attempt at humor trailed off. "Sorry about that. Look, just find out where Rollo is and give me a call."

Jimmy rubbed his chest.

"You want to go out and grab a few beers?" asked Macklen. "I still haven't thanked you for that article you wrote on the wrestling match last week. I got a shitload of calls when that one came out; now everybody wants to book the hall."

"Thanks, but I'm tired. It's been a long day."

"Come on, Jimmy, I said I was sorry." The welt along Macklen's jaw darkened. "It's not like you to hold a grudge."

"Let's get together next week—we'll catch up," said Jimmy.

"It's a date." Macklen's cane slipped on the polished wood floor as he started for the door, and he almost fell.

In his haste to help his boss, Great White brushed against the wall and knocked down one of the framed photographs, shattering the glass.

"Goddammit, Great White, be careful with Jimmy's things."

"It's OK," Jimmy said hastily. "I'll clean it up later."

Macklen stood over the graduation photo, staring down, the tips of his anteater-skin cowboy boots dragging on the carpet.

Jimmy got down on one knee, reached for the photo. "Don't worry about it—"

Macklen pinned Jimmy's hand to the floor with the tip of his cane, driving it into the broken glass. "Not so fast." He ground down on Jimmy's hand, putting his whole weight on it, oblivious to Jimmy's howling. "I seen this picture before."

Jimmy tore himself free and tried to bolt for the door, but Great White blocked him, wrapped his enormous arms around him, and drew him close, squeezing the wind out of him in a rush. Jimmy's vision sparkled as under Great White's soft leather coat he felt a smooth, armored chest. Like Blaine had said, it wasn't fair.

Macklen picked up the graduation photo, his face unreadable.

Great White released his grip slightly, and Jimmy was able to breathe again. Great White smelled like grease in an industrial deep fryer, old grease that needed to be changed.

Macklen nodded at the photograph. "This here's the junkie I popped. The *Register* ran this very same picture the day he got planted." He beamed at Jimmy. "He didn't look nearly so good the last time I saw him."

"What's going on, Mack?" asked Great White.

Macklen stared at Jimmy. "I'm not sure."

"What's the big deal?" said Jimmy. "I bought that photo at a garage sale, along with the posters. It was cheaper than buying new stuff."

"Why did you panic?" asked Macklen.

"You almost broke my hand," said Jimmy. "I didn't know what you were up to. It's been a long time; how was I supposed to know what you were thinking?"

Macklen held on to the framed photograph. "Let's take slick here back to the office, Great White."

"I'm not going anywhere with you," Jimmy said quietly.

Macklen grinned at Jimmy. "Hey, if I were you, I wouldn't want to go with me, either."

Chapter 40

"I *know* you're awake, slick."

Jimmy opened his eyes. He lay on the floor of Macklen's office, still feeling finger impressions on the scruff of his neck. Great White had dragged him out of his apartment, ignoring his kicks and punches for a few moments before stopping him with a head butt. Jimmy had regained consciousness hearing a cover of Bob Marley's "Woman No Cry" and had thought for a moment he was dead, then realized it was Reggae Night at the Big Orange Arena. He sat up awkwardly, his wrists bound with duct tape. "You got new carpeting since I was here last."

"Painted the walls, too," said Macklen, leaning over him. "Had to. Couldn't get the bloodstains out."

"I read somewhere that club soda does a good job." Jimmy pulled himself onto the leather sofa and saw Great White perched on a beer keg beside the door, a sketch pad on his lap, colored pencils clutched in his bandaged fist. A new Barcalounger faced the television, a high-tech model with electronic lumbar supports and a heated massage unit.

"What did I ever do to you?" asked Macklen. "It must have been something damned important. I'd like to know just what the fuck it was."

Jimmy settled back into the couch, listening to a reggae beat pounding through the walls as he scanned the office, looking for something he could use as a weapon. The office was much the same as it had been a year ago, with maybe a few more of Great White's circus drawings and watercolors thumbtacked to the walls—Macklen as a ringmaster, in a top hat and with two good legs; Macklen as a lion tamer, cracking a whip; and, behind the desk, an unnerving portrait of Claude, one of the dead VC Boyz, in sad-eyed clown makeup, his lips a garish blue.

"I asked you a question," said Macklen.

"I don't know what you're—" One of Macklen's canes slammed into the sofa, and Jimmy jumped. Stuffing seeped from the split cushion, a steady leakage that was more unnerving than an explosion of foam innards would have been.

Macklen held up the framed graduation photograph, Samuel's face now spiderwebbed with broken glass. "I don't believe in coincidences."

"Fifty million sperm swimming after one egg, and the best your daddy's nut sack could produce was *you*?" Jimmy said to Macklen. "Coincidence is all there is."

"You know, I always wondered how anybody could have gotten past the security cameras that night," said Macklen. "Cops even checked on the company that installed the equipment, but they didn't come up with anything. Then, on the way back here tonight, Great White *finally* decided to mention that last week you strolled out from behind the curtains at the wrestling match like you owned the place." He whacked Jimmy across the face with the graduation photo, sending glass flying. "Was that a coincidence, too?"

Jimmy felt blood trickling from a gash in his forehead. "I guess this means you're out of the hospitality business."

Macklen leaned closer to Jimmy. "I spent a lot of time this last year trying to figure out who fucked me up. I made a list of all my enemies, all the people I burned, all the people who wanted to see me dead." He shifted his weight on his crutches, arms bulging. "There were a lot of names on that list, but I never once thought of you."

"You must feel pretty stupid."

Macklen nodded. "I'm starting to feel better now, though."

Jimmy smiled. It was either laugh or cry, and he figured he'd better laugh while he still could.

"What's so funny?" demanded Great White.

"It's OK." Macklen lowered himself down onto the couch, his movements as precise and controlled as those of a gymnast on a pommel horse. "Jimmy just wants to show us what he's made of, let us know he's not scared." He put an arm around Jimmy and squeezed him hard enough to puncture a lung. "Good for you."

Jimmy winced, getting a dose of Macklen's sourness. "You can only kill me once."

Macklen lifted one of his legs with his hands, hoisted it next to the other one. "Well, if we do it right, once is more than enough."

"I've got nosy neighbors," cautioned Jimmy, forcing himself to keep on talking. "Old Mrs. Plesa probably took down your license-plate number and has already called it in to the cops."

Macklen lit a clove cigarette, snapping his lighter shut with the suddenness of a decapitation. "I'm not worried." He glanced at Great White, saw him bent back over his drawing pad. "Great White's not worried, either."

"I guess you're just a couple of happy-go-lucky sociopaths," said Jimmy.

"Couple of what?" asked Great White.

"A couple of twitchy motherfuckers who don't give a shit," Macklen translated, grinning. His cigarette popped, a bit of smoldering clove arcing onto the carpet, but he kept his eyes on Jimmy, blew smoke in his face. "Takes one to know one, slick."

There was a knock on the door.

"Help!" Jimmy tried to stand, but Macklen shoved him down, ground the lit cigarette into his neck. Jimmy howled and punched at him with his bound hands, but Macklen just kept methodically twisting the cigarette into his raw flesh.

Another knock, more tentative this time. "Mr. Macklen?"

"Goddammit, C.J.," said Macklen, fighting to hold Jimmy down, stabbing the cigarette into fresh spots on his neck while Great

White wet one of his colored pencils in his mouth and kept on drawing. "I *told* you I didn't want to be disturbed."

Jimmy tore himself free and scooted to the end of the sofa. His neck felt like it was still smoldering. The ease with which Macklen had manhandled him, his own helplessness, made him want to start screaming again, but he fought down the impulse. Once he started screaming, there would be no stopping.

Macklen's left eye was puffing up where Jimmy had hit him, but he didn't seem to mind. "That's a mean-looking burn you got there, slick. I'm afraid it's going to blister."

"I want to take a turn on him before you're finished, Mack," said Great White, his flat, black eyes fixed on Jimmy. "I want to ask him some things."

Macklen rolled his eyes at Jimmy. "Great White's got this thing about the other side," he explained. "He read somewhere that people on the edge of death can maybe get a glimpse of what they're headed for. Great White wants to get a preview of coming attractions."

Jimmy turned to Great White, shivering even though he wasn't cold. "Here's your preview: you in the middle of a vast cesspool, treading shit for all of eternity."

"Sit down," Macklen said to Great White as he started to get up. "Jimmy's just having some fun with you." He poked Jimmy in the ribs with his cane. "Feel that knot in your chest, getting tighter every time you breathe? That's *fear.* Joking helps, but fear, it's a bitch to control; lose your concentration for a moment, and it's running free, running wild, and nothing you can do but shake and cry—"

"Sounds like you're an expert," said Jimmy.

"You could say that," admitted Macklen. "The first few weeks after I was shot . . . they were bad. I didn't even know how many vertebrae there were in the human body until my doctor explained it to me. Fifth lumbar, Jimmy, that's the one that got nicked. A little higher up and I could probably walk with braces, a little lower and

I'd never have made it out of the chair. Yeah, I know all about fear. Now I'm going to teach you a few things."

Jimmy tensed his muscles to keep himself from shivering. He thought he was doing a good job until he saw Macklen smile.

"So why did you do it?" Macklen nudged the graduation photograph with his cane. "I pop some junkie, and a year later you come after me? What the *fuck* is that all about?"

"Untape my hands, maybe I'll remember."

"One way or the other, you'll remember," promised Macklen.

"Go on, Jimmy," said Great White, his hands moving quickly over the drawing pad, sketching. "Tell Mack about that river in South America with the funny name. Try that one out on him. I want to see what you look like afterward."

"That junkie was crazy." Macklen chuckled. "You should have heard him telling me to stay away from his pussy, *ordering* me like he had serious juice behind him. That boy was just asking for it."

"You should have stayed away from his wife and little girl like he told you to," said Jimmy. "They might have been a family again, and you'd still be walking."

"I don't trust a man who pretends he's not afraid," said Macklen. "That's a man who needs a serious fucking to set him straight."

"Samuel wasn't pretending."

"It was 'Samuel,' was it? Piss-elegant name for a junkie." Macklen cocked his head; with the canes and that posture he looked like a praying mantis. "Did he save your life or something? Pull you out of a burning building?" He picked a fleck of tobacco off his lip. "Did you grow up next door to each other, jack off to *Playboy* together?"

"I liked him."

Macklen stared at him. "Got to be *something* more than that."

"I liked him," Jimmy said simply. "I *liked* him, and you killed him."

Macklen shook his head. "You believe this guy, Great White?"

"Yeah, I believe him," said Great White.

"Me, too." Macklen laughed. "You sure do take shit personally, slick, and I can relate to that." He poked Jimmy again with the cane. "Payback, that's the name of the game. I fucked you first by killing your junkie buddy. Then you fucked me with the VC Boyz, you fucked me *good*—credit where credit is due. Well, guess what? It's my turn again."

Jimmy lunged at Macklen, but the cane cracked against his knee, and he stumbled back onto the floor again, staring at the pointy tips of Macklen's cowboy boots. Out of the corner of his eye, he saw that a long shard of glass from the broken picture frame was lodged in the carpet right beside him.

"Why don't you get started, Mack?" said Great White, bent over his drawing pad. "Ain't nobody can hear nothing with the music going."

"I'm in no hurry, and you'd better not be, either," Macklen warned him. He pointed out the portrait of Claude the clown to Jimmy. "That's the boy I saw through the smoke that night, tears and snot running down my face, knowing I was going to die. All three of them VC Boyz was crazy, but Claude, he was a fucking doodlebug. Even half deaf, my ears ringing like a gong, I could hear him that night, jabbering away in gook to the two others—I couldn't understand anything but my name, and he sure as shit was wearing it out that night." He stood over Jimmy, his face blotchy with hate. "The first few times he shot me, I hardly felt it, it was like a dream, but the last one, that *burned*. I remember flopping around on the floor and seeing Great White grab Claude, just crumple him up like a paper bag." He swung the cane, hit Jimmy in the knee again. "Claude died too quick for what he done to me, but I got all the time in the world with you, slick."

Jimmy palmed the sliver of glass and slowly stood up, his knee throbbing. Whatever happened, he was going to die on his feet.

"Why didn't you just kill me and be done with it?" asked Macklen. "All the trouble you went to dragging in the VC Boyz—"

"I wanted to do it myself." Jimmy cupped his hands, sawing at the tape around his wrists. "I was just using the VC Boyz for cover, but . . ."

"Hard work pulling that trigger, isn't it?" said Macklen with a sneer, right in his face again. "Not like those movies you write about."

Jimmy maintained eye contact with Macklen as he cut away at the tape. "Why don't you give me a gun? I think I could get it right this time."

"No can do," said Macklen. "Why did you steal the memory chips, though?"

"Spur-of-the moment decision. I thought it might confuse the cops."

"It had me stumped, too," admitted Macklen. "Pretty smart, thinking on your feet and all, that wasn't bad, but I bet you didn't figure on me and Great White coming out heroes." He grinned at Jimmy. "The mayor himself gave me a plaque for the TV cameras, even shook my hand, told me I had the right stuff. He had soft hands, felt like warm oatmeal."

Jimmy's fingers were cramping as he worked on the tape.

"Things sure haven't turned out like you planned," taunted Macklen. "I mean, look what happened to Pilar. She was just an innocent bystander. I feel bad about that."

"Me, too," Great White said, chuckling. "I feel bad about the Robo-Surfer."

Macklen shook his head. "Why didn't Pilar just tell me Rollo wasn't fronting the memory chips for her? She never said a word, except to tell me to get off her property."

"Would it have done any good?" asked Jimmy.

"Hell, no, but she should have tried," said Macklen. "*I'll* never understand females—"

Jimmy wrenched his hands apart. He slashed at Macklen's throat with the piece of glass but managed only to graze his cheek before one of the canes smacked his shoulder, numbing his fingers.

"You just won't quit, will you?" Macklen wasn't angry; he looked pleased, blood dribbling down his face. "That's good, Jimmy, because you and me got a lot of bad road to travel down before we even things out. Miles and miles—we're going to see the USA in my Chevrolet, you and me."

Jimmy gripped the shard of glass so tightly that his fingers got cut.

Great White carefully set down his drawing pad and colored pencils. "Mack?"

"He's all mine," said Macklen. Blood dripped onto the collar of his shirt, but he paid it no heed, circling Jimmy now, feinting with the cane.

"I'm *glad* I fucked you up," said Jimmy, keeping the sliver of glass close, looking for a chance to cut Macklen's jugular or the nest of veins inside the bend of his arm. "I was at the Vatican a few months ago. All those people lined up asking for forgiveness, and I never even considered lighting a candle for you."

"Keep talking," said Macklen, closing in. "I bet you been talking your way out of trouble your whole life. Well, you got your work cut out for you this time, slick."

"I just wish I had killed you," said Jimmy. A cane shattered an end table he was using as a shield. "You should have seen yourself stumbling around that night. I could have taken you down without a second thought."

"But you *didn't*," said Macklen. "That's the problem with all you smart guys: you can't get the job done." His cane crashed into the wall beside Jimmy, the crook of it lodging in the plasterboard.

Jimmy wrenched the cane away and hit Macklen square across the face with it, dropping him like a bag of shit. He was rearing back to hit him again when he was flung across the room, crashing into a file cabinet.

Someone was knocking on the door again.

"C.J.! Get the fuck out of here!" sputtered Macklen, his head gashed open, blood bubbling from his mouth. Great White tried to help him up, but he just pushed him away.

Jimmy hung on to the file cabinet.

More knocks. "Mr. Macklen, sir?"

"Great White, smack some sense into C.J.," said Macklen, struggling to his feet with one cane, looking around for the other.

Great White opened the door, the reggae music louder now, rolling through the office.

A skinny man in a bad suit stood in the doorway. "I'm sorry, Mr. Macklen, Great White, but I had to do it—"

Holt pushed C.J. aside and pointed her nine-millimeter semiautomatic at Great White. "Police officer. Step back, please." Her hand was shaking slightly. "I said, step *back*."

Great White backed into the room, leather trench coat flapping. He glanced at Macklen.

"Come on in, miss." Macklen tried to wipe the blood off his face but succeeded only in smearing it into a red mask. "Excuse my appearance, but I've been attacked by this man—"

"Jimmy, are you all right?" asked Holt.

"Beating on a cripple," said Macklen, "that's about as low as it gets."

"Head shot, Jane. Head shot," wheezed Jimmy, trying to catch his breath.

Chapter 41

"This is *so* cool," said Rollo, looking around.

Napitano wiggled his toes in the backseat of the armored limousine. "A friend of Jimmy's is a friend of mine, and I am rather pleased that he entrusted your protection to my vehicle."

"This thing is fucking awesome." Rollo bounced on the leather seat beside Napitano as they rolled south on the number 5 freeway, the evening traffic thinning out now. "Feels like we're riding in a battleship."

"My sentiments exactly." Napitano beamed.

"Sink the fucking *Bismarck,* dude."

"Feel free to stay here as long as you like. I have spare toothbrushes and pajamas in the trunk." He pulled the bottle of Cristal out of the ice bucket. The limo had a built-in champagne-refrigeration unit, but Napitano preferred the ceremony of the ice bucket, the delicious rustle of the cubes, the dripping bottle. "Champagne?"

"I'm not really into alcohol, Nino—how about one of those Mountain Dews?" Rollo rapped on the thick bulletproof glass. "Great White, man . . . I don't think even *he* could bust through this. We should drive by the Big O Arena and flip him the bird. It's not that far. You down for that?"

Napitano showed his sharp baby teeth.

"Keep your hands up," ordered Holt, a little too loudly.

Great White's fingers brushed the ceiling. He seemed to think it was funny.

Holt stood just inside the doorway. She was dressed in a sleek knee-length black dress and matching jacket, and Jimmy found himself wondering where she had been on her way to when she decided to save his life. "Can you walk, Jimmy?"

"What about me?" said Macklen. His scalp was open to the bone from Jimmy's blow with the cane, but he seemed more annoyed than wounded. "I'm the one who's been attacked."

Holt swiveled her pistol back and forth between Great White and Macklen. Moving too fast. Better to keep the weapon on one of the suspects, your eyes on the other.

"Call for backup, Jane," croaked Jimmy, still hanging on to the filing cabinet.

" 'Backup, backup,' " mocked Great White. "Ten-four, Eleanor."

"I drove over to your apartment to talk to you," Holt said to Jimmy. "I saw them putting you into a car and wasn't sure what was going on."

"What's going on is that Jimmy just admitted to committing a crime in this very office a year ago," said Macklen, dragging himself over to his other cane. "A fucking felony, lady. You should arrest him before he hurts somebody else—"

"We were making a citizen's arrest." Great White edged closer to Holt. "You ever hear of *posse comitatus?*"

Jimmy stepped away from the filing cabinet. He was unsteady on his feet, but he kept moving.

Holt pointed the gun at Great White's chest. "Get back."

"Head shot," hissed Jimmy.

"I won't warn you again," Holt said to Great White, the gun still trained on his heart.

Jimmy waited until Macklen had pulled himself upright, then kicked one of his canes out from under him, enjoying the sound he made hitting the floor.

"Jimmy!" Holt looked shocked at what he had done, distracted for a moment. Which was all it took.

Great White punched her in the side, bounced her off the wall, then grabbed her by the throat, lifting her off the floor until she was at eye level with him.

Holt still managed to get off three shots—torso shots, just like she'd learned at the academy—while Great White steadily increased the pressure on her throat. She fired once more, the gun dangling from her hand now, her index finger hooked into the trigger guard.

Great White looked into her eyes as she gasped for air, her face getting redder and redder. "Can you see anything?" he asked her.

Macklen pulled himself up again, his face puffed up, a flap of scalp hanging over one ear. "Dammit, Great White, hurry up and finish her."

Jimmy loped across the room, one knee throbbing. He picked up a chair and swung it against Great White's back with all his strength, but Great White didn't even bother turning around, just kept staring at Holt, watching the light die in her eyes. Jimmy clawed at him, but he slid right off Great White's body armor.

Holt's lips were moving, but no sound was coming out.

Great White hoisted her higher. "Can you see anything yet? *Anything?*"

"How is she supposed to answer you?" said Macklen. "Even if she could talk, there's nothing there to see. Nothing to see, nothing to say."

Great White shook Holt. "Look harder. You ain't trying."

Jimmy picked up one of the colored pencils, a sharp green one, and stabbed Great White in the back of the neck with all his strength.

Great White howled, a deep, guttural roar, but he hung on to Holt with one hand and reached around with the other, gingerly touching the pencil that now protruded from his neck.

Jimmy reared back, slammed his palm into the pencil, pushed it farther into the thick white meat, hit it again, and drove the pencil flat, spiked through Great White's spinal cord.

Great White shuddered as though he had been hit by ten thousand volts, muscles twitching in full electrical overload, head jerking. He dropped Holt and turned slowly around, facing Jimmy now, towering over him. The black leather trench coat flapped around Great White like a thunderstorm, but he didn't say a word, the tip of the green pencil sticking out from under his chin.

Jimmy slumped against the couch, out of breath from the enormity of what he had done.

Great White took one step toward Jimmy, then slowly sank to his knees, eyes wide. He stayed like that for several moments, staring at something far beyond the office, and then a vast, deep sigh rolled from his lips and he fell forward onto his face.

Holt sat on the floor. She was trying to say something to Jimmy, but her voice was crushed.

Jimmy heard a sound beside him, looked up, and saw Macklen raising one of his canes overhead, about to splatter his brains across the office. Jimmy thought of Olivia driving the long ball down the fairway. The gunshot made his ears ring. He could see Holt holding the gun with both hands, shaking so hard it looked as if she were applauding. Jimmy felt like applauding, too.

Macklen lay groaning on the carpet, his right shoulder blown open.

Jimmy walked slowly over to her, circling Great White's body, not trusting anything that big to truly be dead. He stepped on something, moved his foot, and saw one of Jane's pearl earrings.

Holt coughed, unable to take a deep breath. She still held her revolver, though.

Jimmy bent down and picked up the earring. It felt like it took hours. He had plenty of time to think.

Holt wheezed.

Jimmy stared at the earring, then sat down beside her.

Holt took the earring from him, touching him with more tenderness than she had last night when they made love. "Thank. You. I. Would. Hate. To. Lose. This." She looked like she was going to cry.

Jimmy kissed her, carefully put his arm around her. "You women and your earrings. Always losing them in the worst possible places."

. . .

"Cops must have busted the coke dealers working the men's room," said Rollo, watching the revolving red and white lights on the police cars outside the Big Orange Arena through the thick glass of the limo, the strobe reflected in his glasses. Caviar dripped off his fingers. "Too bad. I was looking forward to having the manager call Great White out here so I could tell him to kiss my ass."

"Dig deep," said Napitano, as Rollo reached back into the kilo can of beluga, scooping it out with three fingers. "I like a chap with gusto."

"I always wondered what this stuff tasted like," said Rollo, licking his fingers clean as he passed the can back to Napitano. "It's good. Weird, but good."

Napitano scooped up some caviar for himself, slowly pressed his tongue against the roof of his mouth, bursting the black eggs in a flood of ripe sensation.

Rollo washed the caviar down with a swallow of Mountain Dew. "Now what?"

"A friend of mine has some substantial acreage just east of San Diego, a veritable wildlife preserve stocked with zebras, antelopes, giraffes, and other . . . more interesting exotics."

Napitano's smile was dotted with glossy black eggs. "I thought it might be amusing to match my limousine against his particularly ill tempered bull rhinoceros."

"Demolition derby?" Rollo wiped his mouth with the back of his hand. "Nino, man, my camera is locked and loaded. Let's *do* it."

"A veritable clash of the titans, don't you think?"

Rollo considered this. "More like *Terminator Two*."

Chapter 42

Jimmy was floating, drifting in a quiet, peaceful place, when he felt someone take his hand, the coolness of the touch slowly pulling him back to consciousness. He blinked, trying to sharpen his blurred vision, and made out a figure in blue sitting on the edge of the bed. "Hey, Doc. . . ." He moistened his lips. "How am I?" He blinked again, saw Jonathan looking down at him with the same distant expression as in his dream last week, and jerked his hand away.

"You're not going to hit me again, are you, James?"

Jimmy could feel a thick dressing across his neck where Macklen had burned him with the cigarette, and there was another bandage across the heel of his right hand. He tried to sit up, but Jonathan effortlessly pushed him back down.

"Take it easy, you're not going anywhere," soothed Jonathan, his pale face antiseptic under the hospital fluorescents, his short-sleeved surgical scrubs rustling as he smoothed the sheets. "Not for a while, anyway."

Jimmy looked for the call button, but someone had placed it out of reach.

"I was just finishing rounds and thought I would check on you," said Jonathan. "Mother and Father are in Mexico. Mother wanted to cut their vacation short, but I told them your injuries weren't serious."

"Where's Jane?"

"Gallant as always—no matter what your failings, James, I have to give you that. Detective Holt's windpipe was bruised; if the ER hadn't taken aggressive action, she might have suffocated, but she's expected to be released in the next day or so. She was asleep when I looked in on her." He deftly peeled back the bandage on Jimmy's neck, examined the sensitive tissue.

"Please don't—"

"Shhhhh, I know what I'm doing." Jonathan leaned closer. "No sign of infection, that's good. Cigarette burns can leave nasty scars. I'll be happy to do the skin grafts if you like."

"I don't think so."

Jonathan replaced the bandage, his movements so gentle that Jimmy barely felt it. "What's the matter, don't you *trust* me?" He tousled Jimmy's hair, then gave it slight tug, but Jimmy clamped his jaws shut and didn't cry out. "How did it feel, James? I'm really quite curious."

"How did *what* feel?"

Jonathan's eyes were hard and shiny, making Jimmy think of the carapace of a beetle. "How did it feel to kill a man?"

Jimmy didn't answer. He could still see Great White lying face-down in front of him, the green pencil stub sticking out of the back of his neck like the first shoot of springtime. He could still see Holt's pearl earring on the dirty carpet. And he knew, too, that he and Jonathan weren't done with each other yet.

"It wasn't as if you'd used a gun. Your method was so . . . intimate—so grotesque, even." Jonathan checked the stitches in Jimmy's forehead, clucking, displeased with the work. "I'm not criticizing you, of course, but I did read the medical report on Rolf Berger—this Great White fellow, according to the news media. My word, James, you drove a *pencil* right through his brain stem." He tapped the bandage on Jimmy's right hand. "I can't imagine the strength it must have taken to penetrate all that flesh."

"I was highly motivated."

"The man weighed nearly four hundred pounds. If you were a fisherman, you could mount him in your den. If you had a den. That's a joke."

"Ha-ha."

"I just can't imagine what you must have gone through in that office—burned and beaten, fighting for your life. . . . I've never been in a situation even remotely like that. I'm very proud of you, I want you to know that." Jonathan peered down at him. "Any second thoughts now? Any regrets?"

Jimmy watched him. "None."

"That's the spirit. I'm the same way—a surgeon with second thoughts has no business in the operating room. One might as well have a fear of blood." Jonathan continued his painstaking evaluation of Jimmy's injuries, folding down the sheet, poking and prodding, bent over so that Jimmy could see the pattern of hairs in his scalp. Finally satisfied, he pulled the sheet back up. "Dr. Lan, the orthopedist, gave your knee a cortisone injection, and that seems to have worked out nicely. I would imagine you're feeling weak as a kitten, but don't worry, it's mostly the medications, the antiinflammatories in particular. You'll be back tilting at dragons before you know it."

Jimmy's fingers edged toward the call button.

Jonathan patted his hand and pushed it back under the covers, tucking the sheet tightly around him while Jimmy struggled to free himself. "The nursing shift is changing now, and you wouldn't want to disturb them while I'm here to help. What do you need?"

"Nothing."

"How stoic. I don't mean to unnerve you, but Mr. Macklen has been making some wild accusations from his own room in the secure ward. He says you robbed him a year ago as part of some vendetta you had against him. It sounded complicated, but if I remember that case correctly, three young men were killed." He stroked Jimmy's brow with his clean pink fingers, ignoring Jimmy's repugnance. "No one believes Macklen—he's making you out to be some sort of murderous avenging angel. Still, I wanted to alert you in case the police decide to visit. One can never be too cautious in dealing with the authorities." He touched Jimmy lightly on the cheek. "Innuendo can be toxic, James. How close an examination of our lives can any of us stand?"

"I'll take my chances. What about you?"

"*Touché.*" Jonathan patted his arm. "Olivia sends her best, by the way. I'm sure she would have stopped by, but she's preparing for a tournament. She's considering rejoining the pro tour, and this time I think she means it. It might be good for her. She seems . . . distracted lately. Have you noticed?"

"I'm tired, Jonathan."

"Yes, I would imagine you are, laid out like this, not even able to sit up. You must be feeling very vulnerable."

"Not with my big brother here."

Jonathan beamed, his pleasure genuine. "That's the thing I admire most about you, James, that indomitable self-confidence of yours—in spite of all the evidence to the contrary, you maintain your poise."

"Gee, thanks."

"I enjoyed our conversation at my opera party, but you have to admit, you flinched that night." Jonathan glanced at the door, turned back. "The things we said to each other, can you believe it?"

"I'm not sure. *Should* I have believed you?"

Jonathan pointed to a red welt on the side of his jaw. "Look where you hit me. I was showing it off all night; it was all anyone wanted to talk about. I only hope the police don't find out—they latch on to any sign of temper or volatility and start spinning their little webs. I wouldn't want them to start giving credence to Mr. Macklen's tall tales. No telling where their questions would end. There were no more Eggman killings while you were gone; I hesitate to imagine what the police would think if they started up again." He smiled. "See there? You flinched again."

A pretty young nurse popped her head in the door. "I heard you were on the floor, Doctor," she said, flirting. "How is our patient?"

Jonathan stood up, winked at her. "I think he'll live, Elizabeth."

Jimmy waited about two minutes after Jonathan left before hoisting himself out of bed and shuffling over to the nurse's station for directions. Initially they directed him back to bed, but he was adamant.

"Jane?" Jimmy heard the sound of water running when he pushed open the door to Holt's room. He walked in and let the door close behind him. Her bed was empty, but the shower was running. He knocked on the door to the tiny bathroom. "Jane? We need to talk about Jonathan." No response. He opened the door, and steam dappled his face, making the scratches and bruises on it tingle. "Jane?"

Holt peeked out from behind the shower curtain. Her hair was plastered around her face, her necked ringed with purple. You could practically see Great White's fingerprints on her throat.

Jimmy stepped into the bathroom, holding his gown closed in the back.

"Nice ensemble," Holt whispered, her voice hoarse.

"The skinhead's photos, the Polaroids that the cops found in his fight-club album . . . did Forensics match them up to the Laguna Polaroid?"

"You have very strange timing."

"Was it the skinhead, Jane? Did he murder Philip Kinneson?"

Holt shook her head. "No match. That's why I came by your place last night; I wanted to tell you that we still might have a serial killer out there. Why do you ask?"

"I'll tell you about it later." Jimmy turned to leave, but Holt pulled him into the shower, embracing him carefully, the two of them wincing with every move.

"We almost died," she rasped.

"*You* have very strange timing," said Jimmy, his bad knee buckling.

"When that man was strangling me . . . I was closer to death than I was to life." She kissed him. "They say that when you're dying, at a certain point you stop caring and accept the inevitable." She kissed him again. "But Jimmy . . . I *never* stopped wanting to live."

"I didn't head for the white light, either," said Jimmy, gently kissing her bruised throat. "I just wanted to stay here and cause some more trouble."

Holt peeled off his wet hospital gown, all elbows and knees, her hands sliding down past his belly as the warm water sluiced off their bodies. "You can cause all the trouble you want."

Jimmy gasped, leaned back against the shower stall.

"Detective?" The door opened a crack. "Are you all right?" asked the nurse.

Holt stuck her head out the shower curtain, and Jimmy moved behind her, his hands cupping her hips. "Fine," she said. The door closed. "Just fine," she growled as Jimmy entered her.

Chapter 43

"I need your help," said Jimmy.

"I'm so glad to see you—you *scared* me, Jimmy." Olivia stood beside him on the Newport Beach pier, seagulls screaming overhead. She had driven straight over from the golf course after getting his call; her face was still shiny from the heat, leaves stuck to the cuffs of her khakis. She smelled of sweat and fresh-cut grass. "I shouldn't have been surprised that something like this would happen to you; I think it must be what you were trying to prepare me for the last time we talked. You said you had gotten yourself in trouble—"

"We have to talk. This isn't going to be easy."

"When the local news broke into Letterman's monologue, I knew that something bad had happened," Olivia said, not hearing him, her hand on his shoulder as though to reassure herself. "Apartment fire . . . freeway chase . . . armed standoff. . . ." She sounded out of breath, the words tumbling out as though she were afraid of what might happen if she stopped talking. "Then the news anchor said that you and Jane Holt were dead. I started crying, but Jonathan just reached for the phone, getting dressed at the same time—he must have the number of every hospital in the county in his head. When he called from the ER and told me that you were still alive—" She threw her arms around him, held him tight, and he held her back. "I tried reaching you at the hospital yesterday," she sobbed, clinging to him, "but they said you had checked yourself out, so that must mean you're all right. You *are* all right, aren't you?"

Jimmy kissed her on the cheek, then gently disengaged from her. "I need your help."

"Anything, Jimmy, anything you—"

"Did you ever find your diamond earring?"

Olivia stared at him.

"Michelle told me you were looking for it at the office party. I thought maybe if you didn't find it there, you might have gone back to the pool house to check. That was the only thing that could explain what happened with the Polaroids."

Olivia nodded absently. "I knew Jonathan was going there the next day to meet with a contractor. I didn't want him to find it there. He would have known." She lowered her eyes. "I . . . I've always loved the pool house. The Tiki Room, that's what you used to call it. I loved the paint-by-numbers Mauna Loa and the Dole pineapple appliqués your mother put up, the whole Elvis-in–*Blue Hawaii* thing."

"Why did you take the Eggman photos?"

Olivia's gaze wandered across the water, watching the surfers bob on their boards, waiting for a wave.

"Olivia?"

"It was so dark and quiet in the Tiki Room when I went back there that night," said Olivia, still looking out at the water. "I knew Jonathan was going to be at the hospital for hours, so I was just enjoying being there, remembering . . . other times. I didn't even see the Polaroids at first. I was looking for my earring with a flashlight when I saw the first one, of that young man, the track star. Then I saw another: Jonathan being sucked off by some redhead." She looked directly at Jimmy now. "I didn't think much of her technique, but Jonathan seemed to be having a grand time."

"You should have—"

"There must have been a couple of dozen Polaroids of Jonathan with different women. I remember thinking that at least he didn't play favorites." Olivia smiled, but there was no merriment in it. "I still have some of the love letters you sent me. I tried to tell myself that Jonathan and his blow-job photos weren't all that different from me and your letters, but I don't think I was really convinced."

"Why just take the Eggman Polaroids?"

"I took them so Jonathan couldn't use them against you. Those pictures—they were disgusting. I figured you must have found them after I left and thrown them down in a rage. I know how you feel about the people the Eggman murdered, and so does Jonathan." Olivia's voice was rising now. "I thought he was going to use them to hurt you somehow—that's what you do to each other, isn't it? Ripping and tearing. . . . And you're as bad as he is." The breeze off the water was warm, but she was shivering. Jimmy was tempted to put his arms around her. "I left the blow-job photos because I *wanted* him to find them; I wanted him to know he had been discovered. I was going to confront him the next day when he got home. I was going to tell him that I had been there with *you*."

"Why didn't you?"

Olivia shook her head. "I was so sure of myself . . . but then the next day he came home and told me about finding you and Jane Holt here, getting all hot and sweaty pawing through his things."

"It wasn't like—"

"Jonathan told me about his blow-job photos on his own. He *showed* them to me without my even bringing them up. You and Holt shook him; I've never seen him so upset . . . so devastated. He told me you took Holt to the Tiki Room, said you were trying to ruin his reputation. He's my husband, Jimmy, and he had already told me the truth about his . . . souvenirs, and that was hard for him, very hard."

"You're wrong about Jonathan. He's smarter than that."

"Smarter than me, that's what you mean, isn't it?"

"Smarter than the both of us."

"Did you plant those murder Polaroids? You were angry when I walked out that night, and *you're* the one who was obsessed with the Eggman. You probably have lots of photos like that in your files, and you had plenty of time to—"

"Is that what he told you?"

"You're the one who knows the power of the press." Olivia lowered her voice as a family walked past munching from bags of fast food, a little girl throwing French fries at the seagulls while her mother pushed a baby in a stroller. "A blind item in the gossip column, a casual comment to the right people, and Jonathan would be a laughingstock."

"You don't believe that," said Jimmy.

"I *have* to."

"What you have to do is give the Polaroids to Jane Holt. If they're the ones she's looking for, they may help her solve the Eggman killings."

"You and Jonathan . . ." Olivia watched a seagull snatch a French fry from the hand of the little girl just as she went to take a bite. "I never know which one of you is telling the truth."

"Olivia, *please.*"

She looked at him. "I burned them."

"Don't try to protect him."

"I was trying to protect *you.* I burned them as soon as I got home that night. I burned them in the fireplace until there was nothing left. I thought Jonathan was using them to get back at you. I remember how you used to talk about the hate mail you got, the pictures people used to send you—"

"The Eggman. Holt thinks the *Eggman* took Polaroids of his victims."

It took a moment for Olivia to realize what he was saying, then her mouth twisted. "Even for you this is crossing the line. Do you *really* think your brother is a killer?"

"I don't know. That's what I want to find out."

"Do you think it's even a *possibility?*"

"You know him, Olivia. What do *you* think?"

Olivia stood there for a long time, but she didn't respond.

"I need your help," said Jimmy.

Chapter 44

"What are you doing here?" asked Jonathan, his voice echoing, his car keys clutched in his hand.

The underground garage of the Newport Towers was nearly empty—most of the doctors and lawyers who filled the offices had left for the day, Porsches and Lincoln Navigators and Mercedeses circling past, billable hours made manifest. Jimmy had been waiting here for over two hours, breathing stale air and listening to tires squealing on the gray concrete. It was eight days since he'd been assaulted by Macklen, eight days since he'd killed Great White; he was still sore, but his strength was back.

"I just wanted to return your property." Jimmy pulled a stack of Polaroids out of his jacket and shuffled them, the stiff photos rustling like dead leaves. "Pick a card, any card," he said, fanning the photos out upside down. "No?" He riffled the photos, cut, then snapped the top one and held it up: Steve DeGerra sprawled on the running track, mouth slack, one eye wide.

"I've never seen those before," said Jonathan.

"I thought you were just a splatter queen when I first found them." Jimmy shuffled again, did some sleight-of-hand, and plucked Denise Fredericks's ruined face out of Jonathan's ear. "If I'd known you'd taken these yourself, I never would have sicced Holt on you. That lady is a pit bull."

Jonathan glanced around, his skin translucent under the yellow vapor lamps.

"It's a nice night; let's go for a drive. Call Olivia and tell her you're going to be late."

"I think not."

" 'I think not,' " Jimmy mimicked. "Look, Jonathan, I got your nuts in my hands right now," he said, fancy-shuffling. "If I wanted to squeeze, I already would have done it."

"I thought we'd finished this particular game at the opera benefit. You lost, remember?"

Jimmy kept shuffling the crime-scene Polaroids he had borrowed from Jane Holt; the police photos weren't identical to the ones Olivia had burned, but they were close enough to fool Jonathan as he flicked them in the harsh light. "You must have taken two Polaroids of Philip Kinneson, because here's one"—he popped up Kinneson's dead stare, then made it disappear back into the stack—"and Holt has another one just like it. Some kid found it on the beach a few days after the murder and turned it over to the police. It's got a little water damage, a little sun damage, but Holt's not complaining."

Jonathan didn't react. His pupils didn't dilate, his mouth didn't tighten, his brow didn't wrinkle. Perfect control. A red Ferrari drove past, the balding man behind the wheel waving at Jonathan as he slowly negotiated the turns, grinding the gears.

"Every Polaroid camera leaves a unique signature on its photos, a forensic marker as reliable as a fingerprint." Jimmy palmed the Polaroids and showed Jonathan the face of Steve DeGerra again; then he waved his hand, and Steve DeGerra was replaced by the equally dead William Hallberg. Another wave and Elice Santos lay cupped in his hand. "That's why Holt got so excited when I told her what I'd found in the pool house—she wanted to see if your Polaroids matched up with the one from the beach. She's been looking all over for Eggman photos." He spread out the photos, fanned his brow with them. "See what I mean about my having your nuts in my hand?" He grinned. "You *really* should have looked harder for the one you lost on the beach. I hope you're not that sloppy in the operating room. You sure you don't want to go for a drive?"

Jonathan appraised him for a long moment, then pressed his remote entry, and the racing-green BMW beeped like a lapdog. He barely waited for Jimmy to buckle himself in before he peeled down the ramp and out of the parking garage, idling at the signal on the Pacific Coast Highway. It was just after dark, and the air was still warm from the day. A flashing neon sign was reflected on Jonathan's face, the cold blue glare rippling across his cheeks. "Where would you like to go? You must have someplace in mind," he said.

Jimmy cut the Polaroids, flipped up Philip Kinneson. "Laguna it is."

Jonathan drove smoothly through the traffic, making progress without needing to brake, simply finding openings in the flow and exploiting them. "This Macklen fellow has been talking to the newspapers. You're the one who should be worried."

"I slipped up; it happens to the best of us. Look at you, keeping souvenirs." Jimmy pulled out the Polaroids again when Jonathan stopped for a red light; he shuffled and cut the top one. "Carlos Mendoza, come on down!" He waved the photo at Jonathan. "You want to hear something weird? Carlos was at the Big Orange Arena the night before the Eggman killed him. It was Salsa Sunday, and he and his cousin Raoul were checking out the ladies. Carlos got lucky that night; Raoul said it was always that way. Or at least it was until the *next* night, when Carlos ran into *you*." Jimmy put one foot up on the dash. "His mama put up this shrine to him in the family's living room—Carlos's baby shoes, pictures of his First Communion, you name it." He flashed the Polaroid at Jonathan again, the young man's face crowned with a broth of blood and brains. "You think *Mamacita* would like this one for her shrine?"

"I thought you were sympathetic to the victims," said Jonathan. "That watery-eyed prose, the angry interviews—"

"Neither of us is quite what he seems, huh?" Jimmy looked away, confident that he had Jonathan's complete attention. "I've got to do something with these snapshots of yours; I was just playing keepaway at first, but they're too dangerous to have around now. Holt's been dropping by my place unannounced, and I know somebody's been there, looking around—I figure that was probably you, right?" He played with his seat adjustment, riding it up and down, back and forth, while Jonathan pretended not to mind. "You do love your tricks. I was pretty pissed off about your stealing Olivia out from under me. That was a good one; that was even better than your sending me the note from the Eggman."

Jonathan didn't respond.

"I don't blame you for being cautious. I wouldn't trust me, either." Jimmy shuffled. "I was with Olivia before your office party, did she tell you that?"

Jonathan gripped the steering wheel a little tighter.

"I didn't think so." Jimmy snickered. "Lot of good it did me, though. I had hopes, but she's a married woman. That's what she said. A married woman, and she's not married to me." They rode in silence until they reached the outskirts of Laguna Beach. Jimmy sat up as they passed the Paradise Lounge, the windows of the club open wide to catch the ocean breeze, a techno sound track drifting into the night. "There's a small grocery store about a mile down the road. Park there, and we'll walk the rest of the way."

They pulled into the grocery-store parking lot a few minutes later. Jonathan waited outside until his brother came back out with a six-pack of cold beer. Then Jimmy led the way along a narrow path overlooking the beach, stopping halfway down on a large, flat outcropping of rock that was surrounded on three sides by scrub, invisible from the bluffs above but with a good view of the beach below.

Jonathan kicked an empty beer can over the side. "It looks like you've been here before." He cleaned off the rock and sat down beside Jimmy.

Jimmy opened a beer, took a long swallow, passed it to Jonathan. "Were you wearing your surgical scrubs when you played the Eggman? Was that how you got so close? Not one of the victims showed any sign of having resisted."

Jonathan took a sip, looked back up the path.

"Talk to me."

"I don't think I shall, James."

Jimmy stood up unsteadily, unbuttoned his shirt, and threw it onto the ground. "Look, no wires!" He kicked off his shoes, then undid his pants as Jonathan protested. Pants around his ankles, he did a slow pirouette. "Still no wires." Jonathan smiled as Jimmy mooned him. "You see any wires, Doc?" Jonathan pushed him, and Jimmy tripped and fell into the underbrush, the two of them howling now, Jimmy scratched up and bleeding as Jonathan helped him to his feet. Jimmy zipped his pants up and put his shirt back on, leaving it half buttoned, then sat down again, the two of them still laughing.

They passed the can of beer back and forth until it was empty, then popped another one and shared that, too, listening to the waves slapping onto the sand as they worked their way through the six-pack. The breeze rippled the dry grass.

"This is good," said Jimmy, "sitting out here with you. Slam a few brews down your throat, and you're almost human."

"Almost." Jonathan opened another beer, took a long swallow. "You were right about the surgical scrubs," he said softly. "I've underestimated you."

"Pass me that beer, and I'll forgive you." Jimmy pointed to the beach. "That's where the little girl found the first Polaroid you took. It was pretty thrashed, but Forensics could still tell it had been shot with a flash. That's how Holt knew it hadn't been taken by one of her people. Pretty stupid letting it get away from you like that."

Jonathan chewed a thumbnail. "It was windy that night, and I was in a hurry."

"Mistakes happen; don't beat up on yourself." Jimmy pulled out the stack of Polaroids and shuffled them again. "Both of our fingerprints are on these now, but I've got alibis for the killings. Holt's already checked me out." He glanced at Jonathan. "What about you?"

"What is it you want for them?"

Jimmy kept shuffling as he looked out at the Pacific, which beyond the shoreline chop was smooth and glassy all the way to Japan.

When the breeze gusted from the north, it carried snatches of music from the Paradise, tiny bursts of unidentifiable sound, and Jimmy thought of Philip Kinneson making his way home after *Monday Night Football,* feeling good, maybe with a little buzz on, smelling the clean salt air.

"What do you want, James?" The dim light illuminated the curves and planes of Jonathan's face, the arrogant, boneless symmetry. "I've been waiting for you to make your demands ever since I walked in on you and Jane Holt that morning."

Jimmy looked at him. "The DA is investigating Macklen's accusations; any day now I'm going to be indicted for murder. I didn't kill the three VC Boyz myself, but I might as well have. I'd feel a lot better with a *really* expensive defense attorney."

"You could have simply asked me for the money."

"I just did." Jimmy checked his watch, without giving it away. "I should have killed Macklen when I first had the chance. I had the gun pointed right at his head, but I couldn't do it."

Jonathan popped the last beer, suds foaming over his hand. "The first one is the hardest. Best just to step up and get it over with. After that . . ." He shook beer off his fingers.

"You don't tell on me, I won't tell on you," said Jimmy. "Just like when we were kids."

Jonathan passed him the beer. "This Macklen fellow, was it personal?"

"Very."

"No wonder you couldn't pull the trigger. Emotions are too . . . unsettling."

"I'm not like you, Jonathan; I need a reason. I used to look at Macklen sitting around his office, and the whole universe seemed wrong—tilted, somehow. Killing him was going to be like straightening a picture that was out of place."

"James Gage, straightener of the universe, God's own handyman." Jonathan chuckled. "Sorry, brother, but the world is running down, and there's no way you can wind it up again." He patted Jimmy on the back. "You were right at the opera party. Those six people, my half dozen; I didn't care who they were—sinners or saints, cabbages or kings, it made no difference to me. I could have walked right past them, but I didn't, *I* didn't, and that made all the difference." His mouth was a thin sneer. "Do you really think God's making a list, checking it twice? Do you think he keeps *score?*"

Jimmy smiled. "Maybe he should. Then I wouldn't have to."

"If it's godhood you aspire to, forget the personal touch and kill them all, the blameless and the bad, kill every one of them. *Then* you'll know what it's like to be God." They looked into each other's eyes for a long time before Jonathan realized that his cell phone was buzzing. "Speak slower," he said into the phone. "Calm down. Calm *down*. Did they say what they're looking for?" He listened. "Call Barry Slosberg, his home number is in my Rolodex. Tell him to get over to the house immediately." He listened again, for a long time now. "You're certain that's what they said? Call Barry; I'll be home soon." He snapped shut the phone.

"What's happening?"

Jonathan tugged at his lower lip. "That was Olivia. Detective Holt is at our home with a search warrant. She's looking for evidence connected to the Eggman homicides."

"She's looking for these," said Jimmy, holding out the Polaroids. "She's probably got a warrant for my place, too." He tore Denise Fredericks in half.

Jonathan stopped him before he could tear it again, gently taking the ripped photo and the rest of the stack, staring at the faces in the dim light of the stars, slowly going through them, almost tender. "I should never have kept these. It was an indulgence on my part, a vanity." He tilted Steve DeGerra to get a better view. "I watched this boy run laps for about fifteen minutes before I stepped out from the bleachers. It was a cool morning, the dew shiny on the grass, his breath like steam in the air, and it was—"

"We have to destroy them."

"I didn't need to keep them," Jonathan said, talking to himself more than to Jimmy. "I didn't need a reminder of what I had accomplished. I remember every killing, the smells in the air, their skin tones and the expressions on their faces, the sound the gun made. . . ."

Jimmy took the photos from him and started tearing them up while Jonathan first watched, then finally helped him, the two of them working until the Polaroids were bits and pieces on the ground. Jimmy took out his lighter and set the ragged faces on fire.

Jonathan watched the dead blacken and curl in the flames. "Somehow it seems appropriate that you discovered my . . . mementos. We've never had any secrets from each other; there was never enough room in that house for secrets, and not enough room for the two of us, either. 'Share and share alike' is a pleasant sentiment, but it's not realistic." He took a deep breath, as if they were swimming and he were getting ready to dive for the bottom. "Still, I think if I have loved anyone in this life . . . it's you. Don't laugh. I take love seriously."

"So do I."

Jonathan ground the blackened bits of paper into the sand, then stood up. "I have to go. Do you need money for a cab?"

Jimmy stood beside him. "I'll come with you. You and I . . . we're in this together."

"Are we? What game are we playing now?"

"Oh, this is the one where Olivia and I are setting you up so that we can live happily ever after."

"She doesn't love you anymore, James. If that's what you're thinking."

"I know."

Jonathan stared at him until he was convinced that he was telling the truth. "I'm not going home just yet," Jonathan said. He stirred the ashes in the sand, watched the wind carry them away. "Olivia overheard a couple of the police officers talking. There's evidently another search warrant, for another . . . *unnamed* location."

"Like I said, they're going to hit my place, too."

"I don't think so. They're waiting for me to arrive before they serve it." Jonathan looked at the black waves, the whitecaps catching the dim light. "I haven't been quite as cautious as I should have been. There are some other . . . items that I kept."

"Do the police know where they are?"

Jonathan didn't answer.

"The Polaroids can't hurt you now; if the cops don't know where the rest of your '*items*' are, you're in the clear. So what do you want to do?"

Jonathan turned to Jimmy, his eyes deep-set and sad. "All right, James. I'll play along."

"It was pretty stupid of you to leave anything here after I found the Polaroids," said Jimmy as they climbed through the window into the pool house. It was almost eleven o'clock; most of the neighboring houses were dark. They had circled the block on foot, listening, before cutting into the alley. "What were you thinking?"

"I had no place else to put them," Jonathan said, "and besides, you missed them the first time, and there was no reason to think you'd come back again."

The room was darker than when he had been here with Olivia. "Jonathan?"

"So many memories in here—the room is overflowing with them, isn't it?" Jonathan's voice was disembodied in the darkness, a shadow among shadows. "I see images of you and me bent over our desks, images of us soaked with sweat, a knife flashing and your back to the wall . . . images of you and Olivia rolling around on the couch, the two of you groaning away in this dirty little room." Jimmy hadn't heard footsteps, but Jonathan's voice had moved to another part of the room. "Perhaps I'll give her back to you. Would you like that, James?"

"No thanks."

Jonathan laughed, and the sound made Jimmy shiver. "I used to enjoy coming here after work. I'd sit at the desk and go over my pretty pictures for hours and hours. You have no idea how much pleasure they gave me. . . . I think in some way I was erasing what you and Olivia had done here, wiping the slate clean, as it were." The floor creaked. "Did she really turn you down the night of my office party?"

"Turned me down cold."

"But if she had been willing?"

"I'd have fucked her until she forgot all about you. I'd have fucked her until *I* forgot all about you, too."

The grass-skirt curtains rustled, and Jonathan was suddenly closer. "I believe you."

"Get what you came here for, and let's go."

"What's your hurry?"

Jimmy squinted, his eyes adjusting to the dim light now, seeing Jonathan right beside him. "I don't like standing around in the dark waiting for the cops to show up."

"*Are* the police coming?"

"Make a decision, Jonathan, I'm getting bored."

Jonathan walked to the couch, slid it over, and started pressing at the floorboards, using both hands, his nails scrabbling on the wood. One of the floorboards popped up, and Jonathan reached in and brought out an old leather medical bag. He held the bag up for Jimmy, a grinning ghost holding up a trophy. The front porch creaked.

"Come on in, Jane!" shouted Jimmy. "Help!"

A flashlight beam caught Jonathan in the face as he reached into the bag, blinding him, and Jimmy thought of Macklen slumped against his desk in his office, trapped in the flashlight as Claude pumped bullets into him.

"Put your hands up!" Holt was framed in the window, a flashlight in one hand, a pistol in the other.

Jonathan threw an arm over his face to shield himself from the light. From behind his arm, he glared at Jimmy.

The front door was kicked open. "You're under arrest, Dr. Gage," said Desmond, his voice easy and authoritative. "Don't you move, now."

Jonathan pulled a revolver from the bag and pointed it at Jimmy's chest, but for all his vaunted steadiness, his hand trembled. He hesitated, and Jimmy tackled him, the gun clattering across the floor.

Jonathan clawed at him. "Is this the best you can do? This is *nothing*."

"I . . . didn't . . . really believe it," Jimmy grunted, trying to restrain his brother as he kicked and struggled. "Even after everything that had happened, I still didn't believe it." He felt out of breath, his ribs aching, but he tried to hang on. "Olivia didn't want to make the call tonight, but she couldn't live with the doubt. Now we both know who you really are."

"I know who *you* are, too," Jonathan growled, and Jimmy could feel spit peppering his face. "The things you told me on the beach tonight, the things you said about Macklen—I was watching you, and those weren't lies. Not all of them."

"Just some of them. I'll tell you which ones someday."

Jonathan quit fighting, holding on now, pulling Jimmy closer, stronger than Jimmy remembered his being. "Tell me now."

Jimmy hit him and kept hitting him until he let go.

"I didn't flinch, James, you remember that," Jonathan said, his face transparent in the glare of the flashlight, placid as a mask. Only his eyes were alive, burning with an awful, frozen light. "I didn't flinch."

Jimmy stared back at him. "Neither did I."

"Poor James." Jonathan dabbed at his dripping nose, his resonant laughter reduced to a cackle now, sharp and thin. "You always draw blood, but you never win."

Jimmy stood up. He was aware of Holt and Desmond nearby, but he didn't need their help anymore. "Game's over, Jonathan."

Epilogue

Boarding gate number 21 at the Orange County Airport had closed, but Jimmy stayed in front of the window in the terminal, watching the last of the passengers find their seats on the Boeing 777. "What are you doing here, Jane?" he asked, not turning around, smelling her perfume.

"Desmond told me where you were."

"You know me, I'm a sucker for that closure crap."

"Is that what it is?"

Jimmy turned around. Holt looked cool and elegant, as usual, but she was wearing her hair longer these days, a little freer, curling around the shoulders of her suit. He liked it. They had seen plenty of each other in the six months since she arrested Jonathan, their relationship bobbing about in that treacherous zone between professional and personal. "I was going to call you tonight."

Holt watched the plane slowly taxi toward the runway. "Where is she off to?"

"Phoenix Open," said Jimmy. "Then she starts the rest of the tour. I watched her play last weekend, and I think she's got a chance."

Holt nodded at the newspaper someone had left on a nearby seat. HUNG JURY FOR BEAUTY DOC, read the headline. "I talked with the DA's office. They're going to retry the case."

"I have visions of Jonathan getting acquitted again and *me* going to jail."

Holt didn't respond, which was the professional part of their relationship that kept coming between them.

Prosecuting Jonathan should have been a slam-dunk for the district attorney. The doctor's bag Jonathan had retrieved from under the floorboards of the pool house contained a thirty-eight-caliber revolver loaded with Glaser safety slugs, a label maker, and a Polaroid camera, all with Jonathan's fingerprints on them. The slugs were the same type of bullet used in the Eggman homicides, and the label maker was the same brand that had produced the note to Jimmy. Three forensics experts, including one from the FBI crime lab, testified that the Polaroid camera was the same one that had been used to take the Kinneson photo found on the beach at Laguna.

Jonathan, however, had assembled a team of lawyers that made O.J.'s dream team look like Legal Aid clerks. Jonathan's attorneys dismissed the safety slugs and the generic label maker as "merely circumstantial," "a practical joke in poor taste," or "planted evidence"—take your pick. They also brought in three forensics experts of their own who disputed the match between the Laguna Polaroid and Jonathan's camera. The unexplained murders that had occurred in three different South American villages where Jonathan had performed his outreach work were ruled inadmissible.

Jimmy had testified, of course, but he had been destroyed on cross-examination, cast as a marginal writer and occasional drug user, a man jealous of his brother's success and enraged by the loss of his former girlfriend—"a woman who conveniently filed for divorce the day after her husband was arrested," as Jonathan's lead attorney told the jury with a sneer. Jimmy was accused of enlisting his friends in law enforcement in his scheme to frame his brother, and the mention of his arrest in Rome—"with a *thirty-eight-caliber revolver*, ladies and gentlemen of the jury"—caused a noticeable ripple in the courtroom. In TV interviews on the courthouse steps, one of Jonathan's attorneys even suggested that if the district attorney really wanted to determine which of the brothers was capable of murder, he might wish to talk with Lee Macklen, an inmate currently serving a thirty-year sentence at Chino State Prison.

Jonathan, by contrast, had been a stellar defendant, shocked and hurt by the accusations against him, beseeching the jury to give him back his good name. He had looked directly at James from the stand and told him that he forgave him. A panoply of local power brokers had testified as to Jonathan's good character, his kind works, and his selfless devotion to medicine. In the end, three members of the jury had held out for acquittal. Rollo and Napitano had both correctly predicted an acquittal, but Rollo hit the count exactly, winning an undisclosed payoff from Nino.

Holt stood beside Jimmy at the window now, watching the plane gather speed as it raced down the runway. "Desmond says you haven't seen much of Olivia these last few months."

"Desmond talks too much."

"He said you didn't even try."

Jimmy waited until the airplane's wheels had left the ground. "She wasn't right for me."

"No, she wasn't."

Jimmy followed the 777 as it banked toward the ocean, getting smaller and smaller. He turned away, looked at Holt. "Now what?"

"Why don't we start with a movie?" Holt smiled. "Is there anything good playing?"

ABOUT THE AUTHOR

ROBERT FERRIGNO is the author of five previous novels, *The Horse Latitudes, The Cheshire Moon, Dead Man's Dance, Dead Silent,* and *Heartbreaker.* He lives in the Pacific northwest.

MARRIAGE ON THE ROCKS

MARRIAGE ON THE ROCKS

JANET GERINGER WOITITZ

DELACORTE PRESS / NEW YORK

Published by
Delacorte Press
1 Dag Hammarskjold Plaza
New York, New York 10017

Manufactured in the United States of America
First printing

Designed by Oksana Kushnir

LIBRARY OF CONGRESS CATALOGING IN PUBLICATION DATA
Woititz, Janet G
    Marriage on the rocks.

    Includes index.
      1. Alcoholics—United States—Family relationships.
      2. Alcoholism—United States.   3. Alcoholics—Psychology.
I. Title.
HV5132.W64   362.8′2   79-13507
ISBN 0-440-05918-6

ACKNOWLEDGMENTS

I want to thank my children—David, Lisa, and Daniel—for encouraging me in my work and for adding a special quality to my life.

jan

This book is dedicated to those of you who live with alcoholic husbands in the hope that it will lead you out of the maze of hopelessness and despair into a full, rich, and happy life, whether or not your husband stops drinking.

CONTENTS

INTRODUCTION

The National Council on Alcoholism estimates that there are ten million alcoholics in this country. Each one of these profoundly affects the lives of at least six other people. The figures are staggering, and, I suspect, conservative.

Much attention has been given in recent years to understanding alcoholism and working with alcoholics. This work is vitally important. Unfortunately not enough attention has been given to the family. The theory has been that if the alcoholic recovers, the family will recover. This theory is somewhat simplistic for several reasons. First, it dooms the family whose alcoholic does not recover. Second, it assumes that the family recovery can start only after the alcoholic's recovery starts, and third, it does not take into account that the family can be as sick as, if not sicker than, the alcoholic.

A family who comes to grips with the problem can play an important part in the recovery of the alcoholic, but the family's own recovery is important enough to treat separately. That is what this book is about—how families of alcoholics can help themselves to recover.

What I have discussed in this book, for the most part, is the stereotypic American nuclear family. The husband is the primary breadwinner and the wife is the homemaker who takes care of their 2.3 children. Although this is only one domestic style, it is probably the one that is still considered the most common. The discussion of one model also helps to keep the ideas somewhat simple. As you will see, the dynamics operating within the alcoholic family system get very complicated very quickly.

There are many other models that can be developed to look at alcoholism within a family. There is the situation where the wife and not the husband is the alcoholic. There is the situation where both adults are alcoholic. There is the situation where one or more children are alcoholic. There is the situation where one or both parents are alcoholic. There is the situation where a brother or sister is the alcoholic. There is the situation where a lover and/or roommate or the roommate's lover is the alcoholic. There is the situation where the boss is the alcoholic. There is the situation where the wife of an alcoholic is trying to maintain a career. There is the situation where the child has left home physically but not emotionally. And since alcoholism tends to run in families, and since people tend to marry people like those they have known, it is not unusual for the wife of an alcoholic to also be the daughter of an alcoholic, and for her brother or sister to also be an alcoholic, and so on and so on.

Picking only one model also leaves out other complicating variables such as chronic illness, divorce, widowhood, aging dependents, and so on, ad infinitum. The combinations become infinite, the problems too complex to deal with until they are broken down. That is why I have chosen a rather simple model to explore.

Each of the situations described above has its own special needs that cannot be minimized. Just shifting the glass does not mean that nothing else changes. However, many of the generalizations discussed in this book will work regardless of your particular situation. Because it is not outlined precisely as it affects you, does not mean that the principle does not apply.

If you are the husband or the working wife, bear in mind that compulsive over-involvement in activity at one stage and almost indolence at another applies regardless of whether you are running General Motors or scrubbing the kitchen floor.

If you are a child reading this book, it should give you a better understanding of what has happened to you and how it has happened. It should also give you some idea of how you can help yourself to get out of the situation. If you are a child of one alcoholic parent, it might be a good idea to give a copy of this book to your sober parent. If you do not have a sober parent, it may be time to start looking for an adult whom you can trust. If you can't do that for yourself, write me in care of the publisher and we'll find you a way.

If you are a parent reading this book, you will probably go all through it and understand what relates to you and what you should do, and you will close the book and say, "But God help me, it's my kid—there's got to be something more I can do. If I had not been a failure as a parent this would not have happened." It is so hard to step away from our children and see them make mistakes in their lives regardless of whether they are ten or fifty.

I suggest to you that you read everything you can on the disease of alcoholism. Look at your extended family to see if alcoholism is part of a family trend. Until you can begin to accept the fact that you did not cause your child's disease, you cannot be of any help. You will only beat yourself into the ground and you will accomplish nothing. Worse than that—you will close off the lines of communication because your child will be unable to handle the pain he/she sees in your eyes.

If your boss is the alcoholic, you may want to take a good hard look at whether or not you are willing to work in that situation. You will be working with someone who will undermine your self-confidence, and, when you are scrambling to get your act together, will criticize you for not being more aggressive. This book should give you an understanding of what is happening. Only you can estimate the damage that can be done to you. You may decide to use it to your advantage, but I've never known anyone to outmanipulate an alcoholic until the final stages, where the disease is apparent to everyone.

A friend of mine has an alcoholic son who is no longer drinking. He decided about six months ago to join a religious cult which very heavily brainwashes its membership until they become robotlike. Two months ago he returned home, unaffected. His mother was flabbergasted. I said, "Why be surprised? You know as well as I do that *nobody* tells an alcoholic what to think." When his mother asked him to explain this seeming miracle he said, "I took what I liked and left the rest."

To those of you reading this book I would simply say, "Take what you can use and leave the rest." Not everything said will apply to everyone, but at the very least, you will have a better understanding of the enemy, alcoholism, and some of the weapons used in the war against it.

It is important to realize that the enemy *is* alcoholism. It is important to realize that even though the book is about the alcoholic marriage, it is not a male-female issue. It is important to realize that even though the book uses the traditional female role model it is not a liberated-unliberated female issue.

In my office I have seen men and women, old and young, black and white, Christian and non-Christian, gay and straight, professionals and laborers, rich and poor, urban and rural, single and married, and in various combinations thereof. One of the things that I am likely to say at the first interview is, "Before you tell me what is happening, let me tell you."

The response is always the same. After the initial shock has worn off, the vocal cords once again begin to function. "How did you know?"

I know because I understand what happens to the family of an alcoholic. I know because I recognize that it is not an issue of men versus women or traditional versus untraditional life-styles, but of the POWER OF THE SICK OVER THE WELL. This illness is a great equalizer. The people who should be stronger or wiser or more tuned in fall victim just as readily as everybody else. No racism or sexism here. Alcoholism supports the ERA without reservation.

This book should help to make clear when it is the illness one is reacting to and when it is the person. It is only when you can understand that difference and not allow the sickness to take over that you can look at whatever other issues exist.

In most instances in this book the alcoholic spouse is he

and the nonalcoholic is she. I did this for a number of reasons. The first has to do with convenience. It is simpler to write it that way than to say he or she each time it is appropriate. The second has to do with the fact that the majority of my clients have been women, and I naturally think in these terms. Although we are learning that the ratio of women to men alcoholics is more even than previously thought, there is one major difference as it relates to the family. The nonalcoholic wife will more often than not remain in the marriage whereas the nonalcoholic husband will leave. Therefore, there is a higher percentage of women than men who require counseling in order to learn to live healthfully within the alcoholic situation. Although my discussion is slanted toward this model, most of what I say is true regardless of sex and should be recognized as such.

I'm writing this book for all of you who live with a drunk and feel you're all alone. You're not all alone. Millions of women live with alcoholics; it's a private hell but a public problem.

I'm writing to you and about you. You may have picked the book up because you feel desperate. You just don't know what to do anymore. You've tried everything you can think of to get your husband to stop drinking, and nothing has worked. You've tried lecturing: "Look at what you're doing to your body. You're going to rot out your liver." That hasn't worked. After all it's his liver. You've tried tears: "If you really loved me and the children, you wouldn't do this." That hasn't worked either. You've tried hiding the bottles, threatening to leave him, and even drinking with him. You've tried nagging, reminding him about his behavior so that he won't repeat it. You tell him on the way to the party what you expect of him. He promises he won't get drunk, but he does anyway. Nothing works.

And what do you accomplish? Well you induce a little guilt; he can then drown his guilt in booze. Or you make him angry. Who wouldn't drink if he were married to you? Heads the bottle wins—tails you lose. You lose because he still drinks and you lose because you can't stand the person you are turning into. You never imagined you would become a screaming fishwife or a tearful doormat.

Despite all of the above I still have the nerve to say that you can learn to live with an alcoholic. Not only can you live with an alcoholic, you can be happy and productive no matter what he does. Perhaps you don't believe me. I wouldn't if I were in your place. I'd be thinking, "What does she know? If she lived with what I live with she wouldn't hand me that crap!" Well, I *do* know how you can improve your life. Decide whether you want to try it out. If you don't you can keep all your unhappiness. The choice is yours.

1 A LOOK AT THE PROBLEM

We live in a society where drinking alcoholic beverages is encouraged and even expected. A man has difficulty being socially "with it" when ordering club soda or a Coke. "Drinking someone under the table" is manly, and making a martini without "bruising the gin" (whatever that means) is chic. We admire the gourmet who knows the appropriate wine to drink with each course at dinner. And we laugh at the man with the lampshade on his head—unless, of course, he happens to belong to us.

Yet the very men who are so "in" socially are "out" if they become addicted. We treat them as social outcasts and avoid them as if mere contact will taint us. They become social lepers, and so do their wives. We've all heard friends say,

"I'd love to have Sally over, but you know how obnoxious Bill gets when he has a few."

You know what that feels like. You don't really want to go with him, but you don't want to go without him either. Avoiding the issue seems to be the best course to take; as a result, you don't go out at all. No one has been honest about what the problem is. If it is not discussed, you think, it will go away. But the pain of the rejection does not go away—it hurts. It hurts like hell and you are angry. Furthermore somewhere mixed in with all those feelings is the nagging thought that somehow you are responsible. Maybe you are all those terrible things he says you are. Maybe if you were a better person he would stop drinking. At the very least maybe there is something that you haven't thought of that will make him stop.

The alcoholic husband of a friend of mine used to say to her, "You're such a great social worker. You help so many people. Why can't you help me?" She tried. And she believed that she should help him. She knew in her head that a doctor should not treat his own family. But in her gut she felt extremely guilty—he knew how to make her feel that way. Yet she couldn't help him stop drinking. She was not the cause and she could not be the cure!

She was not the cause because he is an alcoholic. Alcoholism is a noncommunicable disease. No one can cause such a disease in another person.

You're probably thinking: Yeah, alcoholism is a disease and all that, but how do I know if my husband really is an alcoholic. Maybe he is just a bastard. Or morally weak or emotionally ill or under so much pressure that he needs the alcohol to slow down. "I *knew* that my husband could *not* be an alcoholic for a number of very good reasons," Wendy R. told me. "He was obviously not a bum. He was always well-

dressed and always looked terrific. I would look like death
warmed over after an all-night brawl, but he looked just fine.
He held a very responsible job. He was an executive in a
company where he had to make split-second decisions without wavering. His work was brilliant and everything he did
won an award. Alcoholics cannot do such things. Everyone
knows that there is brain damage; the brain slows down and
the thinking processes get numbed. I knew he could not be
an alcoholic because it would mean that my mother was
right: I should have married the other guy. I knew he could
not be an alcoholic because he never fooled around with
other women and alcoholics are unfaithful."

One myth after another. "Essentially I knew he wasn't alcoholic because I loved him and he was my husband and the
father of my children and I DIDN'T WANT HIM TO BE!"

You know what? He is. He was and is and always will be.
He has a disease called alcoholism, which is incurable. It can
be arrested, but he will be an alcoholic all his life. It is a fact
of his life—and hers—just as if he had diabetes or blue eyes.

I know that you are still not convinced. That's not important right now because you are thinking about the problem.
The point is: No woman who has consulted me about her
husband's drinking has ever been wrong. No woman ever
says, "I think my husband has a drinking problem," when it's
not a fact. More often than not she has underestimated the
seriousness of his drinking. Many a husband says, "She
doesn't know what the hell she's talking about. I may have
one or two to relax but that's it." The amount of liquor in the
one or two is, of course, not discussed. Winning the argument is not the same as winning the battle.

Alcoholics Anonymous says that if alcohol is interfering
with any area of a person's life, chances are that person is an
alcoholic. You had probably already decided that alcohol is

having a bad effect on your life when you picked up this book. Certainly you can agree that a problem exists. But you still don't know exactly what an alcoholic is.

As in most things what is true for one person is not necessarily true for another. Yes it is true that some alcoholics end up on Skid Row. Not all, but some. It is true that some alcoholics show the effects of the chemical in their physical appearance. Some alcoholics cannot hold a job of any nature. Even some mothers are right! Not Wendy's, though. Wendy married Jim because she was very much in love and, in spite of all her troubles, she would do it again. If you attend an A.A. meeting, you will meet all kinds of people from every walk of life. Just as in any other group of people, you will be drawn to some and others will turn you off. The main things these people have in common are their alcoholism and their desire to come to grips with the disease.

The only statement that applies to all alcoholics is that an alcoholic is a person who cannot drink normally. There is, however, a cluster of personality traits that most alcoholics have in common. Although not every alcoholic has all of these traits, and they are not exclusive to alcoholics, some knowledge of them will help you to understand what is happening to him and you and to those around you. What happens is predictable. Knowing this may make you feel less alone. Later we will talk about what you can do about your situation—what you can do so that you can enjoy your life and enjoy being you. The alcoholic's traits that I am going to discuss include: (a) excessive dependency; (b) emotional immaturity; (c) low frustration tolerance; (d) inability to express emotions; (e) high level of anxiety in interpersonal relationships; (f) low self-esteem; (g) grandiosity; (h) feelings of isolation; (i) perfectionism; (j) ambivalence toward authority; and (k) guilt.

Excessive Dependency

The alcoholic is a very dependent person. He prefers not to take responsibility for his behavior. Let George do it. Then when George does it, if anything goes wrong it's George's fault. He himself would not have made the mistake. The alcoholic prefers to have someone make all his decisions for him, including what he eats and what he wears. Recently I've been working with a family in which the alcoholic husband is continually threatening suicide. This keeps the rest of the family off balance. Every time he makes his threat they get scared and try to talk him out of it. They minister to his every need and whim. This man cannot decide whether to have cornflakes or an egg for breakfast and quite often he eats nothing.

The last time his wife called me in a panic with "This time he really means it," I answered, "Say good-bye. After all if he really means it there's nothing you can do." When she said "Good-bye" he came right home. What else could he do? Thinking he might be ready for some help, I called him the next day. "My family would be better off without me," he lamented. "They probably won't dance in the streets," I answered, "but I will, because at least you have made a decision." I also gave him the name of a doctor who would prescribe medication to ease convulsions while he was making his decision. He still hasn't made it.

He's dying more slowly from alcohol than from the more flamboyant act of suicide, but he's given up the threats. His wife and two oldest daughters started college this fall. One of them is a student of mine and comes in smiling and happy. They are my main interest. They have not abandoned their alcoholic, but they have learned how not to abandon themselves either. He's not too crazy about me because he can't control them anymore. Yet he still does not want to take responsibility for his behavior.

Avoiding responsibility and making decisions is one of the things that causes alcoholics to drink at first. But drinking does not resolve dependency problems. The alcohol itself becomes a need. His "I just need a drink to relax me so I can think clearly" becomes a vicious cycle, creating even worse physical and emotional dependency.

Emotional Immaturity

"When an individual starts drinking alcoholically, he stops developing emotionally" is a common maxim. He just looks like forty. Emotionally he is about seventeen. I'm sure you often feel that your alcoholic husband is just another child in the house. This, as strange as it may sound, is very close to the truth. A client of mine was making wonderful progress, which stopped suddenly. After a month had passed, I finally confronted him. Was there a change in his life that was getting in his way? The only thing he could think of was taking two or three drinks each night in order to get to sleep. Those two or three drinks could have been shot glasses or tumblers. From the moment he started drinking to excess, he stopped developing emotionally. My position was quite clear: I do not counsel chemicals. When he eliminated the alcohol, we were able to move on.

Emotional growth tends to result from confronting discomfort or pain. If we remember clearly, we have to admit that the times we grew the most were during times of trial. The happy times, the carefree times, were not growing times. I have never heard anyone say, "It was a wonderful easygoing time, and boy did I grow." Growth seems to come with a desire to develop or change, along with a discomfort about things the way they are. Since the alcoholic is busy anesthetizing himself against unpleasant reality, he cannot develop emotionally. His chronological age and his emotional age are very different. One is adult and the other, child. You get into trouble when you expect this drunk child to act like a sober adult. How many times have you criticized your alcoholic husband for his behavior? You were, in effect, asking a drunk to act sober when you said, "Don't drive like that!" If you had in you what he had in him, would you drive any differently? Probably worse. "Don't cry like that!" we say to a child. He replies, "It's the only way I know how to cry!" What we are really saying to the child is, "Don't cry!" and what we are really saying to the alcoholic is, "Don't be drunk!" That's a contradiction in terms. It is natural for the child to cry, and it is natural for the alcoholic to drink.

Low Frustration Tolerance

The alcoholic has a short fuse, and you never really know what particular thing is going to set it off. Life itself ignites the fuse. Certainly a wife and children get in the way. The least little thing can set your husband off. Things tend to happen which cause outrageous reactions. The phone has a habit of ringing when someone calls. Alcoholics have been known to rip it off the wall because it has the nerve to intrude. In addition a simple snag can turn the whole day into a nightmare—the baby-sitter is ten minutes late, there is no clean towel in the bathroom, or the mayonnaise is on the wrong piece of bread.

The ordinary frustrations of everyday living are overwhelming to the alcoholic. Have you ever noticed the way children walk through a room, and it immediately looks like a disaster area? They *really* didn't do anything. I'm constantly amazed! Nobody did anything, but the time I spend cleaning up the kitchen that nobody had anything to eat in defies the imagination. The alcoholic cannot handle this kind of frustration. He wants things the way he wants them, when he wants them, and how he wants them. If it doesn't work his way, he either becomes violent and busts up the place before storming out to drink, or, if he is not prone to violence, he simply takes refuge in drink. It is a way, if only temporarily, to dull the nerve endings. Since the frustrations he is unable to handle are not the ones that go away, he invariably has reason to get drunk again.

As a result of your husband's irrational behavior you start to walk on eggs. You don't want to set him off, so you are very careful not to do or say the wrong thing. You also try to get the children to be very careful about what they do and say. You look for the "right" time to tell him about the dentist bill. You become tense trying to keep everything calm, and then something happens to screw it up anyway: The car won't start; a light bulb blows; somebody forgot to put the cap back on the toothpaste. It is all your fault because you are a rotten wife or a rotten mother or a rotten housekeeper. The abuse varies according to the particular drunk, but it does go on and on.

If you're like most people, you can't help thinking that in some way it was your fault. You could have checked the toothpaste; you did have a hard time starting the car yesterday; and if you had only . . . What you are not allowing for is the fact that if it wasn't the toothpaste or the car it would have been that you talk too much or you don't talk enough— but it would have been something. It's hard at the time to think logically, because while you are taking responsibility for whatever he is frustrated and angry about, you are also feeling things like, "No jury in the world would convict me of manslaughter if they knew him." And then since nice people don't commit murder, or even think about it, you feel guilty. You've lost again.

Inability to Express Emotions

The alcoholic is unable to talk about what he is feeling and keeps his feelings "bottled" up. (Forgive the pun. I couldn't resist.) One of the things alcohol does is disinhibit. It makes us feel freer to say and do things that we might not ordinarily say and do. For example, a man who is usually very shy and withdrawn can become very charming and popular after a couple of drinks. This is what happens in the beginning. As the drinking goes on a couple of other things happen. Repressed feelings start to emerge. And perception of reality is distorted. That means purple cows and pink elephants.

Emotions are not properly directed either. Since the alcohol distorts perception, the emotions expressed are not necessarily appropriate to the situation. More often than not the feelings expressed toward others are antagonistic. These feelings are actually feelings that the alcoholic has about himself but which are too painful to deal with, even under the influence of alcohol. Talking about how you feel can take the edge off, but resolving these feelings takes work. The alcoholic goes no further than blowing off steam or dumping his feelings on others. That is, if the feelings he has kept in are feelings of anger, he will behave in an angry manner. But the person he is really angry at is himself. Because he cannot face the fact, he will let you have it.

Whether you believe him or not, you listen and are terribly hurt. You don't realize that even though he is talking to you, he is mainly talking about himself. He is filled with self-hate. "Can someone lie when he is drunk?" I am often asked. "I don't know," I reply. "It doesn't really matter." Since the alcoholic's perceptions are distorted, he may be lying when he thinks he is telling the truth. And telling the truth when he thinks he is lying. Even if what he says is true, you can only believe it for the moment that he is saying it anyway. An alcoholic once told me, "I've lived a lie for so long, I don't know what truth is." *That* I could believe!

We live in a society where it is not considered manly to cry, to be afraid or insecure, to show any of the frailties that make us human. If a man feels these things he certainly doesn't want to admit them—even to himself. Thus if he feels these things and has even more difficulty expressing feelings because he is an alcoholic, he turns to the bottle and exposes his flip side. I have often wondered if *Dr. Jekyll and Mr. Hyde* was modeled after an alcoholic. I would not be at all surprised, because this book so clearly describes much of what we see in the alcoholic personality. "When he is drunk he is not the person I married," many women have told me. "I don't know him at all. He is a stranger to me." My response is something terribly profound like, "He doesn't seem like the man you married because he is not the man you married." That is the reality of the situation.

High Level of Anxiety
in Interpersonal Relationships

Alcoholics tend not to make friends easily. They suffer from feelings of inferiority. They have trouble relating to others for fear of being found out. They don't want people to see beyond the facade of normalcy. As a result they establish short- rather than long-term friendships, and when the friendships start to get close, they end them or become less available. They do, however, have drinking buddies and believe these people are their friends.

When an alcoholic is drinking, he is able to forget his fears and, at least to himself, feel in control. Alcoholics can be very cunning, very charming, and very manipulative. I guess I don't have to tell you about that. You have fallen victim to your husband's charms over and over, only to be shattered when his personality changes. Perhaps he has convinced you that this time he really means it. He'll give the alcohol up. He loves you. And, of course, he can't give it up. You fall for his story every time, as he is exceedingly clever. And you want so badly to believe him. This time it will be different. You think. How vulnerable and trusting you are.

You are not the only one who succumbs. He cons his boss—for a while. He cons those he borrows money from— for a while. He cons the police and the courts. You have to be very careful when you take him to court that you don't end up with egg on your face. How could this good-looking, charming man have thrown you down the stairs in a drunken rage? Even if he admits it, the judge is assured it will never happen again. Boys will be boys.

When your alcoholic husband has difficulty with interpersonal relationships, except at a distance, you will find that your friendships with other couples drop off. As the disease progresses, you will be spending less and less time with people you used to be close to. There are a number of reasons for this. One of them is he just cannot handle the closeness. He will make excuses or decide he doesn't like them. He is simply too uncomfortable in a social situation. He will probably be all right if you push him into accepting an invitation by saying when he gets there he can have a few drinks, but the idea of going at all is very frightening to him. You will be hurt because you cannot continue your friendships very long under this kind of pressure. The truth is, sadly enough, that there is no way to maintain a couple-to-couple friendship with only half a couple. It is too unfair and too hard to make the other couple understand, especially when you are protecting him, covering up for the real problem. A cover-up usually sounds like a cover-up, no matter how convincing you try to be.

Low Self-esteem

Alcoholics generally have very little sense of self-worth. They do not see themselves as people of value. The alcohol gives them a false sense of self-confidence, an "I can do anything!" attitude. This false sense of self-confidence then gives way to the outrageous. I'm sure you've heard alcoholics claim that they can do just about anything. There is no problem too big for them to handle. The presidency is small potatoes. The next day, if they remember their claims, they feel embarrassed, guilty, and remorseful. Since they do not think much of themselves to begin with, their behavior while drunk reinforces their negative self-image. The reasoning goes: A person who is worth something does not behave like that. If I were not a terrible person, I would not have done that. I am just a crumb.

If you're honest enough to admit it, you probably support your husband's feelings of inferiority. When there is any part of that evening he does not remember, you are right there to remind him: "How could you have said that to her? How could you have made a pass at my best friend? Do you think they *really* thought that story was funny?" His inner feelings that he is worthless are again reinforced. Since this is a very painful reality and he runs away from painful realities, he returns to the bottle. And you are flabbergasted. You thought that after the performance he put on last night and the amount of liquor he consumed, if you weren't lucky enough to have him hit by a Mack truck at least he would give up drinking. Not so. Foiled again. The disease beat you. It always will. Face it, he is powerless over alcohol—and so are you.

Grandiosity

I once heard an alcoholic defined as an egomaniac with an inferiority complex. As the alcoholic drinks, this insecure person becomes more and more flamboyant. He goes from Harry to Mr. Harry to Sir Harry to the ruler of the universe. His grandiosity is limitless. He is the king. And don't you forget it. He is also living in a fantasy world. My four-year-old just left the house dressed as Superman, although he believes he is Superman less now than he did at age two. When he was two he tried to fly and chipped his tooth. Now he knows he is playing a game. I'm not so sure that the alcoholic knows he is playing a game. The chemical changes the character, and lo and behold—as one alcoholic described himself—KING BABY!

Grandiose behavior is not limited to verbal obnoxiousness. The grandiose alcoholic thinks nothing of ordering all new furniture for the living room or a newer and bigger car. Paying for it is not a problem because his fantasy includes making a lot of money. When he takes you out he feels free to shout, "This round's on me!" I know one woman who had all she could do to keep from getting completely hysterical when her husband paid for the dinner eaten by the couple at the next table. This incident occurred after she had spent the day hunting for shoes at bargain prices for her children. The wife, as she watches the paycheck fly by, is ignored if she objects with decorum, and considered a shrew if she makes a scene. After all he is just being generous. The promotion is just around the corner. Being poor is a state of mind. There is no limit to the amount of money that an alcoholic with grandiose tendencies can spend. In effect he is trying to buy respect and friendship. He has nothing left of himself to give. But the momentary elation and applause soon fade and the broken pieces follow. The family literally pays the price.

Feelings of Isolation

It has often been said that we can love others only to the degree that we love ourselves. If this is true, and I suspect it is, then the alcoholic is unable to offer love. When one is unable to show love, it becomes more and more difficult to receive love. The love his family gives him makes the alcoholic feel guilty. And because he feels undeserving of love, he retreats to the bottle. His companions at the bar give him a false sense of camaraderie for a while, but that quickly fades as his drinking progresses. He is locked into himself.

As the disease progresses, the isolation he feels takes on another form. People turn away from him. Friends refuse to see him. His family goes the other way when he comes home. He may lose his job. Even his friend, the bartender, may refuse to serve him. The isolation becomes a reality. He is truly alone. In his desperation he turns to his only true friend—the bottle. What a self-feeding disease this is! The alcoholism causes the changes that bring about the excruciating loneliness—and then it offers itself as the only way out.

You watch and feel cut off and lonely too. You start to wonder if you wouldn't feel less lonely than you are now if you were completely without him. You too have become isolated from most of your social contacts, and it's hard to imagine yourself going out and meeting new people, making new friends and being desirable. And you don't even have the bottle for solace. Your pain is raw. Joan L. admitted to me that she ate chocolate to push down those nagging feelings. "The cake wouldn't even have to be thawed out for me to go at it," she said. "I would stuff myself to the point where I was nauseous, and that feeling would prevail over the loneliness." The family can indeed become sicker than the alcoholic. I don't know about you, but Joan was well on her way. If you think about it, you can probably top that story with the crazy stuff you've done.

Perfectionism

The alcoholic is a perfectionist. He cannot tolerate lack of perfection in himself or in others. Working with him is almost impossible because there is no way to meet his standards. Any project he undertakes has to be done perfectly. If he cannot do it perfectly, he may not do it at all. Yet when he makes the attempt he takes so much time doing it that it is hardly worth having it done. "He bought the paint, the brushes, and the drop cloth and prepared the room for painting," Barbara told me. "Two-and-a-half years later I decided I had better do it myself." Perfectionism coupled with low frustration tolerance becomes an excuse to abandon the project and drink. This particular mixture is very explosive, and the family is well advised to keep their distance.

You may be thinking I have described a lot of people you know—that perfectionism is not peculiar to the alcoholic. You are probably right. However the inability to find an effective way of dealing with the frustration caused by the need to be perfect is what makes the alcoholic different. In a more typical personality these feelings are manageable. They blow over, or after a brief outburst the crisis is over. The alcoholic's reactions are all out of proportion to the situation, and they give him an excuse to drink.

You are constantly left with the questions, "Do I wait until he does it or do I get it done myself? I have no doubts that he will do it better, but by the time he gets around to it will I be too old to enjoy it?" Eight months ago an alcoholic I know bought a game that hooks up to the television set. He is waiting for just the right moment to attach it. His oldest child is a sophomore in high school, and I have a feeling that the right moment will not arrive before the boy goes off to college. Periodically his wife suggests he hook the game up. He gets angry and defensive, but they still wait.

The situation above is not very serious. But those of you who have lived with the water turned off for the weekend because your husband was going to fix the plumbing himself, and then it turned out he didn't have the exact wrench he needed, know what I am talking about. "It's a simple job," he says. "Nothing to it!" Those fateful words. And you end up using the neighbor's bathroom, trying to make light of the fact that you want to hit your husband over the head with a sledge hammer. You know you'll end up calling the plumber anyway, because in the middle of the job he will take off and get drunk because the blankety blank something or other won't fit into the blankety blank something.

If he gets through the whole job, it will probably be wonderful. You will, however, have to convince yourself it was worth it. Those gray hairs do not stop appearing. If you tell the story, people will have a good laugh. But you may have to wait five years until it seems funny to you. Pamela L. waited three years for her husband to replace the fallen ceiling in her kitchen. She was determined to wait it out. Her husband called me one day to come over and take a look at the lovely new ceiling. He's very proud of himself. The ceiling looks wonderful—but *three* years! If I were writing for any group of people other than you who are married to alcoholics, most of what I am saying would not be believed. You know that I am not making anything up. I'm just telling it the way it is.

Ambivalence Toward Authority

Authority figures mean nothing to the alcoholic who is drinking. He has the same reactions as you or I when he is sober, but when he is drinking nobody is going to tell him what to do. He doesn't concern himself with the illegality of speeding or hit-and-run driving. The problem is compounded by the police, who tend to be much more sympathetic with alcohol abusers than with drug abusers. I observed an instance in which an alcoholic had been picked up for a hit-and-run collision. He was obviously smashed. But he was charming. The charm of the alcoholic is not to be underestimated. He was so charming that the police refused, over the protests of the man he had hit, to give him a drunkometer test. His wife, Brenda, kept her mouth shut. Enablers all! He got some points on his license, but this sick man was allowed to go back out there on the streets where the next time he might kill himself or somebody else. Sometimes being the nice guy is not the nice thing to do. No wonder the alcoholic is ambivalent. The authorities are ambivalent. I talked to his wife later. She said she simply lacked courage. After worrying all night she was so relieved that he was still in one piece, she just sat down and shook. Brenda would not react that way today because she knows she aided and abetted alcoholism that night. She didn't know any better. You will—so that when it happens to you—and it will—you will have a choice.

There is humor in everything if we allow ourselves to see it. The only concern Brenda's husband had during the ordeal was that he shouldn't lose his keys. Not a thought about her, the other people involved, or the damage to his car. After what seemed like forever he and Brenda got home. He went up to bed and she, unable to sleep, went into the den. Soon the doorbell rang. It was the police. Yes, he had remembered his keys, but he had also picked up the keys to their patrol car. They wondered if she would be so kind as to return them. Even though they told her she had the right to remain silent, she continued to laugh as they meekly walked out to the street with the keys that her husband had not forgotten.

Guilt

Guilt is a mainstay in the alcoholic home. The alcoholic is terribly guilt-ridden. He does not want to behave the way that he does, and he does not like the person he is when he is drunk. He doesn't understand that he has no control over his behavior when he is drunk. He promises, because he really loves his family and wants to keep his job, that he will stop drinking. He is not lying. He really means it when he says it. But he does not have a choice. So he disappoints himself and everyone who cares about him or needs him. This makes him feel very guilty. Unable to confront the pain he must ease it, and consequently he drinks some more. This makes him feel even more guilty. Then you feel guilty because of the part you play in making him feel guilty and he feels yet guiltier . . . and once again the bottle wins. He gets sicker and sicker and YOU GET SICKER AND SICKER!

These traits I've discussed are not true for all alcoholics, nor does any one alcoholic necessarily possess all of them. Nor are these traits exclusive to alcoholics. They are, however, traits that alcoholics seem to exhibit with far greater frequency than a more typical population.

2 WHAT HAPPENS TO YOU

You cannot live with active alcoholism without being profoundly affected. Any human being who is bombarded with what you've been bombarded with is to be commended for sheer survival. You deserve a medal for the mere fact that you're around to tell the story. I know it has not been easy. You don't know from day to day—even hour to hour—what to expect. You imagine all kinds of terrible things and, as often as not, you are right. You become obsessed with what will happen when he gets home (if he gets home). Your day is spent in emotional turmoil. Your head keeps spinning. You can't sleep. You don't eat properly. You look terrible. You withdraw from your friends. You snap at your children.

You're sick. You have developed a disease which we call

near-alcoholism, which is every bit as damaging as alcoholism itself. Like alcoholism it has its own symptoms.
Anyone who has close contact with an alcoholic is affected by
the disease, the degree being directly related to one's emotional nearness. Since you have the most continual and relevant contact with your husband, you are the most
vulnerable.

As there are some patterns which described the alcoholic's
behavior, there are also some patterns in your responses. No
one close to an alcoholic escapes responding in at least some
of the ways I will discuss. It is only a matter of degree. The
following are the symptoms of near-alcoholism: denial; protectiveness, pity-concern about the drinker; embarrassment,
avoiding drinking occasions; shift in relationship; guilt; obsession, continual worry; fear; lying; false hope, disappointment, euphoria; confusion; sex problems; anger; lethargy,
hopelessness, self-pity, remorse, and despair. As you read
about these symptoms, try to identify the ones you have.
Recognizing a problem is the first step in getting rid of it.

Denial

Denial is your biggest enemy. It seems impossible to believe
that you are involved with an alcoholic. It simply cannot be
true. If it cannot be true, it isn't true. You believe what you
want to believe. You ignore reality. Because the alcoholic
wants to face reality even less than you do, he helps you to
be unrealistic. Denial is part of the disease for both you and
your husband. He expends a great deal of energy denying
the fact that he cannot control his drinking. He seems to

control it for long periods of time. These periods grow shorter as the disease progresses, but he will convince both you and himself that he is the master of the bottle. Pure fantasy! The alcoholic does not seek help until he can no longer deny his lack of control and until the results of his behavior have been so horrifying he feels the pain despite the drug.

You don't look at the problem honestly either. You don't seek help until you are overwhelmed by fear of violence, loss of income, and uncertainty about what each day will bring. As the disease progresses, you take over more and more of the family responsibility. You try to maintain control over the situation and act as if everything is manageable. You deny the turmoil that exists within, as well as without, because denial is the most tolerable way to cope with an otherwise intolerable situation.

You go around in circles until the denial no longer works. You have no choice but to face facts when the weight of the evidence is overwhelming and the pain is too great to handle. Denial is part of the process that enables the disease to progress. This is true of any disease. How many unnecessary deaths have there been because people would not, for example, accept the fact that they had cancer? Disease flourishes in the virus of denial.

In order to combat near-alcoholism you must first admit that the problem exists. I say that glibly, but I know how hard it is. Cindy M. takes a hard look at herself: "I was one of the most skillful deniers around. I just couldn't admit there was a problem. I just couldn't let go of the idea that I could figure out a way to make it disappear just like a bad dream. I denied in the face of the undeniable.

"My husband had a drinking problem before we were married," Cindy relates. "Every time I broke off with him, it was as a result of a drunken episode. I discounted those episodes because I loved him. I discounted them until about five years ago when there was nothing else I could do. That was thirteen years into the marriage. I made excuses for him. The pressures at work were incredible, and he needed a few drinks in order to unwind. Made perfect sense. I would even mix his drinks for him. He complained about the job and went over and over the same story, never reaching a solution. I would sit with him very sympathetically. I always got to bed later than was good for me, but after all, he needed me.

"I denied that the problem was alcohol. It's hard to believe how naive I was. When I tried to go to bed, he would wake me up. I'd get up rather than risk waking the children. Night after night this went on. I told no one. Who could I trust? I had created the image of the ideal couple and didn't want that damaged. And I didn't want anyone to think less of him.

"He started getting violent. With one stroke of his arm he could clear the kitchen table or break everything on a shelf. Then I'd stay up most of the night picking up the broken glass and scrubbing the mustard off the walls. I didn't want the children to find it when they woke up in the morning. They had to be protected.

"My mother started nagging me that my skin looked bad and my house wasn't clean. But I didn't tell. What could she do anyway? I was afraid of an 'I told you so.'

"Deny, deny, deny. I was seven months pregnant when I landed in the emergency room to get my arm stitched up. He threw a glass at me when I wouldn't get out of bed at two in the morning to talk to him. He threw it with such force that it shattered. I covered for him. I protected him. I denied. I just couldn't face the truth.

"I denied until I could deny no more. The neighbors saw

him staggering home. Who was I fooling? My mother spent a night with me. Why had I shut her out? My children knew something was terribly wrong. I had accomplished nothing. I simply couldn't face up to what was happening until I had no choice. My stubbornness only made it worse. My seeming strength was really only lack of courage. My ignorance was appalling. The person I am today would have behaved very differently. The person I am today demands the right to her personhood. Reality must be dealt with. Pretending it doesn't exist does not make it go away. I learned that the hard way."

That's an example of what denial can do to a person. I gave you Cindy's story. It could have been Barbara's or Joan's or Nancy's. They are all variations on the same theme. Denial makes life a lie. It distorts reality every bit as much for the nonalcoholic as the alcohol distorts reality for the alcoholic. If you choose to give denial up, you will experience an almost immediate sense of relief—get that monkey off your back. You can adjust to truth. You don't have to like it, but you cannot deny it and be healthy.

Protectiveness, Pity-concern About the Drinker

In the early stages of alcoholism we are all very understanding. "Yes, dear, I know it's a jungle out there. Yes, you should have gotten the promotion. You work so hard with so little appreciation. Let me fix you a drink." You feel very sorry for your husband and his suffering. You worry about him and try to find solutions to his problems. There is no way to solve his problems, however, as he becomes more

and more skillful at snatching defeat from the jaws of victory.
If there is something to worry about or be angry about he
will find it. The injustice can be real or imagined. It doesn't
matter.

Night after night you get sucked in and lose sight of yourself in an attempt to pacify your alcoholic. After all, he *is* out
there bringing home the paycheck and you owe it to him to
make things as smooth for him at home as you possibly can.
The fact that you've had a rough day too is not important. It
is part of your role to make the world right for your husband.
Your needs are not important. Jean B. remembers: "That's
what my husband told me. You know what else? I believed
him. And more and more I became less and less. I became a
servant in my own home. I had no needs. But I sure had a
good case of colitis. Those feelings that I denied I had were
eating my guts out. I was so concerned for my husband that
I would bleed. Everything was being drained out of me. We
nonpersons do things like that. But not anymore."

Embarrassment, Avoiding Drinking Occasions

What other people think of us seems to be very important—
far more important, in fact, than what we think of ourselves.
We assume that others are judging us by our own behavior
and by the behavior of those around us, especially that of our
family. When I bragged about my youngest son walking at
nine months, was I saying, "He's terrific," or was I saying, "I'm
terrific"? By the same token when the older kids run into
trouble at school, unless I make a conscious effort to separate
myself from them, I consider it a negative reflection on me

as a parent. Since you are probably like most people, when your alcoholic husband behaves outrageously, you're embarrassed. You make excuses and wish you were invisible. You don't feel that you can go home, leaving the "life of the party" behind. A number of these experiences will cause you to feel insecure and afraid of social situations where there is drinking. Eventually you want to avoid such situations altogether. The embarrassment is too great. You are, in effect, taking responsibility for his behavior. The truth is that you can really only take responsibility for your own behavior. At this point that statement doesn't make much sense. You also don't understand that other people often don't know that your husband's behavior humiliates you. Other people's drunken husbands don't bother me. Sometimes I enjoy them because I don't have to go home with them.

You also can't enjoy the party because you're watching him all the time, suggesting that maybe he's had enough, trying to get him to leave, insisting on driving. It reaches a point where it's just not worth going in the first place. If you can't have a good time, why bother. Consequently you feel sorry for yourself and nurse your wounds.

Shift in Relationship—Domination, Takeover, Self-absorptive Activities

As the disease progresses, the alcoholic assumes less and less responsibility. The relationship between you and your husband and you and your children changes. You take over more and more. You try to become both mother and father to your children. This is not possible. A mother simply cannot be a father. She is just not built for it. A mother can only be the best mother she is able to be. When she tries to be a father too, she takes on an impossible task. Not only is it unrealistic, it is destructive to the children. She causes confusion in their minds and wears herself out.

You become more and more in charge and make virtually all the decisions in the house. The alcoholic eventually becomes yet another child. And although you dominate him as you would a child, you become angry and resentful when he does not behave like an adult. You're afraid that everything will fall apart if you don't take charge. So you run the house and care for the kids; you handle the finances, paint the walls, mow the lawn—in effect you do it all. You may even go to work so you can be sure there is enough income. You are definitely in control and running the show. When I watch women doing this, I am reminded of Joan of Arc. It really makes you stop and think. There's not too much satisfaction in martyrdom, not for most people anyway.

After taking over it is not unusual for you to get involved in lots of activities outside of the home. You are continually busy. These self-absorptive activities are a form of escape. Even if what you are doing is very productive, your motive is less to be helpful than to avoid thinking. Mary N. is a highly skilled teacher specializing in children with learning problems. She says, "I did tutoring with neurologically impaired children at one time. Although I did a good job, I did it more because it afforded me a little financial independence than out of concern for the children. I would do anything in order to avoid an issue that might be potentially explosive."

Even though your outside activities may benefit others, the satisfaction to you is limited. It is limited because you are running away from, not toward, something. It also can make the situation at home more difficult to bear. On the outside you are respected and appreciated. You forget that you will not be respected and appreciated at home. Anything that you are involved in that does not revolve around him is a threat. He is so needy, he resents any of your energy being directed elsewhere. You are never ready for his criticisms. Zapped again!

You are vulnerable. Thus you feel guilty not only because of what your husband is doing, but because you know that you'll fight not to give up your bridge game, garden club, or part-time job. A part of you knows that you are not doing such a bad thing. But just how strong is that part? Mary N. compromised: "I gave up the bridge game and kept the job. I also lied to my friends. I even forgot what I told them, but they didn't believe it and neither did I. I would not do that today. I might or might not compromise, but I know I wouldn't lie. I also know that if I chose to compromise, it would be out of a desire to accommodate and not out of fear. The *reason* for what I do is every bit as important as the thing itself. I want to act out of strength and not weakness. I want a choice and today I have it." And you will too.

Guilt

The alcoholic is expert at projecting his own guilt feelings onto you. You become expert at accepting them. When he avoids responsibility for his behavior, yelling, "You drive me to drink!" you take it on yourself.

You begin to think that if you were a better wife he would

not drink. He agrees. The children start to think that if they were better kids, he would not drink. He agrees with them too. You tread carefully in order not to set off your alcoholic. Of course this does not work either. One of my favorite stories involves an alcoholic who asked his dutiful wife to fix him two eggs, one sunny side up and the other over easy. When she presented him with the eggs, he refused to eat them, complaining, "You turned the wrong one!"

When you hear how terrible you are over a period of time, it is almost impossible not to believe it. As a result, much of what the alcoholic says is internalized and you become ridden with guilt. The alcoholic knows just where you are vulnerable and pushes those buttons.

Guilt is a very strong manipulative force. Gloria told me how guilt affected her: "I felt guilty because I couldn't stop my husband from drinking. I felt guilty because I couldn't always control my children's behavior. I felt guilty when I was ten minutes late getting home from a tennis lesson. I felt guilty if I played cards at night when he wanted me at home. I felt guilty for crimes I didn't understand. I found ways to apologize when I didn't know what I did, even when I was in the right. I didn't want a hassle and I couldn't stand his rejecting me when he was angry. My thinking was as off as his. The difference was that he was acting and I was reacting. He dished out the guilt and I swallowed it whole. I became so filled with guilt that I reached the point I just couldn't handle it anymore. So I gave it all up. Today my conscience tells me right from wrong, but my guilt button no longer operates. When I'm wrong I promptly admit it, but when I believe I'm right I can stand by it." You can do it too.

Obsession, Continual Worry

As the disease occupies more and more of the alcoholic's thoughts, it has the same effect on you. Life is no longer predictable and you are continually worried. What will happen next? Will he be caught drinking on the job? Will he be fired? Where is he? Will he be home on time? Will he get hurt? Where will he go? Will he be violent? How can I get him to stop drinking? Where have I gone wrong? Is there another woman? Should I leave him? Why do I love him? Is there a way out?

These worrisome thoughts crowd out all other thoughts. You're in a squirrel cage. You go through the motions of living, but your mind is elsewhere—always on the alcoholic. This obsession is a waste of energy because it solves nothing. It only makes the whole family sicker, more involved in the emotional orbit of your husband. Knowing this does not help much. You are trapped. You have lost control of your thoughts and life is a nightmare. After several weeks in counseling Linda B. confided, "I remember driving past a cemetery and feeling envy. I saw a funeral procession and thought, At least *he's* got friends. That's the pit of despair and the height of self-pity. The one advantage to feeling that low is that if you choose to go on, there is no place to go but up. I don't ever want to feel that way again. I will never allow that to happen." And you don't have to either.

Fear

Anxiety and fear are usually present in the alcoholic home. Some of these fears are groundless, and some are well-

founded, such as: Can I make it alone? Will he beat me? What
if he loses his job? I know a woman whose husband chained
the doors when she left the house so she couldn't get back
in. At first she was afraid to leave because the thought of
being locked out with her children locked in terrified her.
Later on she learned to carry a screwdriver and undo the
latch. Her fear, once confronted, was manageable.

Charlotte S. describes her fear: "I found that most of the
things I was afraid of happened. I also found that I was anxious much of the time but couldn't figure out why. If I ate
lunch and the feeling went away, it was hunger; if it didn't,
it was anxiety. Fear became a way of life for me. I hid it well
from outsiders, but my stomach knew. I found that the time
and energy I spent being afraid was not good for me, so I
tried to put my energies elsewhere for as long as I could.
When I was attending classes, I found that I was in a panic
on the way to school. After all I was leaving my three children behind—with him. I was nauseous during class, and
then I would race home. I would travel an hour each way to
hear a man I respected, and my head would be elsewhere.
Four wasted hours! With that awareness came a commit-
ment to myself. I decided to be where I was at the moment.
I could not change what was happening at home but I *could*
decide whether to waste my time where I was or to concentrate and get something out of it. It was hard work but I
won."

Many women lose confidence in themselves as a result of
living with an alcoholic. Then they become very fearful and
anxious. Situations that at one time were not at all threatening become overwhelming. These women become more and
more the victims of their nameless fears. I know some
women living with active alcoholics who are terrified of
being alone, others who are afraid to leave the house. They

can't explain why, but the fear overwhelms them. It's terrible to live in fear. It renders us immobile. It makes us behave in irrational ways. One act out of fear leads to another, and we lose control of our lives. We start spinning our wheels with no place to go.

Lying

Lying is a way of life in the alcoholic home. You lie in order to protect the alcoholic. You tell his boss, "I'm sorry, he won't be in to work today. He has the flu." You explain to your neighbor, "I don't know how the lamp got broken. The cat must have knocked it over."

The alcoholic lies to you, his boss, and himself, saying such things as, "I have no liquor in the house." "I had only one beer." I know of one alcoholic who had thirty-five members of his family die in three years. Some of the same people died two or three times. He missed many days of work with the excuse that he had to attend a funeral.

The most destructive of all are the lies that are not really lies. They are truthful in intent but not in execution. The alcoholic says, "I will be home at 6:00 for dinner!" He is not lying. He fully intends to be home at 6:00 for dinner. But he does not arrive home at 6:00, because there is a world of difference between his intent and his ability to carry it out. He tells the children he will take them to the ball game on Saturday. He means it when he says it. When Saturday comes he is passed out on the floor. What is a lie? What is the truth? Who is responsible?

This kind of behavior adds greatly to the confusion and

disorganization of your family. Truth loses its meaning, and perceptions of reality become distorted. You simply do not know what to believe. In the end you believe pretty much what you want to believe. This leads to continually setting yourself up for a letdown. He is so convincing, and you would rather believe him than the evidence of last week's burnt dinner or unused theater tickets. That can all change, however. You can learn to eat and go to the theater alone if you have to. But you have to get well first.

False Hope, Disappointment, Euphoria

Part of what throws the alcoholic's family into confusion and despair is the building up of hopes and the subsequent disappointment. The family, unable to accept reality, lives in fantasy. You think of your alcoholic husband in terms of what he was or could be. When he makes a promise you respond as if he were that person. When he does not fulfill his promise, you are let down much more than you would be if you had not believed him in the first place. If he does keep his promise, you are so excited you become euphoric. This, of course, sets you up for greater disappointment the next time. The alternating feelings of false hope, disappointment, and euphoria add to your confusion and fear.

You have, in effect, given him control over your happiness. He now has the power to make you happy or miserable. He uses and abuses this power as a way of manipulating you. If you do not behave according to his desires, he will not take you to the party. If he has decided ahead of time that he wants a way out, there is nothing you can do. He sometimes withholds his manipulative moves until the very last minute. And there you are all dressed up with no place to go.

You really believed that *this* time he would follow through. You were getting along so well. He hadn't had a drink in two weeks. *This time it would be different.* How many times have you said those words to yourself? How many times has the alcoholic said those words to himself? Yes, it's different. It's worse. The disease progresses. You are not in control. Your husband is not really in control. The alcohol is in control—if you allow it to be.

Confusion

You become confused when you live with an alcoholic. You don't know what to believe or what to expect. Since he is pulling the strings, you are dancing to a very inconsistent tune. Your sense of what is real becomes distorted. Every day is more unmanageable, a living nightmare.

In your confusion you may decide that you will drink with your husband. Having tried everything else you could think of, you decide, "If I can't lick him, I'll join him." You think that maybe this way he will cut down or become less abusive. The results are predictable. You can't keep up with him. If your children see you drinking with their father, they become even more fearful and confused. They think that their mother too will become an alcoholic. Thus everyone gets sucked a little deeper into the alcoholic abyss.

It is very hard for you to think straight. In fact it is very hard for you to think at all. You can't turn your head off and

yet can't come up with any answers. You're on a treadmill;
but you don't know where you got on, and you don't know
how to get off. You start to wonder where it is all going to
end. "Am I losing my mind?" you ask yourself. "Maybe I am
going crazy. No sane person would live this way." And you
just may be right.

Sex Problems

As communication in other areas of your marriage breaks
down, the physical expression of closeness breaks down as
well. You use sex as a weapon. You withhold sex if your husband doesn't behave himself. He can't have you in bed if
he's going to drink like that. "Go to bed with your mistress
or the bottle!" you think.

You may be repulsed by the smell of the liquor, which is
reason enough to reject his overtures. You assume he wants
you out of lust and not love anyway. You may, however, submit to him because you figure that if he is sexually satisfied
he will go to sleep and leave you alone. You may also think
in terms of your wifely role and responsibility. So you have
the choice of feeling guilty or degraded. Once again your
self-esteem has been reduced.

Sexual abuse is not uncommon. Women submit to behavior they would resist if they had any self-respect left. Clients
tell me of actions resulting in the need for medical attention.
It is hard for them even to tell me what happened. But these
unfortunate women gather their courage to tell me so that I
can give them permission not to allow it to happen again. I
give my client permission to be a person. "I just couldn't live

anymore without telling someone," Judy D. said to me. "And I know that you're not allowed to tell anybody." I don't have to be more specific. You know what I'm talking about. You know the difference between creative sex that is pleasurable, and abuse. In the sexual sphere, as in every other sphere in your life, you lose a sense of yourself as a worthy person and become afraid and confused.

It is not unusual for an alcoholic to have an affair. He complains, "My wife doesn't understand me." You sure as hell don't! "She doesn't want me in bed." Well, he's right. "She won't drink with me." You tried it, but you've developed an aversion to the stuff by this time. It doesn't matter that the affair is a symptom of the disease—you are shattered. Your identity is so tied up with him that you are beside yourself. "I'm obviously not much of a woman," you conclude. "If I were, this affair would not have happened." Your self-image thus takes another downward plunge. You're a bad wife, mother, housekeeper, and now—you've lost your sexuality. You're a nothing. Baloney! You're a victim. You're a casualty of near-alcoholism.

Some couples are able to maintain a satisfying sex life until the later stages of the disease, when the husband becomes impotent. The problem here is that you think that because you can be so loving in bed, everything else will be all right. This hope too is shattered. Your expectations get you into trouble. And you can only be disappointed. There can be no winning until you learn how to give up your false hopes and live in the moment. You will.

Anger

Anger, in one form or another, is always present in the alcoholic home. The tension is thick enough to cut with a knife. What will he say? What will he do? I'll kill him if he doesn't leave me alone. Will he damage the car? Will he wake up the kids? Should I ask him for the money? All these uncertainties lead to anger with people you are not really angry at. A simple request from your child turns you into a screaming shrew. "I only asked if I . . . You didn't have to . . . ," the poor kid cries. Then when you realize what you've done, you are angry with yourself.

Quarreling is almost constant. The alcoholic quarrels in order to find an excuse to drink and the nonalcoholic quarrels because everything he says or does turns her off. It seems that no other kind of conversation is possible. "Pass the peas," he snarls, only to be answered with, "What, is your arm broken?"

You punish: "Fix your own dinner. I've had it!" You try to get even: "You won't see my folks. I won't see yours!" You threaten to leave. If you actually do, you find yourself out in the car in the middle of the night with no place to go. You become rigid and distrustful. Rage consumes you without a satisfying outlet. Anyone who walks into your house can feel the angry vibrations. There is no escape from it. Who ever thought you would turn into such a self-righteous witch?

This tension, however, does not always show itself in your behavior. If you are living with violence, you may keep it inside rather than risk an assault. It's a difficult but realistic choice. If it is inner directed, that is, if you continually keep your mouth shut even though you feel the need to explode, the tension will probably make you physically ill. Colitis, gastritis, and ulcers are not uncommon in families of alcoholics. Anger that is not let out can literally eat your guts out. I am not advocating that you open up your mouth. The consequences may not be worth it. I will, in a later chapter, talk about productive ways to get rid of your anger.

Lethargy, Hopelessness, Self-pity, Remorse, Despair

No matter what you do, no matter how hard you try, it isn't enough. You give and you give as if the well has no bottom. After a while you give up. What's the difference? Nothing you do will change anything. You are physically and mentally exhausted. You are tired of carrying the world on your shoulders. You just can't do it anymore. You reach a point where you lose interest in everything. Your emotional energy is drained, and you feel hopeless and alone. You are filled with self-pity and remorse. Getting through each day becomes a chore. Getting out of bed and getting dressed are overwhelming tasks. What's the use of going on? It simply isn't worth it, you think. Consequently you give up. You withdraw into an isolated existence.

When you reach this point of despair, you yourself may start drinking or taking drugs. It's incredible, but the alcohol wins again. You don't care anymore, and you feel as if you can't face another day. Your problems are too great. Your life has become totally unmanageable. You want out.

Identify with any of this? Any of it have any special meaning to you? You betcha! I give you my word I haven't been in your house. But I've been in a hundred other houses, and I've talked to a hundred other women who have lived your life. You're not alone. It's a big and not very exclusive club.

I am reminded of the airline pilot who said to his passengers, "I have some bad news and some good news. The bad news is . . . we're lost. The good news is . . . we're making excellent time." It's amazing how much you expend going round and round in circles. You may not believe it now, but you have the power to say, "Hey, wait a minute. I want to get off." This book will show you how.

3 WHAT HAPPENS TO THE CHILDREN

What about the children? They are the most vulnerable of all. They are victims and they are powerless. They are dependent and defenseless. They know no other way of life. You and your husband are the most important people in their world. You are the ones they turn to to know that they are loved, that they are worthy, and that no harm will come to them. What do they get? They get a lot of mixed messages. You say, "I love you—leave me alone." You say, "Don't worry," as the lines dig deep in your forehead. You feel their pain but don't know how to take it away. It's hard for a child to know what is really being said. What happens goes something like this: You spend much of your time and energy reacting to your husband both when he is there and

when he is not. So do your children. They also spend time
and energy reacting to you. They react not only to you and
to your reactions to their father, but to your actions and reactions toward them. Sound confusing? You bet. They cannot think clearly when their life is so muddled. Nothing
makes a lot of sense. The only certainty is the uncertainty.
The only consistency is the inconsistency.

So they become confused. If you live with confusion you
get confused. There is no alternative. The smoke does not
clear. Children imitate their parents. This is one of the ways
that they learn who they are. Somebody is always saying,
"You have your mother's eyes," or, "You're built just like
your father." Kids don't say, "Hey, wait a minute! These are
my eyes," or, "This is my body." We tend to look toward
family to explain certain things we see in our children. My
daughter has played the piano since she was five years old.
My mother said, "She gets that from your brother." It may
or may not be true, but it's a nice feeling. It's a nice feeling
because they share something special. These comparisons
are also made in destructive ways. "I wasn't surprised when
Johnny Jones got busted for drugs. After all his father's a
drunken bum." This happens a lot. I bite my lip a lot too,
because I know that the son of this self-righteous person was
Johnny Jones's connection. The point is that even in this age
of individuality, adages like a chip off the old block, or the
apple doesn't fall far from the tree, carry a degree of truth.

They carry truth not only because of what I've just said
but because that is the way that children learn. They learn
through identification. As I write this book my oldest son is
working on a short story, my daughter a song, and my baby a
godknowswhat. He can't read it back. They may be conscious or unconscious of what they are doing, but they pat-

tern themselves anyway. We communicate to them what our values are and they pick them up as their own. If we are unclear they will be unclear. They will role-play the adult. House is a favorite game among children. Let's take a look at what your children have to model their dolls after. It's not the Brady Bunch.

The alcoholic father is inconsistent. He is thought of mostly in terms of broken promises. When he is sober he makes commitments to the children. "I'd love to take you to the game Saturday." "Sure, I'll buy you that toy." When he says this he really means it. But it rarely comes about. The children never know what to believe. They do not know from day to day, hour to hour, how he is going to treat them. When he is sober he acts like the ideal parent. He tries especially hard because he feels rotten about his behavior when he was drinking. He is loving, affectionate, understanding, indulgent, and companionable. He is all the things a child would want. He makes the child feel that everything will be okay. He will make it so. The child takes this all in. He needs this and it makes him feel good inside. Then when the drunken episode occurs, and his father is mean and brutal, he is shattered. His whole world falls apart. He doesn't know what is real. He doesn't know what to depend on or what to trust. He wants to believe in the good father but he can't. He can't stand the thought of believing in the bad one. He bounces back and forth not knowing that this isn't the way things have to be. After all this is what he knows. Since the idea of what a father is is all mixed up, and since this is all the child knows, the son of an alcoholic father has trouble seeing himself as a more typical adult male. He simply doesn't know what it is. The horror is that alcoholism itself becomes part of the father role that the boy identifies with.

As a result we find that a high percentage of alcoholics also come from homes where one or more parents abused alcohol.

On the surface you would think that just the opposite would be true. You would think that the children would develop an aversion to alcohol. Some do, but more do not. Unless these children experience other alternatives they will repeat the same mistakes. "I can hold my liquor. I'll never be a drunk like my father." Chances are his father said the same thing.

The daughter gets confused too. She may think of a man who drinks as manly and independent. It doesn't make a lot of sense, but that's what happens. As a result we find that daughters of alcoholics are more likely to marry active or potential alcoholics than daughters of nonalcoholics. Here again they don't do it on purpose. They are not consciously aware of what they are doing. Many girls marry their "fathers." It is not unusual, but in this instance, it is unfortunate.

So much for the child's view of the alcoholic. Now let's take a look at how the children see you. They do not see you as terrific either. You are in an impossible position. You try to shield your children, but it doesn't work out the way you want. Your protection of the children leads to a lot of half truths and white lies. After all you don't want them to worry. You don't want their father's drinking to become *their* problem, if you can help it. Since children react to feelings as much as to words, they know something is not quite right. They know you are not being completely honest with them. They want to know and yet they don't want to know. If they ask, you snap at them, "Nothing is bothering me!" "If nothing is bothering you, why are you snapping at me? I didn't do anything." It goes downhill from there. Or they don't ask, but that doesn't mean they are not concerned. They are con-

cerned because they know, and yet they don't know, what is
going on. They know something is wrong but they don't
know what. They really don't understand. And you can't
make them understand because you don't really understand
yourself, and besides you'd rather not get into it. After all
what good would it do?

Even though, in your moments of anger, you have let the
children know what a horror their father is, it is not unusual
for them to be more angry with you than with him. After all
you are the one responsible for saying no to them. The discipline is not often shared. You are the one who is tired and
irritable and takes it out on them. How can you possibly
have the patience that children require when you have been
up all the night before with a drunken husband who has followed you from room to room? I know one woman who was
up night after night cleaning up the mess so the children
wouldn't find it, indulging the alcoholic so he wouldn't be
noisy and wake up the children, and waiting up until he was
ready to pass out so that she could get him to bed and the
children wouldn't find him passed out on the floor the next
morning. She overheard her children talking about her.
They said, "My mother's always so tired. I hardly ever see
her anymore." They didn't know. Even if they did they
would still feel the loss.

You are also the safest one to be angry at. They know what
will happen if they are angry at you. They may not like it,
but with their father anything can happen. So you get all of
it. They cling to you, and yet hold you responsible. You
weep for them, but wish they would leave you alone. Just a
few minutes' peace. Isn't there an end to it?

The alcoholic home is not hard to identify. It goes something like this:

The air is fraught with tension. It is only a matter of time before the quarreling begins. It begins for reasons that don't make sense. The alcoholic will start an argument as an excuse to go out and drink. You will start an argument because of something that happened five days or five months or five years ago. The argument itself will be over some dumb thing that doesn't matter anyway. "What time is it?" "What, are you blind?"

Mary was telling me that her parents were arguing about what her curfew should be. She was furious because they wouldn't listen to her. She wanted to express her point of view since it was her curfew. I explained to her that the argument was really not about her. It was a power play. The argument itself had to do not with Mary, but with her mother putting the drunk down where he belonged, and his fighting the bitch who was driving him to drink. Mary is the victim of the decision, but she is not relevant to the argument. After a while these arguments become just words to the child—angry words. Right or wrong doesn't matter because none of it makes any sense. The child responds with fear and soon learns that grown-ups don't always say what they mean or mean what they say.

Eventually truth loses its meaning. In my own research with children from alcoholic homes, I found that they had lost a sense of truth. They didn't know what was true and what not true. It also wasn't very important to them. They would guess at what they were supposed to feel. I gave a questionnaire to 150 children. One hundred of these children came from alcoholic homes. The fifty that did not were the same as the others in terms of age, sex, and background. The only difference was that they did not have a parent who abused alcohol. Within this questionnaire is a lie scale. It is a way of finding out if someone is giving you the answers they think you want rather than telling the truth. They do this in order to get a high score. The results showed that the children from nonalcoholic homes who lied, lied for just that reason. The children from alcoholic homes had much higher lie scores. These results showed that they were not lying. Their scores came out low whether they lied or not. This result pointed to the fact that their world is not a typical world. Therefore their answers are not typical answers.

Beyond that, to complicate the issue still further, behaviors and attitudes that one would consider strange in a more typical home situation can be even healthy in the alcoholic home situation.

I had a twelve-year-old boy referred to me about a year ago. George had been disruptive in school. All the stories he wrote and drawings he made had to do with death and murder. There was lots of blood and violence and stabbing and shooting. He was doing poor school work as well. Both his parents and the school were concerned. He went to a summer program for special help and was then sent to me for emotional problems.

He came willingly. It has been my experience that children from alcoholic homes are very anxious to be able to talk to someone that they can trust. Keeping it all inside is almost too much to bear. As he spoke, he told me of a dream he had. The dream involved man-eating ants attacking his home. He, because of his bravery, was able to lead his mother and grandmother to safety. For some reason his father remained stuck in the house and when they returned, all that was left of him was a part of an intestine. Interesting dream? Yes. Interesting in a lot of ways. Sound like a kid in trouble? Yes. No question of that. But the dream itself is not a sign of mental illness.

This boy was living in a home where his father was an active alcoholic. His life was a living hell. He could not show his anger to his father. He was afraid of him. His mother chose to avoid the issue and became overprotective of the boy.

No wonder the boy was screaming "KILL!" He was very angry. Who wouldn't be? If he had not shown any outward signs of his anger he would have been far more disturbed.

I saw the boy for a short period of time and then I began to see his mother. If the climate in the home could be changed the boy would react differently. If I could get her healthy, the boy could be healthy. And that's just about the way it went. The mother's changed attitudes allowed the boy to grow and to talk about his feelings. He was able to find ways of behaving that were more acceptable. The dreams stopped and so did the drawings. I saw him last week. His father is no longer drinking and they are all working hard at being a family. He smiles now. He no longer hates the world. He's doing better in school. He's in less trouble. Now when he fails a test, or gets into a fight, it's because he didn't study or because boys get into fights. It's not because he couldn't concentrate while worrying about his mother worrying about his father, or because he wanted to beat up the world.

In this case the child cried out for help and it was recognized. Other children withdraw and are left alone because they are no trouble. Others end up in jail. "Who cares what I do!" Others are referred to child guidance clinics. The prognosis for mental health is very poor without help. And with your help we can perform miracles. The results are almost immediate. But before you can help, it is important to look at the full picture.

It does not get less complicated, but it all falls into place so that you can understand what is happening. As you read further you may start to feel depressed and guilty. Don't be discouraged. These children can be helped. Just between you and me that's why I love working with families of alcoholics. I have success. I will give you the tools and you will have success too.

As our environment acts on us in negative ways, it can act on us in positive ways. These children have very few consistent supportive experiences in their lives. As a result their self-esteem is badly damaged. It has to be. The way that we learn to think that we are worth something depends on a number of things. A person's self-esteem has to do with the degree to which he thinks he is capable, significant, successful, and worthy. Much of this is determined by the way he is treated by others. He takes on the ideas and attitudes of the important people in his life as his own.

The child from the alcoholic home does not see himself as capable. If he was truly capable he would be able to figure out a way to get his father to stop drinking. Everything else pales by comparison. He dismisses anything that he does as unimportant. What difference does it make if he can build something, or can get A's in math, if his father is drunk all the time and his mother is preoccupied and nobody really cares.

I was shown a self-portrait made by a very bright fourth-grade boy who lived with a violent, abusive alcoholic father. Under the drawing the child had written, "I wish I was dead. I'm so stupid." His self-image was far from his capabilities. He was behaving according to his self-image.

He had been placed with an insensitive teacher who did not understand his pleas for help. We were able to change his class. His new teacher was made familiar with his home situation and with warmth and reassurance the boy began to improve.

Significant? To whom? His father is more concerned with

his next drunk. His mother is thinking up ways to try to prevent that. How can he be significant? He gets in the way. And he feels in the way.

I was asked by a family to interview their sixteen-year-old son, who was being held in a youth detention center. It was their hope that if I wrote a favorable report it could be used in the boy's defense when he came to trial.

Ned had been involved with a very serious crime and the whole community was outraged. As we sat and talked I said to him, "I don't understand what made you do it. I've known you a long time and it just doesn't sound like your style." He said, "I did it so they'd notice me."

Does that send chills up your spine? It did mine. His family had been so consumed with his father's drinking that they really had paid no attention. He had gotten expelled from school. They paid no attention. He was involved in petty crimes, each time leaving evidence for his parents to find. Nothing. And finally he did something that got their attention. It got a lot of people's attention. And it cost a boy a year in jail. For him, for children who act out in order to be noticed, the nature of the attention is not nearly as important as the attention itself. At least they know I'm alive. Let them worry about me for a change.

They feel worthless because they feel responsible for their father's illness. If they were better kids their father would not drink. And, of course, there is no way that they can be good enough. So these feelings are continually reinforced.

What happens in terms of their attitudes toward home is interesting. You would assume that the kids would want to run away. You would assume that they would want to get just as far away from that situation as they possibly could. This is not true. These kids have very mixed feelings. Although they are unhappy at home, they feel needed. How can their mother manage without them? They worry about their father. Although they are angry with the alcoholic or the irritable nonalcoholic, they feel somehow responsible. They hunger for the love of the rejecting parent, and this binds them up emotionally. This has an effect on their self-concept. They feel guilty. They can't let go of the feeling that it is something wrong with them that caused their parent to drink. There must be something they can do to get their father to stop drinking. These attitudes are supported by the alcoholic who does not want to take responsibility for his behavior. This is also an attitude that they picked up from you because you are thinking the same things for yourself. It gets complicated. The children want to protect their mother. They want to be protected by their mother. Their father isn't *always* horrible. Maybe he'll stop as he promised. Their emotions are greatly tied up in their home. Even when they leave the home they have not left emotionally. The college students that I have who come from alcoholic homes are far more concerned with what is happening at home than those students from more typical homes. The phone calls are traumatic. They need me. I owe them. Can they get along without me? It is a different feeling than I get from the other students. From them I get comments such as, "My folks are trying to lay a guilt trip on me 'cause I don't call or come home as often as they want me to." They may feel guilty but it doesn't appear, in general, to be as wrenching. It is the struggle to grow up and be independent, even if it means being selfish and thoughtless. Although, as a parent, none of us like that stage because it feels like a kick in the teeth, it is healthier than the constant checking up and running home to be sure that everything is still there.

Social relationships must of necessity suffer. The children are afraid to establish friendships because they are embarrassed to invite their friends home. They don't know what will happen, or how their friends will be treated when they arrive. And they have cause to be concerned. Since they cannot explain ahead of time, and since eventually invitations from others must be returned, they are embarrassed. I know of one little girl who brought a friend home with her from school and found her father passed out on the living-room floor. Her mother told the friend that he had a bad back and the doctor had told him that sleeping on the floor would be good for it. The girl seemed to believe it at the time, but she never returned.

What happens to these kids is that they withdraw so that they do not have to face others, or they act out in such a manner that others will reject them. It is just too painful to deal with. This adds to the feeling of aloneness and lack of worth. "Everybody hates me. I have no friends. No matter what I do I get into trouble."

School performance and attitudes suffer as well. It is hard to imagine how one can concentrate on schoolwork when he is worried about what is going on at home, or has been kept up most of the night by an alcoholic parent. Attention span is something that is learned and developed. Under these circumstances it is almost impossible.

A teacher who is sensitive to the needs of children—who establishes an accepting, caring climate—can provide a haven for these children. I think this is shown by the following essay written by a seventh-grade girl from an alcoholic home. Although she doesn't state it, she is reflecting back on a time when her father was actively drinking.

DREAMS

I seldom remember my dreams. I think dreams are just things you think about while you are asleep. I am pretty sure that I am accurate. I once had a dream that a huge monster came to town. He killed everyone in sight, and smashed up houses with people in them. I would see him before anyone did, it always turned out that no one else noticed that he was there except for me. I would run to the Seniors' house two houses away, and hide on their new porch. They had just added a porch in real life when I had the dream. Anyway I would hear screams and really get scared. I started to cry, when all of a sudden, the monster picks me up and starts talking to me. I was really scared then, I was sure he'd trample me. But he didn't. I'm sure he would have if I wasn't crying. He became very sentimental, and was very nice to me. It turned out that I was all alone because the monster had killed everyone in the world except for me. The monster kept me company, then one day I turned and he was gone, I was all alone again, but this time it was for good.

What that dream seems to mean is that I was angry and I wanted to get back at people who had hurt me in any way. So I was really the monster getting back at those people by killing them. Then, after I had killed them I was all alone, which is where I started from. When I had that dream I was in third grade. I had no friends at home, because I was shy and very sensitive. Whenever someone did something mean to me, I'd really get upset. I hated a lot of people. I was a real mess. Probably the reason I liked school was because it was a way to get away from problems around home. In school

I was the comedian, and had a lot of friends. I tried to
be funny to hide my real feelings.

It is hard for the teachers to identify these children as suf-
ferers of near-alcoholism. They don't want it known. I have
asked kids of varying ages if they would join a group in
school to help them live with this problem if their names
were kept confidential. Each has said, "Forget it! I won't
take the risk of someone finding out!" I am starting such a
group at the college where I teach. I find that out of every
ten students I see, at least two are somehow touched by this
problem. Astounding figures, but true. I don't know how
many will join the group. The admission to others is devastating, but the response of "I know exactly what you're talking about because it happened to me too," brings with it
such enormous relief you can almost observe a great weight
being lifted. They stand taller.

Although the picture I've painted may look pretty grim, it
is far from hopeless. Just as soon as you begin to get better,
your children will get better. It is practically automatic. You
can recover as a family. The very illness that has divided the
family can bring it together. I have seen it work so often.

Alcoholism is a family disease. Part of its strategy is to
divide and conquer. It gains strength when each member of
the family retreats into his own private hell. But when the
family joins as a unit to combat it, it loses its power to control and dominate. It becomes neutralized. It loses the sick
energy that it needs to feed on. The struggle it puts up is
enormous, but once the family is not afraid, it can only feed
on itself. Eventually it loses its power, and you gain yours
back.

This book will give you the tools to work with. It will give you a way to help yourself and then, more specifically, it will give you the tools that will help the children.

As I said earlier, children learn through identification and role modeling. They give back what is given to them. As you change, you present to them a person that they can feel good about. You become a person they want to be like. As you are better able to share your thoughts and feelings, so will they. As you learn to accept yourself, so will they be better able to accept themselves. When you learn to love yourself, they will learn to love themselves. And finally you will learn to make your energy work for you and not against you. It's not easy—but it's worth it.

4 COMING TO GRIPS WITH THE PROBLEM

The first step in making your life manageable is to accept alcoholism as a disease. It is a disease as diabetes is a disease or cancer is a disease. It is a progressive disease. It gets worse by stages. It is a fatal disease. It can be arrested, but it cannot be cured.

Nobody can really pinpoint what happens in the body of an alcoholic when he takes a drink. Something happens that is not the same as when a nonalcoholic takes a drink. The alcohol does not follow the same digestive process that it does in a nonalcoholic. I recently heard an alcoholic say, "I took a swallow and felt it in my toes." "I tried a taste of chocolate mousse that I didn't know had brandy in it and I started to tingle." The sensitivity to the drug is immediately apparent.

I know of an alcoholic man who had not had a drink in eight years. He started working in a paint factory. The alcohol in the paint fumes triggered off his addiction and he went on a bender.

I have an alcoholic student who bounces off the walls when she takes antihistamine for a cold. Her body reacts the same way to all drugs.

I know of many recovering alcoholics who will not use aspirin for a headache, refuse Novocain at the dentist, watch the mouthwash labels, and take other extreme precautions because they are terrified that the slightest ingestion of any drug into their system will cause them to lose control. The fact of the matter is that there is a good chance that they are right.

Alcohol addicts its victims both psychologically and physically. Usually the psychological addiction is the most apparent in the early stages. In R. D. Laing's book *Knots,* he describes the pattern of psychological addiction. Although there may be variations on the theme, I find what he says to be pretty much the way it is (I have changed she to he).

He has started to drink
                as a way to cope
                that makes him less able to cope

the more he drinks
the more frightened he is of
                becoming a drunkard
the more drunk
the less frightened of being drunk

the more frightened of being drunk
                when not drunk
        the more not frightened drunk
        the more frightened not drunk

Round and round we go. I think you get the picture. The victim gets sucked in deeper and deeper. The image that comes to mind is that of quicksand, but I've been told you can float on top of quicksand. There's no floating with alcoholism. Things may appear to stabilize, but that's a part of the deception.

As the psychological addiction progresses, so does the physical. Consider this. Alcohol is made up of both ethyl and methyl alcohol. The ethyl alcohol is what makes us feel good and is absorbed quickly into the system. Methyl alcohol is similar to embalming fluid. This takes longer to break down. Because of its nature, it is the methyl alcohol that is responsible for the morning-after hangover. I'm sure you've been told that the best remedy for a hangover is a drink. This is so because it slows down the methyl alcohol and the ethyl alcohol is absorbed. You feel better for a time. Then, if you continue to choose to avoid the pain, you just have another drink. This slows down the process of the methyl alcohol and the ethyl alcohol is absorbed and you feel better for a time—and then if you want to avoid the painyoujusthaveanotherdrinkandthisslowsdowntheprocessofthemethylalcoholandtheethylalcohol. . . . Many alcoholics don't have hangovers because the level of alcohol in their bloodstream never gets low enough for the methyl alcohol to start to break down.

What I have talked about so far are the early stages. The disease gets progressively worse. As it takes greater hold, there is the physical compulsion. Many develop physical symptoms, such as the shakes, which are calmed by alcohol. Others hallucinate. Alcohol causes the devils and then offers itself as the only thing the alcoholic can use to drive them away.

Many alcoholics die from damage to body organs such as

the liver or the pancreas. Alcohol takes such a strong hold on the sick alcoholic that he can even risk death when he tries to withdraw. Cold-turkey withdrawal from alcohol can be dangerous. One does not die from cold-turkey withdrawal from heroin, but one can with alcohol. Detoxification centers watch alcoholics very carefully when they are going through withdrawal. Rehabilitation centers, in general, will not accept an alcoholic until he has been detoxified. The risks of convulsion are too great for nonmedical people to handle. I cannot believe that a person who was not insane would poison himself to this degree. This is not an act of moral weakness. This is a sickness.

If you believe nothing else that I have told you in this book, believe that alcoholism is a disease. I know it is difficult to accept, but the evidence is overwhelming. I have spoken to so many women who just cannot believe it. No matter what I say, and no matter how much they trust me, they still can't stop thinking, "If he *really* wanted to, he could quit!" Interestingly enough while these women cannot accept the disease concept for their husbands, they are scared to death that their children will inherit it.

One thing that may get in the way of your accepting alcoholism as a disease is the stereotype of the Skid Row bum—out of work, no family, cruddy clothes, grubby beard, brown bag hiding a bottle, wiping windshields of cars for change to buy more rot gut.

The stereotype is true—for a few. I admit I used to believe it myself, but then I got to know some alcoholics. Some were out of work. Some were working. There were unskilled laborers and high corporate executives, doctors, lawyers, you name it. Incomes ranged from being on welfare to $200,000 a year. Some were Irish Catholics, some Protestants, some Jews, white, black, old, young, brilliant, slow. The only statement that can be made for all these people is that THEY ALL HAVE A PROBLEM WITH ALCOHOL.

The stereotype is not the only myth that gets in the way of your accepting the disease. There are a number of others. "He never drinks during the day," "He doesn't drink all that much," "He only drinks on the weekend," or, "He never drinks on the weekend." The fact remains that it doesn't matter when he drinks, how much he drinks, or what time of the day he begins. What matters is whether he loses control once he takes the first drink. As the disease progresses, he will drink earlier and earlier. The fact that he delays the first one does not mean he is not alcoholic.

"He only drinks beer." A bottle of beer has the same amount of alcohol as a shot of whiskey. A six-pack of beer is like three double shots. You get more bloat, but you don't get less alcohol.

"He's too young to be an alcoholic." Alcoholism is not a function of age. As a matter of fact the disease progresses faster in a young person than in an older one. I recently heard a man in his early twenties proclaim that he didn't start drinking seriously until he was eight. Incredible? Believe it.

Attend an open meeting of Alcoholics Anonymous. You'll see the same assortment of people that you see at a PTA meeting, or a church group, or on the beach. Some of them will be the identical people. You will hear them talk about the things they did when they were drinking, because they are afraid that if they don't "keep their memories green" they will repeat them.

At the first A.A. meeting that I attended I heard an elderly woman speak. She talked about attending a wake many years ago. At that time they still packed bodies in ice, and she hid some beer bottles under the ice in the casket. Now she knew how alcoholic that thinking was. Alcoholism, if left unchecked, will drive you insane—if it does not kill you first.

Who is an alcoholic? It comes down to this: An alcoholic is anybody who is suffering from the disease of alcoholism. That's it. I know that sounds much too simple, but the understanding and acceptance of that statement are the beginning steps toward *your* recovery.

I mention once again how important it is to realize that alcoholism is a disease. The alcoholic is a sick person. He does not choose to behave the way he does. It is the chemical within his system that dictates his behavior. It is not his choice. Ingesting the chemical is not his choice. It is not a sign of moral weakness. He has a compulsion over which he has no control. No one chooses to be an alcoholic. Someone may choose to take a drink. If that someone is not alcoholic, he still has a choice after the first one as to whether or not he will have a second. The alcoholic does not have such a choice. After the first drink, the compulsion sets in, and even though he may be able to control his drinking for certain periods of time, the compulsion will eventually take over and he will drink until he can drink no more.

The other key word in that sentence is suffering. The alcoholic is not a happy person. Alcohol is a depressant. So regardless of the real or imagined reasons he uses in order to justify his drinking, he is miserable much of the time, if only because of the effect of the chemical. The initial feeling of freedom that allows him to be the life of the party gives way to depression. It is an emotional depression if he is embarrassed by his behavior, and a chemical depression because of the nature of the drug.

There are many definitions of alcoholism. None of them is entirely satisfactory. It is not really necessary for us to know them all. We all know what an alcohol abuser looks like. We can all make some assumptions about what an alcohol abuser behaves like. And we all know, when the subject of alcohol abuse comes up, what we are talking about.

For our purposes an alcoholic is best defined as someone whose drinking causes a continuing and growing problem in any area of his life—more specifically someone whose drinking is causing a continuing and growing problem in *your* life. It may be seen as a problem by you long before it is seen as a problem by him. And furthermore what really truly matters is not whether your husband is an alcoholic by whatever definition, but your reaction to his drinking. Nancy H. called me the other day. She said, "Maybe it's me. Maybe he's not an alcoholic. He says he isn't but I treat him as if he is!"

I say to you what I said to Nancy. It doesn't matter whether or not your husband is an alcoholic. You are reacting to him as if he is and therefore you have to work on yourself.

And so we begin.

The first thing to do is to begin to work on changing your attitude. If your husband were dying of cancer and his disease was causing him to be obnoxious, the obnoxious behavior would make you upset and angry, but you would not hold him responsible for his cancer. The same thing holds true with alcoholism. You cannot hold an alcoholic responsible for his alcoholism. You can hold him responsible for his behavior. Chances are you have done the reverse. You have thought of him as a bastard when he drank himself blotto, and then found a way to blame yourself for his ranting and raving. In so doing you have enabled the disease.

What a harsh thing for me to say to you—harsh, but true. You have probably been an unwilling accomplice to alcoholism. You have, for all the right reasons, done all the wrong things. You have probably covered up for him, blamed him and not the disease, made aimless threats, joined him in drinking, become extremely emotional, used self-pity and self-deception, tried to control his drinking, and taken over his responsibilities.

All of those responses are understandable. All of those responses are perfectly normal. All of those responses help to make his continued drinking possible. It may not make sense to you yet, but it should as we go on. Even when you see how these responses enable the disease, you may not choose, for your own survival, to eliminate all of them. But you will be aware, and being aware will open up new options for you.

There are two physical responses to alcohol that are helpful for you to understand before you can stop enabling his alcoholism and feel good about it. The first has to do with the anesthetic nature of the drug, and the second response is blackouts.

Alcohol is an anesthetic. Before the development of more sophisticated anesthetics it was used for this purpose. It insulates one physically and emotionally against pain. The pain that you or I feel when someone is hurtful to us goes unfelt by the alcoholic who is drinking. What that means is that anything that we do that lessens the consequences of his drinking helps him to continue drinking. He has to be hurt so badly that he can feel the hurt through the drug. He has to hurt so badly that he will cry for help. You don't know what it is that will make him hurt badly enough, but the enabling stops the pain and delays the moment of truth.

Alcoholics are also prone to blackouts. A blackout is a period of time when an individual functions in a seemingly normal manner, but has no memory of it. He only knows he has been in one when he comes out of it, and he doesn't have any sense of how he got where he is. A blackout is a very frightening experience. I have heard some of the most incredible stories of what has gone on during blackouts. One man told me of being transferred by his company from Newark to Boston. He was happy about the transfer and went out to celebrate. When he came out of the blackout he found that he had enlisted in the Canadian army. That blackout cost that man five years.

Many a businessman will make a series of phone calls while in a blackout. Then, the next day, remake those same calls. Not too good for business. But he had no recollection of having done it before.

I know a man who claims his last child was conceived in a blackout. His wife called it rape, and his friends have a great time teasing him that he can never be completely sure that it is his child.

Blackouts are strong evidence of alcoholism. Nonalcoholics will pass out before they black out, or they will stop drinking when they have had enough.

I bring up these two examples of the effects of alcohol to help you understand the importance of changing your behavior. Many of us who work in this field maintain that an alcoholic will not seek help until he has hit his "bottom." He will only hit his bottom when the repercussions of his behavior are too overwhelming for him to ignore. Keep in mind that any behavior of yours that allows the alcoholic to avoid the consequences of his actions lengthens the life of the disease. Any behavior of yours that causes the alcoholic to take responsibility for his behavior *may* help shorten it. We don't know for sure what will make a difference, but we know the direction. Since we are dealing with such an insidious disease, the opposite of the usual rules apply. You will behave in ways that are contrary to your nature if you are a loving, supportive, caring, nurturing person. The way you demonstrate your love is by letting your alcoholic endure his own suffering. If you cushion that for him because you love him, and want to make him feel better because you are a good person, *you are helping to kill him.* I recognize that this is a very strong statement. I don't know how to make it any stronger. I would if I could.

I know of one man who had to go away on a business trip in order to crash to his bottom and seek help. Somehow his wife, no matter how hard she tried not to, found a way to patch up his wounds, and his disease continued to progress. When he finally got away and there was no one to apply the emotional bandages, he had a psychotic break—technical term for "he lost his mind"—and was finally able to get help. His wife, recognizing this was beyond her scope, had him hospitalized. Since he was crazy as a result of the alcohol, his hallucinations ceased after a few days and his paranoid delusions stopped. He then went to a rehabilitation center to begin his recovery. The point here is that his wife, with the best of intentions, was only doing harm.

There are many ways that you enable the disease. Most of them are ways in which you thought you were being helpful. You may also have been afraid to act differently. It may be that the risks of behaving differently are too great for you. You must be prepared to handle the outcome of your behavior. As I discuss enabling or rescuing behaviors be aware of this behavior in yourself. Then look at it, and see if it is truly in your best interest to continue. You know that it is not in the best interest of your husband *regardless of what he says.* He will try to tell you otherwise. When trying to convince you, he will try to lay guilt on you and may threaten you. At that point, if you stand your ground, he will either back off or attack. More often than not the surprise at your assertion will cause him to back off, but, as I've said many times, the behavior is unpredictable and you have to be prepared for whatever happens. The preparation is part of the learning, but for now, let's just look at the enabling behaviors. Let's look at what it is that you do that enables him to avoid taking responsibility for his actions and thereby facing their consequences.

The first of these is covering up for him. How many times have you called his boss and told him that your husband was not feeling well when he was hungover? He's big enough to make that call for himself. How many phone calls have come in when you have said that he was out because he was too drunk to come to the phone? Why not hand him the phone and let him find a way to struggle through the call?

Sheila's husband went out to play poker. She stayed up most of the night worrying. When he ambled in at about four in the morning, he had blood on his forehead. Her fears were realized. He had been in an accident. A taxi had had the misfortune to stop at a red light and Rob had driven right into it. There was minor damage to the cab, Rob's windshield was smashed, and his forehead was cut. Sheila was so relieved that he was not seriously hurt that any thought of herself went out the window. Do you start to smell the setup? "Sheila, dear, do you think you could take care of having the car repaired?" "Of course, honey; all that matters is that you're not hurt."

So Sheila told the men at the body shop that it was her fault. She did all the paper work for the insurance company. She suffered all the aggravations one suffers when a car is repaired. Bob gets off free. His wife has covered for him and taken over his responsibility. He has not had to feel any consequences. He has paid no emotional price for drunken driving. Is that fair to him? The disease is the only beneficiary because Rob has lost out on an opportunity to feel the results of uncontrolled drinking. He must experience it if he is to get well. Sheila's loving act was, in reality, very cruel.

Another way that you may cover up is in not letting him find the fruits of his drunken labor. If he has smashed up the furniture the night before, or broken some dishes, it is important that when he awakens he sees them. There are a couple of reasons for this. The first has to do with you and your self-respect. Why should you clean up after him? Are you a servant in your own home? The second reason is that since alcoholics are prone to blackouts, there is a very real possibility that he simply will not remember. He would prefer to forget the whole thing as if it never happened. Your cleaning it up will help him to do that. Telling him about it will not have the same impact and may open up a whole other can of worms. The same applies to helping him to bed. Let him find himself on the floor when he awakens. That way he will know that he really did pass out on the floor. Otherwise you cannot be sure that he will believe it. It is a very painful memory. Alcoholics would prefer to avoid unpleasant memories.

You are naturally concerned about the children. You don't want the children to awaken and find the mess. You want to protect them from the harsh reality. Perfectly understandable. It just doesn't work. First of all you make the assumption that the children slept through the whole thing. That is highly unlikely. Secondly you are making the assumption that knowing something is wrong and not knowing what it is is better than knowing the truth. Rethink that. They know that something is wrong because they are not as sophisticated as adults. They feel it. They pick up what you are feeling and it is unsettling to them. If you want your kids to grow up strong and emotionally healthy, they *must* con-

front reality. Life is not always pleasant. You know for yourself that you can handle the truth more easily than a
well-meaning lie. Children are not different in this regard.
What you do is simply tell them the truth *without anger*.
"This is what happened last night when Daddy was drunk. I
feel very sad that you have to see it, but I am not going to
pick it up and I don't want you to either."

Let your husband see the mess. Let your husband clean
up the mess. Let your husband be embarrassed for the children. He has a right to his humiliation. He earned it.

When you blame him and not his disease, you play into it.
You act in accusatory ways that give him an excuse to get
drunk. He feels guilty and resentful. He can hold you responsible. And he goes off to drink. If you accept the fact
that he has a disease, you can blame the disease and not
him. You can have compassion for him. Then you separate
him from his illness. When he smashes up the furniture you
know that this is not the person you love smashing it up but
the disease. The person who wakes up the next morning and
is horrified at what his disease caused him to do is the one
you care about. All those angry feelings are gone and he cannot even believe himself that he could have done that. If you
tell him about it, he may need to think that you are exagger-
ating. And well you might be. He will also respond to your
tone.

When you truly separate the person from the disease, and
detach yourself from that part of it, you will send out different vibrations. Alcoholics are very sensitive people. They
wait for a reaction from you. If you feel hostile, even if your
words are kind, they feel the hostility and use it as an excuse
to drink. Remember they are like children in this regard. If
you are truly compassionate and they do not feel tension
coming from you, they have no excuse. This does not mean

he will stay home and remain sober, but what it does mean
is that he cannot use you as an excuse for his drinking. He
has to admit, if only a little, that he is doing it for his own
reasons, and not because of something that you have said or
that you have done.

Remember Beth? It is entirely possible that Beth would
not have required twenty-six stitches in her arm if she had
been detached. This detachment that I speak of—and it is
hard work—can save you a lot of grief. I don't know what
words she said to her husband when he came upstairs and
awakened her, but I do know that she was angry. He picked
up on her tone and acted against it. If she had had compassion for his illness, even though she may have refused to
leave her bed, her vibrations would not have said *kill;* they
would have shown sympathy. He would not then have had
anger to react to. This may not seem realistic to you yet, but
keep reading. The pieces will fall into place.

Any behavior that allows him to use you as an excuse for
drinking enables his disease. Crying, berating, inducing
guilt—all give him an excuse to drink. He promises he'll
stop and controls it for a while, but he can't, and your attitude plays into his need for a drink.

Hiding his bottles and pouring them down the sink only
add to the expense. He'll learn to hide them better. *"She's*
not gonna decide if I can have liquor in my own house!"

If you truly want him to get well, it is important that you
do *nothing* to get in the way of his drinking. Read this again.
I said what you think I said. If you really care about him,
you will not find ways to get him to drink less. Any action of
yours that causes him to control his drinking prolongs the
life of the illness. Alcoholics, with few exceptions, need to
get very sick before they get well. The faster they get very
sick, the greater the chances of their recovery. So do not

hide his bottles or extract "good behavior" promises. He has
to stop by and for himself. He has to reach the point when
the pain of drinking is greater than the pain of not drinking.
Only he can know when that point is.

Your own ability to stay in touch with reality is essential.
When you make excuses for his behavior you don't help him
know the situation for what it really is. You help him deny
his addiction. He doesn't want to believe it, and if he cons
you into thinking, "Things will work out all right," or, "I can
control it," he can also con himself.

Drinking with him is a way of saying that his behavior is
acceptable. If you can't lick 'em join 'em is a questionable
hypothesis at best. You know that you're really only doing it
to keep an eye on him. Maybe if you're with him he won't
drink as much.

More and more you take over his responsibilities. You
take over the checkbook. You mow the lawn. You do all the
things you no longer trust him to do. This frees him to drink.
This also means he doesn't have to answer to the bank. It
also means he doesn't have to look at the overgrown grass. It
may be that for yourself you cannot leave these things unat-
tended, and that's okay. Just be aware that it is a rescuing
behavior. Be very sure you take over these responsibilities
because you feel you must, for your own good and the good
of your family. Martyrs are not appreciated during their lifetimes.

I realize that while you are reading this section you are
saying a lot of "yeah buts." I've heard them all. No, your situation is *not* different. No, your husband is *not* worse. No,
you're no more afraid than anyone else in the same situation.

You're afraid you can't live with him.

You're afraid you can't live without him.

You're afraid he'll lose his job.

You're afraid he'll get killed.

You're afraid he'll kill you.

You're afraid of being alone.

You're afraid of a hundred things you can't even name. What if . . . what if . . . what if . . .

That spinning feeling is not yours alone. And you don't have to be lonely. There is help. There is Al-Anon. Al-Anon is a self-help group for families and friends of alcoholics. When you can muster up the courage, give them a call. You won't be asked to tell them anything you don't want them to know. They won't even ask you your name. They will just be happy that you've reached out for help. You will feel at home. You will tell these women (and men) of the horrors only you are living with, and they'll finish your sentences. They've been there. You'll hear someone talk and you'll think, "My God, they're talking about me!" You will feel a tremendous burden lifted. Once again you have friends. The difference is that you have no secrets from these friends. They've lived your life because they're married to men like your husband. They know how you feel. At first there will be one big difference between you and them. They'll know you're new to the group because of the pain on your face and your nearness to tears. You'll know who is not new because their eyes will be bright and they can laugh. You'll get there too, and the next chapter will start you off.

5 HOW YOU CAN BE HELPED

This is the hard part. Concentrating on yourself is new to you. You have not been the center of your own universe. You have been spinning in your husband's orbit. You have been revolving around him.

You have been reacting to him. His reactions to you have been his reactions to your reactions to him. You have not been your own person. You have, in effect, become a non-person.

This is not at all surprising. Even with the advent of the women's movement many women still choose to live in the shadow of their husbands. For many women it is a satisfying way of life. In your situation it is unhealthy. It will destroy you. In our society it is not unusual for a woman to define

herself in terms of her man and her children. You are so-
and-so's wife and so-and-so's mother. Your husband's success
is your success. The notion of the woman behind the man is
still with us. His approval of you is your approval of you.

Your day is focused around his comings and goings. Pleasing him is all important. Since pleasing him is the most important thing in your life, you do not want to displease him.
Since pleasing him becomes more and more difficult as he
gets sicker and sicker, you try harder and harder. As a result
you too get sicker and sicker. You gradually lose your sense
of worth. You have not determined for yourself what your
worth is, so when you are continually put down by your husband, you lose a sense of yourself. It doesn't happen overnight. The erosion process is so gradual as to go unnoticed.
You have unwillingly allowed the disease of alcoholism to
decide your value as a human being.

Now that you are becoming aware, let us begin to put all
that in the past. It will not be easy. Start with today. You
will begin to live in the present, one day at a time. This
moment right now belongs to you. Grab on to it and make
the most of it. Do it for yourself.

You will be faced with a new question. This question
sounds very simple, but you will find it most difficult. You
may not even understand it at first. The question is, "What
do I want?" It is hard because you don't know for sure who
"I" is. How long can you talk about yourself without men-
tioning another person? How many sentences can you write
that start with the word I? How much of a conversation can
you carry on talking about only your own thoughts and feelings? Take a look at how much of your conversation revolves
around your husband and children. I'm not saying that is
right or wrong. What I am saying is, can you make a conscious choice to talk only about yourself and be able to do it?

Linda discovered that she was pregnant. At first she refused to believe it. But, as you and I both know, there are certain things that cannot be denied. Her marriage was a mess. Chuck's drinking was getting worse and he continued to be violent. Linda's obstetrician had told her that she was not strong enough to carry to term. Her older children were frightened because she had miscarried before and it was very upsetting to them. Her mother had said, "What do you want to have a baby for?" The other women where she worked had said, "Your other kids are launched. You're starting a career. A baby will tie you down." There seemed to be a consensus that having a baby would not be a good idea.

Finally someone said, "Linda, what do *you* want?" She was dumbfounded. What a strange question. That was the one question she had not considered. "What do I want?" She felt turned inside out. "What do I want?"

She gave it careful thought. She was seven months along and still thinking. Decisions are rough. It finally came to her. "I want to have a baby! After all I'm the one who will have to live with whatever decision I make. I'm also the one who will have to take care of the baby once it is born." She finally knew that having the baby was the right decision for her.

I was with her when she delivered. I had never heard a mother laugh all through the labor and delivery. She had natural childbirth. It was only fitting. She was awake for the first time in a long time.

The baby is four now and he's wonderful. All the people who advised her against it love him dearly. She did what was right for *her* and everyone else benefited. They reacted to her joy and her positive attitude. Good feelings can be just as contagious as tension and anxiety. The bonus is that her husband is now sober and is a good father to the boy. But that's only a bonus. She had the baby because it was right for her and that's the best reason to do anything. She was able to answer the question, "What do I want?" Now it's your turn.

Let's take a look at some of the symptoms of near-alcoholism that we went over in the second chapter. Those things that drove you to despair can be examined in a new light. You can use your energy to work either for you or against you now that you know you have the choice. Isn't that a powerful place to be? A person has choices. A person has options. You are a person. You will now become aware of what some of those options may be.

Denial

Isn't it about time you faced up to what's really happening? Cinderella is only a fairy tale. Your Prince Charming will probably puke in your glass slipper. The energy that you use to deny the truth can be put into facing it and not being victimized by it.

If you accept the fact that he will probably come home drunk, you are prepared if he does, and pleasantly surprised if he does not. If you deny the probable, even though he swore to you that he would never drink again, you will be shattered if he disappoints you. You have, in effect, set yourself up. It is unfair to blame him.

Reality may be rough, but it's the only way to keep sane. I'm not suggesting that you give up hope. I'm just suggesting you give up fantasy. "If only"—these two words can lead to nothing but trouble. Some people live out their whole lives with if only's. What happened happened. What you did you did. You did some things well. Other things you screwed up. That is now in the past. Today is today. I give you permission to make a fresh start, a chance to make new mistakes rather than relive the old ones. I also offer you a chance to do things that will make *you* feel better. That is today. Yesterday is gone. You can relive it and relive it, but you lose this day and that is all you really have. It's hard to change that which has already happened. You can only change it if it is repeated today and you behave differently.

When you accept the fact that your husband is suffering from an illness today and that chances are pretty good that he will still be sick tomorrow, you are in a better position not only to help yourself but to help him. Pick a time when you are not angry, and he is not drinking, and share with him some of your concerns. He may or may not listen, but the seed will have been planted. Literature about alcoholism or A.A. left around the house may get an angry response but is seldom left unread. You are not preaching but looking at reality. There is a difference. He'll probably continue to deny even after you've stopped, but you will no longer be part of his denial system. And a suggestion will have been made as to where the help is—when he's ready to ask for it.

Embarrassment, Avoiding Drinking Occasions

You cannot take responsibility for anyone's behavior but your own. You are a person in your own right. You are not merely a reflection of your husband. He is a person in his own right. When you go to a party he'll do what he does and you'll do what you do. Concentrate on having a good time for yourself. STOP WATCHING HIM. STOP TRYING TO CONTROL THE AMOUNT HE DRINKS. That is not your problem. He is an adult and as an adult he must make that decision for himself. The only decision you have to make as far as he's concerned is who drives home. You may have to assert yourself here, but the rest is up to him and to you.

If you find that having a good time with him is too much for you to handle, go without him. Yes, you may have to start going places alone. As his disease progresses he will become more and more antisocial and you will find yourself home and isolated until you learn to go out by yourself.

I gave a large party about six months ago. As one of my guests was leaving, she thanked me and apologized for her husband's absence. I hid my embarrassment because, until that moment, I had not realized he was missing.

It will be hard, at first, to go places without him. It will get easier. Go with a friend if you are too uncomfortable to go alone, but go. You don't have to withdraw from outside contact because of your husband. If he doesn't want to go to the family wedding, to your sister's on Sunday, or whatever, take the kids (if they're invited) and go. You'll be amazed but no one will ask for any great big explanation. They'll be happy to see you. They'll express appropriate regrets that your husband couldn't make it and that'll be the end of it. Believe me, he's the central figure in your life but nobody else's. Why deprive yourself of having a good time? Why be punished because he is sick? It's unfortunate that your husband is ill, but alcoholism is *not* contagious.

I understand that the things I am suggesting to you are a little scary. You've been very dependent and I'm telling you to go places alone. It's like jumping into a pool. At first the water feels cold, but it warms up once you start to splash around. The idea of going off the diving board is threatening, but once done, you feel a sense of accomplishment. And of course the more you work at it, the easier it becomes.

Shift in Relationship, Domination, Takeover, Self-absorptive Activities

Even Superman didn't want to be Superman all of the time. He only wanted to be Superman when it served his purpose. The rest of the time he was content to be a regular person. The same goes for you. You don't have to do everything all the time. Just because your husband abdicates a responsibility does not mean you have to pick it up. If he has promised to paint the kitchen and isn't doing it, you don't have to do it unless you cannot live with it the way it is.

If he loses his job it doesn't automatically mean that you *have* to go to work. Taking over the role of the breadwinner is not necessarily the most desirable alternative. Before you panic, find out the circumstances of his losing his job. The fault may or may not lie with him. The reason may not be alcoholism.

There are a number of questions. Is there severance pay? Is he eligible for unemployment? Will the company rehire him if he enters a rehabilitation program? More and more companies are becoming aware of the savings involved if they do this.

Do you have savings? Are you eligible for public assistance? Will your family help out for a while? Attend an Al-Anon meeting. Ask the women you meet how they handled this particular problem. Job loss is no stranger to those who live with alcoholism.

What I am suggesting is that rather than pick up the gauntlet that he has dropped, you may make better use of this time to take a good hard look at yourself and your situation and think about what you want to do with your life.

There is the possibility, depending on how sick he is, that he may find another job. It may shock him into facing himself. Your act of heroism may be perceived by him as castrating. Examine your motives. Buy a little time.

This may be the point when you decide that you've had it. You may decide that you are no longer willing to live in this situation. You may decide you want to go to work because it is good for you and for your children. It may be a desirable solution for many reasons. But one of those reasons should not be to take the burden off your husband. Chances are that he will not make things any easier for you at home, and what may have the potential to be a wonderful growth experience for you will end up making you even more resentful. And just when you are feeling terribly, terribly sorry for yourself because of the burden you carry, somebody like me will come along and say, "Martyrs are rarely appreciated during their lifetimes, but women who have careers and also run households are among the most exciting people I've ever known."

How long can you do it all? Do you really want to? What's in it for you? Just who is impressed or who do you want to impress? Do you want to drain yourself physically and emotionally? Where are you in all of this? Or are you?

What did you do for yourself today? What did you do just because it made *you* feel good. Nobody else, just you. You may resist the idea. That's very selfish. Yes, it is. It is selfish but not in a negative sense. If you do something for yourself that causes harm to another, that may not be a good idea. But most of the things that we do that are selfish are fulfilling of the self. These things not only benefit us, but those around us. If you feel good you will influence those around you. You know that others react to your irritability; they also react to a feeling of well-being.

Why not make a list of ten things that you like to do. Most of them probably aren't even costly. Promise yourself that you will do at least one of them every day. Doing something for yourself will help make you feel better about yourself.

This list will probably be hard for you to write. Thinking about yourself in other than a pitying way is a new idea. Try it. There's nothing to lose but a few minutes of misery.

These are the first steps in building a life for yourself in which your husband may or may not be a part. You start with the simple little things that give you pleasure. Then, when doing for yourself becomes a part of your daily routine, when seeing others is a part of your entitlement, you may then start to think in terms of what more productive things you can do with your time. You may want to think in terms of volunteer work, taking a course, or looking for a job that you will enjoy.

The change in focus is what is so important. Do what you do—whatever it is, because *you* want to do it—because it is good for *you*—not because you are afraid to ask him for money or because you think you should. Do what feels right for you. All other things will fall into place.

Guilt

Give it up. It is a worthless emotion. You didn't cause his disease. You can't cure it, nor can you control it.

Let your conscience be your guide. That comes from the inside. That gives you the true measure of what is right for you and what is wrong for you. Guilt is imposed by the outside. Who has the right to decide for you how you should or should not feel, or how you should or should not act? After all you are an adult.

At about this point you must be thinking, "That all sounds well and good, but it's easier said than done!" You're right. There's nothing easy about becoming your own person. It's hard work.

Essentially what I'm telling you to do is to take your power back. You have *given* him the power to make you feel guilty. He cannot do it to you unless *you allow it*. Butbutbut . . . Think about it. The next time he pushes that guilt button say to yourself, "Do I want to feel guilty about that? I'm sorry he feels that way but that is only my problem if I choose to make it so." See what happens. The pain may be a little less.

Obsession, Continual Worry

Obsession is really rough to combat. It is such a relief if you find that you are thinking of something other than your alcoholic and your problems, if only for a moment. These consume you. They overpower you.

As you begin to think of yourself a little more, the obsession will begin to lose its hold on you. You can, essentially, only think about one thing at a time. If you are thinking about something else you cannot be thinking about your problems. Concentration under stress is extremely difficult so do not be too demanding on yourself. Try to concentrate on something else if only for five minutes at a time. If that is too long try it for two minutes or even one minute. The time will build up. Just stay with it.

Many women have told me that they use the Serenity Prayer to help slow down and relax. They just repeat it over and over. It contains a wonderful message.

> God grant me the serenity to accept the things
> > I cannot change
> The courage to change the things I can
> And the wisdom to know the difference

Try it. Or pick up a book on relaxation responses or attend a yoga class or a lecture on meditation. When was the last time you enjoyed the quiet solitude of a church? What about a hot bath? Ride a bicycle around the block. Find something that will help slow down those spinning wheels in your head and divert your mind. It will only work for short periods of time in the beginning, but the time will grow. Gradually you will be in control of your own mind. After all it belongs to you.

The worry doesn't do you much good either. I've never heard anyone say, "Boy, am I glad I worried about that. It really helped." I have heard the reverse. "Why did I waste all that time worrying? It didn't change anything."

That's very true but it's not going to make you stop worrying. Instead of spending your whole day worrying about what kind of shape he's going to be in when he gets home, tell yourself you'll start worrying at five. It takes a lot of energy to decide not to worry at all when you've conditioned yourself to worry. It may take a little less to put it off. "I'm not going to worry about that problem just yet." The problem at the moment is, "What shall I make for dinner?"

Another thing to keep in mind when you start to worry is the simple question, "Whose problem is it?" It is very important to know where somebody else ends and you begin. Whether or not your husband gets home safe is not your problem. You have no control over that. If you've decided he should be home at six for dinner that's *your* problem. If you believe his promises that's *your* problem. If you cover up for him that's *your* problem. If he doesn't show up for dinner that's *his* problem. You're not a short-order cook. If he's hungover after an all-night drunk that's *his* problem. It belongs to him. Let him have it. You've got enough that belongs to you. You don't have to take any more on. When you start to worry don't forget to ask, "Whose problem is it?"

Fear

Fear is your constant companion. Some of your fears are rational, some irrational. Some of the things you are afraid of are real. Some are imagined. Some of your fears you can identify. Some are nameless. Some of your fears are healthy and necessary; others are destructive to you.

The first thing you have to do is try and sort out the fears that are working for you and those that are working against you.

Do you have a friend you can trust? Is there someone who will listen to you, without giving advice, and let you hear yourself out? Just talking about what's going on in your head will help to take the edge off.

You may resist the idea because you don't want to burden your friends. Is that fair to them? When a friend confides her

problems to you, how does it make you feel? I venture to say
it makes you feel good. Why deny your friends the right to
be your friend? Kathy told me of her resistance to burdening
her friends. One night her husband laid such a trip on her
that she went hysterical and unloaded to her friend Ken.
When she finished she felt greatly relieved but was concerned as to his reaction. "How did it make you feel that I
did that?" she said. "Did you feel I was leaning on you? Just
what did you feel?" His response was simply, "You made me
feel important."

Why deny someone else the chance to feel important
when it will also be helpful to you? Just choose your friend
wisely. Maybe one of the women you met at that Al-Anon
meeting I suggested. Such a person would both respect your
privacy and understand your problem. Secondly take a look
at your fears and differentiate between the immediate ones
and the projected ones. You can, with active alcoholism, live
only in the day. You cannot concern yourself with tomorrow.
You must focus on getting through each day one at a time.
If, for reasons you don't fully understand, you are more
afraid of living without your husband than with him, accept
that as real for now. Don't deny your feelings or judge their
appropriateness. Accept that you are afraid. To deny the
feeling is to waste energy. You have no energy to waste and
you cannot will the fear away. It will return. Admit to yourself, "Yes, I am afraid. Now what am I going to do about it?"

Violence

You may fear for your life. Many women who suffer from
physical abuse are the victims of alcoholic behavior. Al-

though not all alcoholics are violent and not all violent people are alcoholic, more often than not abused wives will say that he "had a couple."

If you live with violence, or the threat of violence, it is very important to do your homework.

The first thing to do if he is physically abusive to you is to stop making excuses for him. You did *not* deserve it. You may have provoked it, but you did not *deserve* it. The fact that he is sorry and promises never to do it again does not make it all right, that is if he even remembers what he did. You are a person. This behavior is unacceptable. The "If I hadn't said, he wouldn't have" doesn't cut it. Either he would have or he wouldn't have, but the responsibility for the violence is his. His violence is his fault. What you can do is look at what you do to trigger it.

Arguing with him when he is drunk is asking for trouble. There is no reasoning. Remember you are arguing with a chemical. Berating him will make him angry. These factors will set you up to get hurt if he is prone to violence. He will find enough reason on his own without your adding fuel to the fire.

He will not like the fact that you are working on becoming a whole person. Manipulative people are very threatened by changes in those around them. He'll try and suck you back in. Standing your ground may momentarily cause more trouble, but as you grow, you will be ready to meet each stage.

Alcoholics are very sensitive to tone. If you say, "I'm going to bed," and what you are thinking is, "I'm going to bed, you sonofabitch," he'll react as if you said what you really meant. Don't play games with yourself. "All I said was . . ." You can fool a lot of people that way and maybe even yourself, but you cannot fool your alcoholic. He is very tuned in.

There are a couple of ways to work on this. The first is to come to realize that you are really angry at the disease and that your husband is a very sick person. Once you can accept this, the vibrations that you send out will not say "Die" and he will not feed on them. Many women have told me that when they were finally able to accept on an emotional level the fact that alcoholism is a disease, the violence stopped. This may or may not be true in your case but it is certainly worth a try. And second, read everything you can about the illness, attend Al-Anon meetings, and talk about it with other people who understand and have been through it. They will be sympathetic but will not offer you sympathy. They will let you talk it out and share your experience with you. It will help to take the edge off the fear and keep you from misdirecting your anger.

At the same time keep in mind that there are other things you can do.

1. You can call the police. They will not take action unless you are willing to press charges, but they can quiet things down for the night. Be honest with yourself when you consider this suggestion. Can you do that or are you more fearful of his reputation or his losing his job or what the neighbors will think than of your own protection? You may be. Many women find it helpful to call; others find they are unable to.

You may be willing to make the call but he may not let you near the phone, or you know that he will tear it out of the wall if you go after it. This is also a very real possibility. You can ask someone that you know and trust to call you and if things are not under control, that person can call the police.

2. Never place yourself where you cannot get out. Do not

allow yourself to be trapped. Have a door between you and him and be ready to get out if you have to.

Think about what you will do when you leave the house. Be prepared when and if the time comes. Is there a friend you can drop in on any time of the night? Is there a women's shelter in your area? Find out. Is there a wife-abuse hot line? Call your local mental health center or local chapter of NOW, and find out. Your problem will not be unique to them. Ask for suggestions. Is there an underground of places for you to go? Stash enough money and have it readily available so that you can spend the night in a motel if you have to. But plan ahead so that you don't find yourself on the street with no place to go but back in.

What about the children? Will he go after the children if you leave? Many women stay and face it in order to protect their children. There are alternatives. One is to take the children with you. Chances are they are not asleep. If you cannot take them with you, call the police from the nearest phone and tell them what is happening so they can help you get them out. If the children are old enough, talk to them before the fact so that you will have a plan should there be violence. The intent is not to alarm them but for all of you to be prepared. The discussion will be both upsetting and reassuring at the same time. It's a very unpleasant thing to contemplate, but so is the situation.

3. Find out your legal rights. They vary from state to state. Call an attorney or your local legal aid society. You will need to know what legal steps you can take to protect yourself from physical abuse. Your position may not be as bleak as you think. Knowing what it is will help you to realistically assess the situation. You are best off talking to a lawyer who understands alcoholism and alcoholics. The National

Council on Alcoholism may be able to recommend someone
to you. If not, they may be able to refer you to someone who
can. Or ask someone who belongs to either A.A. or Al-Anon
for a referral. This does not obligate you. You may not be
ready to call. But have the number handy so that when you
are ready you don't have a delay.

Bear in mind that the decision to live with violence is
yours. If you do not feel strong enough to explore alternatives, all the more reason to continue to work on yourself in
order to reach the point where you can make a choice. At
this point you may be more afraid to be on your own than to
stay. He has helped you to feel this way. All your self-doubts
have been reinforced. You believe him when he promises
that it won't happen again. You want to—so you do. You feel
so isolated. You are embarrassed to discuss what happened
and you are embarrassed to be seen. You don't want to have
to answer any questions. If, after looking at the suggestions
offered on these pages, you still feel as intimidated and out
of hope as you did before, I would encourage you to talk to
someone who is familiar with this particular problem and
how to deal with it. Call that wife-abuse hot line and find out
where and how to get help. You don't have to identify yourself. This is not a simple problem and the answers are not
simple. You deserve better treatment and you need to believe
that you do. You also need to find out how to make that happen. If you knew how to do it yourself, you would have.
Help is available. Take advantage of it.

Another fear that you may have has to do with his getting
himself killed or his killing someone else. This is a contin-
gency over which you have no control. It is also not unrealistic to consider. It is definitely in the realm of possibility. Ask
yourself questions like, How far will his life insurance carry
me? Am I prepared to go out and get a job if I have to?

If you have no skills you might want to consider getting some. Not only would it make you less fearful, it will put your mind on something else and get you out of the house.

Volunteer work may fit the bill if you don't have the courage yet to seek employment. It is a step. It is a step toward becoming a person in your own right. You need to feel that you can take care of yourself. You can never depend on being able to depend on your husband.

Susan totaled her car and landed in the hospital. The doctors examined her, stitched her up, and then told her to call her husband to bring her home. She knew that she could call but that he would be drunk and unsympathetic. As it happened he was angry that she was late and he had not yet had his dinner. She then called a cab to take her home. She was fully prepared to do that from the beginning. She was no longer denying the reality of her life and could automatically, even under these circumstances, take care of herself.

You will learn to count on yourself. You will learn who you can depend on and who you can't. You will learn to have few expectations from others. If you have few expectations, you are less vulnerable. You won't hurt as much. The less easily hurt you are, the less fearful you will become.

You will learn to control your own life forces. You will not give your husband the power to control how you feel. You will have choices.

Anger

Anger is a very powerful emotion. It can be turned inward and can eat your guts out, or it can be turned outward and you can risk his wiping the floor up with you. It is a gruesome choice. There are alternatives.

If you truly accept your husband as sick, you will be less angry at him. You will still be angry at your situation, but not at him. To deny these real feelings is to con yourself. They won't go away. Anger is a form of energy. We know from physics that energy once created cannot be destroyed. It can, however, change form.

So what do you do with this energy? You get rid of it. You get rid of it in productive ways. You may choose to ride your bike. The exercise will do you good. Scrub your kitchen floor. You will be happy to have it done. I know one woman who painted the whole inside of her house in a rage. When the job was done the anger had dissipated and the house looked terrific.

If you're unable to sleep because he's kept you up late and you're too agitated to relax now that he's passed out, why not do the wash? The sheets don't know if they've been folded at three in the morning or three in the afternoon. Nancy once said, "Remember, you don't get the time back. So use it. You'll be too tired tomorrow to do the things you planned. So do them now and rest tomorrow." Makes a lot of sense. You're not living in a normal situation, so it becomes important to be flexible.

Wives of alcoholics have to be flexible. Planning ahead is nice, but don't count on it coming off if your husband has been involved in your plans. You can be sure of following through only if you are only depending on yourself. He may have offered to help with the grocery shopping. If you think of it as more than an expression of positive intent, you risk disappointment with its subsequent feeling of hurt. If you take it as a personal rejection, or anger at the unreliable son of a bitch, you turn your feelings outward. Have you considered that the person you've most reason to be angry at is yourself? After all, you've set yourself up.

You know better. Every time you're angry because you've expected your drunk to act sober, you're really angry at yourself.

Don't judge yourself. Making mistakes is part of being human. Just try not to repeat the same ones.

Remember the trusted friend. Talking to her may help take the edge off your anger. If your friend too lives with an alcoholic she'll know what you're feeling. You won't be alone with it. Of course you may have to offer her equal time to tell you what's upsetting her, but that's what friendship is all about.

Another way to deal with your anger is to get in touch with it while it is still manageable. When something first comes up and you react negatively, it is a different feeling than if you stew with it all day. This is true for any interaction with another person. It can also be true that what you heard is not what was intended. Even in more typical relationships different people look at things differently. That is made much worse in a relationship where perceptions are distorted chemically.

Sometimes you can just let things go. Other times you can't, and it becomes important to check things out. Check before you are enraged, and pick a time that he is not drunk. You may not get a response that is satisfying, but expressing your feeling will be helpful. Bear in mind an expectation as to your husband's reaction can lead to disappointment, but the need to express your feelings will be good for you. "It upset me when you said . . ." Phrase it in terms of "I feel" not in terms of "you did." Remember you are expressing your feelings, not blaming. If you keep this in mind, and this is truly your intent, you will feel better for having said it. I know it's a scary thing for you to do, but the sky will not open and lightning will not strike you down. All that will happen, no matter how your statement is received, is that you will have made another step toward asserting yourself as a person with rights and feelings.

It may also help you to understand your spouse a little better. His thinking may be "off the wall," but he may not be deliberately out to get you. You are so used to being put down by him that you react to everything the same way. It is not unusual for an insecure person to put others down as a way of feeling better about himself. He may even be projecting the negative feelings he has about himself onto you. And there's even an outside chance that sometimes when he criticizes you he may be right.

It is important to take a realistic look at yourself. It gets too convenient to blame everything on the alcoholic and decide that you are a perfect person. As long as he is acting outrageously and irresponsibly, you don't have to look at your own behavior. Certainly, in comparison, you come off smelling like a rose. But are you kidding yourself? Sometimes aren't you even setting him up so that you will look like the long-suffering wife married to the inconsiderate bastard?

Carol told me the other day about spending more than an hour and a half preparing her husband's favorite meal. It was ready at the time that Ken said he would be home, with a little leeway built in. That way they could relax and have a pleasant chat first. Do you see Carol sprouting wings at this point? You know the rest of the story. He came home late and drunk. She felt very justified in letting him have it. How could he do this to her! After all her work she was forced to eat alone and his food was all dried up and on and on and on. Carol was looking to me for sympathy and understanding.

That I will always give her, but here she was looking for sympathy and understanding for her behavior. She wanted me to praise her for holding her ground and letting him know how she felt. That didn't happen. That didn't happen because Carol's anger is not justified. The only person Carol is justified in being angry at is herself. She set her husband up. She knew that she could not depend on him to come home on time. He's an alcoholic. So to let him have it is unfair. It is as if she wanted an excuse to vent anger at him because he is sick. He can't help being sick. She has a right to be angry at the situation. It's a stinkin' lousy situation. But face up to what you're really angry at. You are angry at your situation. You are probably jealous that everybody else's marriage is truly wonderful. Everybody but you is married to Paul Newman. You're angry at that. You're angry because you're jealous. I'll let you in on a little secret. Alcoholic marriages are not the only problem marriages. Other people have problems too. Some of them just as serious. Don't displace your anger. Don't place on your husband anger that doesn't belong to him. You will not end up feeling better about yourself if you do that. Examine your motives. Your thinking has become confused too. You must be able to separate what is from what you want to be.

Another thing to consider about anger is whether a particular remark or behavior is really worth your anger. He has just called you a fucking bitch for the 738th time. Is there any need to respond to that? Is there any need to feel upset or angry about that? It is an old tape. It should be just so much noise. The only thing that it is worth any energy is to ask yourself the question, Is there any truth to what he is saying? If there is, then you may look for ways to change your behavior. If there isn't, the perception belongs to him and he won't remember he said it in the morning anyway.

The reason I ask the question about all angers being worth the energy has to do with how you feel when you're angry. Do you really like yourself when you're angry? If you do, by all means stay with it, but IF THERE IS NOTHING IN IT FOR YOU, WHY NOT LET IT GO? This does not mean that you condone things that you don't like, but it does mean that you are maturing to the point where you will decide what things are worth going to the wall about.

Sometimes the reason we hang onto anger is because we lose perspective. I started this morning with a stuck car and an hour-and-a-half wait for the tow truck, which was promised within the half hour. I don't have to tell you the feeling. Anger—what a mild word. Rage. And I couldn't let the guy in the tow truck have it because he has all the power and he probably was not late in an attempt to deliberately aggravate me. I arrived home livid. My cat took one look at me and slinked down the basement stairs. My daughter has more courage and asked me what was wrong. I told her. In her naïveté—after all at the tender age of twelve she doesn't understand that this thing with the tow truck was merely a part of a grand design to get me—she said, "Is there anything you can do to change what happened or to make it right?" Wiseass kid. "No." I continued to go along. "Then why don't you start your day over right now?" What a marvelous thought. Why should the clock decide when my day is gonna start? I'd had a crummy couple of hours but I could start my day all over again. And that's just what I did. And the feeling shifted. I lost the feeling of anger that I had, and allowed myself to be filled up with love for a child who, in the infinite wisdom that only children possess, had given me the day. You too can start your day over whenever you choose. You can start it at eight or five or whenever you need to get a fresh start. I give it to you as my Lisa gave it to me.

The truth is that you are in a very difficult situation to deal honestly with your anger. Your husband is sick and it is unkind to be angry with someone who is sick. He cannot be held accountable for his behavior. Yet you are furious. You are really furious at the situation in which you find yourself, but it is nearly impossible to separate the situation from the person. After all the chemical is self-inflicted. No one is doing it to him but him. You also know that that is not realistic because compulsion is part of the disease. Nevertheless if he didn't pick up the drink with his own hand he would not get drunk, and you would not be living in this godawful situation. The anger is real. The discharging of it is what is most difficult. Don't deny that it exists. Find ways to channel it that will be good for you. Eventually a lot of it will leave you and you will start to feel more serene within yourself and more compassionate toward your alcoholic. That will come with time and understanding and honest appraisal and reappraisal of yourself.

Sex Problems

This is an area of increasing concern to women in alcoholic marriages. I don't know if the concern is new, but the willingness to discuss it openly is new. Women are waking up to the fact that they have sexual needs, desires, and rights as well as men. Women are waking up to the fact that they are not possessions, but partners. They are realizing that they don't have to do anything that they do not want to do and can do anything that they want to do. It's a whole new ball game. I must admit I love it.

It is important to try to keep your thinking simple in this area as in all others. The subject of sex gets very complicated very quickly. In this area, like all others, decide what is good for you and stick with it. If you have a satisfying sex life, enjoy it. If you find his sexual behavior, while drunk, to be degrading to you, there is no reason to submit. Be sure that you do what you do for the right reasons. If you are repelled when he smells of liquor but are not turned off otherwise— tell him. It would be best to tell him during a time that he is not drinking. It is only fair.

If you are turned off by him, chances are he will try to put the problem off on you as he has in all other areas. You are probably no more or no less hung up sexually than anybody else. I have had a number of open, frank discussions with groups of women living with active alcoholism. After the questions about physical abuse and repulsion at the odor, the questions are very much the same as in any other group of women. Women are just beginning to accept that it is okay to masturbate, that it may even be helpful in reducing tension. Women are just beginning to accept that inter-course is not the only way for a man and woman to enjoy each other.

These ideas become important in the alcoholic marriage for a number of reasons. Few women in alcoholic marriages take lovers. Their egos have been so badly damaged and their sense of themselves as sexual beings has been so badly eroded that they run away from involvement. They also re-ally love their husbands and would be unable to handle the guilt if they had an affair. So masturbation or lack of any sex-ual gratification are the available options.

The reason that it is important for a couple to explore op-tions to intercourse has to do with the fact that so many alco-holics become impotent. The alcohol increases desire but seems to decrease the ability to perform. A friend of mine reported a comment to me that she had read in a book on sex for the aged. Poorly paraphrased it went, "The fact that you can no longer run does not mean that you have to stop walking."

Here, as with all other things, ask yourself: What do I want? What is good for me? Once you answer, things should fall into place. Your reasons are your own. You may decide to submit because you know that he falls asleep when he is satisfied and you are rid of him for the night. The romance goes out when the alcohol comes in. Sex, like every other area of communication in the alcoholic marriage, becomes distorted. And you, as in everything else, must focus on yourself and your own needs. Reacting to the alcoholic is no better for you in the sex area than any other. Be true to yourself. This book will help you get to know that self.

As you come to more fully understand the nature of the illness, and as you become more determined to grip reality, many of the other symptoms of near-alcoholism will either disappear or become manageable.

The *protectiveness, pity, and over-concern* that you felt will gain perspective. You now know that the protectiveness that you felt was not good for your alcoholic. It enabled his disease and your disease. Pity and over-concern are not helpful either. Compassion and caring are more healthy and helpful feelings for you to express. Compassion carries with it understanding but does not make us weak. Pity weakens the receiver. To feel pity for someone is almost to say that they can do nothing about what they are, so you, who are above them, feel sorry for them. To feel compassion is to appreciate the difficulty that another person faces but also offers them the opportunity to do something about it. Over-concern suffocates us and makes us want to push others away. In the case of the alcoholic, it gives him another excuse to drink. The concern that one human being has for another is interpreted as caring and gives the object of the concern options as to what to do about it. We gain strength through love, provided that love is freely given. Both the giver and receiver become richer. No disease has the power to combat the power of love. It is the most powerful weapon in the world. If I love you no matter what you do I become a mirror through which you can look at yourself. If I am not rejecting and hostile but continue to love, you cannot use me as an excuse. I do not have to pretend that I accept behaviors that are unacceptable, but I love you as a person. I do not pity you nor will I protect you from yourself. I care about you too much to help you to be weak.

By the same token, you will no longer automatically lie for him. It is no longer necessary. Your self-respect is important. You are taking responsibility for yourself and that means, in part, that your husband now has the choice to take responsibility for himself. Your sense of self-respect, coupled with the desire to stop enabling, make covering up undesirable. If you choose to lie, you do it fully aware of what you are doing and what the outcome will be. If you lie now, it is not because you have to. It is because you have chosen to. There is a world of difference.

False hope, disappointment, and euphoria no longer have you bouncing off the walls. You have learned that you are the only one who can be responsible for your happiness. You cannot depend on another person to do that for you, nor can another person expect that of you. You are in charge of you and your happiness or unhappiness. You *allow* other people to make you happy or unhappy. It is not automatic. Once you accept this your husband's inconsistent behavior will have less of an effect on you. He can please you or disappoint you only if you choose to allow him to do so. The power over you belongs to him only if you give it to him. Accept the good and let him hang on to the rest.

Much of the *confusion* is gone. You are now able to make decisions. You are calling the shots. You are no longer trying to understand the thinking of someone who is drunk. If you could, either you would be drunk too, or he would not be. You have stopped asking your husband to think *as if* he were sober. You are now asking yourself to think as if you are sane. I think you probably are.

Lethargy, hopelessness, self-pity, remorse, and despair fade into the background. They come up from time to time as they do in all human beings. Healthy people have ups and downs too. But you will find that there are fewer extremes and the downs are more manageable. Gail has admitted to me that she really enjoys a good depression every now and again. She really likes to get into it and feel really sorry for herself and withdraw from the world. However, she gives herself a time limit. She says, "I'm going to allow myself to be depressed until three o'clock and then I will get dressed and pick up the kids and do the other things that I have to do." It works for her. Especially that time of the month that you want to pull your hair out because your body chemistry is askew. Wallow in it but prepare your exit. Sometimes you're better off having that hot fudge sundae and getting it over with. It can save a worse binge later on.

You've looked at yourself in a variety of ways in terms of your alcoholic husband. We've talked about ways that you can adjust and be healthy. This has mostly been in terms of improving your relationship with your husband. Now let's begin to talk about improving your relationship with yourself.

In order to develop as a whole person it is important to

know yourself. It is important to know what you think and what you feel, what you're like as a person. You haven't had much of a chance to look at yourself. It may be the time to take the time.

I'm going to list some traits that help to make up one's self-image. There are no right or wrong answers. It is a chance to get to know yourself a little better. If you become aware of some things about yourself that you are not especially happy about, you will now have a choice. You can choose to work on that particular aspect. There is no high score or low score. It is an attempt to get you to have a little bit of a picture of yourself.

All our lives we've heard expressions like, "You shouldn't feel that way." What gibberish. You feel however you feel. If you don't like the feeling you can make efforts to change it, but it is whatever it is. We may not always behave according to the feelings that we have because appropriateness in behavior is more important. I may want to kick that tow truck driver in the teeth but I may not behave in that way. I will not deny my feeling.

Sometimes we have feelings that are outrageous. Sometimes I feel like chucking my life and taking off for parts unknown. When someone I love dies, my feeling of sorrow is more for myself than that person. I know my children get angry at me when I'm sick. I may not be able to abdicate my responsibilities and take off for Tahiti. I may express my sorrow to the family and say all the right things. I may not consider my children ungrateful if I'm sick because I know that their security is threatened. But I needn't pretend that I feel differently than I do.

If I acknowledge that I want to run to Tahiti I can sit myself down and ask why. Chances are I've overextended myself, which I am prone to do. Then I can work out a way to slow down. Acknowledging that feeling can help me to resolve it. Judging myself and saying to myself that responsible people do not think irresponsible thoughts doesn't get me anywhere.

If I acknowledge that the sorrow at the death of a friend is mine, I can then reflect back on the beauty of that person and how much richer I am for having known him. I can then share this richness with his family and we can all profit from it. If I had decided feeling sorry for myself was selfish and I shouldn't feel that way, I could not have figured out what I could offer to those who were suffering too, as much as I.

If I did not acknowledge my children's right to be angry at the disruption in their lives when I am sick, it would only cause anger and bitterness on my part when what I really need is rest to regain my strength. If I acknowledge their anger and their right to it, then we can work out ways that the family can pitch in to make things go smoothly for a while. This way they can take pride in their contribution and not feel put upon. They also don't have to feel guilt because of their feelings.

The trait checklist that I'd like you to have a go at can be found in Muriel James and Dorothy Jongeward's book *Born to Win*, published by Addison-Wesley.

Move quickly through the following list of traits. Use a check mark (√) beside those that fit your self-image. Use a cross (x) to mark those that do not fit. Use a question mark (?) to indicate the ones that you're unsure about.

___Like myself

___Afraid of or hurt by others

___People can trust me

___Put up a good front

___Usually say the right thing

___Feel bad about myself ✓

___Discouraged about life ✓

___Don't like to be around ✗
people

___Have not developed my ✓
talents

___Glad I'm the sex I am

___Fearful of the future ✓

___Dependent on others for ideas ✓

___Waste time ✓

___Use my talents

___Think for myself

___Know my feelings

___Don't understand myself

___Feel hemmed in

___Use time well

___Can't hold a job ✓

___Trust myself

___Usually say the wrong thing ✓

___Enjoy people

___Don't enjoy being the sex I ✓ am

___Often do the wrong thing ✓

___Involved in solving community problems

___People like to be around me

___Competent on the job

___People avoid me

___Uninterested in community problems ✓

___Enjoy work

___Enjoy nature ✓

___Don't enjoy work

___Control myself

___Enjoy myself

___Trouble controlling myself ✓

___Don't like myself ✓

Now look at those traits you have marked.

Is there a pattern?

Are they good for you? Bad for you? Both?

Which traits would you like to change?

Think about it. How can you change those traits with which you are uncomfortable? How can you encourage and develop those traits which are satisfying to you? Both are equally important.

If you can't say that you like yourself, does it mean that you don't like yourself? Or does it mean that you haven't cared enough about yourself to even know? What could you do that would make you like yourself better? Maybe start with the basics. Do you get enough sleep? Do you eat properly? Do you tend to your physical appearance? At what times have you liked yourself? What were you doing at those times? Why not repeat it? Are you doing those things that you wrote down on that list earlier in the book? How can you expect anyone else to like you if you don't like yourself?

Take a careful look at those traits and see what they mean to you. Make a little contract with yourself. Decide that you are, for example, going to enjoy nature. Then set aside a little time each day and do it. Another goal might be, I'm not going to worry about wasting time. I'm going to choose to "waste" an hour each day and not feel guilty about it. Or, I'm going to work on the xyz committee for the local PTA. Little by little you'll feel like more and more.

You'll gain a real sense of yourself. You'll become a person in your own right and your position in your marriage will change.

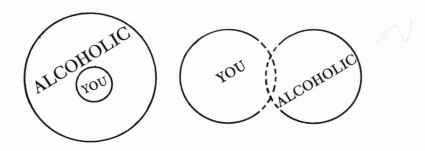

Your position changes from one where you are consumed by the ravages of alcoholism to one where you stand on your own two feet and interact with your husband to the degree and in the ways that are good for you. That interrelationship is flexible, as are all healthy relationships. Healthy relationships allow for breathing space. They do not smother.

In order to build a healthy relationship at least one partner must be healthy. Only you can decide if your being healthy is worth the effort. What I have outlined for you is a lot of hard work. You won't change overnight, but you didn't get into this state overnight either. It can't take any more effort than coping with sickness has taken. But it is a different kind of effort. It is new. The known is safer no matter how dismal. What if I get to know myself and find out I really am a terrible person? There is that risk. There's also the risk that you'll find out you're someone of value. That is just as frightening because that carries new responsibilities. Valuable people take pride in themselves. They don't indulge in self-defeating behaviors. They get their strokes not from the sympathy of others but from what they are able to offer.

Once you believe you are a person of value, you will be able to offer those things that you need. You will learn that the only way to be sure of receiving love is to give it away. The only way to be sure of being understood is by offering understanding to others. If you care, others will care for you. As ye sow so shall ye reap. You don't have to react to what is given to you unless you choose to, unless it is good for you. You can act as well as react. You get back what you give. You have that power. I give it to you.

6 HOW YOUR CHILDREN CAN BE HELPED

You will be amazed at the improvement in your children as soon as you start to get better. In my counseling practice I see many children. As soon as I can, I ask to see the parents, especially the mother. I find that I can be of greater help to the child by working with the mother than directly with the child. Children respond almost immediately to changes in the home climate. When you become more even-tempered and more predictable, so will they. When they see you smile and hear you laugh, so will they. Oh, but where to begin.

Begin with confronting reality. Begin with your children where you began with yourself. Your children have denied as you have denied. If your family is to recover, it must begin with the truth. Use the words that work for you.

When you are ready the words will come. I asked Betsey what she said to her children. They were very young and needed to be told in a way that they could understand. Her children had always asked her questions like, "Why is Daddy doing that?" "Why is Daddy acting so funny?" "Doesn't Daddy love us?" She would answer in such a way as to put them off. They learned that asking these questions would upset their mother and it added to their confusion. Finally Betsey was ready. She sat them down and very simply said, "I haven't been fair to you. I've been keeping something from you and I'm not going to do that anymore. You know that sometimes Daddy acts like he's somebody we don't know and that upsets you. It upsets me too. Daddy is an alcoholic. He has an allergy to alcohol. When he drinks he acts in a funny way that he cannot help."

That was the beginning. From that point on she answered all of their questions frankly and honestly. She offered the older ones literature to help with their understanding of the disease and she made a contract with all of them.

The contract was that they would no longer hide their feelings from one another. If one started to worry that his daddy would come home drunk, he could talk about it. Their father's illness was out in the open. They didn't like it and that was okay. They didn't have to feel guilty about hating their father when he was drunk. They knew now that they didn't hate their father. They hated what the alcohol made their father behave like. A great burden of guilt was lifted.

Children worry. Let them share their worries. The worries will become more manageable. Accept their feelings as valid. "I understand that you're worried your father will have an accident. I worry about it too. But there is nothing we can do about it so let's see if we can think about something that will make us happy."

Children are fearful. If they can share their fears you can reassure them. "No harm will come to you as long as I am here. I give you my word," or, "I was afraid to speak up in class when I was your age too."

The key here is to accept their right to feel whatever they feel. To say, "You shouldn't feel guilty," to a child who believes her father's drinking to be her fault is not to help her resolve the guilt. It is better to explore the feeling with her.

Ginger's mother had called the police to take her father to a locked ward in a local hospital. The alcohol had affected him to such a degree that he had lost his mind. Life in her home had been unbearable the week before he actually snapped. Ginger felt responsible. She didn't want him around. She wished he would go away. She actually had a dream that he had gone to a hospital. Ginger and her mother had good communication. They had learned to be honest with each other. She said to her mother, "It's all my fault. I made it happen. I wanted him to go away to a hospital. I did it."

She felt responsible for what had happened. She wept with guilt. Because she was able to tell this to her mother, her mother was able to reassure her. She told her that she was not responsible. She told her that she too wanted her father in a hospital. Ginger was not alone in her feelings. She had nothing to feel guilty about. They cried together and it was over. Had they been unable to talk it out, the child would have continued to feel guilty about something over which she had no control.

Find out about the Alateen groups in your area. Encourage your children to go. Talking to other children with the same problems will be very helpful. It is also a chance to make social contacts with other children who have similar lives. They can be friends without embarrassment. They will learn more about the disease and how to detach from it, but still love their alcoholic parent. If they are not ready when you first mention it don't be discouraged. They may come around. Bring them Alateen literature anyway. Show them this book. It's so helpful to be able to identify with what you hear or read. The relief I see on the face of a child who says, "Yes, that's exactly the way I feel," is heartwarming.

Understanding their reality is the first step toward turning these children around. They will improve as soon as they no longer feel the weight of the burden as theirs alone. Now it is shared and eventually can be discarded.

Confusion has been the norm. This has to be changed. Consistency must prevail. This can happen quite simply. Dinner should be at a specific time. Establish the time and stick to it. Homework is done at a specific time. Establish the time and stick to it. Bedtime is at a specific time. Establish the time and stick to it. You will probably get some resistance at first, but it is usually more a testing to see if the limit is real rather than a rebellion at the limit itself.

Children should have responsibilities in the home. All family members share in the work. Setting the table or taking out the garbage are simple chores but give a feeling of being needed and belonging.

These behaviors will help to make your children feel more secure. They can now know the parameters of their world and that someone is watching. That someone cares!

This is another key step. There is no way that you can give your children too much love. Tell them how much you love them. Hold them, hug them, kiss them, sit them on your lap. This will not smother them or spoil them. Being overindulgent is not an indication of love. Letting them have unearned privileges to overcompensate for the alcohol is not an indication of love. Buying them things they don't need, because they are emotionally deprived, is not an indication of love. These things satisfy your needs—not the needs of your children. The greatest gift that any parent can give to a child is unconditional love. I love you because you are you. You don't have to earn it and you don't risk losing it. The fact that I love you unconditionally does not mean I approve of everything you do. Sometimes your behavior drives me up the wall. Sometimes it is necessary to punish you. Sometimes your behavior makes me very very angry. Because I love you I may not like what you do, but I always love you.

It may be hard for you to be a loving parent right now. When you are feeling irritable and unhappy it is hard to be warm and understanding. Be honest with your children. "I'm happy to see you but I'm feeling very nervous right now. Maybe I would be better off alone for a while." Then they know, and if you should lose control they won't take it as personally. Also just making the statement will make it easier for you.

Treat your children with respect. If a door is closed knock before you enter. Their private papers are not for your eyes. They know when you have been in their drawers. They need to be able to trust you. Listen to what they have to say when they disagree with you. You don't have to change your mind but your listening helps to make them feel they have worth.

Try to be sure that you say what you mean and mean what you say. To say yes or no to a child's request just for the sake of being done with it encourages manipulative behavior. These children have learned from their parents to be very manipulative and it is not a quality to be encouraged. If you do not offer a reason for your decision, that decision may not be accepted by your child. If you change your mind a lot because you didn't think your answer out to begin with, your answer may not be accepted by your child. Either you will be badgered until you give in or you will become adamant and angry. You need to be able to say, "This is my decision. You may or may not agree with my reasons but this is the way it has to be. I have heard what you have to say and am sticking to my decision anyway." Then the child has a choice. Either he will do as he is told or he will not. If he does not then there are consequences for his behavior.

I was at a showing recently of a new film relating to the family aspect of alcoholism. There were many people there. Among them were a thirteen-year-old boy and his parents. I have known this boy for quite some time and he knows just how to get precisely whatever he wants. He had his mother getting up at 7:30 to fix him a full breakfast that he was capable of making himself—until I came on the scene. I watched him ask his mother for the money to buy a Coke. I heard her refuse. Fifteen minutes later I saw him with the Coke. I went over to him and said, "I knew you'd get the Coke. I was just interested in seeing how long it would take you." He grinned and walked away. This is a minor example, but it does point up the fact that unless you take control of your home, the other forces in your home will take control of you. As you are getting your personal control back in your marriage, it is also necessary to get the control back with your children. They do not want to be able to get everything their way. They won't admit it necessarily, but children would prefer to be children. If they are not allowed to be children, they cannot enjoy the fight to grow up.

They also need you to say no in situations where they want to say no and cannot do it for themselves. Sometimes the peer pressure is very great and they cannot get out of something they do not want to do unless they can say, "I really want to go, but I asked my mother and she freaked out!"

Jerry asked his mother for permission to sleep over at his

friend Peter's house on the Fourth of July. His mother said, "I know the reason you are asking that is so that you can stay out very late and shoot off firecrackers. That makes me very nervous and I cannot give you permission." She expected fireworks from her son. He looked at her and made a remark about how rough it was to live with a mother who knew the score. He also looked relieved. He was afraid of getting into trouble with Peter and his friends but couldn't let them know he wasn't as macho as they. His mother gave him the out he required. She could be the heavy and he could get out of it.

To have said to this child, "Yes, Jerry, I will let you go because I trust you and I know that you will not do anything you shouldn't," is to invite disaster. That statement is implied, if you have a good relationship with your children, every time they get out of your sight. But let's not set them up. Let's not help to put them in positions that require a strength that insecure, troubled children do not have. To let them know you value them is a helpful step in getting them to value themselves. That is the only way you can prevent the things from happening that you are afraid will happen. You cannot stop your children from taking drugs or acting out sexually or committing vandalism or whatever they have decided they have to do. You can help them to value themselves so that these choices are not desirable to them.

I get along very well with the young people I know. My son was curious about this. He couldn't understand why everybody liked his mother, particularly the adolescent boys who didn't like anybody, and whom everybody was turned off to. He decided to check it out. They told him, "We know where she stands. If she says she won't say anything about what we tell her, she won't. If she says if she hears about our brown-bagging it to school once more she'll call the authorities, she will. If she can help she will, but if she thinks we're full of shit she'll tell us that too." They know if they reach out their hand to touch me there will be something there to touch. It will be the same arm that was there the day before and the same one that will be there tomorrow.

What I have discussed here are all ways to first reduce anxiety and second to build self-esteem. You play a key role in both these aspects. After a while the children will not only feel better about themselves, they will be able to tune in to you. I was there when Mary Jane said to her mother, "I know that look in your eyes, Mom. You are starting to worry if Daddy will come home drunk." Her mother swallowed her up in her arms and said, "You're right. And if you try not to worry I'll try not to worry with you. Let's go bake some cookies."

Many of you are very worried that your children will inherit alcoholism. We do not really know if they can or cannot. What we do know is that the home environment can either encourage or discourage alcohol abuse. It is not through a discussion of the horrors of alcohol that this happens necessarily, but through the value one places on himself. You can take preventive measures. If there is one trait that predominates among alcoholics it is an avoidance of responsibility. You can teach your children to take responsibility for their behavior. If Johnny breaks the neighbor's window it is up to him to call the neighbor, own up, and find a way to either repair or replace the window. Covering up for him will not help him grow as a person.

Bob and Tim set a minor leaf fire on mischief night. No damage was done. The police and fire department were called. The boys could have lied their way out of it. But they were wrong and admitted it. They also sat through a lecture by the police captain about their behavior. Their mothers went with them. They wanted the boys to feel the full impact of their behavior but to know they were loved. Loved but not overprotected. The act of love, in this case, was to let the boys sweat it out. This way they took responsibility for their behavior.

I have written reports for the court that helped to send an adolescent boy to prison. The following year the parents of the same boy asked me to write another report for the court and this time I was instrumental in getting the boy off. They know that I will be fair and that the best thing for the child is not necessarily to get off.

If you do your chores you earn your allowance. If you don't, you don't. Simple, clear. The responsibility belongs to the child. If you make a mess, you clean it up. Or, at the very least, you help.

If you encourage this responsible attitude toward self, not only can the children manage their own difficulties, they can manage their own successes. When they get that A they get it because they earned it, not because they were nagged into it.

Even the negative stuff can carry a reward. When Johnny told the neighbor he had broken the window, she was flabbergasted. She was so impressed that he had been truthful when there was no way she could find out, that she told him to forget it. He had made a friend.

Encourage your children to talk out their problems so that they can find a way to confront them. Once out in the open, things become more manageable. The solution may be simple—just not thought of.

What I have discussed here are principles that are important in any relationship with parent and child. They are especially important in the alcoholic home because there has been so much damage to the self-concept. This damage is reversible. If you believe nothing else that I have said in this book, believe that. In fact your children *may be better off for having lived with alcoholism.* What a strange thing for a person to say. I did say it. I have heard individuals at A.A. meetings stand up and say, "I am a grateful alcoholic." I have heard women get up at Al-Anon meetings and say, "Had I not married an alcoholic I would be less of a person than I am today." I have heard children at Alateen meetings say, "We are the survivors," and they didn't mean only among children of alcoholics.

These statements are very important and they are not Pollyanna-ish or naive or an attempt to make you feel better. They are important because there are very specific reasons why they can be true. First they are true because accepting the disease of alcoholism has forced these people to concern themselves with their own mental health. Had it not been for this illness, they might not have taken an opportunity for self-growth and self-awareness. They might never have been as aware of proper parenting and how important that really is. We are not trained to be parents and it is a very difficult task under the best of circumstances. Coming to grips with a problem of the magnitude of alcoholism makes one aware of how essential it is that children do not bring themselves up, even if they don't cause us any trouble.

The other part of this has to do with developing scar tissue. We grow stronger because of the difficulties that we have encountered, faced right on, and come to grips with. We do not become stronger if life goes on with relative ease. We don't even know how to appreciate the good things if we have not experienced adversity. These children, your children, as they confront the reality of their lives, will become stronger. The things that bother other children will not get to them. I have seen many children devastated when another child says, "I don't want to play with you." The child of an alcoholic who is working on himself and his own growth and is detaching from the feelings of rejection by his father cannot take that kind of remark seriously. "If that kid doesn't want to play with me I'll find someone else or I'll play by myself." Those little hurts of growing up diminish in meaning.

If they have joined Alateen they can talk about these feelings with other kids in the same boat. They can talk about that teacher who is out to get them. The other kids will talk about ways of dealing with the teacher and also, *in a caring climate,* will determine if it's really the teacher who is the problem.

I believe in the wisdom of children. I believe in asking children what they think—especially in the areas that affect their lives. I asked some children I know who have at least one alcoholic parent what the best thing their mother could do for them would be or would have been.

These kids are on their way to recovery. They can be up front with their feelings. They still feel the pain but they are learning to talk it out. That makes it easier for them to hear. I simply made a list of what they said as they said it.

1. Stop the B.S. Tell the kid what's happening. Don't hide anything because that makes it worse.

2. Get the kids into the program (Alateen).

3. Don't put the kids into a state of confusion. Answer the questions they want answered—not the ones you want them to know, the ones *they* want to know.

4. Show the kids a little patience and understanding. They suffer but they don't know why.

5. Don't play God—play Mommy.

6. Don't confront him when he's drunk. It takes two to fight and the alcoholic is always looking for someone to fight with. If he's violent, it'll be your teeth on the ground.

7. Don't make excuses to us. No B.S., please.

8. Don't let the kids know how scared you are. It'll only make them more scared. Try to keep yourself together.

9. Don't have us confront the alcoholic when you don't want to. When my father fell down the stairs she told me to find out if he was all right. He told me to "get the hell out." If she wanted to know she should have done it herself.

10. Don't use us to get to the alcoholic. Don't say stuff like, "If you won't stop drinking for me, do it for the kids." Leave us out of it.

Children tell it how it is. They are not sophisticated enough to cover up the truth with niceness. Thank heaven for that. We can learn so much from them. They can learn so much from us. We can learn so much from each other. You can learn to love—without strings. You can learn to rejoice in each other's development—without expectations. You can experience the adventure of life together and alone. And if by chance your alcoholic husband should recover, he can join you. Because without him to make you so terribly aware of how precious a healthy family is, you may have missed out on this opportunity.

7 WHAT "THEY" WILL SAY

Alcoholism is a disease of paradoxes. It defies logic. The opposites of the usual rules apply. What would make sense in a normal situation simply doesn't in the alcoholic situation. It is all mixed up. When the alcoholic starts to recover and looks back at what he did and why he did it he can't understand it either. Pete shared with me the following; author unknown, people who identify—thousands.

POSITIVELY NEGATIVE
WE DRANK FOR HAPPINESS AND BECAME UNHAPPY.
WE DRANK FOR JOY AND BECAME MISERABLE.
WE DRANK FOR SOCIABILITY AND BECAME ARGUMENTATIVE.
WE DRANK FOR SOPHISTICATION AND BECAME OBNOXIOUS.

WE DRANK FOR FRIENDSHIP AND MADE ENEMIES.

WE DRANK FOR SLEEP AND AWAKENED WITHOUT REST.

WE DRANK FOR STRENGTH AND FELT WEAK.

WE DRANK "MEDICINALLY" AND ACQUIRED HEALTH PROB-
LEMS.

WE DRANK FOR BRAVERY AND BECAME AFRAID.

WE DRANK FOR CONFIDENCE AND BECAME DOUBTFUL.

WE DRANK TO MAKE CONVERSATION AND SLURRED OUR
SPEECH.

WE DRANK TO FEEL HEAVENLY AND ENDED UP FEELING
LIKE HELL.

WE DRANK TO FORGET AND WERE FOREVER HAUNTED.

WE DRANK FOR FREEDOM AND BECAME SLAVES.

WE DRANK TO ERASE PROBLEMS AND SAW THEM MULTIPLY.

WE DRANK TO COPE WITH LIFE AND INVITED DEATH.

You know, because of what you've learned in reading this book, not to say, "If that's what happens, why don't you stop drinking?" You know to leave it alone. You know that the opposite of the usual rules apply. You know that if you care about your husband and want him to stop drinking, you will do nothing to get in the way of his drinking. You also know, because you care about him, that he has to face whatever happens as a result of his drinking. You know that enabling is destructive to both you and your husband.

You know and I know and the people in Al-Anon know and the people in A.A. know and the National Council on Alcoholism knows and anybody who understands the disease knows. But that is not the general public. To those around you who do not understand alcoholism, your behavior may look strange. You may be thought of as uncaring. "How could she let him spend the night in the drunk tank and not go down and bail him out? What kind of a person does something like that to another person?" A person who loves an alcoholic may do that. But try telling people "I loved him enough not to bail him out!" People will look at you as if you are crazy.

You may receive phone calls from relatives and friends. They will express genuine concern for your husband. They will tell you about the money they've loaned him or the bed they gave him when you threw him out. They will not be too happy with you. You will then explain to them that your husband is a very sick alcoholic and you are doing the things that you have been told to do if he is to get well. They will say that they understand what you're saying but if you really cared about him you would. . . . They will not understand and to some you will become the problem. "Who wouldn't be driven to drink if he lived with a bitch like that?" What a blow—I never told you that any part of what I'm telling you to do would be easy. It's not.

Your husband will encourage others to put you down. He will turn to them to enable his drinking when you stop. *Enter the enablers.* You're not the only one who has played into this disease.

FRIEND-RELATIVE

This person, because of guilt or genuine caring, moves in to rescue the alcoholic from his predicament of the moment. He wants to take the pressure off so that his friend will not have to live with this unbearable tension. He pays the overdue bill or makes the phone call or provides the bed. He handles whatever it is that the alcoholic does not want to confront. He says he does this because he cares. I suspect it is to serve his own need rather than the need of the alcoholic. What's a friend for? Families must stick together! How could I turn him away and live with myself? And so on. Eventually the alcoholic will run out of these people. They will go just so far and then they will be forced to reject him to protect themselves. Then they will understand you better. "She was right all along."

THE OTHER WOMAN

Enter the villain of the piece. In your eyes she is the villain, but there is some predictability to this particular enabler. It may not happen to you. It may. It's not a threat to your marriage. It's a symptom of the disease. After all you don't want to drink with him anymore. You don't want to go to bed with him anymore. You don't want to save him from himself. You know better. She doesn't. She feels she's the only one who understands him. And she will help him to get sicker. The best thing you can do is to leave it alone. Do nothing to get in the way of it. His guilt will take over or she'll put pressure on for a more permanent relationship. Neither of which is manageable for him.

Jack tried to reduce his guilt by telling Alice all about his affair. He also wanted her to end it for him. Alice knew that this woman was not a reflection on her. She knew enough about alcoholism to know that what he did was not unusual. She knew that she should let him get himself out of it. After all it was *his* problem. She did just as any normal wife would. First she let him have it with both barrels right between the eyes in a volume usually reserved for Madison Square Garden. Then she called up the woman and let her know exactly what she thought of her and what she would do to her if she ever again came near her husband. Right on, Alice! Sometimes you just have to do what you have to do. She felt a lot better. She can go back to being understanding tomorrow. For today she lost her cool and it felt really good.

EMPLOYER AND FELLOW WORKERS

Since it takes a long time to develop alcoholism to the degree that it affects your job performance, a man may have been on the same job for ten to fifteen years. During this time he has developed friendships and loyalties. It is only natural for fellow workers to say he came in on time when he was late or pick up the slack in his work. His employer will overlook infractions because he remembers how valuable this man has been to him in the past and wants to believe that he will be again. Without this continued protection and cover-up the alcoholic could not continue in his job. He would have to give up either his job or his irresponsible drinking. These people are victims of his drinking but help it to continue. "There but for the grace of God go I." Eventually the cover-up becomes impossible, but it takes awhile.

THE PROFESSIONALS

It hurts me to have to tell you how few professionals understand alcoholism and as a result do more harm than good. Your husband may start to become concerned about how mixed up his life is becoming and with your urging he will seek help. The doctor who offers him tranquilizers to get off the booze is helping to get him polyaddicted. The psychologist who tells him that early toilet training and not drinking is his problem is giving him a reason to continue to drink. He starts to believe that when he resolves his emotional problems then he will no longer have the desire to drink. Professionals who understand alcoholism will not indiscriminately prescribe drugs or deny alcoholism as a cause of the other problems. They will refer patients to rehabilitation centers or A.A. or attack alcoholism as the problem. Once the alcoholism has been arrested other problems can be explored. Until then it is wasted time and money.

It may be small comfort to you at this point to know that you have given up carrying the medicinal cask of brandy under your neck and that is the most helpful thing for you to do. The other enablers make it that much harder for you to keep firm in your resolve. You naturally want people to like you. Since you are still feeling vulnerable and insecure you may start to doubt yourself. It is only human. How much pressure can you take? You will start to get confused. It is essential at this point, unless you are made of steel, to surround yourself with people who understand alcoholism. Talk only to these people about what is happening in your marriage. They are with you. Go to a lot of Al-Anon meetings or open A.A. meetings or call the National Council on Alcoholism for a mental health referral. Do not try to handle it all alone. You will need constant reassurance that you are doing the best thing for you and for your family. You need to be with the people who are on the same wavelength as you are, people who will reassure you that you're not crazy. It may be that, for a time, these people will be your only social contacts. That is not such a terrible thing. After all they are people like yourself who want to enjoy life. They know they are not strong enough alone to combat alcoholism but their strength comes from sharing with each other. There is a feeling of warmth and security that will help to carry you over the rough spots. *You are not alone.*

You are not alone but you are little understood by the general public. Although schools have instituted many fine drug and alcohol education programs, there is little or no emphasis on the struggles of the family. Most of the literature in the field is on alcohol and alcoholism. Gail Milgram, who is at Rutgers' Center of Alcohol Studies, has put together a fine bibliography of alcohol education materials. It includes 873 references. Of these 873 only 38 deal with the effects on the family. Of these 38 the majority are pamphlets circulated by the Al-Anon family groups. This lack saddens me and makes me angry. It also drives me to write. When you feel stronger and more courageous why not explore the alcohol and drug education programs in your community? What exposure is your child getting in school? Why not encourage your school system to include the effects on the family as part of their program? The school systems do not leave it out deliberately. They just don't think about it. Maybe it is up to you to plant the seed.

Industry is starting to wise up. Companies are beginning to become aware of the dollars that it is costing them in missed work days and inefficiency. They also know that the investment they have in many of those workers makes it worth making an investment in their recovery, rather than dismissing them. Many large companies are establishing alcohol rehabilitation programs of their own. Employers are learning to offer rehabilitation as an alternative to firing. This is an important step. I don't know of much concern being placed on the worker whose spouse is drinking and who is spending the day worrying about it. This is just as costly to business.

Education of the public is so much of the answer here, as it is in so many things. This is one area where every little bit of knowledge helps. Authorities in the state of New Jersey have decriminalized drunken driving. They are learning that alcoholics are sick people and not criminals. It is a slow process, and an even slower process is that of bringing about public awareness of the profound effects on the family. As you grow more comfortable with yourself you may feel freer to talk more openly about the awareness that you've gained. Educating the public is the responsibility of each and every one of us. That is, provided that you have reached the point where you are comfortable within yourself on the subject and are not concerned about having others know about your particular situation. It gets tricky because of the social stigmas attached. You may be ready to overcome it, but is the rest of your family ready? Many of the people who speak on alcohol-related subjects from their own personal experience do so using only their first name. Their alcoholic has a right to privacy. You will find that after a while you will feel compelled to do your part. You will begin to see needless suffering around you. You will begin to be aware of neighbors and friends who have your same problem but have not come as far as you have. It will become important to you to find a way to offer them help without invading their privacy. You will find a way. You will have to. And you will find the way that works best for you. You will know how to help and what to say because you have been there—in the same muck as they.

I remember giving a series of lectures on alcoholism and its effects on the family to a group of my counseling students. At the end they handed in reaction papers. At the bottom of one a student had written, "If I had known ten years ago what I know today, I would not have hated my father until the day he died." I wept for my student and strengthened my resolve to awaken people to the realities of living with this disease in any way I can.

8 WHAT ABOUT THE FUTURE?

That is such a hard question. Who knows? What I do know is that unless you are living in a situation where you are in fear of your life, you are better off not making a decision today. In order to make an intelligent decision that will affect the rest of your life, you need to have your head on straight. It is best at this point to use your energies to get yourself healthy. Once you feel in control of your thoughts and feelings you are in a better position to make a decision.

Many women enter into a game of "If I . . . then he." This is dangerous. What they hope to do is to create a crisis that will cause him to stop drinking. Laudable goal. It just doesn't work.

Mary decided she was leaving Jim. She couldn't live with his drunkenness any longer. Or so she said. What she really felt was that once she left he would be so miserable that he would beg her to come back and never drink again. She left. She left for a week. She was so miserable during that time that she came running home. She wanted him on any terms. Jim hadn't even missed her. She walked in and he acknowledged her as he always had. Her grandstand play only added to her turmoil.

Another variation on this theme is when you ask him to leave. "If I throw him out then he will come to his senses. He will appreciate me and the kids and will stop drinking forever and ever." Talk to Marcia about that one. She threw him out all right. Right into the arms of an enabler. And he's still drinking himself to death. Marcia regrets her action. She was not prepared for the outcome.

I'm not saying never take these kinds of actions. All I'm saying is be sure that if you do it, it is because it is good for you, and not because it will bring him to his senses. You have to be able to deal with whatever the consequences of your behavior may be. It is not usually the loss of a wife that causes the crisis that may lead to sobriety. It is more often the loss of a job. Men identify themselves in terms of occupation. A loss of employment is very emotionally disruptive. This doesn't mean that you should cost him his job. You don't know what will make the difference in your particular situation—if anything.

I've seen so many things that I thought would make the difference and they haven't. I was sure when Joe woke up in a pool of his own blood that he would be frightened enough to get help. He talked about it, but that wasn't his crisis. A year later when his youngest child looked at him with scorn he said, "I surrender." There is no way to know. And it is a mistake for you to speculate about what, if anything, will make the difference.

There are a couple of things that you can do. You can be prepared if the moment ever does arrive that he comes to you and tells you that he needs help with his drinking problem. Have the 800 number of Alcoholics Anonymous at your fingertips if it is nighttime. Have the local number available if it is during the day. Know about detoxification and rehabilitation centers in your area. Know what your insurance coverage is. Have all these details clear in your head so that when you feel that he is sincere you can act quickly in order to get him help. That's about all you can do, but it can make the whole difference. If you can move quickly he will not have an opportunity to reconsider and decide that he can really do it himself. You can't push him into it, but you can make the resources available so that he cannot make excuses. You may go through this more than once, but the major role that you can play in the early stage of his recovery is to have him know that help is available and you want to help him get it.

It may be that you don't believe that this day will ever arrive. There are no guarantees that it will. What if he never gets sober? Do you love him enough to stay with him even if he never gets sober? Can you adjust to alcoholism as a way of life? This is not a loaded question. If you can answer yes your adjustment will be a lot easier. Rosemarie said that when she answered yes to that question it changed her whole life. She became much more accepting of her husband and stopped living in a fantasy world. Ironically enough it wasn't long after this that he became dry. Maybe the fact that she had stopped flailing at windmills made the difference.

If your answer to that question is no, then you need time to plan a life for yourself that will not include your husband. You need to figure out just how you will effect the changes that you need to make. You will need to know what your legal rights are. You will need to know what your financial position will be. You will need to know a number of things. You can talk to other women who have been in your position and who have chosen to leave.

Staying or leaving are individual decisions. All I suggest is that you make the decision on the basis of what is best for you and not because of the impact it will have on him. If you opt out, do it not out of anger, but because of careful consideration.

Part of your fantasy is that "If he only stops drinking, everything will be terrific." Forget it. Recovery is hard. Life doesn't become wonderful just because he is no longer drinking. It will take him a few months to be able to think about more than just not having a drink. If he joins A.A. they will recommend to him that he attend ninety meetings in ninety days. That leaves you feeling neglected. You will have to adjust. He may be irritable. After all, he is facing life now. He has to look at all the things he had been avoiding with alcohol. The bowl of cherries is part of another life. I have no intentions of going into a big thing about the problems involved with sobriety. That would not be helpful. I only mention it to let you know that sobriety is not instant bliss. As it took you and your husband a long time to get sick, you will not get well overnight. Facing oneself is rough. But as difficult as recovery may be, it is certainly preferable to drunkenness.

The future belongs to you. You decide, one day at a time, what you want to do with it. You have a whole full life to live, if you allow yourself to do it, with or without your alcoholic husband. As you recover you will begin to see the ways in which you used your husband's alcoholism as an excuse for your immobility. That will no longer work. You will have to look at yourself. You will take that class because *you* want it, or you won't take it because *you* don't want to—not because he won't like it. You won't stay home because of what he will say if *you* want to go out. You will find out how much you have hidden behind him. If he didn't get in your way would you have had to face your own fears? What I am saying is this: If you don't join the tennis group because he will have a fit if you're not home when he gets there, you don't have to look at the fact that you're afraid to join the tennis group because you are nervous about your game. You don't have to look at your fear that when they find out how terrible a player you are they will be sorry they asked you to join. It is a whole other place. Alcoholism can be a wonderful excuse to avoid looking at things on a deeper level. It becomes a habit. You may not even be aware that you are doing it. Can it be that the part of you that doesn't want to grow up doesn't want him sober? Can it be that the part of you that wants to be his mother rather than his wife doesn't want him sober? What a terrible thought.

What I'm saying to you—in every way I know how—is *get yourself healthy*. If you get healthy you can do anything; the future is yours. If you don't get healthy it doesn't matter what you do. Stay with him or leave him. You will make the same mistakes. I know many women who have traded off one alcoholic marriage for another. Working on yourself is the answer. Self-discovery is such a delicious life adventure. You will learn your good points and your bad points. Whatever they are, they are you and you can change what you need to, and enhance what you need to, and work to be the best you can be. That's what being healthy is all about. Are you worth it? Only you can answer that!

9 GETTING IT ALL TOGETHER

After reading this far you must have a sense of how David must have felt when he came up against Goliath. You have been coping in a situation of enormous difficulty. As miserable as you feel, you have to give yourself credit for just surviving. You have been going up against the giant with a slingshot. The way that you're feeling today makes it difficult for you to believe how many women have used the principles in this book and are much happier for it. It's a lot of hard work but it's worth it. I asked a number of these women to offer their thoughts. I knew them all when they were feeling hopeless and alone. I knew them all when their husbands were actively drinking and there was no end in sight. Many of these men are no longer drinking. Some even

admit that it was their wives' change of attitude that made
sobriety possible. Others continue to drink but their wives
are no longer sick.

I asked husbands and wives the question, "What is the
best advice that you can give to someone living with an active problem?"

I include their answers just as they were given to me.

Ruth is a sixty-four-year-old housewife. Her husband is retired and still actively drinking. He does not admit to being
an alcoholic.

> Keep healthy yourself. I could go on for hours and
> hours but that's not the main point. The first thing is for
> me to realize that I am not responsible for this illness.
> The treatment for this disease is so different than that of
> any other. It is contrary to everything I ever learned. If
> he had the flu I would make him soup; I would fluff up
> his pillow and make him feel comfortable. With this
> disease I have to let him make his own soup and fluff up
> his own pillow. It is contrary to anything I have ever
> learned.

Donna is a registered nurse. She has chosen to work only
occasionally as she prefers to be home with her four-year-old
son. Her husband has been without a drink for about eight
months.

> I'd tell them to get out to Al-Anon meetings so that they
> can share their feelings with people who understand
> what their situation is. People who have lived through it
> or are in it themselves. That's where I started getting
> the idea of detachment, not feeling responsible for the
> alcoholic's problem, and learning that I needed a great
> deal of help myself—that I finally caught on that I

wasn't there for his benefit—that I needed help too. That's also where I learned to live one day at a time— that I can't do more than that—that's my biggie. When I try to I really get into a bind. Basically that's it in a nutshell.

Pat is the mother of five children. She works as a teacher's aide in a class for retarded children. Pat and her husband are both recovering alcoholics.

Detachment is the only word that comes to my mind. Verbal when necessary and physical when necessary. And a complete mental detachment from the disease. Probably the whole thing should be prefaced with compassion for the diseased alcoholic followed by detachment. The thing would be to build their own personal strength to the best of their ability. That's all I can think of.

Elaine is an executive in a major company in New Jersey. She and her husband have been happily married for eighteen years. He is recently sober.

Plan to get away—plan to get out—direct all your efforts in that way—financial, job, family. That makes now— today—more tolerable. You are really living for your future and you have resigned your mind and emotions to that. Also you don't have to go through with your plan, you can always change it and stay, but you've made all the mental and emotional and physical plans to leave. A person with an active problem has to have the ability to survive now and you can't survive now if you're living someone else's life. By making a mental resignation that you must do something with *your* life, it takes up the problem of today and living through today and also plans for tomorrow. Time is on your side. You can take all the time you want to plan your future in slow degrees or as fast as you want to, or have to. Be selfish about it. Most people would not leave a terminal cancer patient but that is different because you know when the end will be. We know with the disease of alcoholism we could be talking fifteen or twenty years, depending on the person, and it will never get better without abstinence. So the decision is what do you want to do with your life. The other life is out of your hands.

Donna is a licensed real estate broker. When her husband stopped drinking she gave up her career and is now at home. They have a thirteen-year-old son.

I feel that the most important thing is to learn to accept alcoholism as a disease. You learn that through reading and Al-Anon. Something that really shook me up was when someone said that the alcoholic is addicted to alcohol and the spouse is addicted to the alcoholic. I remember hearing it after I had gone on and on talking about my alcoholic. I was so embarrassed and angry to hear that. But once you accept it as a disease and realize how involved you were in their lives—only then can you start working on yourself and learn how to detach. I think the best thing is to find yourself and detach from the alcoholic. I found that for detaching and learning to live with myself I had to seek outside help, a counselor, and then Al-Anon, a combination of the two. I think those are the important things for me.

Phyllis is the mother of five children. She works for the local newspaper.

I think that the biggest problem is the fear. That's the most difficult thing, I think. That's what you have to overcome or work at overcoming. That is the most important thing to do. As long as you show it the active person will use it to his advantage. As long as they know that they can't create this, then they won't use it. In twenty-five words or less that's the biggest problem as far as I'm concerned.

Elisa is a first grade teacher. Her husband is still actively drinking.

Stay out of his orbit and stop trying to find a way to get him sober.

Rosemarie is a registered nurse working in a public school. She is the mother of four. Her oldest daughter is about to be married. They have decided not to serve liquor at the wedding. The father of the bride is working hard at staying sober and his needs take priority.

Besides going to Al-Anon, make your own life, which makes detaching much easier to achieve. For me having a job was the answer. I was able to be me—not the wife of an alcoholic. No one at work knew of my problem. I was able to be free for seven hours a day. That gave me a breather so that I could have the strength to face the rest of the day. Gradually I was able to learn detachment twenty-four hours a day.

Marty has four boys. She teaches piano at home and has a newly sober husband.

When they call on the phone to say they'll be late, or when they go out "for a while," *never* ask what time they'll be back. Just say, "Thanks for calling. I'll see you later."

Pauline is a recovering alcoholic. Her husband is still drinking. She suggests to you what helped her get sober.

Learn to detach from the alcohol and not from the alcoholic. Until an alcoholic is left alone to look at himself, he will use you as his excuse to drink.

Bernadette has two teen-age daughters. She is a secondary school teacher. She has determined that her situation is unlivable and is now in the process of divorce.

Al-Anon. Eight hours consecutive sleep if possible. At least one short rest period per day. At least two peaceful meals a day—alone if necessary. Necessary steps toward financial independence (quietly). Cash accumulation (quietly).

Pat is a dental assistant and the mother of three children. Her husband has been dry for five years.

I think that one of the biggest mistakes is to think that there is nothing you can do but detach and mind your own business. You have got to be a little level-headed before you can do anything. I got to the point where I decided I was worth more than this and simply said straighten up or leave. My husband left, got help, and then returned. I was willing to take the risk with whatever he decided.

Gail runs a medical office. She has been married thirty years and has two grown children. Her husband is very active in Alcoholics Anonymous.

Find out about alcoholism. In other words know what you're dealing with. Get with people who have lived with it and understand it. Share and get feedback. *Do* something. Getting it out is the hardest step for some people. To decide to look for help is the hardest thing. Keeping it in the closet so long that it must be terrible for some people to bring it out into the open.

Connie is the mother of six children. Her husband is currently in a rehabilitation center for alcoholics.

Stay out of his problem. Get help yourself *immediately*. That's all that I can think of. Isn't that it?

Yes, Connie. You're right. That is indeed *it*. That's it in a nutshell. That's the whole story. It's all been said. Now it is up to you. I could have offered you hundreds of other thoughts, each one saying the same thing in different words. The ideas presented in this book are really very simple. Learn everything you can about the disease of alcoholism. Devote your energy to becoming emotionally healthy yourself, and don't enable the disease. You have nothing to lose but a lot of pain. You have nothing to gain but peace of mind. Today is a beautiful day. Allow yourself to experience the joy of being alive. Live in and for the day, each and every day, starting right now.

INDEX

JANET GERINGER WOITITZ, Ed.D.

is Adjunct Professor, Department of Counseling, Human Services, and Guidance, at Montclair State College and an instructor at Rutgers University's Summer School of Alcohol Studies. She is also in private practice in New Jersey, specializing in counseling families affected by alcoholism. For her doctoral dissertation at Rutgers, she made a study of the effects of alcoholism on the self-esteem of children of alcoholics. She is a contributor to the Al-Anon newsletter and has a certificate of award from the New Jersey Alcoholism Association.